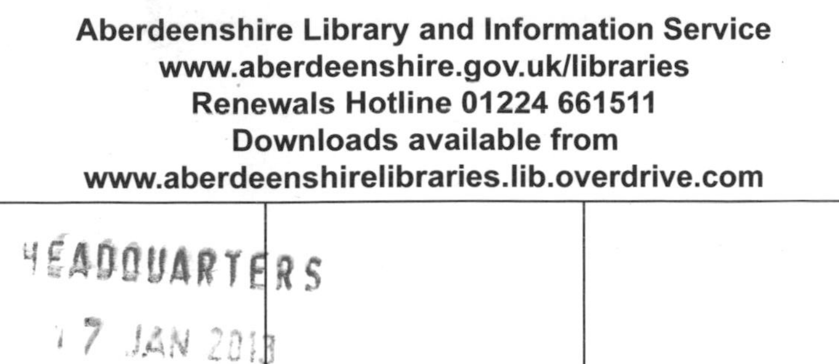

I0257942

THE
SILVER
BOUGH

THE
SILVER
BOUGH

Lisa
Tuttle

JF
Jo Fletcher
BOOKS

First published in the USA in 2006 by Spectra Books
This edition published in Great Britain in 2012 by

Jo Fletcher Books
an imprint of Quercus
55 Baker Street
7th Floor, South Block
London
W1U 8EW

A CIP catalogue record for this book is available from the British Library

ISBN 978 1 78087 439 5

10 9 8 7 6 5 4 3 2 1

Typeset by Ellipsis Digital Limited, Glasgow

Printed and bound in Great Britain by
Clays Ltd, St Ives plc

FT

In memory of Campbeltown Public Library and Museum, this book is dedicated to all who sailed in her, most especially Sue, Florence, Caroline, Christine and Barbara

From the Appleton Advertiser

Ferry Hopes 'On Hold'

The latest attempt to establish a ferry service between Appleton and Northern Ireland has met with no takers.

'This would open Appleton to the world. It would be a great thing for Appleton residents and visitors alike to have regular, speedy access to Ireland, as well as giving a great boost to tourism in Northern Ireland,' said Trevor Burns, speaking for Appleton Aye! a community group dedicated to improving and upgrading the area's economy. 'It would also attract more visitors, year-round. Unfortunately, none of the major ferry companies we approached consider the route commercially viable. I call this very short-sighted of them.'

Applications for government funding for this and previous proposed ferry projects to give the town a sea-link to other parts of Scotland have all been rejected. A matching grant from the European Union might be available, said Burns, 'but for that to happen we need a major business investment first.'

Burns insisted that this is not the end of the Appleton Ferry Project. 'The need is still there. The plan is still there. We are not giving up, just putting things on hold for a while.'

Farewell to Farmhouse Cider

It's the end of an era. There are no cider-makers left in Scotland now that Martin MacDonald has closed his doors.

'I'm just too old to carry on,' said Mr MacDonald, 94. 'I've earned my rest.'

His daughter, Martina Gregory, said they had considered giving up cider production after her husband, Barry Gregory, died two years ago, but had struggled on because 'Cider-making has been my father's whole life. It was a labour of love for Barry, too. Even though we have many faithful customers who love our cider, it has never been a profitable business. We can't compete with the cider factories down south.'

Appleton was once famous for its apples, and an apple is still the symbol of 'the wee toon.' Asked to comment on this latest closure, local councillor Duncan MacInnes remarked, 'I should point out that neither apple-growing nor cider-making have been of economic significance to the area since the 1950s. No jobs have been lost, either, as members of the MacDonald and Gregory families involved in the cider-making were all pensioners. You could say the cider company was a hobby for them. Of course it is a sad loss to Appleton and to everyone who ever enjoyed a bottle of "Old MacDonald's Finest." Truly, this is the end of an era.'

an excerpt from 'Aboot th' Toon'
A big Appleton welcome to our latest incomer, **Mrs Kathleen Mullaroy**, who started work last week as Appleton's librarian. Mrs Mullaroy comes to us from London, where she spent the last seven years working as a librarian for the London Borough of Brent, but, as one can tell from her lovely accent, she comes from much farther abroad, being an American, born and raised in sunny Tucson, Arizona. Let's hope the weather here doesn't scare her off, and that she disnae hae too hard a time unnerstannin' th' patter roun aboot th' toon!

Chapter One

Ashley Kaldis leaned her head against the cool glass and gazed through the bus window at the Glasgow streets. Although this was her first foreign city, she couldn't get excited about it; she just didn't feel she was really *here*. Something about the quality of the milky light, the grey-ness of the streets, reminded her of old black-and-white movies made long before she was born – before her own parents were born – from a vanished, untouchable era. She looked at it all as if from a very great distance, and wondered if what she felt – or didn't feel – was simply the effect of exhaustion and jet lag.

It was late September. At home, it was still summer, with everyone wearing shorts and T-shirts or bright summer dresses, but here it looked like winter already with people on the streets all bundled up in coats and jackets. The chilly air carried the scent of rain mixed in with traffic exhaust and fuel smells.

She sank a little farther into her seat and shut her eyes as the bus grumbled and shuddered and made its slow, complaining way from one traffic light to another through the teeming city streets. She'd made it to the last leg of her journey and there was nothing else she had to do, nothing to worry about for the next four hours and fifteen minutes until the bus delivered her to her final destination. She should sleep.

But after so long awake – she'd been too excited and anxious to get much rest the night before she left, and too uncomfortable on the plane, sandwiched between two strangers – sleep seemed like a skill she'd lost. Her nerves were jangling and her heart pounding, probably from that horrible coffee she'd had in the bus station, forcing herself to drink in an attempt to keep herself warm and alert while she waited.

With a sigh, she sat up again and dug into her rucksack for some distraction. She missed her phone; its absence emphasized how far she was from everything she'd ever known, in a foreign country where it wouldn't work. She reminded herself that it was only for six weeks; not worth changing to a more expensive contract. And, anyway, who was she going to call? Her best friend was dead, and she'd split up with her boyfriend. Her parents wanted her to check in with them, but if she did that too often, they might start thinking she was lonely or something.

She pulled out the cute, old-fashioned travel diary, which had been a present from her mother. So far, she'd only noted down her itinerary, and a few details about the long-lost relatives she was going to visit: Shona Walker (Daddy's first cousin; daughter of Phemie's brother), her husband Graeme, their children: Jade (6), Ewan (10), Callum (12). She wondered what they were like, and if she'd be expected to babysit. She had their home address, and two telephone numbers in case some unforeseen emergency kept them from meeting her at the village bus stop as planned. Also in her bag was her purse, with five hundred dollars in traveller's checks, a credit card linked to her father's account (for emergency use only), an AT&T International Calling Card, and *The Rough Guide to Scotland*. She'd be fine; nobody who knew her could doubt it. She could take care of herself.

But the thought of her own self-sufficiency made her feel a little bleak. She put the diary away and turned her attention back to the passing scene. They'd left the centre of town and were in the suburbs, which looked oddly crushed and miniaturized to eyes that took Texas landscapes as the default setting. She gazed at row upon row of nearly identical houses with front lawns the size of doormats, *bijoux* shops, petrol stations, a supermarket, a car dealership, and, finally, the first appearance of open space: bits and scraps of empty land, vacant lots, and something that looked like a long-abandoned factory with a sign advertising a unique site available for redevelopment.

The bus continued to trundle along slowly, muttering under its breath, air brakes squealing every time it was forced to stop. She looked down on the cars in the next lane and saw a man with a ponytail behind the wheel of a small red car, nodding and smiling to unheard music. It felt strange to have such an elevated and detached view. She was used to going everywhere by car, and had flown half a dozen times, but bus travel was weirdly exotic. It was something old-fashioned, a routine from another age, like travelling by train or steamer. Apart from a few school field trips – and there was no glamour in thirty kids packed into a yellow school bus to be ferried across town – she'd been on one other bus journey in her life.

The memory of that trip to San Antonio gave the empty seat beside her a sinister aspect. Freya should have been sitting there. But, no, that was wrong, because if Freya were still alive, neither of them would be on this bus; they'd both be back at school in Dallas, planning their great escape to France. France was where they'd wanted to go, France or Italy. Scotland was never in the running. Freya had no great opinion of the home of oatmeal and bagpipes and men in plaid. The fact that Ashley was one-quarter Scottish was of no more significance than Freya's half-Swedish heritage. Their long-dreamed-of, long-discussed trip abroad had nothing to do with 'finding their roots' – an urge which, she believed, did not strike normal people until middle age – but with fun and adventure, the desire to see lots of great art and sit in sidewalk cafés sipping cappuccino and flirting with the local talent.

She turned her face back to the window, watching urban wasteland give way to open countryside, feeling the bus pick up speed on the empty road. No art museums, no famous landmarks, no pavement cafés, no best friend, and nobody so far worth a flirtatious second glance; nothing to see but rolling fields dotted with grazing sheep, the gentle hills a luminous green beneath the milky sky. This was Phemie's country; this was the land her grandmother had departed more than half a century ago, left behind so utterly that she'd never had a word – good or bad – to say about it.

Ashley was here because Phemie and Freya were dead, although neither of them would have wanted her to go to Scotland. Really, this should have been her father's journey.

Since his mother's death, Jesse Kaldis had been trying to find out where he came from. He knew a fair amount about his father's family, which combined Greek and German stock, but about his mother's origins he knew very little. When she was alive, she'd discouraged his interest. The past was past, she'd say, and hers was not very interesting. She claimed her parents had been dead for years, and gave vague and contradictory answers to questions about exactly when, why, and how she'd come to America. He knew that his father had met her in California and married her in 1952. She'd acquired American citizenship and what was sometimes taken for a Canadian accent by the time Jesse was born. He knew that 'Phemie' – which everyone called her – was short for Euphemia; that her maiden name was MacFarlane, and that she'd been born somewhere in Scotland in 1931. It wasn't a lot to go on, but within six months of her death he'd discovered that one Euphemia MacFarlane, born in 1931, had disappeared from her hometown of Appleton, on the west coast of Scotland, in the autumn of 1950, and that people still remembered her there.

Phemie's parents were long dead – although nothing like as long as she'd always implied. Her mother had survived until 1975, never knowing she had a grandson in America. Phemie's older brother, Hugh, had died three years ago, but his three children were all alive and well, with families of their own. One was in England, one in Australia, but the third, Shona, had remained in Appleton. She was married to a man called Graeme Walker, who worked as a postman and turned out to have a passion for local history. He was even more thrilled than his wife to learn what had become of Phemie, and no sooner had Jesse made contact with Graeme than he'd been invited to visit Appleton and offered free accommodation and introductions to the town's oldest inhabitants, some of whom could surely tell him more about his mother's early life.

Jesse meant to do it – but now was not a good time for him to be away from work. (It never was, thought Ashley.) Maybe next year, he said. Strangely, as the quest lost its urgency for her father, Ashley became more interested. She'd loved her grandmother Phemie, but she'd never been especially curious about her, taking her for granted the way kids did. She hadn't even realized that 'Phemie' was short for 'Euphemia' – she'd thought it was a peculiar family variant on 'Granny,' like Freya's grandmothers being known as 'Gaga' and 'Mimi.' To Ashley it had come as a shock to learn that the sweet, rather dull old lady she had known and loved had once been an impulsive, smouldering young beauty whose flight had made a deep and permanent impact on her local community.

She remembered telling Freya about it shortly before Christmas, as they sat together in her room wrapping presents.

'Nobody had any idea she was planning to leave; they all thought she was perfectly happy. Everybody liked her, and she was engaged to be married to the richest guy in town.'

'Rich isn't everything. Maybe he was a creep,' Freya suggested, pausing in her ribbon-curling to examine the small black-and-white photograph Ashley had borrowed from her father. It showed Phemie as a vibrant young mother in the early fifties, holding up her baby boy and laughing, her hair hanging in dark, lustrous waves around her face, looking at once glamorous and maternal. She nodded slowly, approving. 'She was gorgeous. What about the guy she left?'

'I don't know. Dad didn't say much about him. I think he was older than she was . . . anyway, it sounds like he was pretty shattered when she dumped him; he left town himself within a couple of months, and the family business went to pot without him. That was bad news – it was a major employer. From what my dad's cousin says, it was the beginning of the end for the town. Local economy in ruins, all on account of this one girl deciding to run off. Although, of course, they didn't know for sure that she *had* run off – some people thought she'd been done away with. Maybe that's why her fiancé left – too many suspicious looks, like they all thought he'd killed her and buried her in the woods and was just pretending to be heartbroken.'

'Well, it usually is the boyfriend – although, of course, Phemie wasn't murdered! But who knows what might have happened if she'd stayed?' Freya looked thoughtful. 'Could it have been like an arranged marriage? You know, she was supposed to save the town by keeping him there and giving him an heir or whatever? So she couldn't see any other way of getting out of it? And even though he was rich, he was maybe a lot older than her, and really awful, but she had to do it because the families insisted?'

Ashley frowned, uncertain. 'Could Scotland have been that feudal in 1950?'

'Not an official arranged marriage, then. Maybe more like a done deal between him and her dad. Women didn't have that many options back then. And there must have been some reason why Phemie wouldn't talk about where she came from. Seems like she was scared of something, even after she was married to somebody else. She didn't want to be found. Because she knew they'd never forgive her, and the town would rise up and take revenge, no matter how much time had passed.'

Freya laughed suddenly and rested her warm hand on Ashley's. 'Ooh, or maybe her dad abused her, and she wiped it all from her memory. Or maybe . . . maybe I just watch too much TV! Probably it was just a really dull, boring place, and she felt guilty about dumping her fiancé, so she just decided she'd pretend none of it had ever happened. Did your Phemie seem to you like somebody hiding a deep, dark secret?'

'Not really. But she never would talk about her past – nothing about her family, or anything that happened before she met Grampa.'

Freya shrugged. 'Still . . . now she's gone, I bet she wouldn't mind your dad finding his relatives. It's made him feel better. He's made some new friends, and he's got a project. It's always good to have a project. Takes your mind off being unhappy.' She spoke, as she sometimes did, with absolute assurance, like someone wiser than her years. Two weeks later, she was dead after losing control of the dark green Camry she was accustomed to driving so fast and skillfully around the crowded, chaotic Houston freeways.

They'd been best friends since they were eleven. Losing her was like losing her soul or half her brain, Ashley thought despairingly. She couldn't believe she was still alive, left alone. Nothing made sense any more. But she remembered Freya's comment about having a project, so she went back to school two days after the funeral, because at least there she would have something to do. Teachers were understanding, everyone was sympathetic, but without Freya she was just the ghost of herself. She experimented a bit with drugs and sex, trying to jump-start her life. When that failed, she threw herself into schoolwork, attended every class and lecture, took copious notes, did extra reading, and turned in every assignment on time. She also acquired a steady boyfriend, Brandon, to occupy the hours when she couldn't work; but well before the end of the semester she knew it wasn't working, that it couldn't work. More than willpower was required. She needed a change.

On the last day of classes, she'd arranged to meet Brandon at four o'clock in the sandwich bar – it was a crummy little place with few customers except at lunchtime, conveniently located halfway between her place and his. He was resigned, if not happily, to the fact that they'd be spending the summer apart, and wanted to talk about getting together over the Fourth of July weekend.

She ignored this opening gambit, and plunged in with her news without pausing for a sip of her usual Diet Coke.

'I'm not coming back to school in the autumn. I can't take business classes any more; I just can't think in those terms. Nobody knows what's going to happen; I always thought I could be practical and plan things out, but it's impossible. How can I take five-year plans seriously when I don't know what's going to happen in five years? When nobody knows?'

He looked pained. 'Ash, it's just *work*. You can't take it personally. It's not meant to be applied to your personal life.'

'I *want* to take it personally. I want to learn something that matters to me.'

'Like what?'

How could he not know? 'Art.'

He looked even more pained. 'Drawing pictures? Painting?'

'I've always liked . . .'

'I know that,' he jumped in. 'Your drawings are good. But I thought it was more like a hobby. You never said anything about doing it professionally. Can you make a living from drawing?'

She shrugged impatiently. She wasn't ready for a big discussion about career possibilities, but it was her own fault for starting it. 'I like *looking* at art, too, so maybe I should learn more about it. I could see myself maybe working in a gallery or something.' She imagined spending her days surrounded by beauty, saw herself moving confidently through a large, well-lit space, the white walls hung with paintings.

'You want to be an art major?' His eyes flickered; she imagined him consulting a mental database of all the colleges in the area. 'Where would you go for that? SMU? That's good, I think, but pricey. Could your parents afford it? Could you get in there?'

'I don't know.' Majoring in art was something she'd decided against in high school, on practical grounds. Leaving aside the whole question of talent (if she could), she didn't have the right temperament for an artist *or* a teacher. There were other possibilities, which she'd discussed with Freya, but she felt no need to rehearse them with him. 'I need time to think. That's why I'm going to take a year off. I can get a job and live at home.'

'Thanks for telling me.'

'What do you mean? I *am* telling you.'

'But you made up your mind without talking to me.'

'I'm sorry.' She sighed heavily, bored and guilty. 'But it's my life, my problem, and I have to solve it.'

'I thought I was part of your life.'

There was nothing she could say to that. He *had* been a part of her life for almost four months, but really only in the way that a bandage or a wound dressing is after a major accident. It doesn't replace the missing part, and eventually has to be peeled away and discarded. He was a nice guy and deserved better, but knowing that made her no less cold. 'I need time to think. I need to get away from everything for a while.'

'Including me. I see.' His shoulders sagged; he looked as if he would crumple and fall forward, grabbing on to her for support, but he stood up, steadying himself by resting his knuckles against the table where their two drinks waited, still untouched and sweating onto the pale Formica. 'If it'd been me who'd died, I bet you wouldn't have dumped your best friend like this.'

She caught her breath. '*She* wouldn't have tried to make me feel guilty if I needed to leave.'

'So I make you feel guilty?' He groaned. 'Is that supposed to make me feel worse, or better? I can't win, can I?'

'No, you can't. I'm sorry, Brandon.'

She'd expected to have a much harder time getting her parents to accept her decision; they'd always been so firm about the importance of college. For the first month she was home she worked hard at two jobs, at Kinko's in the daytime and in the evenings as a waitress at Chili's, and scarcely had time to talk to her parents.

When it finally came out that she didn't intend to return to school in the autumn, she was surprised by how calmly they took it.

'Only for a year,' she said quickly. 'I just want a year off, to think about things and . . . well, I'd like to do some painting. Maybe I could take an art course somewhere.'

'You were thinking of staying here?' asked her mother.

'Yeah ... if that's all right. I mean, you weren't planning to rent out my room, were you?'

'The thought crossed our minds,' said her dad with a straight face. 'But then I thought of how much it would cost to put all your things in storage and decided against it. But wouldn't you rather go somewhere else? Travel?'

She stared at him in surprise. 'Well . . . yes. That's kind of what I'm saving up for . . .'

'I've got enough frequent flyer miles to get you to Scotland.'

She wasn't sure she'd heard right. 'To get *me* to Scotland?'

'You'd like to see where your grandmother grew up, wouldn't you? You could take pictures. Maybe even solve the mystery of why she left.'

'Paint the Scottish landscape,' suggested her mother.

'The Walkers would be happy to put you up. After you've tasted the delights of Appleton you could check out the museums and galleries in Glasgow and Edinburgh.'

'You can be our advance scout. Tell us what to see and what to avoid – because we are definitely going next year.'

It was completely unexpected, and, unexpectedly, she decided it was perfect: exactly what she needed. A complete break from the world she knew, yet with relatives to provide a link. Investigating her grandmother's past would give her a project to work on, supplying a reason to be there instead of somewhere else.

Now she gazed out the window at the famously beautiful Loch Lomond. She remembered learning a song about it in elementary school: a lifetime ago, in another century. The scenery beyond the bus window belonged to an even more distant past; it looked like something in a movie, and she felt rather as if she was watching one now, as if this bus was a theme park ride, and everything outside created to give pleasure. It was even her favourite kind of weather, cool, cloudy and mysterious, with the tops of the hills – or were they mountains? – hidden in low cloud.

The road narrowed and began to wind through the craggy heights. The bus slowed and grumbled with effort. Her ears popped.

Some of the slopes were barren landscapes, the huge boulders jutting out of the thin soil reminding her of an illustration from a geology textbook. She decided they were definitely too steep to be hills, so must be mountains, the first she'd ever seen in real life. Hardy shrubs and tough grasses sprouted between the rocks, nibbled by big-horned, bedraggled-looking sheep or goats. Some of them looked up as the bus lumbered past, staring across the distance from slotted yellow devil's eyes. Veils of mist shivered and parted, floating away like ghostly spirits. At any moment, she thought, a couple of animatronic skeletons should lurch out at them, clanking and moaning to give the passengers a pleasurable fright.

Finally, the bus stopped labouring so hard as the road levelled out, but then, almost immediately, it began winding downward in a long, slow descent. She looked down at a mountainside covered in dark green pines like a pelt of thick fur, and up at a glittering, roaring cascade of water that tumbled steeply down over rocks. There were no buildings anywhere. It was all wilderness, with nothing man-made in sight but the long and winding road.

Except for the traffic, there was nothing to fix you to a particular era. The scene was magically timeless. Wander off across that rocky meadow, or into the shelter of that dark forest, far enough to lose the sight and sound of the road, and you might find yourself in another century, meeting some hunky, shaggy, kilted Highlander . . .

The fantasy was barely taking shape when she noticed the solitary figure of a man walking by the roadside ahead of the bus. He had a purposeful stride, like a man who had been walking a long time with a clear aim in view, yet he wasn't dressed like a recreational hiker. He wasn't wearing a rucksack or a brightly coloured windbreaker or hiking boots. His clothes were nondescript, but wrong for the setting; like his leather slip-ons, they belonged to an indoor life. *He might have dashed out like that to pick up a pizza, but what is he doing out here in the mountains? Where is his car?*

She leaned forward, pressing her face close to the window, wondering if he'd signal to the bus driver to pick him up. Sure enough, she saw him stop and half turn, looking up at the noisy approach. But his look was not for the driver. Instead, it skated across the passenger windows until it found hers.

The feeling–

Later, trying to describe it to herself, she compared it to the description in one of the *Harry Potter* books of the effect of the magical portkey. She remembered Harry's feeling that a hook just behind his navel had been yanked to pull him forward – yes, it was like that, something at once magical and visceral, although for herself the location of the hook was somewhat lower down.

It happened in an instant, when his eyes met hers, and it was over almost as quickly – and unlike the fictional portkey, it did not carry her out of the bus and to another place. It couldn't have lasted, that connection, more than a second or two, because by then the bus had roared past, and although she twisted around in her seat to keep him in view, in a matter of moments, tilting vertiginously, the bus swept around another bend, and the walking man was out of sight.

She fell back in her seat and tried to breathe normally. She felt herself throbbing all over. *What the hell was that?*

But she knew, all right.

Lust. Pure lust.

She put her hand on the empty seat beside her, imagining Freya's raucous laughter. *Get over it! He was a hunk, so what? Do you think he spoke English? There'll be another one along in about fifteen minutes, if you can wait that long.*

Maybe this was another product of jet lag and sleep deprivation, an emotion out of the same stable as the remote detachment with which she'd viewed Glasgow. It was movie time again, where a single, sexually charged look between strangers turned into the tragedy of *Romeo and Juliet.*

Or maybe . . . maybe it hadn't happened at all. Maybe she'd been asleep and dreaming.

Frowning, she sat up straighter. Now that was ridiculous. She would know if she'd been asleep. He had been real. She remembered a pair of dark, rather narrow eyes, and how they'd found hers. Like an aftershock, she felt the power of his look again: the feeling had been mutual.

Yet, although she remembered how the sight of him – and his look – had affected her, she found it oddly difficult to recall what he had looked like. How would she describe him to someone? How would she draw him?

A stranger, she thought. She felt sure he wasn't Scottish – not with that dark, almost honey-coloured skin and those faintly slanting eyes – but she'd be hard-pressed to assign him to any particular race. Maybe he was an American dropout, hitchhiking around the world; maybe he was one of the Romany, heading for his people's encampment down some hidden byway; maybe he was an asylum-seeker fleeing an oppressive foreign regime, a romantic exile . . .

She closed her eyes and took herself back to her first sighting of the solitary figure, determined to know more. She saw his back, wide shoulders in a drab-coloured shirt worn over a dark-coloured T-shirt and straight-legged, khaki pants. No hat; short, thick, straight black hair. Loafers on his feet.

He stopped and turned as the bus approached and looked up, giving her a perfectly clear view of his face in the moment before his eyes burned into hers.

'Inveraray. Fifteen minutes. Public toilets located directly ahead, across from the paper shop. No chips or other fried foods on the bus. Departing promptly in fifteen minutes. Thank you.'

She woke when the throb of the bus engine cut out, in time to hear the driver's announcement, and saw and felt the people around her getting up and moving slowly toward the door. She yawned, blinked, and stretched, disoriented. *How long did I sleep?* She remembered the solitary hiker she'd seen on the road and shivered with desire, even as she wondered if he'd been anything more than a dream.

The bus had emptied out. She noticed that most people

had left behind something to mark their seats: a newspaper, a scarf, a book, even handbags and one portable CD player, as if they'd just strolled out of their own living rooms and there was no danger of theft. She didn't feel confident enough to do the same, and took her small rucksack with her as she made her way off the empty bus.

Outside the air was chillier than she'd expected, and it was raining. The bus was parked beside a small shelter where several passengers were huddled, smoking cigarettes; others made their way toward the whitewashed concrete block of public conveniences. Zipping up the front of her brushed-cotton jacket and pulling up the hood against the rain, she stepped out onto soggy grass and strolled toward the water's edge. She walked just long enough to stretch some of the kinks out of her legs, but by the time she got back to the bus her jacket was soaked through. The rain was not heavy, but it was unrelenting.

The cool air and brief exercise woke her up for the rest of the journey. She was glad she didn't suffer from motion sickness because after Inverary the bus never stopped swaying from side to side. Although they had left the mountains behind, the road ahead unfurled like a wandering river, never running straight, and full of switchbacks as it followed the natural line of the rugged coast, always taking the route of least resistance – going around lakes and the rockiest hills, never over or through them. Obviously, when this road was built, bridges and tunnels had not been budgeted for. It was narrow, too, not made with any large vehicles in mind. On occasion it ran along a narrow ledge, close to a rise of solid rock, with a drop down to the water on the other side, and very little in the way of verge or guardrails. She wondered what would happen if they happened to meet another bus going in the other direction on one of those bends, and hoped she would not have to find out.

The bus made about a dozen stops along the way to let people on or off; usually in tiny villages, once at a ferry terminus, and once to let a man off in what seemed to be the middle of nowhere: no house in view, not even a bus shelter or a sign to indicate that there was any reason to stop. At first all the land between the villages looked like uninhabited wilderness: steep hills, empty rocky moorlands, or stretches of thick, dark conifer forest on the side of the road not bordered by the sea. But at some point this changed. The land became more obviously arable, and the rolling green fields were dotted with grazing sheep or cattle – including some long-horned, long-haired, ginger-coloured shaggy beasts like a cartoonist's notion of cows suitable for a cold climate – all looking rather miserable in churned, muddy fields beneath lashing rain.

Although it still hugged the coast, the road became

straighter and flatter for a short while. Then, about fifteen minutes before they were due to arrive in Appleton, the bus began to labour up another hill, shuddering slightly as it geared down and wobbled around yet another tight bend.

Ashley felt her stomach lurch as she looked out at the precipitous drop to the sea below, lashed by rain that now fell in torrents, foaming and churning around the rough teeth of sharp rocks. More tall, jagged rock thrust up on the other side of the road in the narrowest hairpin bend she'd ever seen. Water gushed from a crack in the hill-side, spurting down to splash against the side of the bus, and she flinched and shut her eyes, feeling that the journey had become just a little too much like a theme park ride: 'Will the stagecoach make it through to Dodge City?'

She didn't open her eyes again until she could tell from the movement of the bus that it was again travelling a relatively straight and level path. They were back amid homely-looking farmland, with a few houses dotted here and there among the sodden green fields, a glitter of grey sea in the distance, but no sign of those weird rock formations.

She sighed in relief and checked her watch again: *Not long now.*

They passed what was obviously a working farm, big white house standing foursquare among a system of barns and sheds, and a strong smell of manure hanging in the air. Someone wrapped in bright yellow rain gear was leading a weary-looking grey horse across a field. Across the road, two black-and-white dogs and a man on a quad-bike were herding sheep.

A row of multicoloured cottages: pink, blue, and white. A very suburban-looking redbrick bungalow, with a garage beside it, a swing set and bicycles in the front yard. An abandoned stone house, the windows boarded over. A sign saying PRIVATE ROAD, then a gatepost with the name ORCHARD HOUSE. Then there was something that looked like an abandoned factory, and then the sign: WELCOME TO APPLETON on top, and below a line of foreign text: '*failte a innis ubhall.*'

The road descended. Appleton was in a sheltered valley, with high hills looming around it, but she saw them for only a few moments, for then she was in the town and the buildings, although none were more than three storeys high, blocked them out. It was beginning to grow dark, and rain was falling harder than ever. The streets were empty of pedestrians, and the shops all seemed to be closed although it was only just five o'clock. In general, the impression was of a deserted and rather miserable town hunched in on itself, not offering anything to the visitor. Yet her heart began to beat faster as the bus carried her deeper into the narrow streets, and a tingling warmth spread throughout her body as if she'd been looking for something all her life and had just recognized the place where it might be found.

From *A Visitor's Guide, to Appleton*
(Women's Institute, 1972)

Appleton Public Library and Museum
(Esplanade and Wall Street)

UNDOUBTEDLY the most striking and memorable building in the whole town, and one no visitor should miss. Also known as 'the Wall building,' it was a gift to the town and people of Appleton by the local philanthropist Lachlan Wall, and designed by his nephew, the Glasgow-trained architect Alexander Wall (1855–1930). It took more than three years to construct, and was officially opened in 1899. The golden dome is a well-known local landmark, and this, with the elaborate carved stone pillars on the exterior (decorative rather than structurally necessary), led to a local wit dubbing the library 'Solomon's Temple,' a nickname you may find is still in use today. There are certainly Classical and Eastern influences in the exterior design which would make it look more at home in a country far distant from Scotland; however, the interior decorative details are very much in the famous 'Glasgow Style' Art Nouveau. The symbol of an apple with the intertwined letters APL was designed by Margaret Macdonald Mackintosh (wife of Charles Rennie Mackintosh), and the stained-glass window in the towering foyer, as well as the classical frieze above the fireplace in the Ladies' Reading Room, are by her sister, Frances Macdonald.

The building was constructed on an L-plan, with the library and museum to the left of the foyer, an octagonal reading room on the right, and, straight ahead, a two-storey wing (the upstairs, at present used for meetings and storage, is closed to the general public). Also accessible from the foyer is a long loggia, open on one side to an inner garden, which leads to the Library House, adjoining the Museum.

The Museum is well worth at least one visit during your stay, and will delight all ages. It is very educational, with displays relating to the past of the town, the once-important apple orchards and cider industry, as well as the old fishing fleet, farming, and so on. Local wildlife is also represented in a realistic diorama featuring many stuffed birds and beasts – always a hit with the youngsters. In addition, the original 'cabinet of curiosities,' begun by James Alexander Wall and forming the core of the Museum's collection when it was first opened, contains things you're unlikely to see anywhere else, including what are said to be a mermaid's comb, a fairy's purse, several fairy eggs, and a unicorn horn.

Alexander Wall also designed Appleton Grammar School, the Grand Hotel (now ruined) in Southport, and almost a dozen fine houses in the area, including three of the most striking villas located on the Esplanade (see page 11).

Chapter Two

It had been raining in Appleton for four days solid. Locals took the rainy weather as inevitable; some even welcomed it after a summer they'd found 'close' or 'too dry.' 'Can't complain,' they said cheerfully, bringing their books up to the library counter to be stamped out. 'We had a lovely summer, and here it is almost October. Makes a break from the heat. The ground was awful dry, you know; my garden's been crying out for it.'

When she heard this, Kathleen had to smile and bite her tongue. As a newcomer to Appleton she didn't want to sound critical; nobody had made her come here to live. But her own opinion of the summer just past was that it had been far from dry, not to mention unseasonably chilly – and she *liked* rain. Growing up in the dry American Southwest, she'd found wet days refreshing. The smell of rain in the air made her hopeful. Even ten years spent living in England had not cured her of these feelings, but life on the west coast of Scotland might.

A child swathed in a large, shiny red raincoat came in, banging the door loudly, holding a plastic bag up to the desk. 'Here, I put my books in a bag to keep 'em dry, see?'

'That was clever.' She smiled and moved to take the bag, but he'd already started pulling books out, and his jerky movements released torrents of water from folds in the stiff, shiny fabric of his sleeves, drenching the books. She went on smiling and handed them on to Miranda, the assistant librarian, already waiting with a cloth.

The relentless, steady drum of raindrops on the roof, a sound she'd once found soothing, now made her prickle anxiously at the thought of more leaks. She had discovered three since the rain began, and her supply of buckets was now exhausted. She didn't know what she'd do if a fourth one appeared. She'd reported the leaks to the head office, faxed through as *urgent*, but her hopes were not high. In a building as large and old as this one, repairs could be expensive, and everybody knew the county council was strapped for cash; they'd been cutting corners and eliminating 'nonessential services' for more than twenty years.

Things were tough all over; having worked for nearly a decade in locally funded libraries, Kathleen was used to being on the receiving end of budget cuts, but Appleton had, in addition, its own particular problems, in consequence of its situation: 'the farthest from anywhere, the closest to nowhere' as the local description had it. It had seemed a wonderfully distant and romantic place on her first visit. She'd been bewitched by the scenery, charmed by the clean, bright emptiness of the landscape and the peaceful, old-fashioned little town, and three months of living here had only made her fondness for it grow. But there was a price attached to living so far from everywhere else – a hundred miles from library headquarters, the farthest-flung of all council outposts. Even the most basic supplies cost more and took longer to arrive. The drivers of delivery vans didn't like going to Appleton. It was the end of the road; nothing to do when you got there but turn around and go back. There were no alternative routes – nothing but a private airfield used mostly to ferry patients to hospitals in Glasgow – and the only road was no motorway but a narrow, winding, often badly rutted track that ran along the sea, where it was swept by high waves during storms, except when it climbed to higher, rocky ground, where there were a couple of tight and dangerous bends.

'Hear the weather report this morning?' Miranda asked when they were alone again.

'Let me guess: set to continue.'

'Worse, actually.' She put on a broadcasters voice: 'Bad news for listeners in Scotland, with the fine, bright weather coming to an end as a heavy band of rain sweeps in from the west, affecting all parts by early Saturday morning.'

'*What* fine, bright weather?'

'That's what they've been having in Glasgow, apparently. A real Indian summer. It was even on the news. Sunbathers outside the People's Palace, didn't you see –' She stopped, giving Kathleen a slightly wary look. 'Um, do you *have* a television?'

'Oh, yes. But the reception in the Library House is terrible – the walls are too thick or something. I can't get cable, because you're not allowed to fix a satellite dish to the wall of a listed building; there's even a problem with putting an aerial on the roof – it might pose a risk to the museum skylights . . .' She frowned. 'You're looking relieved. That's not kind.'

'I was worried in case you were like Mr Dean, with a *thing* against television.' Mr Dean was the previous librarian. He had died six months short of his anticipated retirement, and seemed to have been an eccentric character, not generally adored.

'Of course, television wasn't the only thing he disapproved of,' Miranda went on. 'Although he was always railing against *old-fashioned superstition*, he also hated anything *too modern*. It was all decadence to him; I'm sure we could have had computers in the library by now – I'm sure there were central government funds available for that Millennium project to get everybody online – but, thanks to Arnold Dean, Appleton Public Library remains stuck in the past.' She picked up a date stamp and crashed it down savagely onto a pad of pink Post-its. 'We'll *never* get funding for it now; not from the council.'

Fraser Mann, the head of library services for the county, had told Kathleen before he hired her that both a computerized checkout system and Internet access for the public were in the pipeline at long last. Appleton Public Library would be the last in the county to go online, but the day was coming – although he wouldn't be drawn into giving a specific date. He'd stressed that, although the salary was low compared with what she'd been making in London, she shouldn't imagine she was walking into an undemanding job. The library was at present antiquated and under-equipped, and, despite funding problems, it had to be brought up to date and into line with modern needs. Should she accept the job, Kathleen would be in the enviable position of presiding over the dawning of a new era in Appleton.

But since she'd taken on the job more than three months ago she'd not heard another word from him on the subject. She decided to say nothing about it to Miranda now, but to raise the issue with Fraser next week. She was well settled in now, and it was time to look to the library's future.

'I get my news from the radio,' she said, bringing the conversation back to their original point. 'I can even get Radio Four if I put it on the windowsill in the living room and point the aerial just exactly *so*. But I didn't hear about the sunshine in Glasgow. I don't hear much of the Scottish news, I'm afraid; I'm kind of a *Today* addict. Very London-centric of me, I know.'

'My dear, you don't have to apologize to *me*!' Miranda was English, and still had a rather posh, home-counties accent despite having lived in Appleton for eighteen years.

Kathleen glanced up at the clock and saw it was only half an hour until closing time. 'I'd better go check on the buckets again.'

'I'll write the notices so I can post them on my way home. Somehow, I don't think I'll be interrupted.'

They both gazed around the empty library and sighed. It was a day for sitting indoors with a good book, not going out in search of one, she mused, as she went out of the main room of the library into the imposing foyer. It was a large, echoing space with a high, vaulted ceiling, and felt as grand as a cathedral. Her eyes were naturally drawn upward, even when she wasn't concerned about leaks. But she could hear the sound of splashing, and so for once did not pause to admire the magnificent stained-glass depiction of Adam and Eve and the Tree of the Knowledge of Good and Evil above the front entrance, but instead snatched up the mop she'd left close at hand and dealt with the puddle that had spread around the red plastic bucket.

Next she marched off to monitor the problem in the Ladies' Reading Room. Although it had not been reserved for the use of females only since before she was born – it was now officially 'the reading room' – she preferred to think of it by the name etched into the beautiful, glass-panelled door. It was not the coziest of rooms, although she imagined that it might have been, once, when fires were lit daily in the big fireplace (now boarded up). And there would have been a regularly changing display of magazines, and at least a dozen newspapers hanging from the reading poles instead of the three the current budget allowed for. The many-paned, leaded-glass windows, rattling under the assault of wind and rain, gave a view of the wide, palm-tree-lined Esplanade and, beyond it, the harbour. Today the view was a murky one, the sea and sky both grey and practically indistinguishable. She turned her back on the depressing sight to admire the panel above the fireplace. It was a mixed-media work, an oil painting on wood inset with coloured glass and metal, depicting the Judgment of Paris in the faintly eerie, elegant Art Nouveau style that had been all the rage when the library was built.

Neither of the two leaks in this room seemed any worse than in the morning, when she'd discovered them. There was no mopping up required, and the buckets would likely be all right until morning. Much relieved, she went back to the counter in the main library where she found Miranda gazing thoughtfully at some sheets of paper.

'You look worried.'

She looked up, shaking her head. 'I just found this. It's a photocopy from the British Library – a reader's request.

I think it must have come in last week with some other things, only it slipped down behind the shelf, and I'm not sure if Connie sent out a notice about it – I know *I* didn't.'

'Who's the reader?'

'Mrs Westray'

Kathleen bent down to the card index of membership details kept on a shelf below the counter and pulled out the drawer marked T–Z. For her first few weeks in this job the reliance on such a traditional system of file cards and ledger books and book tickets had seemed impossibly primitive, as if she'd been thrown back in time to an age of hand-drawn water and quill pens, but by now it was second nature.

'The thing is,' Miranda went on, 'I can send her a card, of course, but she wouldn't get it until Monday, when we're closed, and if she's in any kind of hurry for it – she's already had to wait, and it's only a few sheets of paper. It wouldn't cost more than a second-class stamp to mail it to her.'

Kathleen had found her card:

Westray, Eleanor Rowan (Mrs)

Orchard House
Fairview Hill
Appleton

tel: 777 802

'Remind me who she is?'

'American lady, early thirties, attractive, rather tall, doesn't say much, favours classics and the more literary modern fiction.'

'Oh, I know who you mean. I'll give her a call.'

Miranda put the photocopy down on the desk in front of her, and Kathleen ran her eye over the top sheet as she waited for the phone to be answered. It was an extract from a book and an author completely unknown to her: *Pleasures of the Table* by Percival M. Lingerton.

'Hello, is that Mrs Westray? It's Kathleen Mullaroy from the Library here. I think you requested something from the British Library . . . a photocopied extract . . .'

'Oh, yes.'

'Well, it's arrived. Now, I could mail it to you, or –'

'I was planning on coming in tomorrow.'

'Oh, that's fine! You can pick it up then. Just ask at the counter. You know our opening hours?'

That settled, she wrote 'Mrs E. Westray' on a Post-it note and stuck that to the top sheet before putting it on the shelf allotted to readers' requests. Then she picked up her heavy ring of keys, and told Miranda, 'I'm just going to check the museum and lock it up now; somehow, I don't think we'll get a last-minute surge of visitors today.'

'That does seem a bit unlikely.'

The entrance to the museum was located at the far end of the room, just past the children's section. The big wooden door had been carved with a riot of Celtic-style intertwined forms, animals, birds, and foliage revolving around a central tree of life. Beyond it, the roof-lit museum was a dim and shadowy chamber, despite the banks of spotlights, echoing to the relentless drum of the rain. Ignoring the high-hanging oil paintings and the glass cases with their displays of stuffed birds, old coins, tools, and pottery, she peered up at the vaulted ceiling, painted a Wedgwood blue between the white struts and skylights, and held her breath to listen for the sound of an intrusive drip. A swift but careful circuit of the long gallery satisfied her that it was all still watertight, so she switched off the lights and locked up.

'I'll be in my office if you need me,' she said as she passed the counter.

'I'll ring if the crowds get too much for me to handle alone.'

As she stepped out into the foyer again, hearing the loud echo of the steady drip of water into the bucket, she became aware of how cold it was, and shivered unhappily at the thought of the long winter drawing in. The library was a great place to work in the summer, always cool on the hottest days, but she did wonder how much use the antiquated storage heaters would be in combating an extended cold spell, especially with winter gales blowing off the sea and howling in the eaves.

Her office was also the staff room, a narrow room at

the end of the shorter leg of the L-shaped building, most of that space occupied by the reference library and local collection. She went breezing through, expecting it to be empty, and was brought up short by the sight of a man working at one of the tables, surrounded by piles of books and papers.

Graeme Walker looked up as she approached, blinked owlishly, and grinned. 'You look like you've just seen the library ghost.'

'What ghost? No, don't tell me. I don't need anything else making me nervous when the wind howls.' She spoke lightly; despite the age and size of the building, she found it a friendly, almost cozy space and had never imagined it could be haunted. 'You startled me; I thought I was alone. I'm surprised you came out in this weather.'

'Neither wind, nor sleet, nor hail, nor – how does it go?'

'I don't know; you're the postman. But you can't call this your appointed round?'

'A labour of love,' he conceded, cocking his head to one side and regarding the notebook page before him, half-filled with his scratchy writing. 'And I'm on a new trail now.'

'This is your history of Appleton?'

'Yep. Only right now I'm into the time before it was Appleton, before it was a town. What you might call the prehistoric past. Except not what's *generally* known as prehistory because Appleton was founded in the seventeenth century, so I'm talking about the late Middle Ages. And what I'm finding – well, it's major. It could change the way we think about all kinds of things if I'm right; you would not believe!'

Almost certainly not, she thought, careful not to show her dismay. She'd liked Graeme from the moment she'd met him. He was a chatty, charming, intelligent, largely self-taught Glaswegian who had come to Appleton about fifteen years ago for a holiday and stayed on after falling in love with a local girl. When he'd told her he was researching local history with a view to writing a book, she'd thought that it sounded like a good idea. She hoped he wasn't turning into a crank; she'd met quite a few of them over the years, pursuing some mad theory or other, and his latest remarks set off a warning bell in her mind.

'Say, do you have a few minutes? Sit down, and I'll tell you about it.' He got up; she put out her hand to forestall him pulling out another chair.

'Sorry, but we're closing in fifteen.'

'It's a quarter to five already? Jings!' He capped his pen and bent over the table, sorting through the papers and books scattered there. 'I'm supposed to meet Shona and the kids at the bus stop – Shona's wee cousin's meant to be on that bus, come all the way from America!' He closed his notebook and thrust it with a bundle of papers into a shabby canvas briefcase. 'I lost all track of time. Lucky it's only a five-minute walk to the bus stop from here. Now, this book is from the main part of the library, but these others were off the shelves around here.'

'It's all right, Graeme, just leave them on the table; I'll put them back.'

'Ye sure?'

'Of course.'

'Aye, and you'll put them all back in the right places, whereas I might not.' He grinned like a mischievous boy.

She didn't contradict him, although the truth was she was still learning her way around the local collection. In the main library, the system of classification and shelving was perfectly standard, but back here many of the books had been filed according to a different plan, the key to which she suspected had gone with the late Mr Dean to his grave.

'Or you could just leave the books on the table to use again tomorrow,' she said.

'*If* I get in tomorrow. Family obligations at the weekends, you know.' Then he perked up again. 'Although, if Ashley wants a tour guide – well, I'd have to bring her here, wouldn't I? I mean, this is the finest building in the town. I remember my first visit after I'd met Shona and she got Miss McClusky to take us upstairs.'

She frowned. 'Miss McClusky? I thought you came to Appleton fifteen years ago.'

'Yeah, that'd be about right.'

'Mr Dean was in charge by then.' She thought of Miss Ina McClusky – a spry old bird, certainly, and still an enthusiastic talker and reader, but now well into her eighties. 'Miss McClusky was long past retirement age.'

'Oh, aye,' he said, nodding vigorously. 'She was, but she came back to work part-time – retirement didn't suit her, and she missed this place. So she used to help out. Mr Dean was in charge. Mr Dean-from-Aberdeen. I never got on with that man. He was such an old stick-in-the-mud, and he took all the most interesting things out of the museum, because, according to him, they "weren't appropriate" – he meant, not connected with *his* view of Appleton's history – or they weren't "educational" – meaning they didn't teach the lessons he wanted taught.' He leaned confidingly toward her. 'So he put all that stuff away in storage, where it's just waiting to be rediscovered. There's forgotten treasures in there that really ought to be on view. He ruined a unique, small museum, made it bland and ordinary. It's a shame.'

She nodded sympathetically. Although she couldn't judge whether Mr Dean's long-ago changes had been toward improvement or ruin, she knew nothing else had been done in twenty years, and thought it a crying shame that such a potentially important resource was so neglected. 'The museum should have a curator,' she said. 'Even if I had the right professional qualifications, I don't have time to do anything about it. There's no budget for it.'

'You don't have to tell *me*. I've tried to nobble my local representative, but he's just not interested. Funny thing, but he thinks money for education and health care is that much more important! Ah, well.' He sighed and pulled over the biggest book on the table. 'May I take this one out? Or is it still for reference only?'

She picked it up. *The Ancient Volcanoes of Great Britain, Vol. 2*, published in 1897, and seemingly never issued. 'Well, I don't see why you shouldn't take it home with you. I don't suppose anyone else will come in needing to use it. But how is this part of your research? Surely there aren't any volcanoes around here?'

'Under the sea there are. Did you know that the geology of the Appleton peninsula is *completely different* from the rest of Scotland's? There's nothing else like it anywhere in Britain, or the European mainland.'

'Really?'

'Closest match is the other side of the world – the New World, where you came from. And I'm thinking there could have been some volcanic action under the sea that gave rise to a new island, long after the rest of Scotland was formed.'

'But Appleton isn't an island.'

'It almost is. We're only linked to the mainland by a narrow little strip – barely half a mile wide. You know those rocks there by the side of the road?'

She remembered the final tight, high bend in the road

between the sea and the rocky hills just before the descent into the gentler farmland around the town, and she didn't have to ask what rocks he meant. They inevitably snagged the eye, rising like weird, jagged towers at the edge of the sea.

'Don't they look like fallout from some major geological event? Land erupting out of the sea, or sheared off one landmass and sent crashing against another?'

'They are pretty dramatic,' she said noncommittally, glancing at her watch.

'And another thing: the Gaelic name for Appleton is *Innis Ubhall*. That doesn't mean Apple *Town*, it means Apple Island, and by all accounts it's what the folks from round about all called this area well before the Earl of Argyll got his Royal Charter and imported a load of Lowland farmers to bring civilization, aka loyalty to the crown, to these wild parts.'

As soon as he paused for breath she jumped in. 'Why don't I stamp this for you. Did you want anything else?'

'That'll do for now.' He followed her as far as the fire exit, where an old map of Scotland had been hung, before he stopped and called her back. 'Here, look at this, and you'll see what I'm talking about.'

She looked with him at the pink-and-blue patchwork of land and sea that made up the west coast. Appleton had been built on a plumply rounded spur of land at the very end of a long, skinny peninsula; the frequent description of it as an apple hanging from a branch was as apt as it was inevitable.

Appleton was old enough by American standards, but relatively new in European terms. It was one of several new towns founded in the seventeenth century in Scotland, settled by incomers – mostly English-speaking Lowland Scots who brought their loyalty to the British throne with them into the wild and troublesome Highlands. Before then, although the area must certainly have been occupied by someone, there had been not so much as a named village.

'What's the date of this map?' Graeme asked.

'Eighteen sixty-five, I think.'

'There are older maps of Scotland. Do you know about Timothy Pont?'

'Oh, yes.' She'd boned up on Scottish history at the same time as she'd applied for this job. 'His maps are wonderful. Amazingly accurate for the time – the 1590s, wasn't it? – and he was the first to map all of Scotland. He travelled absolutely everywhere.' She stopped and frowned at the map in front of her, recalling her disappointment when she'd checked out the brilliant, searchable Web site where she'd first seen Pont's maps and discovered he'd missed out the Appleton peninsula. 'At least, that was the general idea. Obviously, he missed a few places.'

'No. He came to this part of the coast, and he mapped it in his usual accurate way – but Appleton wasn't there.'

'Well, but Appleton *wasn't* here. Not for a few more decades yet.'

'I don't mean the town. I mean the apple itself is missing. *Innis Ubhall*. This whole chunk of land.' Graeme traced the distinctive curve of coastland with his fingertip. 'It's just not there on his map. Not in the Joan Blaeu atlas of 1654, either.'

It was not hard, looking at the small 'stem' of land that connected the apple to the mainland, to imagine an earthquake or underwater eruption that might cause it to break away, turning Appleton into an island, but it was harder to conceive of it happening the other way around, to imagine an island forcibly pushed against the mainland and made to grow there, like a grafted branch. Did such things even happen? Mistakes made by a couple of early mapmakers were far more likely.

'Interesting,' she said neutrally, turning away from the map. It was not her job to attempt to debunk anybody's pet theory, no matter how wild. She accompanied Graeme to the circulation desk, feeling, as she sometimes did, like a keeper at a very genteel loony bin.

'You found the secret room yet?' he asked, pausing in the foyer to look back at her.

She saw the mischief in his eyes. 'I guess Miss McClusky showed it to you?'

He laughed. 'No, she didn't include it on the tour. But if it exists, I'll bet you she's seen it! Shona says the story is that the architect designed this building with a hidden room, a room without a door, to keep his daughter safe.'

'Safe?'

'She was crazy She ran off, came back with an illegitimate son, then a few years later she killed herself – or else it was an accident – or maybe she was rescued at the brink of death, her mind gone. Some said she ended her days in a hidden room in the library – maybe inside the dome.'

'The dome is purely decorative; there's no way to get inside it.' She knew she sounded pedantic, because she'd said it so often. It was amazing how many times she'd heard the question.

'I know that. But there must be a space underneath: the original room without a door. Of course, if Alexander Wall *did* create a special, hidden room for his daughter, he must have been psychic, to know she'd grow up crazy, because she'd only just been born when he designed it.'

His eyes were glittering now, making Kathleen think of Coleridge's Ancient Mariner. 'I'd give a lot to read his journal – it ought to be in the local collection. It's listed in the card catalogue, but I can't find it. I think that Mr Dean took it off the open shelves and hid it away. It's not right, you know; it was left to the public library and it belongs to the people.' He gave her an affronted glare, and had the air of a man winding himself up for a good, long rant.

Unhand me, grey-beard loon, she thought, glancing at her watch. 'I don't want to rush you, Graeme, but it's four minutes to five. If you're meeting someone off the bus . . .'

He let out a comical yelp and slapped himself on the forehead. 'Late again! Thanks. Look, I'd really like to have a word with you about Wall's journal . . .'

'Of course. Any time.'

She watched him pull up his hood, tuck his briefcase securely under one arm, then dash, shoulders hunched and head down, through the front door, out into the pouring rain. Then she went back to the counter, where Miranda was counting up the day's issue and entering the total in the big red ledger.

'Why is it that nothing at all happens for hours and hours, then, in the last fifteen minutes, you get enough to keep you thinking all day?'

'Sod's Law,' said Miranda, shutting the ledger and putting it back beneath the counter. 'Which five rare and valuable books did he want you to order for him today?'

Kathleen smiled and shook her head. 'He's all right, though – isn't he?'

'Oh, sure. He's a joker, and he gets awfully intense sometimes, but he means well. Never stolen a book – not from us, anyway. His kids are great readers, which I call a good sign. His wife's a lovely girl. He and Mr Dean didn't get along, but I wouldn't call that Mr Walker's fault.'

'Do you know anything about Alexander Wall's journal?'

'I know he'd like to read it.'

'Is there some reason why he can't?'

She held up empty hands. 'I don't know where it is. Arnold Dean hid it somewhere and took the secret to his grave.' She smiled to show she wasn't serious. 'It's probably in that locked bookcase upstairs. It's just a matter of looking – but Connie and I haven't had time to do anything but keep this place ticking over. Those three months before you were hired were awfully difficult. Of course, it didn't help that Mr Dean had been unwell for a while before he died. There were too many things he'd always done himself, in his own way, and he just wouldn't *let go*. I'm not sure you're caught up yet – are you?'

'Just about.'

Miranda gave her a motherly look. 'Unpaid overtime. You shouldn't do it, you know.'

'We'd be closed another day a week if I didn't. Anyway, it won't be like this forever. And speaking of overtime . . . Isn't that Mark waiting for you out front?'

They both looked through the window at the car idling in the rain.

'Bless,' said Miranda fondly.

After she'd gone, Kathleen locked up the front, turning off the lights in the reading room and main library, and went back to the office to do whatever it was she'd forgotten earlier. It wasn't important and could certainly have waited until the morning, but she would feel more comfortable with her desk cleared. Half an hour later she reminded herself that she was working on her own time and should go home. But with home only a few steps away – the Library House, built onto the side end of the museum – and no one waiting for her there, she couldn't work up any urgency. She stood hesitating in the empty reference room, listening to the relentless downpour and the faint, eerie whistle of the wind in the eaves. She liked having the library to herself, felt both stimulated and at peace in the company of all the silent books. She loved the look, the heft, the weight, the smell, and the fact of books – all those miniature embodiments of other lives, other times. Thoughts and dreams preserved for posterity to be summoned back to life through the act of reading. The buzz these days was all about the Internet, the world of online, digital knowledge, the necessity of being connected. But even though she accepted that the Net was not merely the wave of the future but the fact of present-day life, and did miss the access to it that she'd taken for granted in her old job, on an emotional level it could not compare, for her, with the magic of an old-fashioned, printed, real book. It was that, and a child-hood fantasy of being able to live in a library, which had really decided her choice of career, no matter what sensible reasons she might tell other people.

She walked among the shelves that housed the local

collection, touching the backs of old books, occasionally taking one down. Some remnant of childhood animism made her feel sorry for those which were overlooked, left too long untouched. She'd been pleased to see *The Ancient Volcanoes of Great Britain* taken out at last. Now, like a determined matchmaker, she browsed for something else to tempt Graeme. There were some volumes of the *Scottish Journal of Geology* and *Transactions of the Geological Society of Glasgow* with essays about this area, but nothing looked as exciting as underwater volcanoes.

A sudden howl startled her. It might have been a banshee wailing upstairs, but looking through the street-side window she saw the fronds of the palm trees along the Esplanade shaking wildly in a sudden, fierce gust of wind. It had grown dark; the line of yellowish lights strung along the harbour front shuddered and bounced. She was lucky she didn't have to go far in this weather. But this reminder that it was past time for going home did not move her. She *was* home, standing right at the heart of it.

The job had not been appealing by objective standards, and her friends and former colleagues all thought she was mad to take it. The salary was considerably lower than what she'd been earning in London, and although the title of Area Librarian implied a grander job than her old one (where she had been just one of six librarians), and seemed to give her more authority, she actually had only three part-time assistants, none with qualifications in library science, and all the really important decisions were made at headquarters, and handed down to her. According to the advertisement, the new Area Librarian would 'preside over the modernization of the system and help to bring Appleton Library up to modern COSLA standards; a demanding and rewarding task.'

'Translation: you will be overworked and underpaid, and we expect you to be grateful for the opportunity,' said Louise, a children's librarian and her friend for the past four years.

She sent off her CV with the application anyway, and despite all the well-meaning advice from her friends, held her breath and wished on a star and felt enormously grateful when she was called for an interview.

The bleak truth was that she didn't have a lot of choice. She couldn't stay in the job she had. Even with the 'London weighting' on her salary, she could not afford to live in the greater London area without a husband to share the mortgage. It hadn't been easy even when she and Geoff were together, and now that they'd split up it was impossible. She'd thought about moving back to America, but the economic situation, or employers' attitudes, had changed a lot in the decade since she'd left. Out of forty applications, she received only one offer, and that was for a one-year contract in Indiana. She got the message. Like Thomas Wolfe said, *You Can't Go Home Again.*

Driving in the rental car from Glasgow to Appleton, her first time in Scotland, she was immediately seduced by the scenery, but it was when she set eyes on the library building that she fell in love. It was a weird, architectural fantasy, with its golden dome, carved stone, and the sort of imposing, pillared front that had been popular on early 'Picture Palaces,' suggesting that through these portals all your fantasies would be met. It would have been completely unremarkable in Las Vegas, but in a small Scottish seaside town it was an astonishment and a perpetual wonder. She understood perfectly why a local mythology would have grown up around it, stories of ghosts and secret rooms and madwomen in the attic. She wanted to work here; she wanted to make the library her own.

Replacing *Megalithic Enquiries in* the *West of Britain* on the shelf, she decided to do just one more task before going home. She would look for Alexander Wall's journal. Overtime was only onerous when you were forced into it, and personally there were few things she loved more than treasure-hunting among shelves of old books.

So, through the door with the map on it into a chilly stone antechamber, past the fire door (painted red, with the sign THIS DOOR IS ALARMED – EMERGENCY USE ONLY) and up the high, wide, sturdy staircase to another locked room she went.

The smell of lavender beeswax and old books welcomed her in. Officially, this was the 'meeting room,' with a large, highly polished wooden table and matching chairs in the centre ready to accommodate any passing committee. In practice, it had not been used in many years for anything but storage. Cardboard boxes had been stacked as neatly as possible beneath and on top of almost a third of the table. Much of their contents was withdrawn stock, either waiting for its turn on the sales table in the foyer or put aside as 'reserve,' by Mr Dean – reserve stock without reserve stock shelving. At some point it would be her job to go through them all with a ruthless hand. She didn't expect to find any treasures there; it would be a lot of once-popular fiction long past its sell-by date. And yet, although the books had to be removed to make space for new acquisitions, and book culls were a necessary part of a librarian's life, she had been putting the task off. Libraries should be about conserving and preserving books; selling them off cheaply went against the grain. She guessed the late Mr Dean had felt the same, and felt a little more kindly toward her predecessor, even if he had left her with a mountainous backlog to sort out.

Far more interesting than the boxed books were the glass-fronted cases that covered one wall from floor to ceiling. They contained the Wall collection, and other books, which had been donated years ago. Some appropriate volumes had been integrated into the local collection downstairs, but the rest had been left here to languish out of sight. That would soon change. Kathleen's boss had told her that there was a plan to sell the collection and use the money to fund improvements to the library. Most of the books were probably of little value – there were an awful lot of collected sermons and memoirs of long-forgotten worthies – but there were bound to be a few treasures among the dross. The first step, now that the sale had been agreed to by the local authorities, was to bring in an expert to assess the value of the books. But, as usual when Appleton needed something from outside, the expert was taking his time about getting here.

From the huge bunch she carried, Kathleen isolated the stubby little key that unlocked the bookcases, and allowed herself the fantasy of discovering a first edition of Darwin's *Origin of Species*, or something beautiful, hand-lettered and illuminated on vellum by some long-ago monk. In fact, she knew how far-fetched her fantasy was, because the contents of these bookcases had been listed in a small, hard-backed notebook by an earlier librarian, and transcribed in the last year by some council employee to be submitted with the draft resolution. There could be nothing obviously, *famously* valuable here, or she'd have heard about it. She thought it likely that it was the distinct lack of anything really 'sexy' that made their Edinburgh-based expert reluctant to make the long, tedious journey across country to spend a day holed up in here. Which didn't mean there weren't a few books worth more than a hundred pounds apiece to the right collector; only that this consignment wasn't going to make anyone's fortune.

None of the books had been marred by reference numbers on their spines, but guessing that it would have gone against the grain of a professional librarian to shelve the journal of Alexander Wall out of alphabetical order, she looked for the far end of the alphabet, and very quickly spotted a slim, pale brown book without a title, almost invisible between *Country Rambles* by Malcolm Waddell and *The Collected Sermons of the Revd S. Wallace.*

'Aw, there you are, darlin',' she murmured, feeling pleased with herself as she extracted the little book. The first page confirmed her discovery. Handwritten in clear, although rather faded, brown ink on creamy paper was:

Recollections
of
Alexander (McNeill) Wall,
member, R.I.B.A.
and long resident
in
Appleton

She turned to the next page:

I have never claimed, nor wanted, any homeland but this, my beloved Appleton. My parents both were born here, and my father's father and his father before him. I, however, was born on the other side of the world, on my father's sugar plantation on the island of Trinidad, and did not set foot on Scottish soil until the ripe old age of ten when, after my father's untimely death, my dear mother removed us to Appleton. I had been a somewhat sickly child, but I flourished as never before in the cool, balmy ocean air, like a sapling transplanted to more nourishing soil. However, barely had I put down roots before they were wrenched up again; after only four years in Appleton I was sent away to Glasgow, where I was apprenticed to a firm of architects, and thus learned my trade. Lost and lonely as I often felt in the big city, I cannot truthfully regret it, as it is that training which prepared me to become the architect I am now, and fitted me not only to make a living, but allowed me to return at last, to live and flourish in Appleton, and, as well, to make my own contribution to the 'wee toon'.

Reading the words written so long ago by the man who had built this library gave her a thrill; it was as if the building *did* contain a secret room, and he was still alive inside it. His handwriting was neat and clear, almost as easy to decipher as some printed books. She closed it and held it pressed for a second against her chest, deciding that she would read it quickly herself before mentioning to Graeme Walker that she'd found it.

The rain was still coming down in sheets, so that when she went out the back door of the library she had the impression that it had been built behind a waterfall. A contrary wind even blew it into the shelter of the loggia that ran between the library and the house, so she was showered with spray in the few moments it took her to lock up and wrestle the heavy storm doors into place before dashing home.

The Library House was a charming miniature, built with the same attention to decorative design as the bigger building and echoing its architecture. Although the rooms were small, she loved all the doll's house details. There was a stained-glass panel above the front door, an Art Deco-style fireplace in the living room, and a decorative glass domed cupola on the roof, which filled the stairway and the tiny upstairs hallway with light. There wasn't room for half her furniture, but she reasoned that selling it off had not only saved her money on moving and storage, but gave her a welcome excuse for buying new things that were not saturated with memories of her failed marriage.

Originally the house had been occupied by a caretaker who had tended the garden, seen to cleaning and repairs, and acted as a night watchman, but that job had gone to an earlier round of budget cuts. The house was not tied to the librarian's job, but when she'd been told that she could rent it from the council, Kathleen had eagerly accepted. She reasoned that she'd been impulsive about accepting the job and should not also rush into buying a house. If life in remotest Scotland was not to her taste, she might want to move again after only a year. She'd be better off without the burden of a mortgage; it would be wise to wait and look around a little.

This, at any rate, was what she told her concerned friends.

But, really, what other house could compete with this one? She'd achieved her childhood dream of living in a library.

She let herself in and switched on the light, admiring the reproduction Art Deco chandelier she'd installed only two weeks ago. It was so much nicer and more in keeping with the style of the house than the ugly, utilitarian plastic fixture that had been there before. The long hallway had looked gloomy and unwelcoming when she'd first seen it, but she'd painted the walls a fresh, pale lilac and given the yellowish woodwork a coat of fresh white gloss, then hung a couple of framed Mucha prints, and thought that Alexander Wall himself might have approved.

Chapter Three

It was well past midnight when Mario turned off the lights and locked the chip shop, his working day finally at an end. The last customers had come in not long after eleven, as he'd expected: young men who'd shouted or made slurred, incomprehensible remarks as they ordered battered deep-fried sausages, meat pies, and large portions of chips to add to stomachs distended with beer. Once they'd gone, he might just as well have turned the door sign over to CLOSED and hurried through the cleaning, but his uncle – free to leave when he felt like it and untroubled by the need to pay a decent wage to the blood relative he'd taken in as a favour – set the opening hours and the menu, and didn't respond well to helpful suggestions.

'You're not here to tell me my business,' he said sharply. 'You're here to learn. Do your work, pay attention, and maybe you'll gain some understanding of how to make a living.'

One thing Mario understood perfectly well was that he hadn't been sent to this remote backwater to learn anything. If his English improved – as it had – that was a bonus; but his parents thought no more than he did of the importance of the arcane mysteries of preparing, serving, and selling cheap and disgusting fried food. He was here for no other reason than to be kept out of harm's way. It was true – as some ignorant drunk had once shouted at him, meaning to give offense; probably imagining it to be some new term of racial abuse – he *was* an asylum-seeker, although not for the usual reasons.

In his final year of school, Mario had fallen in love with his music teacher, and she with him. It was the most wonderful thing that had ever happened, and he'd thought he was in heaven on earth until, quite suddenly, she told him that her husband was getting suspicious and she couldn't see him any more. He'd refused to accept it, even when she insisted it was too dangerous. His life was at risk – *her* life, too. She pleaded with him not to call; her husband was monitoring the phone. Together, he was sure they could overcome all obstacles; her timidity maddened him. Why didn't she just leave the brute? Who cared what the world thought? If the age difference hadn't mattered at the beginning, why should it matter now? She couldn't explain, and she wouldn't fight. It was all down to him. If he didn't act, he'd lose her – and having once tasted paradise, he wasn't prepared to let it go. So he'd become ever more cunning in arranging 'accidental' meetings, at first by hanging around in all the places he knew she was likely to visit, and later, when leaving it to chance stopped working, by following her. And although, in the end, he'd been forced to stop, at least she was safe, she still had a job, and her marriage was preserved. Her husband might be suspicious, but he had no proof of his wife's misconduct. Mario had taken all the blame; he'd let them brand him a stalker, a confused, fantasizing youth, never revealing the truth, that Anna had seduced *him*. And his reward? An even deeper loneliness, and exile to this bleak, wet Siberia.

After locking up, Mario went for a walk, as he usually did, to get the stink of frying out of his nose and the stiffness from long standing out of his legs. It was raining hard, as it had been for most of the week, but he couldn't face going directly from the chip shop to the narrow, damp-smelling spare bedroom in his uncle's house yet again, and nowhere else in the town would be open to him at this hour. Walking – which had never held much appeal for him at home – was his major leisure activity in this foreign backwater. Walking, listening to music, and writing letters to his love – letters which, of course, he could never post.

He put on the baseball cap his sister had given him, back when a year of study at an American university had been a beckoning opportunity, and shrugged into the denim jacket still damp from his afternoon's dash down the street. He could have bought a waterproof jacket – his parents had given him money for things like that – but that would have felt like giving in, accepting his fate as the resident of a rainy country. He preferred to do without, like someone merely passing through, forever surprised by the weather.

Head down, hands in his pockets, he walked through the driving rain, heading for the harbour. *Anna*, he thought, in time with his footsteps. *Anna, Anna, Anna, Anna.*

He was soaking wet and shivering before he reached Front Street. The rain hurled itself against him with a fury that seemed personally vindictive. He pulled the bill of his cap lower to protect his eyes and made his way across the harbour parking lot. The rain on the few cars parked there sounded like the work of a demonic drummer. When he reached the metal guardrail he gripped it hard, as if the force of the weather might just lift him up and throw him down into the water if he wasn't securely anchored.

The routes of his walks varied, but they always ended with the same view. On his first night in Appleton he'd been drawn instinctively to the sea. Tears had pricked behind his eyes as he stared out at the water. It was greyer and wilder than the sea at home, and yet he'd imagined it was the same sea and that somewhere . . . over there

... Anna might at the very same moment be looking at it, too, and thinking of him.

There was no globe in his uncle's house, and the only maps were concerned with British motorways, so it was a few days before he found out how wrong he was. He'd gone to the library – a strangely magnificent building that struck him as being completely out of place in this dour little northern town – and looked into an atlas. It had made his heart sink to see how far Sicily was from Scotland. And despite his fond wishes, *their* sea was not *this* sea, and when he gazed out from Appleton harbour his view went due west, completely opposite to the direction home. Travelling west there was nothing but the great, wide, cold Atlantic Ocean for miles and miles until you came to Canada. Only by turning his back on the ocean and aligning himself to face, roughly, southeast, would he be gazing in the direction of Sicily, and with that came the heavy knowledge that between him and his heart's desire lay almost the entire landmass of Britain, all of France, most of Italy, not to mention certain legal, social, and economic barriers, the disappointment of his family, and the vindictiveness of Anna's.

He was so cold and wet now that he hardly felt it. The rain ran down his face like tears, and as he stared out at the water he could scarcely see through the night and the heavy curtains of rain, he remembered again, as he often did, that cold winter's day standing on a rocky beach overlooking the Mediterranean with Anna; how she'd taken his hand and played with his fingers and then, while he was still paralysed with confusion, how she'd reached up to touch his face, then pulled his head down to kiss him. Her warm, soft, open mouth. How she'd guided his hand to her breast, and the suggestions she'd whispered in his ear: the instructions and promises. And, a little while later, making love with her for the first time in the backseat of her car.

That was the real Anna; the warm, passionate, half-naked girl trembling with desire, clutching and clinging to him; that was the Anna he'd always remember and believe in, not the cold, older, respectably married woman who spoke so coolly of her 'concern' about his 'inappropriate attachment' to her, pretending she had never shared it.

The rain drumming on the cars behind him now sounded like mocking laughter. *She never loved you, fool. She used you. Forget her.*

He shoved a hand into his jacket pocket, closing it around the little bottle. It was a vodka miniature he'd found in the street in front of the chip shop a week ago, empty and missing its cap, but whole. It was filled now with a tightly rolled-up letter to Anna, and sealed with a piece of whittled-down candle and a piece of strapping tape. He'd been meaning to throw it out to sea for days, but between the bad weather and his changeable, rotating shifts, he'd kept missing the tide. He thought it should be going out now, but he wasn't sure, and he couldn't see well enough to guess.

But did it matter? Whether the tide was going in or out, the chances of this little bottle – or any of the others he'd launched in previous weeks – actually reaching any Mediterranean shore in his lifetime must be vanishingly small. He wasn't worried about some local lout reading it – how many people around here could read Italian?

It didn't matter. It was a meaningless gesture, he was going through the motions of unrequited love for nobody's sake but his own. He might as well burn the letters after he wrote them as throw them in the sea.

He brought his hand out of his pocket, hauled back, and threw the little bottle as hard as he could into the darkness, toward the unseen empty west. Then he turned his back on it and, head down in the blinding rain, unable to see where he was going, retraced his steps, heading for his uncle's house. He'd so often thought, since he came here, that he couldn't get wetter, or colder, or feel any worse, and still it seemed there were new depths of misery and further extremes of bad weather to be experienced. He didn't think he could bear to write and throw away another yearning love letter to someone who didn't care, but he also didn't know how he could survive without that last, small pretense at communication.

Later that night, when a small seismic shock woke him abruptly out of shallow, unhappy sleep, he dreamed for a moment that what he'd felt was his own heart breaking.

From *What Grows in Scotland*
by Mairi Smith and F. B. Lockhart
(Baillie, 1991)

Apples

ALTHOUGH the native crab-apple (*Mains sylvestris*) was known to the Celts, who associated it in their mythology with love, fertility, immortality, and the existence of an earthly paradise, it was the invading Romans who planted the first cultivated orchards in Britain. This tradition was revived and expanded by the Church, particularly Benedictine monks, who planted apple orchards wherever they settled . . .

. . . An exception to the connection between monasteries and established orchards lies on the west coast, not a location usually hospitable to fruit trees, in aptly named Appleton. There are no abbeys or medieval settlements in the area, which was only sparsely populated in early times, without even a named village on the peninsula dubbed 'Apple Island' (*Innis Ubhall*) by the Gaelic-speaking natives. When the first apples were grown there is a matter of some dispute, but by Victorian times Appleton was famous for cider and several particularly fine varieties of eating apple. However, despite a folk tradition that the Lowland settlers named their new town after the wild apple orchards they found there, it seems likely the first apple orchards were planted no earlier than 1669, with stock imported from eastern and central-southern Scotland. The annual Apple Fayre, which attracted visitors from many parts (*see picture, below*), was almost certainly a Victorian invention inspired by similar English festivals, with a few Scottish traditions rather obviously grafted on. (The 'dark stranger' who brings good fortune to the whole town by crowning the Apple Queen will be recognized as the preferred 'first-footer' of New Year celebrations.)

Mass importation of apples from America and Australia hit the home-grown industry in Britain hard, but Appleton remained miraculously immune from the worst effects for many years, with a growing demand for Appleton cider in all parts of Great Britain right up to 1950; in addition, a small but loyal group of buyers continued to favour 'Appleton's Fairest,' an eating apple never successfully grown outside the orchards of Appleton and now, sadly, lost for ever.

Chapter Four

Nell woke suddenly in the depths of night, alarmed out of sleep by a noise that was more than mere sound, as if an invasive, physical presence had shaken the house. For a moment, disoriented, she thought a drunken stranger had broken in and commenced smashing furniture in the rooms below. The noise continued to die away with a bouncing, pattering sound, as of bits and pieces falling and sliding across the floor. There was something visceral and deeply disturbing about it.

As she became more alert, she recognized how unlikely this nightmare scenario was. She lived in the peaceful countryside, with no enemies or drunken relatives to fear. Even if some mad stranger had made his way up the hill to her house, there would be no need to break in, as she'd almost certainly left her door unlocked, as usual. Besides, the noise was not coming from inside.

She pushed herself up in bed and held her breath, but there was nothing to hear except the ordinary natural sounds she'd grown used to; the sounds she'd once called silence. The rain had stopped, allowing the low, urgent murmuring of the stream to come through more clearly She tried to remember what had disturbed her sleep: something cracking and breaking; something falling and sliding and settling; something large and very close.

Her thoughts flew to the old walled garden. Of course, the trees would be all right; they were young and healthy, and although the recent steady downpour meant the ground was waterlogged, they were in no immediate danger. They were fine when she saw them yesterday afternoon, and even if the night's gusts had been of gale force – which she was sure they hadn't – the walls would protect them. But if one of the walls had fallen?

As soon as she thought it, the image was disturbingly clear in her mind. It would be the south wall: the one she'd thought too sound to need repairing. Or perhaps the west wall, which had been rebuilt from scratch. It had seemed so strong and solid; but what if the builders had used some kind of cheap, inferior cement that the past four days of rain had turned to mush . . .

Although she knew she could do nothing about it by herself in the middle of the night, she would not be able to sleep again until she *knew*. Switching on the bedside lamp, she got up and rooted about in the pile on the armchair in the corner until she unearthed some leggings, socks, and a heavy sweatshirt, then quickly pulled them on.

Downstairs the house lay still, quiet and undisturbed. In the storm porch she pushed her feet into the pair of green rubber boots waiting for her beside the back door, and wrapped up in her knee-length Barbour coat. She picked up the largest of the two torches, checked that it was working, and let herself out the back door, which she hadn't locked.

The air was dry and unexpectedly warm. There was a mildness to the night that she associated with the beginning rather than the end of summer, and as she moved away from the house she smelled the gentle, domestic perfume of mint, oregano, and thyme from the edge of the kitchen garden. She made her way slowly across the lawn and into the meadow, treading down the high grass whenever she missed the path in the darkness, and was assailed by a sudden memory from her adolescence of sneaking out of the dorms with two other girls for illicit trysts with town boys. They had been oddly innocent meetings, at least for her. She'd never compared notes with the other girls, but assumed that, like her, they did no more than kiss and cuddle. She'd been just thirteen, and to her 'sex' was heavy breathing and woozy feelings and slightly scary-looking athletic encounters between gorgeous movie stars, or else – for an unmarried girl – it was something dangerous that would end in disgrace, illness, or death. Kissing was different; kissing was love and liking, and any chance to practise it and prepare yourself for falling in love was too important to pass up. She remembered how intensely physical, yet emotionally detached, those make-out sessions had been, recalling the taste of cigarettes and spearmint gum on his breath, the feel of his tongue in her mouth. Once he had tasted of beer, which she thought disgusting, and she wouldn't let him kiss her again that night. He'd accepted her ban meekly, and they'd spent an hour or more just cuddling. He'd stroked her hair and her back and arms, then, for the first time, her breasts. How sweet that night had been.

What on earth had made her think of that?

She stopped short, staring into darkness, overcome by nostalgia for something she had not thought of since . . . well, hardly at all in her adult life. She couldn't even recall the boy's name.

Forcing herself back to the moment, she raised the heavy light. The door into the orchard was directly in front of her, and there was no sign, at least on this side, of any damage to the dark brick wall. She pressed down on the latch and pulled the door open. The smell of growing apples and wet earth welcomed her, and as soon as she stepped inside the warmth of the sheltered orchard she knew it had not been breached.

All the same, *something* had startled her awake, so she

paced out the boundaries and swept each wall with the powerful beam in search of any gaps or cracks. They were all whole and undamaged. The trees, too, were as she had left them in yesterday's light: no injuries, no branches broken, no sudden fall of late-ripening apples. About a third of the trees were bare of fruit, which had ripened in August and the first half of September. The others were midseason or late-ripening varieties and as the rain had set in and continued she had worried that they'd lost the chance to develop their best flavour.

Everything she knew about apples she had learned from books or, in the last five years, from her self-taught, unpaid apprenticeship as a gardener determined to create an orchard at Orchard House.

It had started almost as a whim – although that word was too light for someone who approached life with her seriousness. Self-imposed task, even penance, might be a better term. She didn't have to work for a living, so she needed something to do, to fill in the time. The idea of buying and restoring an old house had always appealed to her, and Orchard House had fit the bill. It was structurally sound but in crying need of lots of minor repairs and complete redecoration. From the look of the interior, nothing much had been done to it since the 1950s and, apart from having central heating installed, Nell reckoned she could handle most of the work herself. She much preferred that to hiring and supervising others. She wanted to go to bed tired every night, and she had a high tolerance for repetitive manual tasks like sanding down, stripping and painting.

By now, the house should have been finished, a show-piece, and Nell looking for something else to do, but the gardens had changed her plans, as they had changed her.

In the beginning, when she bought the house, there was nothing that could be called a garden, just a lot of overgrown land at the back of the house where, some-time in the past, there had been vegetable plots, rose beds, a rockery, a greenhouse (long ruined), and a lawn. The apple orchards that gave the house its name had been on land in the valley down below – land sold off for other uses in the 1960s. As the pleasant young man from the estate agent's had gestured toward the fields and woods that stretched away behind the house, pointing out the boundaries of her property, she'd noticed what she thought was a ruined building, only a few hundred yards away.

'What's that?'

'Oh, yes, that comes with the house; that's the old walled garden.'

'May I see it?'

'It's not much to look at; I don't think it's been touched in thirty years.' But, as obliging as ever to this potential purchaser, he'd let her satisfy her curiosity, leading her on a tortuous journey across a boggy, rutted field, and then scratching himself rather badly on the thorns that barred the door.

'Brambles,' he muttered, finally wrenching the splintered old wooden door open to reveal the way inside still blocked by a particularly wicked-looking bush. 'Devil's own job to dig them out once they take hold.'

'I need a prince on a white charger, brandishing a sword,' she said. She was thinking of the castle surrounded by a thorny hedge in 'Sleeping Beauty' and was surprised to see him blush. She turned away, annoyed by his presumption. 'Never mind,' she said, staring over the hill at the road far below. 'I'm not a gardener, anyway.'

It was true, she'd never grown anything except a tray of cress at school. It had been Sam's fantasy to potter around tending vegetables in his retirement, not hers. But *The Secret Garden* had been her favourite book when she was small, and the existence of the walled garden in the grounds of Orchard House tipped the balance. And once she was the owner-occupier, responsible for the upkeep of the property, things began to happen that made the restoration of the orchard almost inevitable.

A spell of fine weather when she first moved in meant that she began with outdoor jobs, and once she'd cleared away the worst of the weeds and the rubble, she found herself thinking about what to put in their place: patio, flower beds, lawn? After all, the setting of the house was important, and it had been abandoned for so long that she was denied the easy option of leaving things as they were. She ordered books on garden design, drew up plans, searched through gardening catalogues, and took a trip down to Scotland's central belt in order to scout through the bigger gardening centres and do-it-yourself stores to see what was available.

In Stirling she got to talking to a knowledgeable nurseryman about what plants would and would not suit the southern west coast, on a hill above the sea, and unexpectedly she found herself confiding, 'But there's a walled garden, too, so the sea winds don't have to be a problem.'

'Where is it that you stay?'

'Appleton.' She wouldn't have been surprised by a blank look; no one outside of Scotland had ever heard of Appleton, and even Scots outside the immediate area were vague about where it might be, usually confusing it with Applecross, which was much farther to the north.

But he knew it; his eyebrows went up to his hairline in surprise. 'With a walled garden, you say? That wouldn't be Orchard House?'

'How did you know?'

'My father came from Appleton. He left the day he turned eighteen, but he was forever talking about it, and he sent us kids to stay with his parents in the summer holidays every year. We ran wild; there was nowhere we didn't go. I remember that garden. It must have been very formal and beautifully tended at one time, but it was starting to go a bit to seed when I saw it.'

'When was that?'

'The seventies. Two old ladies lived there – well, they seemed old to me then! I think they grew most of their own food. I stole fruit from the garden – there were fruits I'd never seen before. Figs and apricots . . . I'd had them both, but only dried. I'd never realized before that you could pick and eat them fresh. But no apples. I thought that was really strange; it was called Orchard House, but there was no orchard. Not a single apple tree.'

She had started to explain that the commercial apple orchards had been on land well away from the house and sold off before his time, but stopped when she saw he already knew.

'You could certainly grow all kinds of fruit there, if you wanted,' he said. 'I know Appleton gets a lot of rain, but that spot on the hill is a sun trap. Or were you thinking of something purely decorative?'

'No, I like the idea of growing things I can eat.' She didn't mention her qualms about clearing out the wilderness within the crumbling walls, or her original intention to leave it alone. None of that mattered. She should have known she wouldn't be able to resist the chance to create her very own secret garden.

They went on to discuss what she might plant, combinations of colour and size and scent, how to make sure that everything didn't come into bloom or ripen all at once but was staggered for longer-term enjoyment; bulbs, perennials, herbaceous borders, ornamental vs. edible; whether she'd have paved or gravelled or grassy paths, with a bower at the centre, perhaps, so she could sit and enjoy it all, and maybe a fountain . . . until she felt overwhelmed.

'Look, hang on, it all sounds wonderful, but I'm going to be doing all this myself – and I've never actually gardened before! I have a house to fix up as well. Either I leave the walled garden for later, or I start with something simpler.'

He was silent for a moment, then he said, 'You know, the simplest thing *would* be an orchard. Apples are the easiest of all the fruit trees, and they've always been grown in Appleton. There's loads of varieties to choose from, and within two or three years you should have your first crop. It's best to plant in November, which gives you nearly four months to prepare.'

Now, standing in the quiet, breathing darkness, listening to her trees murmur and softly creak, Nell was as close to happiness as she could ever be. The apple trees were like her children, although she would never have said so, not even to herself. She tended them and cared for them, and yet they needed her less than she needed them, which was as it should be. They'd given back a focus to her life, given her a reason for getting out of bed in the morning – and, indeed, in the middle of the night. She still had no idea what had shocked her awake – a distant explosion? a car crash on the road below? – but she'd seen for herself there was nothing wrong in *her* domain. Easy in her mind, she made her way back to bed.

In the morning she didn't give a second thought to what had disturbed her sleep but set off in her car for the town after her usual quick shower and frugal breakfast. The car park of the supermarket was crowded, and there were no spare trolleys in the bay where they were usually stored, but that was not particularly remarkable for a Saturday morning. She only guessed at something wrong when she walked through the automatic doors and heard the unusually high level of sound, a babble of half-hysterical shouting as people raced through the aisles, throwing cans of soup and jars of instant coffee and rolls of toilet paper into their trolleys as if stocking for a siege. She stood still, puzzled, gazing in surprise at the ranks of empty stalls that lined the first aisle. Normally the fresh fruit and vegetables were displayed here, but today there was nothing, not a single bag of potatoes, not a solitary orange.

She walked down to the bakery section, where the racks

that usually displayed the fresh-baked rolls, pastries, and specialty breads were just as bare. The shelves of prepackaged breads held only one loaf of whole wheat and a vacuum pack of pita breads. She noticed a store employee in a white apron, behind the bakery counter, standing with her arms folded tightly across her full breasts, her cheeks flushed and a look of barely contained excitement on her round, young face. Nell caught her eye. 'What happened?'

'Haven't you heard?'

'Heard what?'

'There was an earthquake!'

Nell shook her head, making no sense of it. 'Where?'

'Here! Under the sea, off the coast, actually. Didn't you feel it last night? *I* did. My dog started howling and woke me up a minute before it happened.'

'The store's still standing,' Nell pointed out, not trying to hide her scepticism.

The young woman rolled her eyes. 'It only caused a landslide, didn't it? Blocked the road, up at that narrow bit below what they call Fairview. Our first delivery gets here at four o'clock in the morning, but not today. He couldn't get past the rock. Nobody can. So we're not getting our ten o'clock either. Nobody knows how long that road'll be closed for.'

A woman hurried up the aisle pushing a laden trolley ahead of her. With a wary, sideways glance at Nell, as if expecting argument, she reached past her and snatched the whole wheat loaf off the shelf before rushing away.

'As soon as word got round, people went absolutely mental,' said the store employee in a curiously satisfied way. 'We sold out of fresh milk in five minutes, and since then they've been buying absolutely everything. I shouldn't think there'll be anything left by lunchtime. We'll have to close early'

Nell left without trying to buy anything. Even if there had been a few things on the shelves that she needed, she shrank away from the feverish hunter-gatherer mentality now ruling the aisles. She didn't know if things would be any better at the smaller shops – in her view, big stores brought out the worst in people – but even if she went home empty-handed, she could survive for a week or more on home-grown produce and the contents of her freezer.

The streets of Appleton were as crowded and lively as she had ever seen them, even at the height of the summer tourist season. In the glorious sunshine and unreasonably warm weather, everyone seemed to be on holiday. She was usually confident about finding a place to park in the old marketplace (which had been turned over entirely to parking since the demise of the weekly street market) but today it was double-parked and impossible to enter. She found a place to leave the car on a side street near the library, and, deciding that might as well be her first call, lifted the heavy book bag out of the backseat.

Like the supermarket, the library was a hive of activity on Saturday morning, mostly for the elderly and parents with young children. Entering the cool, spacious foyer, she heard the chatter and hum of talk, definitely up a few decibels from the usual sedate exchange of remarks about the weather. But the feverish, hysterical edge she'd sensed in the store was absent. The people here weren't worried, only pleased to have something new to talk about.

The new librarian – American like herself – was behind the counter, and her smile of recognition was so warm and welcoming that Nell felt disconcerted. No one had responded to her like that in years. People in the town knew her to speak to, but she'd never felt that her presence mattered to anyone, and that was how she liked it.

'Mrs Westray! I've got your photocopy here.'

'Thanks,' she said automatically, reaching to take it.

'There's a charge of fifty pence for the photocopying, and you'll need to sign this form, Mrs Westray.'

'Call me Nell. Do you have change for a pound? Um, I don't know your name . . .'

'Kathleen. Kathleen Mullaroy.'

'Where do you want me to sign this, Kathleen?'

'Just there. Are these books for return?'

'Yes.'

'Ah,' said the librarian, sounding pleased as she opened the book on top of the stack. '*The Club Dumas*. Did you like it?'

'Very much. Do you have any more by him?'

'Yes. He's terrific. You won't find them on the regular fiction shelves, though. There's a copy of *The Nautical Chart* in large print, and *The Flanders Panel* and at least one other should be on that paperback rack by the door if they're checked in.'

'Thanks, I'll look for them.'

The last book on the pile was *Villette*. 'Oh, that's one of my favourites.'

'Mine, too. I used to have a copy, but I must have lost it somewhere along the way.'

'Where are you from?'

'Oh . . .' She made a meaningless gesture, caught off guard by the abrupt change in subject, and uneasy with it. 'I've lived a lot of places. I was born in Massachusetts.' She edged away from the desk, anticipating more intrusive questions.

'Do you like biographies?'

She stopped. 'Yes.'

'We have a very good one of Charlotte Bronte.'

'Is that the one by Lyndall Gordon?'

'Yes. Did you read her on Virginia Woolf?' As Nell nodded,

they exchanged the book-lover's complicit glance, and Kathleen said, lowering her voice slightly, 'Her new book about Mary Wollstonecraft is wonderful. It's out at the moment, but I could put it aside for you if you like.'

'Thanks.' Nell smiled uncertainly. 'Well . . . I'd better find myself something to read now.'

It had been only a brief, casual exchange of views. For all she knew, it was the sort of conversation the librarian had half a dozen times every day, but for her it had been rare and oddly seductive. When she brought her books to the desk to be stamped out, the librarian was again moved to comment, and they wound up discussing the comparative merits of works by Paul Auster, Alice Hoffman and Russell Hoban.

'It seems we have similar tastes,' said Kathleen, and her friendly, pretty face glowed with pleasure. 'And it sounds like you read a lot – more than I have time for.'

Nell shrugged. 'I have to have something for when it's too dark or too wet to work in the garden. I can't stand much television.'

'I've been thinking about starting a book group. They're so popular everywhere these days; it's strange there isn't one in Appleton.' The librarian leaned across the counter, her eyes fixed eagerly on Nell's. 'Would you be interested?'

'No.' The word came out more vehemently than she'd intended. 'No, I don't like clubs; that's not my kind of thing.' The librarian's bright, hopeful expression collapsed, and Nell felt as if she'd kicked a dog for wagging its tail.

'Look, I'm sorry, I didn't mean it like that; I'm sure it's a good idea – I'm just not good in groups, that's all. I'm not good in any kind of company – well, I've just made that obvious, haven't I?' She struggled to make amends, trying to smile. 'I've lived alone too long. I didn't mean to be rude, I've just forgotten how to talk to people.'

'You weren't rude! And as for forgetting how to talk to people – it was the way you were talking to me about books that made me think you'd be perfect in a book group.'

Nell imagined turning and walking out without another word – but she couldn't do it. Although she bought books nearly every time she went for a break to the city, there were no bookstores in Appleton; she needed this library. And, anyway, it was never her intention to hurt anyone. While she hesitated, still struggling with the problem, someone came up to the counter with a stack of books to be checked out. She moved aside, but the librarian let her assistant deal with them and did not release Nell from her gaze. 'Won't you think about it?'

'I'm better talking one-on-one than with groups.' As she spoke, she wondered if she shouldn't just agree and make her escape. She could always find excuses later for not attending.

'Me, too, actually,' said Kathleen, with another disconcertingly warm smile. 'Do you want to meet up for lunch sometime? We close between one and two for lunch. How about today?'

Her eyes went to the golden sunlight streaming through the window behind Kathleen. 'Not today; not with this sunshine. After the weather we've had, I can't *wait* to get back in the garden.'

'Oh, of course. Well, maybe another time? When it's raining? I'm here the same hours every day except Monday and Sunday.'

'Actually, I don't really *do* lunch. It puts such a big hole in the day.'

That should have been the end of it. Two flat refusals were generally enough to kill any hopes. She hadn't even apologized or left an obvious opening for her to try again; Kathleen could only retire, more or less defeated, which was what she'd wanted.

So Nell didn't understand what made her say, 'Why don't you come to my house for dinner? Tomorrow evening?' She spoke so casually that no one could have guessed what a big thing it was; the first time she'd ever invited anyone to Orchard House.

Kathleen's face lit up. 'I'd love to! What time?'

'Six o'clock? It won't be anything fancy; probably more or less vegetarian.'

'That's fine with me.'

They gazed at each other for a moment, both smiling shyly. Nell felt nervous and hopeful and confused by what she'd just done. She became aware that people were jostling behind her; looking around, she saw that a small queue had formed: mothers and children and pensioners struggling with their piles of books and waiting for her to get out of the way.

'I'll take those over here,' said Kathleen, moving to help her overworked assistant. She cast a final, bright-eyed look at Nell. 'See you Sunday!'

In a daze, Nell left the library. She hoped she wasn't going to regret the invitation. It would be harder, in a small town, to avoid someone once the first overtures had been made if you didn't want to be friends. She thought of Sam, who'd never understood what he called her 'shyness' but which others recognized, more accurately, as a carefully maintained aloofness; he'd always thought it the most natural thing in the world to have and keep friends. As she put her library books into the car, as she got out her shopping bags and walked down to the shops, she felt, for the first time in years, the warmth of her husband's approval, as if it were his sorely missed presence at her side.

From *The Living Magic of Scotland*
by Daphne Holdstock
(Mythril Press, 1979)

ALTHOUGH scholars have argued over whether or not the apple tree was represented in the Ogham tree-alphabet discussed earlier, there is no doubt about the veneration with which the apple was regarded by the ancient peoples of Scotland. Even the slightest acquaintance with folklore and fairy tale will bring a dozen references to mind. Apples were the fruit of life and immortality; the earthly paradise was 'Avalon' (apple-land), and a branch bearing silver leaves, crystal blossom, and ripe red fruit was the magical passport which admitted mortals into the Other-World.

This all sounds lovely, and yet the living traces of the long-ago apple-tree cult we can see in the Scotland of today bear a curiously sinister import. The game of 'dooking for apples' played at Hallowe'en is believed by many to be the survival of an ancient Druidic rite, and it also suggests a connection with the water ordeal once used for testing witches, who drowned if they were innocent, but were burnt to death if they managed to survive their ducking.

Old fertility rituals and festivals have long been associated with English apple orchards, but I know of only one such recorded in Scotland. The orchards of Appleton, on the west coast of Argyll, no longer exist, but the last Appleton Apple Fair was held in 1950, so I was able, on my visit to Appleton, to talk to many who remembered it.

From my reading about the Fair I'd been led to suppose it was a Victorian invention that would prove, on closer inspection, to contain nothing authentically Scottish. After all, the town's very name is English, and the orchards were planted by incomers in the seventeenth century. Yet a visit to Appleton changed my mind, especially when I ventured into the surrounding hills, and particularly into the high valley they call the 'reul.' There is *real* magic there; deep mysteries of earth and stone and plant and water.

Even if the Apple Fair was invented to attract tourists, however artificial its beginnings, it could not remain cut off but would soon have been pulled into the service of the local magic. Some aspects are recognizable from other Scottish traditions: that it was supposed to be a dark-haired stranger who crowned the Apple Queen reminds me of the preferred 'first-footer' on Hogmanay. My mother always used to say that the first person to step across the threshold of the house on New Year's Day should be a tall, dark-haired man. If the first caller chanced to be fair-haired, bad luck could be averted by tossing a lump of coal in ahead of him, but if it was a woman, we'd have bad luck all year.

'After the last Apple Fair, we never had any luck in the town,' one elderly woman told me. 'It was *her* fault, the Apple Queen. If she'd married her man, everything would have gone on as it always had. But she went away. They *both* did – only not together as they were meant to. And ever since, nothing's gone right with the town.'

Chapter Five

Ashley slept through it all: earthquake, landslide, sunrise, voices outside, the pounding on her door. She woke at last when she felt someone prodding at her shoulder to the accompaniment of a soft, childish voice repeating, 'It's time to get up. Time to get up, Cousin Ashley.'

She rolled over. Blinking the sleep out of her eyes, she saw a little girl, brown hair pulled into tight pigtails, staring solemnly at her, and she smiled, feeling the sides of her mouth crack with the effort. 'Good morning, Jade,' she said, and heard the croak in her voice. 'What time is it?'

'It's gone ten!'

'In the morning?'

'Of course in the morning! Can't you see the sun?'

She looked. Even though the curtains were drawn, sunlight rippled like water on the rough white plaster of the ceiling. She sat up, stretching her arms above her head as she yawned. 'Mmm. Well, I am on holiday, you know. If I was at home I might sleep till noon.'

'But it's *such* a beautiful day, it's a sin, that's what my granny would say, a sin to waste the best part of the day by sleeping. My granny used to live here, you know,' Jade confided, leaning against the bed.

'Here' – it was all coming back to her now – was a tiny two-room cottage located a short distance behind the house where Jade and her family lived, and which Ashley had been told she was to treat as her own home for as long as she liked.

'I didn't know your granny lived here. I thought your folks just rented it out.'

'Yes, it's a holiday house now, since Granny died. Passed,' Jade corrected herself. 'My granny passed last year.'

The phrase made her envision an old lady in a long nightgown hovering in the sky above the house like an elderly angel. 'So did mine.'

Jade's brow knitted. 'But did we have the same granny?'

'Oh, no. My grandmother was . . .' she paused to work it out. 'She would have been your granny's sister-in-law. I think.' More details of the night before came back to her – arriving in the rain, the friendly chaos of the Walkers' house, the noisy family dinner, how remote everything had seemed through waves of tiredness, until Shona had taken her, beneath an umbrella, across the path behind their house to this one, Graeme following behind with her luggage. 'Our kids get up awfully early,' he'd said. 'You'll get more rest over here.'

Shona had shown her where everything was, how to work the shower and the electric heaters, and told her that she'd made sure there were a few basic food supplies in the kitchen. 'But come over for breakfast with us in the morning if you like, or any time you need anything. Back door's always open.'

Remembering, she fixed the little girl with a look. 'How did you get in? I locked the door.'

'I know where Granny kept a spare key. It was still there.'

'You shouldn't let yourself into somebody else's house.'

Jade was unimpressed. 'It's *our* house. It belongs to the Walkers, and I'm a Walker.'

'I know, but when somebody else is staying here – when your parents rent it out to someone, you don't let yourself in then, do you?'

She shook her head.

'Well, then.'

'But you're *family*.'

Ashley laughed. She liked having been accepted, even absorbed, so quickly into this friendly Scottish clan, but it looked like there might be a few drawbacks. 'Even family members deserve some privacy!'

Jade stared as if this concept made no sense. Ashley put out her hand, palm flat and facing up. 'Give me the key.'

The small mouth set mutinously.

'Or I can tell your mom, and you can give it to her.'

Jade sighed and handed over a small, tarnished key.

'Thank you.'

'Aren't you *ever* getting up? I had breakfast ages ago, but Mum's got some rolls in the oven, and she says you can have whatever you want.'

'Go and tell her thank you, and I'll be over in a few minutes.'

'I'll wait for you.'

'But I don't want you to. I'd rather get dressed by myself. Remember what I said about privacy? Run along, now.' She tried to sound friendly but stern, someone not to be argued with, and it seemed to work.

Jade sighed heavily and moved away from the bed at last, head and shoulders drooping like a cartoon indicating rejection as she left the room. When she heard the door to the outside shut, Ashley got up. She showered, dressed, and applied a minimum of makeup. Her hair would just have to dry naturally because she couldn't find a hair dryer anywhere; she hadn't brought her own because she'd been warned that electrical goods needed an adaptor to work on British current, and it had seemed too complicated. She regretted it now, faced with the prospect of living with frizzy hair, but maybe Shona could lend her one.

She stepped outside into bright sunshine. For a moment

the light was dazzling, and then the view took her breath away.

It had been dark on her arrival, and although she'd been aware of being driven up a sloping incline, she hadn't guessed that her cousin's house – an unimposing modern bungalow – would command such a magnificent vista. She looked out at the gentle curve of the harbour, the sapphire glitter of the water, the quaintness of the small fishing boats and sailboats resting at anchor. The town of Appleton was contained within the natural boundaries created by the sea and the steep curve of the farther hills. It looked like a doll's town by comparison with the immense modern sprawls of the cities she was used to – Houston, Dallas, Los Angeles. It was like nowhere she'd ever been, and she was utterly charmed by it.

She took in a deep breath of the cool, fresh air, tangy with the smell of the sea and something faintly chemical she thought might be coal, and strode down the path to the back door of the bigger house. When she knocked, there was a volley of high, excited barks and several voices called out at once, scolding the dog and inviting her in.

The kitchen was only slightly less crowded than it had been the night before with the two boys missing. The dog, a Jack Russell terrier called Tia, rushed forward to give her a welcoming wag and sniff before retiring to her basket by the stove.

'Good morning,' said Shona. 'I hope you slept well?'

'Yes, thanks,' she murmured, once again made shy by the unexpectedly powerful surge of affectionate recognition she felt for someone she'd only just met. As soon as she'd set eyes on Shona she'd known her. It wasn't only that in the shape of her face and her eyes she bore a striking resemblance to pictures of Phemie as a young woman; when she smiled, and the hidden dimple flashed below the left side of her mouth, she reminded Ashley of her father.

'Coffee or tea?'

'No thanks.'

'Milk? Juice? There's orange or apple.'

'Orange juice would be nice, thanks.'

'I'll get it,' said Jade. She'd been curled on her father's lap, and scrambled to her feet. Ashley noticed that Graeme was dressed in his postman's uniform, complete with cap.

'Are you through with your round already?'

'Nothing to deliver,' he said, reaching to take off his cap. 'I was just telling my girls the news. We're cut off. Appleton's been cut off by road.'

She saw a giant hand equipped with a small, sharp pruning knife, lopping off a skinny apple-bearing bough. 'What do you mean?'

'There was an earthquake–'

'Maybe you felt it in the night?' said Shona. 'Tia certainly did – she got into bed with us!'

'Not a big one, just a tremor, down on the sea bottom, but add that to all the rain we've been having, and there was a landslide, a big one. The road's completely blocked.'

She remembered that final hairpin bend on the bus journey, the high, jagged rocks with the split in them, water spilling down the side. 'But there must be another . . .?'

'Nope. Only one way in and out of this town, apart from the sea road. I think that's what the Vikings called it. In the old days it was more usual to travel by sea than land around here, and I reckon that's what we'll have to do again.'

'Surely it won't take them long to clear the road,' said Shona.

'Oh, no? You haven't seen it. There's a boulder the size of a house blocking the way. I don't even want to think about what it's done to the road beneath. It won't be easy or quick to repair. Just moving the blockage is going to take weeks with heavy equipment. An awful spot to try to manoeuvre in, on a slope and that tight bend . . . dynamite could even make it worse, bring down more of the hillside.' He shook his head. 'I reckon we'll have to find alternatives to road travel for two or three months, minimum. They'll be flying in the post, come Monday – or at least by Tuesday.'

'So there's an airport.'

He grinned. 'There's an old airfield, used during the war, which has clearance for use by small private planes. Maybe some bright spark will set up a regular service between here and the mainland. Next stop, Appleton International Airport!'

'Dream on,' said Shona. 'Nobody outside will care; they weren't that bothered to come here when the road was open! The dozen or so folks who could afford airfare out at this end won't make it economically viable.'

'It's lucky you came on the bus yesterday, Ashley,' said Jade, setting a small, very full glass of orange juice carefully down on the table in front of her.

'Lucky?' said Shona, raising her eyebrows. 'I don't know if she'll think it's so lucky if she can't get away.'

'I don't want to get away. I just got here.' She took a small, cautious sip of the juice, which tasted unpleasantly sharp contrasted with the toothpaste flavour still on her tongue.

'Let's hope you go on happy here. What would you like for breakfast? Eggs, bacon, sausage . . .'

'Fried tomatoes, fried mushrooms, baked beans,' Jade chipped in.

The thought of a plateful of cooked food was amazingly unappetizing. It always took her stomach a while to wake up. 'No thanks, I don't,' she began, but something in Shona's look recalled her mother's ardent belief in the importance of breakfast, and she modified what she'd been about to say. 'I don't want a big meal. I think my body hasn't adjusted to the time difference yet. Just a piece of toast, or . . . do I smell fresh bread?'

Shona gave a gasp, and rushed across to the stove. 'I nearly forgot! Whew, they're all right. Just! When Graeme came in, I forgot I'd put the rolls in. Jade, love, would you fetch the butter, and some jam?'

Graeme decided he could do with a midmorning snack, and put the kettle on. 'Sure you won't have a cuppa, Ashley? There's coffee, tea, or some kind of herbal brew Shona likes.'

'No thanks.' She sat breaking a crispy roll into bits, buttering the pieces, and slowly munching her way through it as she listened. Jade disappeared with a buttered roll in one hand.

'If it really is going to take months to clear the road, it's the end of the town,' said Shona flatly.

'Ach, we'll manage. It might even do us good,' said Graeme. After spending only a few hours in his company, Ashley could tell he was the sort of natural optimist who would always see the silver lining. 'We've already got the air ambulance, for emergencies, and if the post's going to be brought in and out by air, there's the potential for a few paying passengers every day as well. But a ferry's the obvious solution, for goods deliveries and for passengers. In fact, it could be the making of this town – put us back on the tourist map good and proper.'

Shona sighed. 'It's the last nail in the coffin.' She turned to Ashley and explained. 'This town has been dying by inches for years; for decades, really. With the road gone, it's like cutting off the intravenous drip, our last link to life. Without visitors, even as few as they are now, the economy is dead.' She turned back to her husband. 'And if we *do* get a ferry, what's betting the council decides it's not worth the expense of repairing the road? Or it takes them five years to plan and fund and build a road that will meet updated safety standards, by which time this will be a ghost town.'

It was obviously an old disagreement. As they went on rehearsing it, Ashley understood they saw their beloved home differently. To Graeme, Appleton's strength lay in its uniqueness, its isolation, its old-fashioned indifference to the modern world – this was what had drawn him from the big city to become a small-town postman, father, and local historian. To Shona, who had grown up in the town, seen many schemes and small businesses begin in hope and collapse in failure, watched her friends move away in search of jobs and better opportunities, its size, antiquated attitudes, and isolation – attractive though they might be to some – were the symptoms of a fatal disease.

Despite her decision to get out of business studies, Ashley couldn't help responding like the student she'd once been. She remembered a lecture on the drawbacks of a local economy solely reliant upon tourism, and wondered what judgment one particularly dynamic teacher would have made on Appleton's chances.

She asked a few questions; Shona seemed grateful for a chance to break out of the accustomed deadlock with her husband to answer.

'In some ways, the town is exactly the same as it was when I was a wee girl.'

'Like Brigadoon,' said Graeme. 'Frozen in time. So what are you complaining about, lass? If it's lasted fine for so long –'

'It's not been fine at all, and you know it,' she interrupted. 'A healthy organism changes and grows. This town's not changed except to shrivel and age. Every year it gets smaller, and more people move away because there are even fewer reasons to stay. I can remember when there were two cinemas, three bakeries, four hairdressers', and five butcher shops.'

'A lot of meat-eaters left town.'

She ignored this. 'I know shopping patterns have changed. People have big freezers, and they'd rather go a long distance and buy in bulk once a month – get exactly what they need at the lowest price – not trawl around the local shops every day and make do with whatever happens to be available. But nothing's come in to replace the things we've lost. Other towns manage; it's not like this everywhere. And it's such a lovely place – people who come here fall in love with it.'

'Or we fall in love with her daughters.' Graeme moved his chair closer and put an arm around his wife.

She smiled and let her head drop briefly onto his shoulder before going on. 'Maybe it's just the right person hasn't come yet. We need somebody to come along, love the town for what it is, but also see what it *could* be and set out to make it happen. It would only take one.'

'Calling Richard Branson,' Graeme intoned. 'Would Mr Bill Gates please report to Appleton Town Hall? We have a business proposition for you . . .'

They invited her to stay for lunch, and Graeme offered to take her around and show her sights, including the landslide.

'Ach, Graeme, she doesn't want to see a load of mud and rock!'

'Everybody else does. Where do you think the boys were off to on their bikes?'

'I don't want to take up your time,' Ashley said. 'You must have other things to do. Maybe later . . . but right now, I'll just go out and have a wander.'

'You'll get to know the town better that way,' Shona agreed. 'Come back here whenever you want. Don't stand on ceremony The wee house is for you to use, but drop in here whenever you want a bit of company, or something to eat.'

A few minutes later, she was outside in the fresh, bright, foreign air, making her way down the gentle slope to a street of houses. The sweep of shoreline down to her right looked appealing in the sunshine, but she turned left, more curious about the town.

On her arrival, dusk and heavy rain had veiled the scene, allowing her only vague glimpses of a bleak, sleepy seaside town huddled against harsh, barren hills. It looked very different on a sunny day. The rocky hills still loomed above, but they seemed warm and sheltering now, and the streets were thronged with people in light, bright clothing, strolling and shopping, congregating in clumps and clusters on street corners to talk. The predominant mood was cheerful, even festive, despite a few complaints about disrupted plans caused by the landslide.

There were more small shops than Shona's gloomy description had led her to expect, and they all seemed to be doing a roaring trade. She didn't see anything she could identify as part of a chain; every single business seemed to be independent and locally run. It was a bit like travelling back in time, she thought. Even the ubiquitous McDonald's and Starbucks had made no inroads here. Instead, fast-food outlets were represented by the Syracusa Fish Bar, the Chat 'n' Chew, and Bud's Burgers.

The main thoroughfares had been planned on wide, straight lines, although they'd been narrowed in practice by a general disregard for road signs and markings, and an amazingly casual attitude toward parking. Behind the main roads she discovered narrow, winding streets, some of them cobbled and barely more than a single lane wide. Here she saw the first signs of decay: two empty shops with boarded-up doors and soaped-over windows, one on either side of Curl Up & Dye, a feverishly busy hair salon. Across the narrow, cobbled lane was an antique shop with a cardboard sign in the window announcing WINTER HOURS: BY APPOINTMENT ONLY.

And for all its bustle, even on Main Street there were gaps. One large vacant property still bore a faded wooden sign identifying it as Tartan Tunes. In the big window was a board offering the shop for sale or lease. A former jeweller's had closed, and an Indian restaurant, and she saw three other shop fronts that gave no hint about what they'd once housed.

Eventually she tired of wandering and looked for somewhere to have lunch. The word 'botulism' sprang alliteratively to mind when she glanced into the grimy little storefront burger bar, so she followed her nose to the Syracusa Fish Bar. It was obviously popular, with a line of customers snaking out the door and along the front of the shop beneath the blue-and-white sign with its image of a happy, cartoon fish leaping out of the waves. She stepped around the line to peer through the front window, and saw no tables inside, just a counter with two men working furiously behind it. One man was elderly, with white hair and tattooed arms; the other was a good-looking, olive-skinned boy with eyelashes to die for. She watched for a moment as the boy wrapped steaming fried fish and fat golden french fries in pale brown paper, and her mouth watered. He looked up and, very briefly, their eyes met through the glass. She smiled. When he did not respond she turned away, watching a couple of teenagers come out of the shop, already eating their take-away fries. It might have been fun with a friend, she thought, to picnic on a grassy spot overlooking the sea, but it made her too sad to think of doing it alone.

Every table in Chat 'n' Chew was full, so she headed down to the harbour at last. Past the pier she came to a broad avenue bisected by a strip of green where palm trees grew. They were few and puny by comparison with the ones she remembered in Galveston, but she supposed the very fact of their survival this far north said something about the mildness of the winters. Across the street, on a corner, with big bay windows to fulfill the promise of its name, was the Harbour View Café.

'Sit anywhere you like,' said the woman engaged in fitting a new roll of paper into the cash register, so she headed for one of the empty tables at the front beside the window, passing a couple of family groups and one man seated by himself, reading a newspaper and sipping a cup of coffee. Looking again, she recognized him as the man she'd seen from the bus.

She felt it like a blow to her chest but managed to keep moving past him, towards her table. By the time she'd seated herself she knew, from the heat in her face, that she must be bright red. Facing the window, she couldn't see him at all, and if he ever looked up from his newspaper, he'd just see the back of her head. He couldn't recognize her from that. Had he noticed her passing? Did he remember? Had the look that had passed between them on the road affected him at all?

'Are you ready to order?'

She'd been so obsessed by her thoughts about *him* that she hadn't even glanced at the laminated menu resting in a stand on the table in front of her. She decided abruptly that she wouldn't. Phemie had never looked at menus; it had been her custom to ask for whatever she felt like eating, wherever she happened to be, and usually she got what she wanted. Taking the same approach, Ashley asked for a tuna sandwich and a diet cola.

Left alone again, she stared out the window at the people strolling along the waterfront. There was a family like a picture from an old-fashioned children's book, balanced in the traditional way: attractive, youngish mother and father, little girl carrying a doll, little boy with a blue-and-white ball tucked under one arm. They stopped to look at the boats, the father pointing something out to the children, then they moved on, passing out of her view. She hadn't brought anything with her to read, but her sketch pad and pencils were in her day pack, and she got them out. She stared across the curving harbour, at the houses and buildings that lined the other shore, and lifted her eyes to the gentle, undulating line of hills. It was a lovely line. She began to trace it, then shaded in the dips and hollows of the hills, added the outlines of a few houses, and sketched a palm tree in the foreground, for perspective. She began to add a few more details, becoming so absorbed that she hardly noticed when the waitress brought her food to the table. On top of the highest hill was a transmitting tower

– presumably for television and radio, although it had so many different attachments and extensions that it might have been a telephone mast as well. She'd ignored it when she'd started sketching in the line of the hills; but she wondered if she should put it in, for truth, or leave it out for beauty's sake. Would that spikiness add interest or spoil the composition? Her hand hovered above the page.

'You're an artist.'

The low male voice so close to her ear made her jerk; there, in place of the tower, was a jagged pencil slash.

'Oh, now you've spoiled it – I'm sorry!'

'It's not spoiled, it's only pencil, and it's not anything – I'm not really an artist.' She flipped the cover shut to end the discussion, but he didn't move away, and she had to look up at him. This was the chance she'd hoped for, but she couldn't think of a thing to say.

Her look seemed to be enough. She saw the pupils of his eyes expand: he liked what he saw. He touched the back of the chair beside her. 'Do you mind if I sit down?'

She shrugged.

She was intensely aware of his nearness as he settled into the chair: the heat of his body, his leg barely an inch away from hers, the faint sigh of his breath. He was staring at the table, not looking at her, and she let her eyes trace his strong profile, drinking in his rather exotic features. The line of his nose and chin made her think of old Mayan sculptures, but there was more delicacy to his bone structure.

She wondered if he was half-Indonesian, or Hawaiian, or what. She couldn't work out if he had any sort of accent.

'I saw you yesterday,' she said.

'Oh? Where?'

'On the road. I was on the bus that passed you.'

'That was you!' Their eyes met and once again she felt the powerful tug of pure, physical desire. 'I remember. I felt like I knew you. Like we'd met before.' He looked puzzled, which made him seem both younger and more ordinary.

'So did I,' she said eagerly. 'But I'm sure I'd remember if we had. This is my first time in Scotland.' She thought for a moment. 'Maybe we met in California? I used to go there every year to visit my grandparents. San Diego – but also L.A. Have you been there?'

'Oh, yes. I've been just about everywhere.' He sounded vague, distracted, and he looked at the table, not at her.

'Where are you from? I can't pin down your accent. You don't sound American – *or* Scottish.'

'I'm not, quite.'

'So what are you?'

He turned his head and gave her a wistful, curiously sweet smile. 'Desperately hungry, if you want to know the truth. Are you going to eat that?'

It was her sandwich he'd been staring at, and she thought she could take it that it had been the chief attraction all along; those four neat triangles of toasted bread and tuna mayonnaise meant more to him than anything about her. Chastened, embarrassed, she gave a sharp hoot of laughter. 'Go ahead. I don't want it.'

He didn't need to be asked twice. He picked up one segment and devoured it in two bites, then did the same to a second. She sipped her drink and watched him eat, wondering if she looked like a pushover, or if he was really so desperate. When he'd finished the whole sandwich, he polished off the garnish of cucumber, cress, and tomato slices and sighed. It was a sigh more of sadness than satiation.

'Do you want more?'

He hesitated, then nodded.

'How long since you last ate?'

'Not so long, really. I had a meal the night before last, but I've walked a long way since then.'

'You walked all the way to Appleton? From where? Why? Not just for fun.' She was trying to figure him out. His clothes were old, but not especially dirty or cheap-looking. He was youngish – she guessed early twenties – and looked fit and healthy. He said he was hungry, but that could be a ploy.

He didn't answer. Looking down at the white oval plate where the sandwich had been, he spotted a green comma of cress, pressed his thumb down on it, and raised it to his mouth.

'I don't mind buying you lunch,' she said. 'I'm just

curious – don't you have enough money?' She turned around to look back at the table, where he'd abandoned a white china mug and a folded newspaper.

'The paper was there,' he said. 'I ordered a cup of coffee knowing I couldn't pay for it. I don't have any money. I came back to Appleton with nothing but the clothes I'm wearing.'

This wasn't working out as she would have wished, but it wasn't a crime to be short of cash.

'Order what you want; but remember, I'm on a budget. I'm not Miss Richie Rich, OK?'

'OK.' His eyes flashed into hers again before he turned around to catch the eye of the middle-aged waitress.

'What sort of soup do you have?' he asked.

'Chicken and vegetable broth.'

'Sounds good; two of those.'

'Anything to drink with that?'

'A glass of water would be nice. And apple pie for afters; I've never been able to resist a piece of sweet apple pie.' He looked intimately into her eyes, and Ashley felt a disturbing curl of jealousy in the pit of her stomach. She knew, by the smile on the waitress's face and the spring in her step as she departed, that she hadn't misinterpreted the look, and before she could stop herself she'd snapped, 'I bet she'd have given you that cup of coffee on the house.'

'Oh, I was counting on it,' he said carelessly, and she

glared at him, well aware that she had no right to mind, but already enthralled, unable to leave it. She wanted to be special to him, not just an easy touch, a generic pickup.

'So what made you come here, of all places, if you're so broke?' she quizzed him sharply. 'Wait a minute, you said came *back* to Appleton. This is your home?'

'This is where I grew up. I wouldn't call it my *home* – I never felt it was that.'

'But you have family here.'

He shook his head. 'None. My mother died when I was very young. My grandfather raised me, or paid others to do it. After he died, there wasn't anyone left to care what happened to me. I left as soon as I could.'

'So why did you come back?'

He shrugged, gazing out the window at the view she'd so recently been sketching. 'It felt like the right time. I'd been out wandering the wide world for so long, always just passing through, always a stranger . . . I don't know. I've never been settled anywhere; I've been used to moving on at the slightest whim, so why not?'

Their soup arrived with a basket of bread. Ashley had meant to put her bowl aside and pointedly leave it, since he hadn't even asked her what she wanted, but the smell of it revived her hunger. She stirred it and blew gently on a spoonful, and said, 'OK, so you're a travellin' kind of guy – I still don't get what made you come back *here*, especially if you're so broke.'

'Something made me. I had to come. I can't explain it.'

She decided he had to be telling the truth because it was a ridiculous lie. He could have made up a dying grandmother or a delayed inheritance, a stolen wallet or a job interview – anything that might convince her she was doing a good deed. She thought of Shona's deep affection for Appleton and compared it with her own lukewarm feelings for Houston. That was her home, all right, she'd never known another, and if she was broke or in trouble, that's where she'd head – but only because she had friends and family there, people who'd known her since she was a baby. Remove them all, and she didn't think the memory of Houston's skyscrapers and pine forests, crowded freeways and flat coastal plains baking in the hot sun would draw her back across the miles if she had other alternatives. Maybe Appleton was different when the memory of its hills and harbour, cobbled streets and fine old buildings were planted in your heart.

As if he'd been following her thoughts, or perhaps because he was trying to explain it to himself, he said, hesitantly, 'It was different this time, an urge rather than a whim. It was time for me to return. I just knew I had to come back. I'm ready, I think, to – well, to put down roots, at last.' He smiled to himself.

'Well, then, it's lucky you got here before the landslide.'

'Lucky?' he echoed, his eyebrows rising.

'Well, I mean, it's lucky you want to stay, because–'

'Because now I can't leave? Oh, well, I never meant to leave by *that* road, anyway.'

Guessing he was teasing, she concentrated on her soup and didn't ask what he meant. When they'd finished, the waitress brought them two pieces of apple pie.

'Mmm, this is good,' she said after the first bite. 'Really fresh and homemade.'

'Ah, Scotland's a great place for home baking,' he said, sounding as smug as if he'd invented the tradition. 'And Appleton apples are the best.'

'Those apples came from New Zealand, or maybe England,' said the waitress, who was clearing the table behind them. 'They surely weren't local.'

'Really? But why?' He twisted around in his chair to stare at her. 'Why not use local apples?'

She stopped and put her hands on her hips, a sarcastic smile playing about her mouth. 'Why? Because, my love, there *aren't* any Appleton apples, unless you're thinking of the MacDonald orchard over in the White Glen, and those have always gone for cider. I think he tried to branch out into eaters a while back but they didn't take.'

He gaped at her like a caught fish. 'But what about the Wall orchards? They're not all for cider – and anyway, I heard the cider mill closed down.'

'You heard that, and you didn't hear what happened to the orchards?'

'What happened?'

'All sold off, dug over, and planted with other crops. None very successful. A lot of that land is conifer forest now; farmer who bought it got a tax break.' She gave him a puzzled frown. 'Those apple trees stopped bearing before I was even born. Maybe the climate changed, I don't know, but apples don't seem to do so well here now, though the stories say they used to. My neighbour had a couple of Bramleys. The trees were fine and healthy at first, but after a few years the apples were useless, just full of canker and brown rot; nothing to do but burn 'em. He cut the trees down seven or eight years ago and switched to soft fruit.'

'No apples.' He sounded really shocked, which Ashley found mystifying after what the woman had said.

The waitress shrugged. 'Well, I suppose some people have them in their gardens . . . I've been told that the lady who bought Orchard House put some apple trees into her walled garden. She's American, like you,' she added, nodding at Ashley. 'Or are you Canadian?'

'American. From Texas.'

'Texas! My son went there last year with his girlfriend. Some kind of music festival. Austin, that's right, isn't it? He loved it. Can't wait to go back.'

Ashley smiled politely but said nothing, wanting to be left alone with her mystery man, and the waitress backed away. 'Let me know if you want anything else.'

He resumed eating his piece of apple pie, although it had clearly lost its savour.

'Did you *really* grow up here?'

He looked startled. 'Of course. But it was a long time ago. Things have changed more than I imagined.'

'Or else you've forgotten a lot.'

'That's possible.'

She tried again to guess how old he was. He might be as old as twenty-six, and if he'd run away at fifteen his memories of this place might well be vague. Maybe he remembered the cider orchards and confused them with stories his grandfather told about the old days, when Appleton had been famous for its apples.

'Well. Thank you for my lunch.' He wiped the corners of his mouth with a paper napkin and let it flutter down to lie atop his empty plate. 'Next time, it's my treat.'

She went to the cash register to pay. When she turned around she found him waiting for her. 'Shall we go for a walk?'

She'd been on the verge of inviting him back to her place, but she agreed to his suggestion, sure their walk would bring them there in the end.

They went out and turned to the right. Immediately next door to the café was the Victoria Hotel, a building that had seen better days and could have done with a fresh coat of paint, at the very least.

'The café used to be part of the hotel; I think it was a

resident's lounge, or maybe it was the public bar. They must have sold it off when times got hard,' he said, gazing at an upstairs window. 'There are a lot of hotels in Appleton.'

'I noticed that, when I was walking around before. I was amazed. There must be about ten, although most of them were pretty small.'

'The grandest hotel wasn't even in the town. It was out at Southport.'

'Where's that?'

'South side of the apple.'

'Oh, duh!' She grinned and struck herself lightly on the side of the head. 'Southport, south. So there's another town close by?'

'Hardly a town. A village. Not much there but a fabulous beach. There's a golf course – at least there used to be. Once the motor buses were running, it was an obvious place to build a grand hotel, and it was quite successful until it was hit by a stray bomb in the Second World War.' He stepped back, gazing at the hotel before them. 'It's hard to believe now, but in the old days, at the height of the tourist season everyone in the town with a spare bedroom would hang out a sign offering bed and breakfast. Children were made to sleep out in the garden so their parents could let their beds, especially during Appleton Fair week.'

'When was that?'

'Now. Late September.'

They walked on, past a charity shop and a vacant premises with a FOR LEASE sign in the streaked and dusty window. Up ahead, majestically occupying the corner site, was a most impressive building made of dark red stone, with cream-coloured pillars and decorative carvings.

'Wow, what's that?'

'The public library.' His voice was tight with some repressed emotion, and he began to take longer strides so that she had to half run to keep up with him. He was not in a hurry to reach the library but to get away from it, she realized, as he began to cross the street.

'Wait – is it open? Can we go in?' She hurried after him despite her wish to linger and drink in the details of this unexpected architectural glory.

'Not now.'

Once across the street she looked back. Clearly the library *was* open; she saw people going up the wide steps to the entrance. Equally clearly her companion couldn't wait to get away. 'Why?' she asked, hurrying to catch up. 'What's wrong?'

'Unhappy memories.' He slowed his pace. 'I'm sorry. I was never welcome there. It was my grandfather's place, built to keep people like me *out*.'

'That's horrible!' She thought of the welcoming libraries and librarians of her childhood. 'But if your granddad was a librarian . . . what do you mean, "people like me"?'

'I never knew my father. I didn't *have* a father, as far as society was concerned.'

She didn't know what to say. Glancing down at her feet, she saw a tiled mosaic picture set in the middle of the sidewalk. It depicted a mermaid holding a comb in one hand and a looking glass in the other. 'What on earth is this doing here?'

'That used to be a cinema.' He gestured at the empty, weed-covered piece of land. 'There should be a name, too.' He bent down and raised a clump of moss and grass to reveal the letters picked out in blue, red, and gold tiles: RIALTO.

'What does that mean?'

'I dunno. It's a bridge in Venice . . . It was the sort of name cinemas had back then. The other one, down on First Street, was the Ritzy.'

They continued to walk along the wide Esplanade along the curve of the shoreline. The houses built on the landward side, well away from the road, became larger and more elegant, fine old Victorian and Edwardian villas, very handsome, most of them, although there were some with more fantastic pretensions. One house had towers, turrets, and crenellations like a miniature castle; another was an oriental-inspired folly, with Chinese dragons on the gateposts and all four corners and a pagoda in the garden. Most had clearly seen better days, were in need of fresh paint and obvious repairs even when the gardens were rigorously maintained.

They came to the last house, standing at the top of a weed-infested drive guarded by a couple of crumbling stone lions. The road branched in two, with one fork continuing to follow the shoreline, curving away out of sight, and the other leading uphill.

'Where does it go?'

'The cemetery's up there, and beyond that, the old quarry, and the moor. It's great up there. Down along there . . . we'd come to Southport eventually.'

She was enjoying being with him, without pressure, and wasn't tired yet, but walking out of town seemed pointless.

'Let's go back. I saw lots of interesting buildings this morning – you could tell me what they are.'

'I thought you'd want to see the cemetery.'

She wrinkled her nose. 'Why?'

He smiled. 'Look for your ancestors? Find your roots? Isn't that why you came?'

Her mouth dropped open a little as she stared at him. 'How did you know?'

He laughed teasingly. 'I don't have to be psychic! This is Appleton, not Edinburgh. Why else would a lass from Texas come here . . . how else would you have heard of it if you didn't have ancestors born on the apple?'

She began to smile again. 'Well, you're right. But I'd

rather leave the cemetery for later. I don't care about family trees. I'd just like to get to know the place Phemie came from.'

She saw the instant flare of shocked recognition in his eyes. His expression didn't change, he said nothing to give himself away, but the name had hit him when he wasn't prepared.

This reaction, so unexpected, startled her. 'What? You've heard of her?'

He gazed thoughtfully out to sea. 'Phemie is a very Scottish name, very old-fashioned. You don't hear it much nowadays.'

'My Grandma Phemie was old. Her name was Euphemia MacFarlane.' She caught her breath as an idea struck her. 'We're not *related*, are we?'

'Of course not.'

'How do you know? How did you know about Phemie? What's your name?'

'I'm not a MacFarlane.'

'You could stand here all day telling me what your name *isn't*.'

'I told you I never knew my father.'

'So what? You knew your grandfather. What was his name? What's *your* name?'

When he still wouldn't answer, or even meet her eye, she exploded. 'I don't *believe* you! If you think I'm going to waste any more time with somebody who won't even tell me his name . . .' She turned abruptly and stalked away. Her anger held an edge of fear. What was he hiding? Was he a psychopath, with some hideous plan for what he meant to do to her if he could lure her into the cemetery? She'd seen and heard too many stories about attractive yet dangerous men to completely dismiss the idea, yet she couldn't believe she could be so attracted to a man who meant her only harm. So she clung to the hope that this was some esoteric form of flirtation. Surely he wouldn't just let her go. She began to walk more slowly, tiring in the hot sun, and listened for the sound of footsteps behind her. But he'd better have a really good explanation.

She'd reached the mosaic mermaid. It wasn't going to happen. He'd let her go. She stood for a moment, staring down at the picture made of chips of coloured tile, telling herself it was for the best, and she'd had a very lucky escape, but unable to believe it, feeling only a great disappointment, a hollow sense of loss. A voice called her name.

Her head jerked up, but she knew already that it was not *his* voice, and it had come from the wrong direction. She saw Graeme across the street, waving and beaming at her from his rather pointed, pixieish face.

'Ashley! Perfect timing. Come on over, let me show you the museum.'

From *The Life and Letters of Clarence Arnold Fortune*
edited by Florence Fortune McPhee
(London, 1881)

... MR WALL showed me his 'cabinet of curiosities' before dinner, and it provided much for us to talk about over our repast. Let me see if I can recall the contents for you: I know you'd love to see the 'mermaid's comb' (as the little housemaid called it) – a very beautifully worked ivory comb, inset with red coral – a priceless little gem, really. Also fine were the matched bowl and chalice of beaten silver with a marvellous chased design of leaves and fruits; then there was the narwhal tooth, tipped in gold, and in appearance very like one I saw many years ago in Staffordshire, in Lord D—'s possession, believed by his forbears to be a veritable Unicorn horn and therefore prophylactic against all poisons; also half a dozen small glass vessels of some antiquity; coins from an unrecognisable (by me!) currency; various bits of primitive-appearing ceramic work and stone-carving – some rather engagingly fantastic creatures represented here – and half-a-dozen Mollukah beans, which the local people call 'fairy eggs' and use as lucky charms, or amulets. Perhaps most amazingly, all of these treasures were discovered locally, for Mr Lachlan Wall is no traveller, and has spent all his life here in the Highlands, indeed, within a radius of some twenty miles. All these things – and others, which I've forgot to list – were gathered on the sea-shore not far from his house, either by himself, or by one of the local children, who've learned that this odd and solitary bachelor will reward them handsomely for any interesting treasures that they bring ...

Chapter Six

Kathleen heard about the earth tremor and resultant land-slide from Miranda when she came in to work on Saturday morning, and suddenly the dream she'd had a few hours earlier made sense.

She had dreamed she was working in the library as usual, but in her dream the building was actually an enormous ship, bigger even than the *Titanic*. Although Kathleen recognized most of the library users, lining up patiently to have their books stamped, she was aware of a number of people she'd never seen before, oddly small and quick as they slipped behind shelves or rushed past the doors.

Leonardo DiCaprio came behind the counter and put his hands firmly on her waist. 'Come up on deck with me,' he murmured and, although she'd never cared for him on-screen, and he was really not her type at all, she'd agreed, feeling romantic.

They went behind the old counter, and up the winding metal staircase – which extended about three times higher than usual – then had to climb a rope ladder into the crow's nest fixed to a mast high above the library's golden dome.

'Look out there,' he said. 'That's where we're going.'

She had a glimpse of wide, empty ocean gleaming beneath a hard blue sky; no sign of land or life anywhere. Such isolation was unsettling. Turning back to Leonardo, she found he'd turned into Keanu Reeves, an actor she found rather more attractive, but she was still reluctant to let him hold her.

'I have to go back,' she said, trying to remember why she'd ever agreed to embark on this voyage, and realizing that she had no idea of their destination. Then she heard a deep, distant grinding noise, and there came a jolt, which rocked the whole ship and jarred her out of sleep.

'Iceberg,' she whispered, blinking into the familiar darkness of her bedroom. She thought something more real than a dream had awakened her, but had no idea what it could have been until Miranda told her the news that had the whole town buzzing.

The landslide – and what it would mean for the town – was all anyone wanted to talk about that day, but gloomy predictions were accompanied by high spirits; there was a giddy feeling of exhilaration in the air, as if they'd all been cut free, rather than cut off.

'You'd think it was a festival, not a natural disaster,' Kathleen murmured to Miranda as she came back from showing some children where they could find information about earthquakes.

They gazed together at a cluster of white-haired ladies, all with sparkling eyes and roses in their wrinkled cheeks, talking and nodding in vigorous agreement with each other as they departed.

'Well, you have to admit that, as disasters go, it's pretty tame. Nobody injured, no damage to private property or anything except the road. And that's not a local responsibility. People have been complaining and worrying about that road for more than a decade – it was in serious need of upgrading already, and now, finally, something will have to be done; money will have to be found from central government. Of course, I know a few folks have had to put off their shopping trips, and they're not happy about that, but they're sending the air ambulance for Mrs Martin, so she'll make her appointment to see the specialist in Glasgow, and the orthodontist will be flying in on Wednesday to see to the kids' braces.' She gave one of her demure yet mischievous smiles. 'It's that old Blitz spirit, don't you know. Proving our best in adversity, all pulling together. It'll be a positive blessing for the charter boat business. And when you live in a quiet wee place like this, you're grateful for any bit of excitement.'

Gratitude at having something new to talk about would turn quickly to annoyance as time wore on and inconvenience became a regular feature of daily life; but on this first bright, sunny day after the landslide most of the townspeople basked in the novelty of living on an island. Some, it turned out, thought this was the best thing that could have happened to Appleton.

'We'll get our ferry now, just watch and see,' announced Trevor Burns, setting one fat Joan Collins and two even fatter Maeve Binchys down on the counter with an attention-getting slam. He was a slim, dark, driven-looking man who had been campaigning for years for a direct sea link between Scotland and Northern Ireland. The books were his wife's, of course. He had no time for recreational reading. He came into the library on a regular basis to use the photocopier, the fax machine, or the complete set of national telephone books.

'It would be useful to have a ferry,' Kathleen agreed.

'Useful!' He reared his head back as if she'd disagreed, and his little dark eyes flashed. 'It'd be the redemption of this wee town – a rebirth. It would put us back on the map!'

Sandy Brown, a large and amiable man who had organized and spearheaded a number of local groups over the years, all dedicated to encouraging tourism in Appleton, approached. Resting his arms on the counter beside

Trevor, he paused to promote his pet project: 'Daily boats between here and Greenock, that's the ticket. Never mind your Northern Ireland, it's Glasgow and the central belt holds the key. That's where people mostly go by road, and that's our natural supply of folks wanting a short break in the country. Old-fashioned steamers, for personal choice, but really any sort of vessel would do; fast and modern might be best. *Much* better than buses; folks would queue up for tickets. They'll have to put on something like that while the road's out – I've heard it could be as long as six months before it's made good – and once it's established, it'll attract even more passengers. Inside a year, it'll be paying for itself, mark my words.'

'Ach, well, I'll not say you're wrong, Sandy,' began Trevor, when Kathleen interrupted to remind him gently that others were waiting behind him to reach the counter.

'Your wife's tickets, Mr Burns.' She handed over the miniature cardboard folders which were the basis of the library's out-of-date system, and reached to take the pile of Catherine Cooksons old Mrs Ellary was holding up with trembling arms.

'I think this landslide is a blessing in disguise,' whispered Mrs Ellary. 'Maybe now it's not so easy to go gallivanting off abroad, folk will stay put and learn to appreciate what we have here at home. That's how it was when I was a girl, you know. And people were much happier then.'

The only people obviously upset and dismayed about

the landslide were the visitors (as tourists to the area were termed), and their concern was understandable. As the self-catering accommodation was reserved on a weekly basis, with Saturday the changeover day, most of them had been intending to leave today. They were English, Australian, German, Dutch, and even one American couple from North Carolina, and considering the complaints she'd heard from the hotel-owners about how bad business was, and the fact that it was the very tail end of the tourist season, and that those who came to the library probably represented a fraction of those who were stranded here, Kathleen was surprised to see so many coming into the library, seeking Internet access in vain, or wanting to look at maps and phone books. These visits tapered off by afternoon, and the level of anxiety dropped as news spread that they would be offered a way out. Information had been posted in the tourist information office and other places – a teenager dashed in just before the lunchtime closing with a notice for the library's information board – that special flights had been arranged to transport visitors, free of charge, to Glasgow International Airport. One would be leaving the local airfield that evening, and another on Sunday, if necessary. People with cars (that must have been just about everyone), would have to decide whether to leave them behind, or wait for the roll-on, roll-off ferry, which was likely to be up and running between Appleton and Greenock very soon . . . or, at least, eventually.

It was just a matter of bringing the long-disused local ferry terminus up to the necessary safety standards (after finding the funds for that) and allocating a suitable vessel from another route.

The morning was busy, even busier than most Saturdays, and Kathleen was so preoccupied by other people's responses to the landslide that she scarcely had a chance to consider her own feelings about it. She was merely aware of a faint uneasiness, the notion that she'd forgotten something, and the sense that it was somehow connected with her dream of the library as a huge ship sailing out into the vast, empty ocean, until, as she was checking the Ladies' Reading Room prior to locking it up for the lunchtime closing, her gaze went to one of the windows, and she was arrested by the sight of a solitary male figure standing beneath one of the palm trees that grew along the centre strip of the Esplanade. He was just standing there, staring at the library, his head tilted back slightly, his gaze directed upward, towards the roof.

She froze, gripped by a powerful sense of *déjà vu*. Although there was certainly nothing unusual in someone – particularly a stranger, as she sensed him to be – staring at this remarkable building, she knew she had seen him before, last night, in just that pose, gazing up at her bedroom window. She'd thought it a dream.

Then the man moved – perhaps he felt himself observed? Kathleen kept still, watching as he turned and strode away and she remembered the pendant to her dream.

When she woke she'd held her breath and listened for a repeat of whatever noise had awakened her. But it was silent; unusually silent, except for some dogs barking as if they, like she, had been disturbed. It took her a moment or two to realize that it had stopped raining, and without the steady drum of rain on the roof, which had become the norm in recent nights, it seemed *too* quiet.

Glancing at the bedside clock she saw it was a little after 3:00 am. Moving carefully, she'd slipped out of bed, headed toward the yellow glow of the streetlamp, which she could see through the gap in the curtains. When she reached the window, she pulled one side of the curtain back and saw a man standing on the corner, staring up at her.

It was the same man she'd just seen on the Esplanade, in daylight. She only had to close her eyes to see him again, as if his image had been burned in that single moment onto a screen behind her eyes. He was young, in his twenties, with dark hair sleeked back from a narrow, exotic face; she'd had an impression of high cheekbones and rather Asiatic eyes, although that might have been an effect caused by shadows.

She'd felt afraid when she saw him, gripped by the unreasoning fear that this stranger had come looking for her, for some reason she could not guess but which was unlikely to be benign.

After her first sight of him she'd reeled back in shock

and pressed herself flat against the wall, where she couldn't be seen until the pounding of her heart had become less painful, and she'd been able to breathe normally again. When she dared to look again, he was gone. By the time she'd made a quick tour of the house and had seen that the doors and windows were all locked, the motion-sensitive lights in the library garden were dark, and there was nothing obviously amiss, she'd almost convinced herself she'd only dreamed the man below her window.

Until this second sighting proved he was no dream.

Of course, there was no law against a visitor going for a walk late at night and stopping on a corner to look at a public building. Her new home was a structure of architectural interest, one of the landmarks of the town. He might have thought the building empty, never guessing that anyone lived in it. The fact that he'd been out there again in broad daylight did seem to suggest that his interest was in the building, and purely innocent. The odd thing was that he hadn't come in. Most visitors to the town did; even those with the most cursory interest in the big stone building usually came in to ask questions about its purpose, wanting to buy postcard pictures of it, or to ask if they could go inside the dome.

Well, maybe he'd be in during the afternoon, she thought, turning away at last, trying to shake off the unease that her second sighting of him had awakened. She hoped he'd come in and introduce himself as a tourist from Hawaii or an architecture student from France, and dispel the mystery.

But the stranger did not come into the library that afternoon. However, someone else did.

By four o'clock the library had gone quiet. Miranda was shelving books, and Kathleen was thinking of slipping away to the office for a cup of coffee when a man came in. She recognized him immediately with a deep jolt of unexpected pleasure, and as he glanced in her direction she called out a warm and happy 'Hello!'

He smiled back, but it was a reserved, minimal smile; he didn't know her. She felt her own smile congeal with embarrassment, but although she couldn't pin a name to him, she remained certain he was no stranger. At some time in the past, she had known him well.

He walked slowly through the big room, glancing up at the oil paintings by little-known regional artists that hung high above the bookshelves before stopping in the travel and history sections to peruse the spines. He was a man in his late forties or early fifties, lean and fit in faded jeans, a maroon shirt, and a lightweight, beautifully cut leather jacket. His long, greying reddish hair was pulled back in a ponytail, and he had a freckled, lived-in face that might have been unremarkable except that it was so deeply familiar to her. A rush of heat made her thighs tremble and her breath quicken. Yes, she knew what it was to want him, but her longing had been unrequited. She had been a lot younger the last time she'd seen him – but where and when she couldn't exactly remember. In America, before her marriage . . . for some reason, he brought her old boyfriend Hank to mind. In college, then. Could he have been a friend of Hank's? Maybe a teacher?

She watched the leather jacket shift and wrinkle like skin as he reached up to take a book from a shelf, and she stared harder, willing him to turn around so she could see his face again. *Oh, but this is silly.*

Clearing her throat, she called out, 'Can I help you find something?'

'No, thanks, I'm just browsing. Passing the time.'

She knew that voice. No doubt about it. The accent was transatlantic. He could have been an Englishman who'd spent a lot of time in America, or an American educated in Britain. Who had she known like that in college?

'I guess you're trapped here, then.'

He turned to face her, removed his aviator-style dark glasses and slipped them into his inside pocket. 'Trapped? Well, no, I don't see it that way. I wasn't planning to leave for a while.'

'It's not a bad place to be, especially when the weather's like this.'

He smiled. 'You don't sound like a local.'

'Because I'm not bad-mouthing Appleton?'

He gave a soft laugh and took a few steps toward the

counter. 'Tell me, how does an American come to be living here?'

'The usual way. I came, I saw, it conquered me.'

'My experience exactly.'

'Been here long?'

'About ten years.'

That startled her. 'Oh! I'm sorry, I didn't think I'd seen you in here before, and I thought–'

'–I was a visitor. Well, you're not far wrong. I own a house here, but I've never been a full-time resident. And I was away for about a year.' He had been coming gradually closer as he spoke, until he stood directly opposite her on the other side of the counter. She was able to see – without surprise – that his eyes were an odd hybrid of brown and green. He gave her a slightly puzzled, searching look. '*You* weren't here then; I'm sure I'd remember.'

Her heart beat a little faster. Was he flirting? She gave him an encouraging smile. 'I've only been here for three months. But I thought I recognized you when you came in – that's why the big hello.'

'I *liked* that big hello,' he said, leaning a little closer, so she caught a subtle, attractively musky scent.

The sharp, echoing bang of a book being slapped down hard on the counter startled them both. Turning toward the 'Returns' end of the counter, she saw the always-impatient Mr Rand drumming his fingers beside the book.

'Would you excuse me–' But, with a disappointed dip

of her heart, she turned back and saw the ridiculous pony-tail bouncing against black leather as he moved with completely unnecessary haste toward the carved doors to the museum. *I don't bite!* she felt like shouting after him. *And* you *were the one flirting . . .*

But maybe that, like her feeling that she knew him, was a false perception. Put it down to hormones, she thought as she went to deal with Mr Rand. The sexual frustrations of the recently unmarried female . . .

'This is overdue, I'm afraid. That'll be twelve pence, please.'

'I want to renew it,' he snapped before she'd finished speaking.

'I can do that for you, but there's still a fine to pay.'

'What? That's ridiculous. I'm the only one who wants it. Oh, never mind, never mind,' he cut her off, digging into his pocket. 'Ten and two make twelve, there. And I have a request for you.'

Miranda slipped back behind the counter while he was giving her the details of the book he wanted. After he'd gone, she turned to see her hovering, biting back a smile, someone with news to share.

'What?'

'I see you've met our local celebrity.'

Kathleen glanced over at the door, still swinging slightly from the passage of the impatient Mr Rand.

'Not *him*.' She looked significantly in the direction of

the museum. 'I heard you two chatting away.'

She frowned. 'He looked familiar, but I couldn't think why. Local celebrity?'

Miranda whispered, 'Dave Varney.' Mistaking Kathleen's poleaxed stare for incomprehension, she amplified: 'Singer-songwriter, big in the eighties, played drums for–'

'The Stunned Bunnies,' said Kathleen. 'Oh my God. I *loved* them.' No wonder she knew his face and figure, knew those odd browny-green eyes. They'd stared at her out of a poster on her dorm room wall for a full two years. Dear, devoted Hank had driven her all the way to L.A. with tickets to one of their gigs for her twenty-first birthday present. They'd never made it as big as Talking Heads or lasted as long, but she'd adored their intelligent, ironic ballads and offbeat, retro pop tunes.

'That's right. He bought a hill farm on the Apple about, oh, ten years ago, and they spent quite a lot of time there at first. But then his wife died.'

'Oh!'

'You must have read about it, it was in all the papers – brain tumour. About two years ago. Maybe it didn't get as much attention down in London. She was Scottish, his wife, an actress called Kay Riddle.'

'I remember now.' Although the Stunned Bunnies had not lasted long as a group, and Dave Varney's subsequent career had been devoted more to songwriting and production than to performing, his celebrity status revived when his wife, until then a fairly obscure comedienne, got a starring role in what quickly became an extremely popular television series. The following year, she was diagnosed as suffering from a brain tumour, and the two of them became tabloid fodder. It was one of those stories you couldn't help knowing about even if you had no interest in celebrity gossip. He must have thought . . . what? That she was pretending not to know who he was? She felt herself shrivel with embarrassment, and the thought of having to face him again made her feel awful.

'Look, Miranda – do you think you can manage here on your own for the next half hour?'

'Sure, go on. If a coachload of visitors suddenly arrives, I'll ring for help.'

She stayed in her office until closing time, when she emerged to help Miranda with the routine checks to ensure that everyone was off the premises, all doors were closed, and everything electrical switched off before the library was locked up for the weekend. They didn't exchange another word about the afternoon's celebrity visitor. Although Kathleen was longing to talk about it, there wasn't time to explain to Miranda what Dave Varney had meant to her when she was younger, and, anyway, she wasn't sure that her comfortably married assistant was the person she wanted to have such a girly heart-to-heart with: *Was he flirting with me? Did I scare him off? What's the gossip about him? Does he have a girlfriend*?

Instead, she went home to phone Dara, her oldest, closest friend on this side of the Atlantic. It had been nearly a week since they'd spoken, and now, just after five o'clock on a Saturday, would be a good time to catch her in. They had shared their emotional ups and downs for years; losing her regular company had been the hardest thing about moving north. Still, they talked on the phone every weekend, and one of these days – soon, very soon, she promised herself as she settled into her most comfortable chair and pressed in the number sequence she knew by heart – they'd add to that the joys of e-mail and instant messaging, and they wouldn't have to feel they were living in different centuries as well as different countries.

She heard the sound of the phone's distant ringing, hundreds of miles away, and it went on and on. There was no answer, not even from voice mail. With a puzzled frown she broke the connection at last, and tried Dara's mobile phone number. That, too, purred in her ear, and purred and purred without redirecting her to another number or giving her a recorded message.

It was so unlike her friend – could there be a problem with her phone? After a moment's thought, she entered the number for Dara's next-door neighbour, a sweet gay man who fed her cat and watered her plants when she was away, but got a busy signal in response.

So that was that. She looked up, out the window, to where she could see a patch of blue sky between the glossy dark leaves of the holly tree. Sunlight shone on the leaves, making them glisten. One thing she'd learned since moving here was that good weather was ignored at your peril. You had to seize the day. She changed her shoes, tied a light cardigan around her waist, and went out for a walk, choosing to turn her back on the glittering sea and instead climb the hill that rose up at the back of the town.

It was a stiff climb, but rewarding, especially in the fresh, warm air of early evening. From the top she could turn and look down on Appleton, and see the golden dome of her library gleaming in the last, late rays of the sun, and she could also turn her gaze to the moorland and gentle hills that rolled away into the distance. She narrowed her eyes, trying for a glimpse of the sea on the horizon, but, although the sky overhead was still blue and clear, she couldn't make out the line where it met the sea. The far horizon was blurred and misty, as if hidden by gathering cloud. She pulled her gaze back, to the closer hills. Out there, in lush, hidden valleys, were half a dozen hill farms and a few isolated houses, one of which belonged to Dave Varney – songwriter, music producer, one-time drummer, and long-ago star of her youthful romantic fantasies.

A quite unnecessary blush heated her face, and even on the empty hillside where no one could see her, she was glad there was a wind to cool her cheeks. She lived through those few minutes' conversation again. Had her attraction to him been so *obvious*? She supposed it must have been, since he'd taken his first chance to escape without so much as a friendly wave, but it did seem strange that he'd found her carefully restrained interest so threatening that he had to flee. He must get it all the time, not just from his ageing fans, but from younger women with no idea who he was. After all, he was quite an attractive man, even with the ponytail. If he hadn't learned, after his years in the limelight, to take a little minor adoration in his stride, it was hardly *her* fault . . .

She had to stop obsessing about it. He probably hadn't given her a second thought; maybe he'd meant no offence by his sudden rush to visit Appleton Museum. She turned away from the distant view and made her way down to the town again.

When she reached the Hillside Hotel she stopped and gave a considering look to the sign that advertised the bar and restaurant were open to the public. She'd heard that the chef had trained in France, and had worked in good restaurants in London and Edinburgh before coming here; the food was considered the best in town, if also the most expensive. She hesitated, hungry after her walk, and seriously tempted, especially since her choices at home were limited to pasta with cheese or an omelette. Her credit card was in her pocket. If she didn't treat herself, who would? Gravel crunched underfoot as she stepped between the twin brick pillars topped with plaster lions and made her way up the drive. There were eight cars in the parking lot, one an eye-catching red Porsche.

The reception area was deserted, with a sign pointing the way to the bar. It was reasonably full, but not crowded. She spoke to the woman serving there. 'I was wondering if I could get a table for dinner.'

'Just yourself?'

She nodded, slightly apprehensive.

'Sure, no problem. Do you mind eating here, or did you want the restaurant? Only there's nobody in the restaurant; everybody staying in the hotel flew out about an hour ago, if you can believe it!'

She gave her back a sympathetic smile and shrug. 'Sure, I can eat here,' she said, although, looking around, she saw no unoccupied tables.

'There's more tables through in the back room,' the woman explained, nodding toward an arched doorway to her left. 'Today's specials are on the board, or you can order from the menu.'

Kathleen had already noticed the blackboard hanging behind the bar, and made up her mind. 'I'd like the lamb shanks with parsnips and onion mash, please. And a glass of red wine – what do you have?'

A few minutes later she made her way, glass in hand, through the archway, and slipped into a seat at an empty table in the far corner. Only then did she pause to look around and take stock of the room. She froze as she saw Dave Varney at the next table.

He'd seen her, too. 'Well, hello, Madame Librarian!' His face lit up; if she could believe her own eyes, he was genuinely delighted to see her.

She couldn't speak, temporarily silenced by the difference between the aloof, nervous stranger she'd imagined and the friendly, welcoming reality.

'I looked for you when I came out of the museum, but I couldn't find you. It was getting on for closing . . . I could have kicked myself for – anyway, I figured I'd have to wait till next week to talk to you. And here you are!'

'What did you want to talk to me about?'

'Lots of things. For starters, the museum.' He rose. 'Would you like to join me, or – I'm sorry, you're waiting for someone?'

'No. I decided to treat myself to a meal I didn't have to cook.'

His face cleared. 'Me too! Although, to be perfectly honest, I hardly ever cook for myself *except* when I'm up here, so it's a bit of a cheat . . . but here I am. Now, will you make an old man very happy?'

She laughed. 'Are you about to wheel out your aged papa?'

'I was referring to myself, young lady. But we haven't been introduced. I'm Dave Varney.' He pulled out a chair and sat down across from her.

She dipped her head shyly. 'Kathleen Mullaroy.'

'I know. I read about you in the local paper – I have a subscription, so I can keep up with the goings-on in the wee Apple when I'm away. If they'd printed your picture, I wouldn't have left it so long to come back.' He was looking at her with such frank appreciation that she couldn't believe it.

Confused, she blurted, 'I know who you are, too. I *thought* I recognized you when you first came in, but it took me a while to get it. Context: I didn't expect somebody I'd gone to see in concert in L.A. for my twenty-first birthday to walk into Appleton Library.'

'Outta all the libraries in all the world, I hadda walk into yours,' he intoned Bogartishly.

'So what did you want to ask me about the museum?'

He dropped his gaze, moving his wineglass on the table. 'There's a story behind it.'

'Go on.' She smiled encouragingly.

'Well. Are you familiar with J. F Campbell? He was a sort of Scottish version of the Brothers Grimm, who went around the Highlands in Victorian times, collecting Gaelic folktales which he published as *Popular Tales of the West Highlands.*'

As he said the title, she saw the four thick old books covered in sturdy, dark blue library bindings on a shelf in the reference room. 'I know the books you mean.'

'My grandfather had a set, and I read them one summer holiday, every word of them except of course for the Gaelic bits, which I used to stare at and puzzle over as if it were a kind of code that I could break.' He grinned rather shyly, shaking his head. 'Anyway Campbell began his introduction, which was his justification for publishing the sort of stories not normally committed to print and which had not previously been considered worthy of attention, with a discussion of fairy eggs. You know about them?'

She shook her head, intrigued.

'They're large, hard seeds' – he held up his cupped hand to indicate the size – 'found on Scottish beaches and believed by the common folk to have magical powers, and so preserved and handed down as protection against disease or bad luck. The educated disdained them as trash, but botanists studied them. And when they figured out they must come from the New World, that proved the existence of the Gulf Stream. Campbell's point was that even though they weren't magic, there was still some purpose to gathering and studying fairy eggs, and the same applied to stories about the fairies.

'Many years later I was in Edinburgh for the Festival, and the guesthouse where I was staying had stacks of some ancient little magazine extolling the wonders of Scotland – *Aye for Scotland* or *The Tartan* or something like that. Well, I'll read anything–'

She laughed sympathetically, and he grinned.

'Yes, there are worse habits. Better than rolling up the pages and smoking them as I've known some to do. Anyway, I read this old article about the wonders of this tiny Scottish museum, where the core of the collection had come from the architect's family – Mr Wall's Cabinet of Curiosities, it was called, and among the contents were a unicorn horn, a mermaid's comb, and . . . several fairy eggs.' He looked at her expectantly.

She shook her head. 'I never heard of it. I'm sorry. I could ask . . .'

He sighed. 'I asked the old librarian about it. He knew what I meant; he's the one who'd modernized the exhibitions, made them more relevant, supposedly. But as for what he did with the cabinet of curiosities, I couldn't get a straight answer out of him. I suppose he sold the lot off and didn't like to admit it. I'm sure you could get a good price for a unicorn horn on eBay.'

A teenaged boy with a white apron tied on over his clothes approached the table with a tray. 'Lamb shanks?'

'Me,' they replied in chorus, then looked at each other and laughed while the boy stood blankly scowling.

'Great minds,' murmured Dave, then, to the boy, 'Ladies first. And could you bring us a bottle of the Shiraz?' He turned back to Kathleen, pointing to her glass and raising his eyebrows, and she nodded her agreement, although she felt tipsy enough already with the pleasure of his company.

When the boy had gone, she said, 'I really doubt Mr Dean sold anything from the museum. Certainly not on his own authority. If it happened, it would have gone through headquarters, after being ratified by a council meeting – at any rate, there'd be a paper trail, and I can find out. Most likely everything he took out of the museum is in the storage room upstairs. There must be a hundred or more boxes up there.'

'So you think the fairy eggs are still there? Not thrown out as mere trash?'

'I'm sure. I imagine he was cagey because if he admitted he knew where they were, you'd ask to see them, and he didn't want to have to dig them out and fetch them down for you.'

Their young waiter returned with a second plate of lamb shanks. Behind him, the woman bartender came with a bottle of wine and two clean glasses. She poured a small amount into one of the glasses and waited for Dave's approval before filling them both, then left them with the cheerful injunction to enjoy their meal.

'He could have just told me the stuff I wanted to see was in storage, so piss off,' said Dave.

'Maybe he thought you'd be persistent and insist on seeing them.'

'I *can* be persistent,' said Dave. 'And loyal to a fault – two of my doglike qualities.'

She had picked up her fork, but she put it down again unused, caught by his words.

'So . . . you mean . . . you're still determined to see those fairy eggs?'

'Well, yes. I never really stop being interested, once I start. I might seem like a casual sort of guy, but I feel things deeply.' He frowned, looking faintly anxious. 'But I'm not so self-centred that I think it's all about *me* . . . I'm not obsessive in a bad way – at least, I hope not. I mean, I can take no for an answer. If you wanted to tell me to get lost, you could, and I wouldn't bother you again.'

She was assailed by conflicting emotions, realizing he wasn't talking about some old beans.

'I'm not going to tell you to get lost,' she said at last, a little breathlessly.

'I hope I never make you change your mind.' He raised his glass, smiling. 'Can we drink to that?'

She picked up her glass and touched it to his.

'To you not wanting me to get lost,' he said.

From *Pleasures of the Table*
by Percival M. Lingerton
(Baskerville Press, 1892)

WHENEVER business or pleasure takes me north of the border, I seize the chance to savour one (or more) of Appleton's Fairest, as these dappled, cone-shaped beauties are never to be met with in England. The reason is not that they do not travel well, for, in fact, properly packed and stored, they keep beautifully, and indeed for maximum enjoyment they should be eaten not only when fresh from the tree, for although they provide a brisk, juicy, sharply piquant treat in late September, by the New Year the stored apples have become sweeter and drier, with a magnificent yet subtle aroma, and a honeyed, almost nut-like flavour, particularly good taken with cheese and a fine Port wine after dinner, and in this state they will last, as they say 'til the apples come again,' with no diminution in goodness. I myself have partaken of the Fairest as late as August, when the new crop is still a-ripening on the trees. No, the only reason they do not adorn the tables of discerning connoisseurs in England as well as Scotland is that the Scots love them too well to export their small crop for the pleasure of the

'Sassenach,' and keep them a closely guarded treasure.

Now, why should the Scots have this all their own way? Some years ago, I resolved to grow my own. My garden, after all, is in Kent, a county long renowned for apple-growing, and so, although I was warned that Appleton's Fairest would not thrive away from its coastal north-westerly situation, I took several cuttings home with me and gave them to my gardener, a man highly skilled in the propagation and care of fruit trees, with instructions to do his best by them. Alas! Every attempt at propagation failed. I have since learned, from a gardener at Blenheim, that a similar experiment was tried there, on a larger scale, in the 1860s, with the same sad result. Where, on two or three trees, the graft appeared successful, and maiden trees resulted, they proved barren and sickly and had, ultimately, to be destroyed.

Scotsmen have a story for every occasion, and so, naturally, they have one to explain why Appleton's Fairest should be so stubbornly different from all other apples. I heard this from my ghillie on the Ross-shire estate of the Duke of B– where I joined a hunting party a few years ago. The lad had family connections in Argyll-shire, one of whom was a farm-labourer near Appleton. According to him, it was well-established fact that the settlers who came to found the new town discovered the wild crab-apple tree growing in the sheltered glens, and named the place after them. In my experience, most crab-apples are so hard and bitter as to be hardly worth the picking – the cider made from them is unlikely to be worthy of consideration – but *these* wild apples, although quite small, were of a most amazing sweetness; having a sort of raspberry taste, and called by the locals *flann banrigh* (which I understand to mean 'red queen'). Among the first settlers was a pair of brothers from a cider-making family in Melrose. They had brought some small trees with them from their home and built a walled orchard to protect them from the worst of the sea-winds, and, as an experiment, tried crossing a wild apple with one of their own – a variety the ghillie believed was called the Scarlet King, although I've never heard of it.

The result, in any event, was Appleton's Fairest, an apple so delicious that it was reserved for eating, although a few bruised and fallen fruits were thrown into the cider vats on the thrifty Scottish principle, and the resulting batch of cider was so far superior to any they'd produced before that it became a standard inclusion thereafter. Legend had it that the inclusion of just one of the Fairest would raise the quality of the whole vat.

The Fairest is, as you might well imagine from the details given above, a *red* apple, although even at its ripest retaining that undertone of yellowish-green that can appear like a sprinkling or dappling of gold; in colouration it bears affinity to the crimson-over-gold hue of the Worcester Pearmain. An American friend of mine compared the Fairest in both shape and colour to a variety from his homeland called the Mother; I would disagree about the shape, for in my experience, the American Mother is frequently lop-sided, and sometimes flat-sided, and I have never known a Fairest to be less than symmetrical.

And so the ghillie confirmed. And yet, said he, legend had it that once in a lifetime one single *golden* apple would appear among the usual heavy crop of reds. This golden apple could not be treated as part of the common crop. It must be picked at its moment of perfect ripeness, to be shared by two lovers who would thereby be granted their hearts' desire, and peace and prosperity would reign over the land. If, however, the golden apple was selfishly consumed by any one person – or sold – or, worst of all, left to rot, untasted, then, alas, some terrible fate would befall the whole community.

It was for this reason that the annual Appleton Fair always featured the crowning of a 'Queen,' by tradition a respectably betrothed young woman, who would be given an apple to share with her lover. According to the ghillie, his granny recalled the appearance of one special, golden apple in her girlhood, in the year before our beloved Queen ascended to the throne. She remembered it with all the power that accrues with disappointment, because she was then a bonny lass of sixteen, with her eye on her first sweetheart, and she wished with all her might that a magical apple would bind them together in a happy and prosperous marriage.

'Once in a lifetime,' according to that young ghillie, yet not since 1836 has it appeared! They are by all accounts a long-lived race, who spring from the soil of Appleton. Shall we ascribe magical properties to the soil, the air, or to the cider they drink by custom instead of good Scotch Whisky?

Chapter Seven

As she reached the top of her drive after finishing her errands in town on Saturday, Nell looked down and saw the results of the landslide for the first time. She might have seen it earlier if she had been in a mood to notice, but her thoughts did not often turn to the only road out of town. Now, as she put on the handbrake and wound down her window for a better look, she felt a crawling anxiety deep in her stomach. *Trapped.* And yet, had the road been clear, where would she go? Generally she took a short break in Edinburgh or Glasgow every couple of months, but her last such trip had been only two weeks ago. Tearing her eyes away from a sight that made her senselessly uneasy, she drove around to the side of the house and parked beneath the awning.

As soon as she'd unpacked the car and put away her

shopping, she put on the kettle and brewed a handful of mint leaves in the small blue-and-white porcelain pot she'd bought on her first visit to London. She wasn't sure where she'd picked up the habit, but since adolescence, mint tea had been her remedy for half a dozen minor ills, and just going through that minor ritual of brewing a pot worked to calm her.

When the tea was ready, she took it outside to the small paved area behind the house, where she'd set a small table and two chairs near the fragrant herb garden, and settled down to read the photocopied pages she'd picked up from the library.

She'd started reading about apples when she had started her orchard. At first it had been the practical things she'd wanted to know: how to prepare the ground, how to keep the trees healthy, which varieties would do best in a wet and windy climate, and so on. But growing apples did not appear to be a terribly complicated business, and she had quickly read everything she could find on the 'how-to' side of it and moved on to history and folklore.

Their potential variety was practically infinite, because apples don't breed true from seed. Each apple seed is different from all others, and, if planted, may produce a type never known before. If the new apple was special enough, it could be preserved and reproduced either through a root sprout, or by grafting a twig from the new tree onto the trunk of another; they would then fuse together and grow into a tree identical to the one from which the twig was taken.

Nell had been fascinated by the stories of wonderful new apples discovered growing out of rubbish heaps, behind chicken houses, or in old, abandoned gardens: Mannington's Pearmain had come from cider residue tipped beneath a blacksmith's hedge in the eighteenth century; Granny Smith sprouted from a heap of apples dumped into an Australian creek in the 1860s; Bloody Ploughman grew in the 1880s from a rubbish heap where a bag of stolen apples was thrown after the thief was shot . . .

When she'd first started to think beyond the plan of growing a few apples for herself, she'd wondered about creating a new apple; then she'd started to dream of bringing Appleton's Fairest back to life.

Trawling the Internet, she learned of an American pomologist by the name of Creighton Lee Calhoun who had saved hundreds of varieties of old Southern apples from extinction. His method was to drive around North Carolina and Tennessee, looking for old apple trees. Whenever he spotted one, he'd ask the owners if they knew the name of the apple. If they could name it, he took a cutting, grafted it onto rootstock, and planted it in his orchard.

Nell's quest was different because she was looking for one particular apple. It was possible that some people in

Appleton might have a Fairest tree in their gardens, and these isolated examples might have survived after the big orchards were dug up and plowed over in the late 1950s, but she shrank away from the idea of prowling around Appleton, peering over garden walls and knocking on the door and introducing herself whenever she spotted an apple tree. She preferred to keep her distance from the town where she had chosen to live.

She had gone to the library instead and searched until she found maps showing the precise location of the original orchards. They had been bulldozed over, but since the land was to be used for forestry and grazing, it was possible that a few trees had been spared, if only by accident. The trees would be old now, but apple trees could live more than a hundred years, although they usually stopped bearing fruit after fifty.

She had marked the position of the old orchards onto an Ordnance Survey map, and set off on foot to explore. The new forest was a monoculture of softwood pines, planted in rigidly straight rows. It was a silent and weirdly lifeless place – native birds didn't nest in these imported evergreens, and the height and density of the trees shut out light to the forest floor so that only mosses and mushrooms grew there.

But just as she was about to give up and turn back, she found what she had been looking for – although it was outside the boundaries she had drawn, and the sturdy old tree could never have been part of the old orchards, for it was growing alongside a tumbled pile of rocks that, on closer inspection, turned out to be part of a wall. At one time there had been a building here, maybe a small croft house, maybe just some sort of enclosure for animals, but nothing that belonged in an orchard. She had examined the tree closely, cheered by its obviously vigorous life. She knew it could be a seedling, sprouted two or three decades ago from a Golden Delicious or a Granny Smith core tossed aside by a passing hiker, but her discovery filled her with an absurdly optimistic hope, which persisted despite her long experience with disappointment.

She took a cutting with her special knife and carried it safely home. The graft was successful – she'd used a commercial root-stock with a particularly high tolerance for damp – and she had waited for three years, to be rewarded at last this summer, when the new tree's first fruit finally appeared. It was not much of a reward. One apple. One single, yellow apple.

Her first, sour thought was that here was proof that the tree she'd taken her cutting from had, in fact, been a seedling from a picnicker's lunch. Twenty years ago, the Golden Delicious, imported from France, had been the most popular apple with the budget-minded British public and could be found in every packed lunch.

Now, she read over the last page of the photocopied excerpt from Lingerton's book and wondered. Every description she'd found of Appleton's Fairest had emphasized its redness. And she didn't think it was possible for a tree to produce two such distinctly different-looking varieties, unless you got *very* tricksy with the grafting.

But it was a fairy tale. Golden apples were the stuff of myth and legend, and that was all.

She reached for her cup, but the tea had gone cold while she brooded.

When she woke on Sunday morning, Nell's jaw ached with tension: she'd been grinding her teeth all night. What had possessed her to invite that librarian to come for dinner? She *never* did that, ever. Her only other guest in her years at Orchard House had been Lilia, Sam's sister – arguably self-invited – and that weekend, ending in tears, had set no precedent.

She wondered how hard it would be to cry off sick. But the library was closed today, and she didn't have Kathleen's phone number. Anyway, that was the coward's way out, and she loathed cowardice perhaps more than any other human weakness.

She took a deep breath and got up and dressed in the same clothes she'd worn on Saturday. Bathing and what her grandmother had called 'titivating' could wait until after she'd done the housework.

After she'd washed the kitchen floor and vacuumed everywhere else she took a piece of bread and a glass of juice for her breakfast out into the garden. It was another warm, fresh, blue-sky day, promising to shape up into an unseasonable scorcher. The sun on her arms relaxed her, and she strolled around her kitchen-garden kingdom, checking out supplies and planning the evening meal. She could get rid of some of her over-abundant tomatoes in a soup for starters, follow that with some sort of pilaf, and a side dish of courgette cooked with onions, peppers, and tomatoes – or was that too many tomatoes? A simple green salad to follow, in the European fashion, and for dessert . . . it was too hot for baking, so maybe apple snow, or, if there were still enough fresh blackberries to be found . . .

She turned her gaze to the far edge of the garden, where a mass of sprawling wild blackberry bushes remained, after all her savage pruning, like a hedge separating her property from the forest beyond, and went stiff with shock. There was a man. He wasn't in her garden, he was on the other side of the blackberry bush, but what right did he have, what was he *doing*, standing there as still as a statue and staring at her?

Raising her voice, she pitched it at him coldly: 'Can I help you?' Arms crossed defensively over her chest, she walked toward him.

He gave her a friendly wave but did not speak until she drew closer. She took the chance to check him out, even more on her guard because he was definitely her kind of sexy beast. His trousers were old and sloppy, but the plain

T-shirt fitted him snugly, showing off a slender yet muscular build. His short black hair shone in the sun like an animal's thick, glossy pelt, and his skin made her think of a beautiful, fine-grained wood. His features were regular, his nose hawklike, and there was what might have been a faintly Asiatic slant to his dark eyes. He looked young, but she guessed he was past thirty, a man who had his genes to thank for a perpetually youthful appearance. His smile did not reveal his teeth.

'I was just admiring your garden. You've put in a lot of work.'

She didn't smile back. 'Do you live around here?'

'Not for a long time. I've just come back. Someone told me there were apple trees at Orchard House again.'

'I've planted a few.'

'I'd love to see them.'

'Look, I don't want to be rude, but this is private property. I don't do tours.'

'I know, but . . . I'm sorry, I should have introduced myself. You see, this isn't a casual inquiry. I'm Ronan Wall.'

She was no expert on the history of Appleton, but everybody knew the Walls had been one of the major families in the area for a long time. They'd planted the first apple orchards. 'Wall as in . . . the Wall orchards? Wall's Cider?'

'The very same. How are the mighty fallen, eh?' He grinned, showing even white teeth and the smallest glimpse of tongue. She felt a twinge of lust. Well, too bad; she'd just have to control herself.

'Do you know anything about Appleton's Fairest?'

His eyebrows rose. 'I'd be a liar if I said "everything," but – what do you want to know?'

'Everything.' She smiled for the first time and waved her hand over to the right, where there was a gate. 'Come in. I'll show you the orchard, if you'll let me ask you some questions.'

'It's a deal.' He loped along to the gate and came in. 'And you are–?'

'Nell.' She left it at that, just as she did when she'd met someone in a bar or a club in one of the cities she visited from time to time. She turned and led him across the lawn and into the meadow, where clouds of pale butterflies rose and swirled away as they pushed through the high grass.

He quickened his pace and left the path, crushing down wild flowers as he walked beside her. 'How many trees do you have? What are you growing?'

'Two dozen. I've gone for some variety, but I've tried to concentrate on older apples that originated in Scotland.'

'The Fairest?'

They'd come to the door in the wall and stopped. He gazed at her eagerly, and she frowned. What was he playing at?

'*You* should know the answer to that.'

'You mean . . . that's why I've come?'

He was staring at her like she held the answer to life, the universe, and everything. Unsettled, she turned and pulled open the wooden door. 'I *mean* you just told me that you knew everything about Appleton's Fairest, so you must know–'

'I said I don't know *everything*.'

Her mouth quirked sarcastically. 'I thought that was modesty. Was it irony? Are you going to tell me now that actually you don't know *anything* about apples? In that case; what do you want to see my trees for?'

He took a deep breath. 'I'm looking for Appleton's Fairest. I know – I mean, I was *told* that the orchards were all destroyed.' He paused, and she knew he was hoping for contradiction.

'That's right,' she said. 'I've seen where they used to be. It's all pine forest where it's not empty grazing land.'

'But then somebody told me that there were apple trees at Orchard House again, and I thought, I hoped . . .'

An involuntary wave of sympathy for him swept over her. She didn't want to be the one to cut the line he was clinging to, his last, slender dream that the apple which had made his family's fortune was not lost forever. How could she, when it was her dream, too?

Gently, she said, 'I hoped to grow it myself. I did some research. I searched the Internet. I wrote to the Royal Horticultural Society – they've got over five hundred apple varieties in their collection – but they couldn't help; they'd never had it.'

'No, of course not; it would never grow anywhere but here. So, did you manage to find it?'

She gestured at the open doorway. 'Why don't we go in? I'll show you my trees. You can give me your opinion on one.'

She heard his tiny sigh of pleasure as he walked into the orchard behind her, and she warmed to him still more, recognizing a kindred spirit. 'I think it must have been fruit orchards that gave people the idea of paradise,' she said. 'Don't you?'

'There couldn't be a paradise without apple trees.'

They stood for a moment in silence, just drinking in the atmosphere, the heady scent of apples, of damp earth and growth and decay, the drowsy hum of bees like a note of music in the warm, still air.

Tentatively she said, 'I don't suppose you ever tasted an Appleton Fairest?'

'Of course I did. I used to eat them all the time when I was a kid.'

'Really!' She gave him a sharp look. He shrugged and raised his eyebrows at her surprise.

'I told you I grew up here. Why don't you believe me?'

She couldn't remember exactly when the orchards had been bulldozed over, but it could have been no later than the early sixties. If he remembered eating the Fairest – if he wasn't lying – they must have been grown on trees elsewhere, maybe in private gardens. Trees from the 1970s and 1980s could still be bearing fruit today. The idea excited her.

'Unless you're a lot older than you look–'

'I am a lot older than I look.'

'Do you remember *where* the apples came from? Who was growing the Fairest when you were a little boy?'

But his attention had been captured by a small espaliered tree, one of three she'd trained to grow against the wall. It was an Oslin, and she'd harvested its fruits back at the end of August, all except two that had stubbornly refused to ripen. Since then one had fallen, so that now the tree displayed a single, pink-streaked, primrose-yellow globe amid the green leaves. Ronan seemed to go tense at the sight of it, and then approached it with a curious, slow, stalking gait, until he came to an abrupt halt.

'The old Original apple,' he said in a flat voice.

He *did* know his apples. The Oslin was also called the 'Original,' in the belief that it was the first apple ever grown in Scotland.

'You've left it very late.'

She bristled at this note of criticism and felt obliged to explain. 'I picked the others a month ago. That one was late ripening.'

'It's ready now.'

'You can have it if you want. Take it. I've got plenty inside the house.'

He didn't respond; looking around, he'd spotted another solitary apple, her golden mystery fruit. 'What's that one?'

'I hoped maybe you could tell me.'

He moved to face her directly, and she saw, with a startled jolt of excitement, that he was aroused. His pupils were dilated, his lips slightly parted, his nostrils flared; his whole demeanour had been changed by desire. They were standing so close, it would have taken no more than a single step from both of them to bring them together. If they'd been in some club or bar in Glasgow, she wouldn't have waited for second thoughts; she'd have made the move to tell him without words that she felt the same, and they'd have gone somewhere more private. She was aware of the rise and fall of his chest as he breathed, and of a sweet, musky scent that seemed to belong to him. The drowsy, droning hum of bees in leaf-shadowed sunshine was like the buzzing of the blood within her veins. It seemed inevitable, foreordained, out of her control. A man and a woman alone among the apple trees . . .

Not in *her* orchard.

She took several swift steps away from him, walking backward, until she stumbled and nearly fell.

'No! Don't touch me!'

He looked shocked and froze, his arm still outstretched

to arrest her fall. 'I was only trying to help. Are you all right?'

'I'm fine.' She blinked rapidly, trying to clear the spots from her vision, and moved cautiously to establish that she was on solid ground.

'I wouldn't hurt you, Nell.'

She shuddered, and wished she'd never told him her name.

'There's nothing to be afraid of . . .'

'I'm not afraid!' She glared at him angrily; then, because his gaze into her eyes was too intimate, too intrusive, ducked her head and ran a hand through her hair. It felt lank and greasy. 'Look, I'm sorry, but I just remembered – I can't hang around here all day; I've got company coming, and loads to do before then. You have to go now. You've seen the trees.'

'Didn't you want to ask me something?'

She almost denied it. Bringing his attention back to that tree might bring them back to that dangerous moment of desire. But if it did, she would resist it again. She was not afraid. She had good reasons for sticking to the rules she'd set down for herself: sex only without complications, without commitment, away from home.

So she said, as calmly as she could, 'I wanted to ask you if you recognize *that* apple.'

He was still standing beside the tree, which was slightly shorter than he was. He turned to regard it and, as she watched, he reached out a gentle hand to touch the branch from which the single golden apple hung. 'I do.'

'Well?'

'Appleton's Fairest is not extinct.'

'You're saying . . .' She stared at it, caught between cynical disbelief and a tremulous hope. 'But Appleton's Fairest was a *red* apple.'

'Scarlet Kings,' he said. 'And then, once in a lifetime, a single tree produces a sport: a golden queen.'

He'd certainly done his research. Or maybe he really was from the old orcharding family, and they'd brought him up on the ancient lore. 'Well, thanks for your opinion. Now, I don't want to be rude, but I'm going to have to–'

'Wait,' he said, looking distressed. 'This is no ordinary apple. You can't–'

'I know. It's not to be sold for money, or left to rot, or eaten by a single person, only shared between lovers.'

The surprise on his face was almost comical. 'You know?'

'I've read up on the mythology of apples as well as the facts,' she said coolly.

'So what are you going to do with it?'

Raising her chin, she gave him a challenging look. 'I don't think that's any of your business.' She pointed at the door.

His shoulders sagged. After a long moment, when she refused to relent or respond to his pleading look, he moved.

'Expelled from the garden,' he muttered, trying and failing to catch her eye as he went. At the gate, he lingered. 'Can I come back another day?'

'I can't think of any reason why you'd have to,' she said, and her look and her tone were implacable. He didn't try to argue.

She knew that sending him away had been the right thing to do, not just regardless of the feelings he'd aroused in her, but *because* of them. Once upon a time, lust was a deadly, dangerous sin; it made people outcasts from society, broke up families, destroyed lives. These days . . . well, these days society could hardly function without it; lust was not merely acceptable, it was practically a *duty*. You could get by perfectly well without love so long as you were 'in lust' with someone. People thought there was something wrong with you if you weren't constantly moving from one object of desire to another. Maybe the word had simply become debased and misused, maybe it was greed or boredom that made people want so many things they didn't need, but everything was so sexualized now. People 'lusted after' clothes, cars, Godiva chocolates, and new gadgets in the same way that they shopped for new lovers. She'd been guilty of it herself, and she mistrusted the sense she had that, by comparison with what she'd just felt for a stranger in her orchard, her other urges were mere fantasies, nothing more than flickering shadows.

Later, when the image of Ronan came back to her while she was soaking in a hot bath, she banished regret by reminding herself of why it was necessary, why she could never, ever take the risk of letting someone get too close to her.

When she was five years old, her parents had died in a car crash for which Nell still felt responsible. Her mother had been driving, bantering with her husband, ignoring Nell in the backseat, who responded with increasingly noisy demands for attention. Technically, the cause of the accident – which had involved several vehicles – was a truck that had been (inexplicably) driven the wrong way down the motorway, but Nell had known then and always that her mother – a quick-witted and skillful driver – might have taken evasive action and saved her own and her husband's life if she hadn't been fatally distracted by her hysterical child.

She'd lived with relatives after that – people she could somehow never get really close to – and, as she grew older, had been sent to boarding school. She'd had friends there, and at college; she was never totally a loner – but there was no one who mattered to her in the way that (she supposed) her mother and father had, until she met Sam. A few years later, Sam was dead, and although she certainly hadn't caused the accident that had sent him overboard (that was unlucky chance – plus a touch of carelessness on his part) she would always hold herself responsible for his death because she had been unable to save him from the sea.

She believed she'd been born unlucky and the worst thing about her bad luck was that it was directed dangerously outward. It brought her pain – but it killed the people she loved. And it was for this reason that she'd chosen to live without love. But she didn't have to be deprived of a sex life as long as her lovers stayed, safely, strangers.

She thought of Ronan's eyes, dark, the pupils dilated as he looked from the apple to her, and she shivered. As she got out of the bath and quickly towelled herself dry she imagined things she could have said to him: mocking, flirtatious, cruel.

So, you think I ought to share the apple with you? Don't we have to be lovers first?

It doesn't matter. Now, or later. There'll be time.

She could practically hear him saying it, and found herself wondering if he was interested in her at all, apart from the apple.

What's your heart's desire?

You.

He would say that, the charming bastard. Could he really believe in that old wives' tale about a magic apple? And yet, if he didn't, why had he come here; how could she explain what had happened (or nearly happened) in the orchard?

Now tell me yours, Nell.

What I want's impossible.

That's OK. It's magic.

I don't believe in magic. All right, then. (This would put out that smug, mocking light in his warm, dark eyes.) *What I want is for the past to be undone. No death. I want my parents back again. I want my husband Sam in my arms – not you.*

Having satisfactorily routed and crushed her uninvited visitor, she went off to get dressed.

By the time Kathleen arrived, at the tail end of the day, Nell had worked herself back into a better mood. Thinking about life before Sam, she'd remembered the casual, satisfying friendships she'd had at school and in college – none of those people had come to an untimely end because of her, so far as she knew. Since Sam's death she'd worked out a way of accommodating her sexual needs, but she hadn't given similar thought to her social life. Discussions with tradesmen about paint, paving stones, or dwarfing rootstock, and exchanges about the weather with people she met from day to day was about the extent of it. She'd chosen not to join a church or the Women's Institute or any local organization, and without a job or children, nothing threw her in the way of meeting people.

It was clear when Kathleen arrived, clutching a bottle of wine in each hand, that she shared her anxiety about the evening ahead. And recognizing her visitor's nervousness, Nell was able to forget her own as she switched into hostess mode, working to put her guest at her ease.

'Oh, wow, this is a real farmhouse kitchen, isn't it. So big!' Kathleen exclaimed, gazing around as Nell put her bottle of white wine into the fridge. 'Is that an Aga? Did you paint the cupboards yourself? I love the garland and apple motif; I've never seen a stencil like that – where'd you find it?'

'It's my own design.'

'Really? You're good. And you don't do this professionally? Oh, I love your big table!' She ran a hand over the smooth wooden surface, like stroking a horse. 'I wish I had room for something like this.'

The long, sturdy table would have suited a large family. Nell had bought it because the size of the kitchen demanded a substantial table, and because it was a beautiful piece of furniture; she didn't need it.

'I thought we'd eat out in the garden – with all the sunshine we've been having, and the Aga belching out heat as usual, it's awfully warm in here. Do you mind?'

Kathleen grinned. 'Mind? I love eating outside – I didn't get much chance this summer. Seems like whenever the sun was shining, I had to work. Besides, I'm looking forward to seeing your gardens.'

'Shall I show you around the house first? Then we can take our drinks into the garden.' She couldn't help warming to her guest's enthusiastic appreciation; it was unexpectedly flattering to have her hard work so admired. It was in the nature of rewarding her with a special treat that she took her, finally, to the apple room.

'Now, this is something different,' she said, pausing with her hand on the door handle. 'It's kind of old-fashioned, and it's not ideal – but this is where I store my fruit.'

She opened the door. Wooden shelves lined the walls of the cool, unfurnished room. Even this early in the year, with only a few of the shelves filled with recently picked apples, the unmistakable smell perfumed the air. She thought it must be the ghost of last year's crop, for although she kept the window open to prevent the build-up of gases, the odour intensified as the apples matured, and a trace remained behind, perhaps trapped in the porous wood of the shelves, even after the fruit was all gone.

'An apple store,' said Kathleen, gazing at the yellow Oslins and the bright red Lord Roseberys all set out in neat rows in their cozy nests of shredded paper. 'Was this here when you bought the house?'

'Oh, no. This was their dining room. Well – when they used it. The house was empty when I bought it. No, I thought about a purpose-built apple store outside – but it seemed like tempting fate, to go to all that trouble before my trees started cropping, and now – well, this works well enough. It's not like I'm a big commercial venture.'

'But you do sell them?'

'I've taken a stall at the local farmers' markets, and – you know the shop Green Jean's? She agreed to take a few baskets after I swore upon my honour they were organically grown. I'm not trying to make a living out of it, I just don't want them going to waste.'

'How *do* you make your living? If you don't mind me asking?'

'I don't do anything. I don't have to; I was left pretty well-off. Investments and such.' She stepped back and let her guest out of the room before closing the door and leading the way back to the kitchen, feeling grateful that Kathleen made no comment about her 'luck' at being so well-off.

It was as she poured out two glasses of wine in the kitchen that the next, inevitable personal question came. 'What made you decide to settle in Appleton? Is there a family connection?'

She handed her guest a glass of wine. 'Shall we go outside and wander around for a few minutes? Then I'll put the soup on to reheat while I do a few last minute things to the main course.'

'Sure.'

It would be easy enough to redirect the conversation

as they toured the grounds, she knew, but the unanswered question would hang there and take on a more dangerous weight, the longer she left it unanswered. She could give the sort of soundbite answer she'd given to others who'd casually wondered how an American had ended up in such a back-of-beyond part of Scotland, but friendship – even the lightest, most superficial kind of friendship – surely deserved better. So she took a deep breath, and a steadying gulp of wine, and began.

'I first set eyes on Appleton on my honeymoon. We spent it sailing around Britain because Sam loved to sail, and Britain was where he'd learned.'

They paused on the patio, and Nell set her glass down on the mosaic-tiled top of the table and gazed at a lavender bush, a different scene before her mind's eye.

'The sun was low in the sky when we came into Appleton harbour; it made the golden dome on top of the library *blaze*. It was the most astonishing-looking place: the palm trees growing along the wide harbour-front Esplanade, and what looked like a huge, exotic temple plonked down in between some pastel-coloured fishermen's cottages, and a lot of elegant Victorian villas looking down their noses from the hillsides. To top it all, a pod of dolphins were leaping about, chasing along in front of the boat, welcoming us in . . . It was absolutely magical. We felt we'd sailed into another world, a kind of private paradise. And, I don't know why, but after that night we suddenly had this full-blown, shared fantasy of the life we were going to lead after Sam retired. We'd buy a big old house on one of the hills overlooking the town and the sea. It had to have plenty of land, because we'd grow our own fruit and vegetables, and Sam would go fishing in a nearby trout stream, and whenever we felt a bit restless, we'd hop aboard our boat and sail away to somewhere else.'

Kathleen smiled encouragingly. 'Sounds like a beautiful dream.'

'Yes.' She took a cautious sip of wine, just to wet her mouth, while she waited for the inevitable question.

'Your husband . . . ?'

'He died.'

A pained gasp, then, 'Oh, I'm so sorry! Was it . . . was he . . .'

'It was an accident. He drowned. A sailing accident. I was there; I couldn't save him.' She met her eyes for the briefest instant before deliberately turning away, picking up her wineglass to make it perfectly clear she did not wish to be hugged or touched at all.

'How awful. Oh, Nell, how awful for you. I'm so sorry.'

'Yes, it was awful. I'm not really sure why I came back here, except . . . we hadn't really been together all that long, and after he died – well, I was just trying, rather hopelessly, to hang on to him, so I set off on a kind of pilgrimage, visiting places from his past. I'd just been to visit his old school when I noticed Appleton on a map and decided to come here. I saw a picture of Orchard House in the estate agent's window, and on a whim I went in and asked to view the property. And when I saw the place, well . . .' She gestured with both hands, to encompass both house and garden. 'I saw something I could *do*, a place to fix up. I needed a new home, so . . . I bought it.'

'You've done a wonderful job,' said Kathleen warmly. 'I mean, of course I don't know what it was like when you found it, but . . . it's great.'

'Thank you.' She smiled, relieved to have cleared the first hurdle. She guessed Kathleen would be sensitive enough not to bring up the subject of Sam unbidden. 'Now, before I have to go inside and get cooking, would you like to see my orchard?'

They left their drinks on the table and set off. Kathleen gave a soft cry of delight as they approached the door in the wall. 'A walled garden! You've got a walled garden! No wonder you bought Orchard House.'

Nell laughed softly. 'Another fan of *The Secret Garden*?'

'Of course. All the best people are!'

The sun was very low in the sky now, and although it was still daylight in the meadow, inside the orchard dusk had gathered beneath the branches and in the cool embrace of the shadowed wall.

'Kind of dark in here,' said Kathleen, her voice gone thin and uncertain.

Nell felt no anxiety. Day or night, she felt more at home surrounded by her trees than anywhere else on earth. 'It's all right. Take my hand. Your eyes will adjust in a minute.'

'What's that humming, a machine?'

'No, the bees. Wild bees; they live in the wall, and pollinate the blossom.'

'They won't sting us?'

'They won't sting us.'

'I can see now.' Kathleen took back her hand. 'The trees are smaller than I'd thought.' She took a few steps forward. 'Are they espaliered?'

'Some of them – those against the wall.'

'How many are there?'

'Twenty-four trees, ten different varieties – plus one.'

Kathleen looked around. 'What do you mean?'

'I can name the ten varieties I bought, but one is a mystery tree. It fruited for the first time–' She turned toward the tree as she spoke, and what she saw dried the words in her mouth. She narrowed her eyes and stared uncomprehending at a change that had come about in the last few hours. Something new lay clustered along a single branch, something pale white and almost luminous in the gathering darkness.

'Is that the tree with the blossom? Isn't it too late for

blossom? I mean, the other trees have apples . . .'

Although the voice jarred against her ear, she was grateful to it as to a lifeline back to sanity. What she saw was real; she wasn't hallucinating. She managed to speak, and heard herself sounding perfectly calm. 'It happens sometimes. Unseasonable weather can trigger a second blossoming.'

'Huh. I never heard of that. Fruit and blossom on the same branch . . . it reminds me of something; I can't think what. It looks like magic.'

It *was* magic, Nell thought, stunned. Still unable to believe her eyes, she went nearer to make sure what she thought she was seeing was not an optical illusion of some kind, caused, perhaps, by a late ray of sun reflected off the glossy leaves, or a horde of migrating moths who'd chanced to choose this particular branch to settle on. But when she was close enough to smell the heavy scent, which had attracted one or two sleepy bees already, and see the almost purplish flush around the edges of the creamy petals, she had to accept that this was no illusion. As she raised one hand to touch the flowering branch – the very branch that bore the solitary yellow apple – she remembered seeing Ronan touch it hours before, when there had been not the slightest trace of the blossom which now grew so thickly out of season.

From *Mythology of the Celts*
by F. X. Robinson
(Hale, 1902)

AVALON, the idyllic 'Island of Apples' where King Arthur was taken after receiving his fatal wound, is that same Land of Youth, always located on an island on the western horizon, to which Celtic heroes were summoned to dwell in eternity. Bran, as we have seen already, was beckoned by a beautiful woman bearing an apple-branch silver-white with blossom to Emain, described as an island in the west where apple trees are perpetually in flower and fruit at the same time.

The connection between apples and immortality is of course very ancient, and found throughout Europe. In Scandinavian legend, the gods owed their eternal youth to a diet of magic apples, guarded by Idun, the goddess of Spring and renewal. The Greeks, too, had their magical apples of the Hesperides – those Western Isles again. From Ireland comes the tale of how Cu Roi hid his soul in an apple, that he might not be slain in battle, only to be destroyed when Cu Chulain split the fruit with his mighty sword.

For a suggestion of why this should be, we have

only to look at the language of symbolism and its reflection in the natural world. When an apple is halved crosswise, each half reveals the image of a five-pointed star. This, of course, is one of the most ancient and universally recognized emblems of immortality; a sacred sign, like the apple itself, of the Great Goddess and her supernatural realm.

Chapter Eight

The children – Jade especially – were in a bad mood on Sunday morning, because they were missing their weekly cartoon fix. Although at first they assumed a fault in their rather elderly television set, they soon discovered that nobody in Appleton could receive television or radio signals.

'I don't get it,' said the older boy, Callum. 'If it was the earthquake, how come the Johnstones can't get Sky TV? Theirs was out yesterday.'

'Jennifer Connor said the same thing to me,' said Shona. 'That's odd, isn't it? I mean, we've lost reception before – remember that big storm last January? – but it never affected people with satellite dishes.'

Graeme always had an opinion, even on things he admitted knowing nothing about, like modern technology.

'You know, I was reading about earthquakes,' he said. 'And they produce an electromagnetic pulse. That's something that would disrupt *all* transmissions. Remember that disaster movie we saw last year, what was it called?'

Ashley felt sure that a small earth tremor couldn't do anything of the kind, but she didn't bother trying to argue the point. She'd already discovered that Craeme was a slippery debater, impossible to pin down. No sooner had you pointed out a flaw in his argument than he was arguing something else . . . or something that sounded the same, but turned out to be completely different. It was like the theory he'd developed about Appleton's origins. Based on the fact that the Apple was not represented on a couple of early maps and some ambiguous remarks made by early medieval travellers, he'd concluded that this substantial chunk of land had originated somewhere else. According to him, it had been a floating island until some cataclysmic event, taking place roughly around 1655, had pushed it hard against the west coast of Scotland, where it had remained to this day. She was prepared to believe it – why not? – until he started calling on old myths and legends as further proof, and she understood that he wasn't talking about an ordinary chunk of earth that had been grafted onto another in an unusual, yet possible, geological way, but something far more mystical. He seemed to imply that the place now known as Appleton had once been part of a different, supernatural world, and she reckoned that was like somebody in Texas arguing that Galveston Island had been part of Heaven until it fell out of the sky circa 1490. When she objected, he changed his line, shifting from myth to history to psychology to religion and even taking in quantum physics and some obscure, abstruse mathematical theories with hardly a pause for breath. She didn't know if she was too literal-minded or too slow-witted to follow the connections he made, but she soon gave up trying.

After a brief, gloomy discussion of how they would manage if they had to do without TV for ever and ever, the kids were cheered by their father's suggestion of 'a magical mystery tour' to show their American cousin the delights of the 'wee Apple.'

'Southport beach?' asked Ewan, lighting up.

'Certainly.'

'The fairy village?' Jade clasped her hands together in a theatrical pleading pose.

'It wouldn't be much of a magical mystery tour without it.'

'What's the fairy village?' asked Ashley, thinking of miniature golf courses and children's rides.

'You'll have to wait and find out.'

'The beach is more fun,' said Ewan, casting a disgusted look at his little sister.

'We can do both,' said Shona. 'But only if you kids *run* and get your swimming things, and whatever else you want to take. I want everybody ready for the car in ten minutes, got that?'

They scattered, shouting happily.

'Do you have a swimming costume?' Shona asked.

Ashley wrinkled her nose uncertainly. She'd brought one, of course, but as for wearing it when the temperature was barely above seventy degrees Fahrenheit . . . 'Will it be warm enough?'

'This time of year the sea's at its warmest,' said Graeme. 'I thought it was pretty warm yesterday, didn't you?'

'Oh, it was nice,' Ashley agreed. 'But for swimming . . . well, I remember once I went swimming at Galveston at Easter – it was only about eighty – it was all right, I guess, but I'm used to it hotter.'

Shona looked bemused. 'It's not likely to get as high as eighty degrees.'

'If you don't want to swim, I can show you the sights of Southport,' said Graeme.

His wife laughed. 'What sights?'

'Come on! There's the Grand Hotel, and King Arthur's footprints . . .'

'King Arthur? But he was *English* – what would he be doing up here?'

'Oh, it's like "Queen Elizabeth Slept Here,"' said Shona. 'Everywhere in Britain tries to lay claim to our most famous hero.'

Graeme leaned forward, quivering slightly, in his typical

hound-upon-the-scent stance. 'The one thing we can be sure King Arthur was *not* is English! He was a Celtic warlord, and while there are plausible connections linking him to sites in Cornwall and Wales, it is far more likely that he was the leader of a Scottish tribe. You should read a book called *Arthur and the Lost Kingdoms*–'

'Save it for the journey Graeme,' Shona interrupted. 'I need you to help me load the car. And do you know what happened to the big cooler?'

Ashley liked him, but he was kind of exhausting company. She'd never met anyone so full of stories, and so bursting with the need to share them. She thought his obsessive, part-time scholarship had made him a little crazy, and hoped, for his family's sake, that he wasn't so manic *all* the time.

Soon they were all in the car and heading out of the town. Shona drove, which left Graeme free to twist around in the front seat and regale them with more stories of Appleton's far-distant past. Ashley felt herself to be his captive, solitary audience, for although she shared the backseat with the three children, they were all preoccupied: Callum, with earphones, immersed in music; Ewan absorbed in a handheld video game, and Jade in a world of her own as she moved two plastic ponies about in her lap and muttered to herself.

Graeme told her about 'King Arthur's Footprints' – a pair of roughly boot-shaped marks on a rock supposed to have been made when the mortally wounded chieftain was helped out of the boat and onto the shore of Avalon by the great enchantress Morgan Le Fay.

'You're saying Avalon was really Appleton?'

'It was called "the island of apples" or simply "Apple" – which sounds something like "ooh-vall" or "ah-vull" in Gaelic, hear that? not so far from "*Aa vahl-on*". I don't know if the "on" bit was a corruption, or one of those whad-dyecallems – grammatical inflections that you get in languages like Gaelic, where the nouns change as well as the verbs. Anyway – you've got the amazing similarity of the two names; plus the fact that it was located to the west of mainland Britain – and, this is particularly important, it was said to be a place of very great magic, home to a race of immortals. And another interesting thing: this isn't a late attribution. It's not the Victorians playing their sentimental games, because when the very first settlers arrived, before there was a town here, the locals pointed out the imprint left by the great Arthur. And there's a cave . . .'

She tried to look politely attentive, but could feel her eyes glazing over. So many details! She picked up on one of them. 'Um, so what happened to those immortal beings who lived here way back when?'

Jade piped up unexpectedly. '*I* know. They live in the fairy villages, under the ground.' She patted Ashley's arm. 'You probably won't see them, though. I never have, and

I always look. They're very small, and they're very good at hiding.'

She glanced at Graeme, expecting a wink or a tolerant smile, but he was nodding as if Jade had given a perfectly reasonable reply.

It took about twenty minutes to drive to Southport, a tiny village that consisted of two rows of houses, a small, pretty church, and a general store and post office that also advertised home baking, sandwiches, and hot drinks to take away. Spreading away from this were a scattering of houses, a camping site, and trailer park.

The beach was amazing: a huge, curving sweep of pale, silvery sand, dotted here and there with large rocks, which time and tide had worn down to smooth, organic shapes. More rocks could be seen rearing up out of the shallows, barriers against which the rolling breakers smashed into spray and foam. There were probably no more than a dozen people making use of the beach on this fine Sunday morning which showed, thought Ashley, how very far away from everywhere else this underpopulated place was. She noticed three people out on surfboards, all of them in wet suits, and knew by this detail that it was certainly too cold for swimming, despite the sight of the hardy local children who had stripped down to the skin and plunged in.

She left her Scottish relatives arguing the merits of body-surfing over sand castle building and strolled along the beach by herself, enjoying the sun and the wind and the smell of the sea, occasionally bending to pick up a pebble or shell. Very soon, as she followed the shoreline, pale sand gave way to a pebble beach, then to much rougher, rockier ground that looked difficult to traverse without going into the water. She thought at first that she would be forced to turn back, but then she noticed there was a path winding up the cliff side. It looked well-worn and easily accessible, and she decided that rather than retrace her steps she would follow it.

The path took her up to the road, to a deserted spot she supposed was on the far side of the village. A distant glint of light caught her attention, and she looked up and across the road, shading her eyes against the glare. On the hilltop, overlooking the sea, was a very large, white building, with a number of cars parked to one side. It had been the sunlight reflecting off the cars that had caught her eye, but the building was far more interesting. It reminded her at first of a classical Greek temple; a moment later, she recognized that it was a thoroughly modern building, designed by a fanciful architect who was happy to mix elements of Classical Antiquity with Art Moderne, and throw in a dash of Gothic Revival, too. She wondered what it was: hotel? conference centre? or some millionaire's summer villa? Whatever it was, the joint was clearly jumping. As she went on gazing, she realized she could hear music: the lively sound of an old-fashioned swing band. Dance music.

She was assailed by a powerful urge to join in. She loved dancing; since she was nine or so she'd taken just about every dance class offered, and although she preferred salsa, she could do swing – give her a partner and she'd lindy with the best of them.

Staring up at the big white building, listening to the distant music, she wondered what kind of party it was, how accessible or private. Her eyes traced the pale narrow strip of driveway that ran uphill, and she imagined herself going up there, to the big front entrance . . . or maybe she could just slip through an open set of French doors. She was too far away to be certain about such details, but she could see tiny figures going in and out of the building, and from that and the way the sunlight glinted off glass, she guessed that both windows and doors had been left open to the refreshing sea breeze. A place like this, so far from the city, wasn't likely to have bouncers. It wasn't hard to crash a party; all it took was confidence and the ability to blend in.

But her heart sank as she remembered how she was dressed. She looked down at her filthy trainers and knew it for an impossible dream. Turning her back on the music hurt, but what else could she do? She was halfway down the path to the beach when she heard someone call her name, and a moment later saw Graeme, looking rather wild-eyed as he rushed toward her.

'Where've you been? I thought you were lost!'

She shrugged it off. 'How could I get lost? I didn't think I'd been gone that long. I'm sorry. Are we ready to go?'

'Oh, no, the kids are still . . .' he waved a hand toward the sea. 'That's not . . .' He stopped and began again. '*I'm* sorry. I'm so used to riding herd on a group of youngsters that if somebody goes missing at the seaside, well . . .' He gave an uncertain chuckle. 'Do you want a tour guide, or would you rather be left to your own devices?'

Her glimpse of that distant, unattainable party on the hilltop had left her with a craving for company. 'A tour guide would be good.'

He brightened up. 'OK! King Arthur's landing is just around the corner, as it were. Mind, the tide's in, so if you're worried about getting your feet wet . . .'

'I don't mind,' she said, and followed him around the rocky headland, clambering over and around the boulders that, not long before, she'd seen as a barrier to further exploration, until they arrived at another sheltered inlet with a beautiful, unspoiled, empty beach.

'The footprints of King Arthur,' he announced, pointing dramatically to a large, flat rock. She went closer to look at the twin shallow declivities, and measured her own feet against them.

'Hmm, the king had very dainty feet, for a guy,' she said.

The cave, not far away, in the base of the cliff, was also smaller than she'd expected. She peered into the gloomy recess. 'So he's supposed to have been buried here?'

'Not buried. The tradition about the cave is that he went into an enchanted sleep from which he would awake in time of Britain's greatest need.'

'Long way to travel,' she said, turning to stare out to sea. Her sense that she was actually on an island had been growing steadily. She looked back at Graeme. 'Do you have a boat?'

'Me? No. How could I afford it? Why?'

'I just wondered. If the road takes a really, really long time to repair, how will people manage? I mean, how will ordinary supplies get here?'

'Well, the supermarket's part of a chain, you know, and they've already sorted out some sort of vessel to make the regular deliveries. I'm not sure exactly how the smaller shops are going to manage – I guess it might be the end for one or two of 'em. As for the mail, well, I told you we're to get a plane from Glasgow every morning; if not tomorrow, then Tuesday. I imagine it might take passengers as well, in the great Scottish tradition of the rural post-bus, which will help at least until there's a regular ferry service. We *will* get a ferry, of that I have no doubt, unless everyone else has forgotten us so thoroughly that they don't mind cutting us adrift permanently!'

She looked at the cave again, casting her mind back over what she could recall of the Arthurian legends. 'I thought the idea was that after he'd suffered his mortal wound, Arthur was taken off to Avalon to be healed and live for ever – not to be shoved into a hole in the ground.'

'There are different traditions. And I'm not sure the two ideas are totally incompatible. The great hero's saved from death, but he's not alive in the usual sense, he's in another state of being, another world. And to the Celts, that other world was both physically real – a place that you could get in your boat and sail to – but at the same time it was a spiritual realm, insubstantial, accessible to mortals only in dreams, or after death.'

She frowned. 'I don't see how it could be both.'

He nodded. 'It's a hard one to get your brain around, I agree. But . . .' He looked at his watch. 'Maybe we ought to head back.'

As they turned back, Ashley asked about the big white building she'd seen on top of the hill across the road.

'Oh, that's the Grand Hotel – do you want to go up there?'

Her heart gave an unexpected leap. 'Can we?'

'Sure! Why not? We'll drive up – the kids always like it.'

Her spirits lifted even more. If the Walkers went there often – as Graeme's words implied – maybe what she'd glimpsed and heard was not a private party but a standard Sunday afternoon event – dining and dancing. Maybe they could stay for lunch. Although it might be better if she planned to come out on another day, in more suitable clothes, if she wanted to dance.

They found the children draped in multicoloured towels and munching snacks from crackling paper bags.

'This is just to keep them going,' Shona explained when they arrived. 'I've told them, we'll have our picnic lunch soon enough.'

When the children were dried and dressed they set off back to the car; this time, Graeme took the driver's seat.

'Why don't you sit in the front, Ashley?' said Shona. 'You'll see better, and it's more comfortable.'

'I thought we'd go up and have a closer look at the Grand,' Graeme said, starting the car.

'Ooh, the spooky place!' Ewan exclaimed gleefully, and Jade squealed.

'Mum!'

'Ewan, keep your hands to yourself.'

'It wasn't me, it was ghostly fingers!'

'Ghost fingers yourself!'

'Hey!'

'If you two don't settle down, we're going straight home.'

'Why is it spooky?' asked Ashley but, in the turmoil, her question went unanswered, and she soon saw for herself.

As the car toiled up the steep driveway, she was aware of the many potholes, and the fact that the verges were heavily overgrown, some weeds even growing up through the paving, as if it did not get much use. But not until they reached the top did she see that the Grand Hotel was an old, long-abandoned, empty ruin. There was scarcely a whole pane of glass in any of the windows, the white paint was peeling and streaked with ancient soot, and at least half the roof was gone. She gaped in astonishment, unable to speak.

'Shall we go in?'

'No, Graeme, that would not be a good idea,' said Shona swiftly and firmly over the two boys' whoops of excitement.

He twisted around to grin at her. 'Aw, come on.'

'No. Boys, settle down *now*. We are not going in. Graeme, I can't believe you even suggested it,' she went on, exasperated. 'You can see it's not safe. What if a wall suddenly collapsed while one of us was standing under it? Just because it's stood so long . . . just because the council can't be bothered to fence it off or put up proper warning signs . . . who knows what that earthquake might have dislodged?'

He looked penitent. 'I'm sorry.'

At last, Ashley found her tongue. 'What happened to it? Where is everybody?'

They all stared at her.

'There were people here, less than an hour ago. I *saw* them,' she said, and heard the desperation in her voice.

'You must be thinking of another place,' said Shona.

She shook her head hard. 'No! I was down below, standing on the road, staring up at it – I could see loads of cars parked over to the side there, and people going in and out, and I could hear *music* – I couldn't have been mistaken about that – there was a party going on up here, a big, swinging dance party – "In the Mood,"' she finished, as if that clinched it. 'The band was playing "In the Mood."'

'It *is* haunted,' said Ewan, sounding awed. 'It's not b.s., it really *is*. Whoah, boy, wait till I tell Fraser about *this*.'

'They weren't ghosts – it was broad daylight – there were people here; there's bound to be an explanation . . .' Ashley saw her protest made not the slightest impact on the round eyes and pale faces of the three in the back-seat.

Graeme's response was to reverse and head back down the rutted drive, with little or no concern for the effect that speed and potholes might have on his car's suspension.

'Why should it be haunted?' Ashley asked.

'I never thought it was,' said Shona. 'And, Graeme, you've never come across any evidence – I mean, nobody was actually killed in the bombing; the hotel was all but empty at the time . . .'

'What happened?'

'It was bombed during the Second World War,' Graeme replied, frowning through the windshield at the empty road ahead. 'There was a military training base and an airfield nearby – presumably that was the intended target, or maybe one of the bombers heading for the shipyards on Clydeside flew off course. Anyway, there were plans to rebuild after the war, but it never happened. The bottom fell out of the local economy, and although there was talk of reviving the tourist industry with a showpiece hotel, I guess it was always too expensive a risk.'

'And nobody ever held a party in the ruins,' Shona said quietly. 'Nobody ever would.'

'Because of the ghosts,' said Ewan.

'Because it's simply not safe. I'm sure people – kids, mostly – poke around in there from time to time, but you'd never get a band up there today. Anyway, there's nowhere to dance. The ballroom was destroyed – I've seen it.'

Ashley stared out the window, shocked and numb, feeling as if she'd been hit by a bomb herself – a mental bomb, anyway. She wondered what would have happened if she'd climbed up the hill by herself, intent on crashing the party from the past. Would it have disappeared as soon as she approached, like a mirage, or would the revellers have welcomed her in and made her one of them?

She was so absorbed in her thoughts that she did not notice much about the journey that followed, as they left the coast road and headed inland on a very narrow, twisty road that wound up into the hills – almost a small mountain range. Forced to concentrate on his driving, Graeme had little to say, and everyone else kept silent. She had no clear idea of whether it was a long time or short, ten minutes or half an hour, before they pulled into a layby and parked.

It was a relief to be out of the car, which had smelled rather strongly of vinegar, cheese, and spices after the children's snacks, and which had pitched and rolled like a little boat as it navigated a relentless succession of tight bends. Ashley breathed deeply of the good, fresh air, smelling grass and earth and growing things, including something that smelled like a cross between peppermint and coconut. The sun was deliciously warm on her bare arms and the top of her head. Deliberately, she cleared her mind of all thoughts of ghosts and other impossibilities, and pitched in with the others to help unload the trunk of the car.

'Don't worry, it's not far to carry things,' said Jade. 'I could do the walk all by myself when I was only three.'

Walking single file – Ashley went third, behind the two boys – they followed a narrow, well-trodden footpath away from the road across rough moorland. And then, all of a sudden, they were there.

It was a lovely, almost Alpine scene: a very round, small, still lake lay cradled at the base of a mountain wall. The ground before it was covered in a rich green growth of grass, as the rocky, gorse-and-heather-covered hillside gave way to a meadow. Scattered throughout the grass were heaps of stones and also bigger rocks, as smooth as the boulders on the beach, inviting use like Stone Age benches and tables.

'I love it!' she exclaimed.

Jade smiled beatifically, clasping her hands in front of her chest. 'I knew you would,' she said, as if this splendid setting was a gift she'd chosen especially for her cousin.

As Ashley helped Shona lay out the food and drink on an especially flat and well-situated rock, she asked, 'Why do you call it the fairy village?'

'Don't say that word here,' Jade whispered. At normal volume she went on, 'Because this is where they live. That's one of their houses.' She pointed at a pile of stones.

Graeme handed her a can of orange Tango and expanded on his daughter's explanation. 'This is, possibly, the oldest settlement on the Apple. It's never been excavated – not professionally – but it looks like people lived here in stone houses about, oh . . .' He puffed out his cheeks to consider. 'Four or five thousand years ago, I guess. We don't know exactly what happened to them—'

'Yes we do!' Jade objected.

'At the time that Appleton was established as a new town, settled by incomers, there were already people living on the Apple,' he went on. 'But they were incomers, too, mostly from Kintyre and Aran, and even from Ireland. They settled by the sea – some in Southport, and others on the stretch of bay known as the Ob – and they farmed the lower glens. But nobody came up here to settle. These hills belonged to the old, original inhabitants.' He paused to take a swig from his can. 'They had lived all over when the Apple was still an island. Afterward, when the incomers came, they withdrew into the interior – here. And the incomers kept their distance. They were respectful. They knew what most people have forgotten now–'

'Most adults, you mean,' said Jade.

He nodded. 'Yes, indeed. The earlier incomers were wiser than most of us are today. They knew the people who were here first weren't to be messed with. They could do magic, and they were immortal.'

'So where are they now?'

Everyone looked at her like she'd said something stupid, or mildly embarrassing, and she felt her cheeks growing warm, but held her ground. 'Immortal means they live forever. So where are they? If they used to be here, where did they go?'

'They didn't go anywhere,' said Jade. 'This is their home. Just because you can't see them – They can do magic, don't forget.'

'So what are you saying?' She looked at Graeme. 'You believe these magical beings are all around us now, and we can't sense them? You believe that?' She saw him cast a nervous, appealing look at his wife.

Quietly, but with the firm, no-nonsense tone she used with her children, Shona said, 'Talk like that's not respectful. It's not your fault, Ashley; you weren't to know. Graeme has been setting a very bad example. We should be polite when we're on someone else's land.'

She was speechless. Shona – sensible, grown-up cousin Shona, who looked so much like her own practical dad – actually believed in fairies.

Graeme took his wife's rebuke meekly. 'Sorry,' he muttered. He made an odd, bobbing bow towards the pile of stones Jade had pointed out earlier, and added, 'I meant no disrespect.'

'Let's have our picnic now, shall we?' said Shona. 'What sort of sandwich would you like, Ashley? There's cheese and tomato, egg, or ham.'

A few minutes later Jade crept close to Ashley, and whispered, 'Don't be scared of them. They're nice, really. I don't think they mind if we talk about them.'

'I'm not scared,' she said, rather haughtily. What she felt primarily was confusion. It had been one thing to listen to *Graeme* arguing the reality of magical beings; it was something else to find out Shona believed it, too.

'Anyway,' Jade went on, no longer whispering, but still speaking quietly, 'I don't think they're listening to us. I think they sleep most of the time. I know what happened to them: they stopped having babies and got older and older, and littler and littler, and they moved their houses underground, and they don't come out much. They don't mind if people come here and visit, just so long as nobody builds their house up here, because the reul is theirs and always will be.'

'The what?'

'Reul. It means "star" in Gaelic.'

'Star? Why?'

'I'll get Daddy to show you.' She called out to her father. 'Show Ashley the star!'

He slipped off the boulder where he'd been sitting with his wife, picked an apple from a pile of fruit, and took out his pocket knife. 'Do you know what's in the middle of an apple?'

She shrugged. 'The core?'

He cut through it, not in the usual top-to-bottom cut, but across, and held up the two halves for her to see.

She saw the shape made by the pattern of the seeds. 'It's like a five-pointed star.'

'Exactly. And there are five peaks around us – known locally as "the pips."'

'We're right at the very heart of the Apple here,' said Shona, taking one slice of the fruit from her husband's hand and smiling at him as she raised it to her mouth. Taking his cue, he quickly took a bite of the other half, his eyes locked on hers.

Jade rolled her eyes. 'Mushy stuff,' she whispered to Ashley. 'Don't look.'

After returning from the reul, Graeme took them on a

tour of Appleton, including all the notable buildings. Ashley scarcely heard a word of his commentary, too absorbed in scanning the streets for one particular familiar figure. She wanted to meet her stranger again in their company, thinking that either Graeme or Shona would be able to identify him if he really did, as he said, come from Appleton. Graeme had a particularly sharp eye for family resemblances, and despite being an incomer, he was well-informed about the locals. She'd had a taste of his skill on Saturday afternoon in the museum. There was a big oil painting there called *Appleton Fair Day*, one of those technically skilled, highly realistic Victorian pictures that were more interesting as social historical documents than as fine art. It depicted a good cross section of the local society of the time, from the well-to-do landowners and merchant class down to a ragged beggar with his skinny dog, all brought together in the market square. It struck her as a carefully staged snapshot of a vanished world, but, as she paused to examine it, Graeme had pointed out connections to the present-day population.

'If you look, you'll see echoes of most of these folks on the streets of Appleton today,' he said. 'Take a keek at this young lady, here – could be Shona in fancy dress, couldn't it? Although you might not see it as plain as I can – she's a bit older now – but this could have been a portrait of her on our wedding day.'

Staring up at the pretty young thing in a full-skirted,

cream-coloured, lace-trimmed dress, reddish-brown ringlets spilling from the sides of her bonnet, Ashley saw the resemblance. In addition, one of the boys chasing a spaniel in the lower left-hand corner looked uncannily like her cousin Ewan. She didn't know any of the others, although he went on as if she should: 'That dear old soul in black could be the former librarian, Miss McClusky, and that one there, except for the beard, that's Alistair Reid. That gloomy-looking fellow there's the twin of the man who owns the petrol station, and see here–' She took his word for it. In Appleton, at least, it was not merely the buildings and physical landmarks that persisted down through the generations, but also many of the original faces.

When they got home, she declined Shona's dinner invitation, thinking she ought to assert her independence before they took her completely for granted as a member of the family. She was already committed to a 'special tour' of the library building with Graeme on Monday; he'd arranged it with the librarian without asking her if she was interested.

'But I've already *seen* the museum and library,' she'd objected when he told her. 'And I'm sure the librarian can't tell me anything more than *you* could – didn't you say she'd only been here a few months?'

'She can take us behind closed doors, to the parts the public aren't usually allowed to see. She's got the keys to upstairs.'

This piqued her interest. 'Can we go up into the dome?'

He laid a finger alongside his nose and winked.

She decided to have dinner in the Harbour View Café, where she'd had lunch the day before. Maybe history would repeat itself, and her stranger would be there, too.

But at ten past six the café was locked up tight, and a notice in the window gave daily opening hours of nine to five. She set off for the Chat 'n' Chew, which kept the same weirdly office-like hours. She paused, annoyed, and chewed her lip as she tried to recall what else this small town had to offer, and remembered only a fairly filthy-looking burger joint. A young man walked past, hands in his pockets, his head down.

She called out to him. 'Excuse me!'

He looked up, surprised, and she noticed he had beautiful eyes, which seemed familiar.

'Did you speak to me?' he asked, sounding wary, and foreign.

'Yes. I'm a stranger here . . .' She smiled and cocked her head, recalling the faint trace of an accent she'd heard. 'And maybe you are, too? The thing is, I was looking for somewhere to have dinner.'

'Hotel?'

'No, I'm not staying . . .' She stopped. 'You mean . . .?'

'Sunday night.' He shrugged. 'The fish bar's closed. But the hotels, they all have restaurants. You don't have to stay, to eat there. They do bar meals, not too expensive. You know the hotels?'

'There's one on the harbour, isn't there?'

He made a fluttering 'so-so' gesture with one hand. 'The Orchard is better, for food. You know The Orchard?' When she shook her head, he made a little beckoning gesture. 'Come. I'll show you.'

It was not far, and when she saw the big old white-washed building, which sported a three-dimensional, brightly painted apple tree on the ledge above the entrance, she remembered noticing it before.

'You can order food from the bar,' he told her.

'Thank you. Can I buy you a drink?'

He backed away hastily, like he was afraid of catching fleas. 'No. No, thanks.'

Annoyance flared up. What was wrong with the men in this town? Or had something gone wrong with *her*? She didn't think she smelled bad, but some man-repelling vibe seemed to kick in when they got too close.

'Fine,' she said, coolly. 'Thanks for your help.'

She didn't see any familiar faces in the hotel bar, and everybody there looked a lot older than she. She ate up quickly – the food was very good – then went on to check out the other local bars. She found one she preferred – it played better music, had friendly bar staff and a younger clientele – but still no sign of her mysterious stranger.

From *Recollections of Alexander (McNeill) Wall*
(unpublished; no date)

In 1896, several momentous events occurred, with profound consequences for my subsequent life. Not long after the new year had been rung in, my uncle Lachlan died. He'd reached a goodly age, having been born in 1799, and so, although he had spoken jokingly of his expectations of living into his third century, his death could be considered in no way premature. He had left his affairs in order, and upon the reading of his last Will and Testament I learned I had inherited such a fortune as to make it possible for me to retire from the hustle and grime of Glasgow and reside solely in Appleton, which had been, since my marriage, my dearest wish.

I was not the sole beneficiary of Lachlan Wall's Will, for, as he had long discussed with me, he deeded a parcel of land and a generous sum of money to build a Free Library and Museum 'for the continuing education and enrichment of the people of Appleton.' He also donated his personal library, art collection, and cabinet of curiosities to the same, and expressed his desire that the designer of the building should be the selfsame architect with whom he had often discussed his plans, to wit, myself.

These were the important, public events of 1896, but there was another which touched me more profoundly, and that was the birth of my only child, my dearly beloved daughter, Emmeline Mary Florence Wall, in August, on a day when the sun shone hotly down from an enamel-blue sky, the sea lay languid and still, and ripening apples hung heavy on the branches in the drowsing orchards.

Fatherhood was a transformation. From the moment that my dear wife intimated there was to be a happy event, I knew nothing else in life could be as important to me as this unknown child. Everything I did from then on was touched by this knowledge. All that I have done, all I ever wanted, was to keep her safe and happy. If I did wrong, it was for the best reasons.

She is gone now. I can only hope that, wherever she is, she understands and forgives me, understanding that I was driven, as she was herself, by love alone.

Chapter Nine

Dinner at Nell's on Sunday evening was a disaster, although it had started promisingly.

For a woman with her looks and money she was oddly awkward, socially, but she'd done a great job on her house, which obviously meant a lot to her, and when she opened the door to her apple room, Kathleen had the feeling that she'd been offered something very rare and valuable, an entrée to this lonely woman's heart.

And then, inside the walled orchard, something weird had happened. Kathleen didn't understand it. She wasn't a timid or nervous person, and she'd certainly never thought of herself as having psychic tendencies, but as she'd stepped out of the late-evening sunshine into the darker confines of the enclosed garden, the hairs stood up on the back of her neck, and she'd felt immediately that she was in the presence of the numinous. *Numinous*! Now, there was a word from her freshman year in college, a word she rarely had occasion to use, but it seemed appropriate, and more accurate than the other word she'd thought of in connection with the orchard, which was *haunted*. Graeme Walker had suggested the library was haunted, but she'd never felt it. The orchard was different. There was some nonhuman, out-of-the-ordinary power there. She would have turned around and run away except that for a couple of seconds she was so frightened she couldn't move. She didn't know if Nell shared her feeling or only sensed her fear, but, like a real friend, she'd offered her hand, and once Kathleen felt that warm, human touch the terror was gone.

And then they'd seen the branch, so thick with pale blossom that it seemed to gleam like silver in the dim light. Thinking about it later, she recalled a book in the library on the subject of Scottish folklore called *The Silver Bough*. She hadn't read it; she assumed the title implied a Celtic counterpart to Sir James Frazer's great study of myth and religion worldwide – but she didn't know if that was significant. The sight had struck her instantly as magical, impossible – but Nell had said strange weather, like the sudden burst of warmth they were experiencing after such a wet and chilly summer, could cause a second blossoming.

But if that were so, she could think of no reason at all

why Nell's mood had changed so abruptly after their visit to the orchard. She'd withdrawn almost to the point of catatonia, and nothing Kathleen said could get through to her. The food had been very nice, but there was little conversation between them, no connection at all, and so she was home again before nine o'clock, feeling a desperate need for a sympathetic ear. But there was still no answer from Dara's phone, and two other friends she tried in London were equally unavailable, so she went to bed early with the handwritten *Recollections of Alexander (McNeill) Wall* her only companion.

My great-great-grandfather, John James wall, was the first of our name to settle in these parts. He came to Appleton as a young man in the 1660s, bringing with him several small trees from his family's farm in the Borders; by crossing one of these with one of the local wild crab apple trees (so I was told) he created the Scarlet King, which produced a peculiarly delicious cider and which continues to be much grown locally for this purpose.

After John Wall's death his son, James Alexander Wall, took over the running of the family farm and turned it into a thriving, multifaceted business. By his direction, more land was turned over to orchards, and the cider-manufactory was likewise both modernized and increased. Wall of Appleton became well-known for cider, even quite far afield, and the finest eating apples were exported to

Glasgow and other Scottish markets. My great-grandfather may be remembered for his Pomona, a work of much beauty and scholarship, into which he decanted many years of study, and all his passion for apples. But to those who have tasted it, his greatest boon and his lasting legacy must be one of the finest dessert apples ever grown – I mean, of course, Appleton's Fairest.

After a long and apparently contented bachelor existence James Wall took a wife when he was past seventy years of age. The woman's name is not known; it does not appear to be recorded anywhere that I can find – and there must have been some question raised as to the legitimacy of their union, for there does exist a sworn testimonial to the effect that the twin boys, by name Lachlan John and Robertson James, were the legitimate issue, of his lawful marriage, recognized by James Alexander Wall as the fruit of his loins and his lawful heirs. When the boys were about eleven years of age, Robertson (he was named after his paternal grandmother's family) was sent to a school in Edinburgh, but the other lad was kept at home to learn more of the farming business; it was said that he had a great affinity for the apple trees. A year or two later, my great-grandfather suffered his final illness. Not even waiting on the funeral service, his widow, 'the stranger woman' departed for parts unknown with her son Lachlan, and they were never seen again.

The farm and orchards were supervised by a factor until

Robertson came of age. When he finished his schooling, he returned to Appleton, and married a local girl (Mary Brown) with whom he had two children: my uncle Lachlan and my father James.

Kathleen remembered two things when she woke on Monday morning: it was her day off, but she'd agreed to give Graeme Walker and his wife's young American cousin a behind-the-scenes tour of the library building at eleven o'clock. She couldn't remember if she *had* remembered, when he'd wheedled her into it, that this was her Monday off, and it didn't really matter, because she could always take next Monday off instead. Still, while looking at the golden sunlight spilling in around the edges of her bedroom curtains, she thought what a waste of the fine weather it would be to spend her whole day indoors. She'd do it on her own time, then; it wouldn't take long. She was sure Graeme had given the girl a guided tour of the museum already, and he knew more about the exhibits than she did.

After dressing in the bright blue cotton skirt and linen top she'd been on the brink of packing away for the winter, she went out to buy her breakfast from the bakery. Walking through the quiet, waking streets, she became aware of something indefinably different in the atmosphere. Most of the shops and businesses here didn't open until nine or ten – the bakery, which supplied several of the hotels with breakfast rolls and pastries, was a rare exception. But the mood on the streets was anything but sleepy. There was a new air of excitement and hope, she thought, as if the whole town was waiting for something wonderful that was about to happen, holding its collective breath ...

She laughed at herself, recognizing the pathetic fallacy at work. *She* was the one full of hope, expecting something wonderful to come of her meeting with Dave Varney on Saturday evening, and this glorious weather seemed to reflect her mood. She'd almost forgotten how exhilarating the early stages of a relationship could be, before anything as definite as a kiss had yet occurred, when everything remained open and possible. Yet even knowing it for a trick of her own mind, she couldn't shake off the feeling that the town had changed. It didn't seem to be the same place she'd been living in just last week, and yet, for the life of her, she couldn't have said what was different about it.

In the bakery, she bought a fresh, warm loaf of bread, four morning rolls, and – so as to have something to offer Graeme and Ashley – four assorted sweet pastries. She made a change from her usual route on her way back by turning down a back street behind the Orchard Hotel, and saw a shop she'd never noticed before. It was the sort of odd, old-fashioned business she'd occasionally encountered in this country, a shop that offered specialist items, obscure hardware, or obsolete technologies ignored by the profit-driven superstores. Appleton had several small, family-run shops that appeared to operate on the narrowest margin of survival as they sold sweets, sundries, or restaurant supplies to an ever-shrinking market, but Kathleen had not seen this one before. Peering into the dim interior – it wasn't open yet, of course – she tried to work out what it sold. There was no window display, and the ancient wooden shelves that lined the walls were filled with plain cardboard boxes that gave no clue as to their contents. They might have been shoes or fishing tackle or office supplies or even magic wands.

Stepping back, she looked up at the storefront where the name W. P. MACTAGGART & SONS shone out in carved and apparently recently regilded letters, but there was not a hint of what their business might be. There ought to have been a shingle hanging out, with a carved and painted picture of something . . . a wizard, or a bubbling cauldron; then it would have been at home in Diagon Alley. Smiling at her fanciful thoughts about what was probably no more exciting than an out-of-business shoe shop, she went on her way. But it bothered her that she couldn't remember having seen the shop before. She did notice things, usually.

She'd switched on the office coffeemaker a few minutes before Graeme and Ashley arrived, and he sniffed appreciatively as she ushered them into her office.

'Would you like a cup before we start?'

'Mmm, please!' Graeme rubbed his hands and beamed, but Ashley shook her head.

'There are pastries.' She offered the plate.

'No, I'm OK.'

She looked faintly sullen; Kathleen wondered whether Graeme's idea of a special treat had been imposed against her will. 'Juice, water, anything? I think there might be a Diet Coke . . .'

'I'm fine.'

'Why don't you go have a look around the museum?' said Graeme. He glanced at Kathleen. 'Are the doors open?'

'Yes, everything's unlocked.'

'We'll come get you when we're ready,' said Graeme, treating her more like one of his children than the adult she was. 'Or just come back here if you get fed up.'

She shrugged and sighed before wandering off. Graeme took a sip of coffee and turned back to Kathleen. 'She found it hard to get moving this morning. Jet lag, I guess. Plus, I don't think she's really a morning person.'

'I hope she's not going to be bored.'

'Bored? No! She enjoyed the museum on Saturday, I know she did. Plus, she's really interested in art. And she thinks this is a great old building.'

'Well, that's nice. But she's seen the best of it already. There's just a few rooms upstairs . . . it's not the most thrilling tour.'

'Oh, Kathleen, I object! It is *most* thrilling.' He lifted a

Danish and inspected it through narrowed eyes. 'Did you buy this from that funny old bird on the pier?'

'Funny old bird?'

'She was dressed like Whistler's mother. Or do I mean Rembrandt's mother? Long dress and a funny sort of bonnet covering up her head so you couldn't see a single hair, or her ears – I don't know what it was in aid of, but she was selling home baking off a tray on the pier, and doing a roaring trade. They usually do those things in one of the church halls on a Saturday.'

'I didn't see her. I got those from the bakery on Main Street, and I didn't go by the pier at all.' Recalling the route she had taken, she asked him about W P. MacTaggart & Sons.

He shook his head. 'Sure you remembered the name right?'

'I think so.'

'On Kirk Street?'

'If that's the street that runs along behind the Orchard Hotel.'

He nodded. 'But there's nothing like that there. Sure you weren't on the other side of Main, running along to George Square? There's the tobacconist, Peter Marr, which looks old-fashioned.'

'I know the tobacconist's. It's got an amazing display of pipes and exotic cigarettes and jars of peppermints in the window.'

'He might have cleared it out.'

'I wasn't on that side of the street. I was coming back to the library. It was a couple of doors past the chandler's shop, before you get to the dry cleaner's.'

'You've got me,' he said with a shrug. 'I've never noticed it. They must not get post.'

Ashley was in the museum, standing and staring intently up at *Appleton Fair Day*. She scarcely looked around when they came in, as if, thought Kathleen, she was reading the picture and didn't want to lose her place.

'Who is that, do you know? That man kind of lurking in the background there ... you can hardly see him ... it looks like he's got something on his head ... is it a turban?'

Although the figures in the foreground could be seen very clearly beneath the light that came from the two carefully angled lamps fixed to the wall above the picture, details in the background were more obscure. Kathleen fetched the heavy-duty torch from beneath the counter. 'I've never really noticed that man before,' she remarked, before aiming the light at the dark, skulking figure. 'Seems to be my day for seeing things for the first time.'

She heard Ashley gasp at the same moment recognition constricted her own lungs. She thought of the young man she'd seen on the street corner, gazing up at her bedroom window on the night of the earthquake. She'd seen him so briefly, and the painted face was so small, that she couldn't say it for a certainty, but she felt the likeness was undeniable. Which meant, probably . . . her eyes swept back to the young Victorian woman who was the very image of Graeme's wife Shona . . . that far from being a stranger here, the man she'd seen was the descendant of some longtime Appleton family

'Graeme, do you know who that is?' Ashley sounded urgent. 'I'm sure I've seen him – well, his relative – around here.'

'That's not very likely.'

'Why?' Speaking together, they stopped and gave each other a suspicious, assessing glance.

Graeme gave a little laugh at the chorus, although he looked puzzled. 'Well, because, if I'm right – and, mind, I'm just basing this on something I read, and some old photos – that's a Wall. I don't know which one, because he's a young-looking man, and when this was painted Lachlan Wall must have been in his sixties. His younger brother James, if he was still alive at that point, lived in Jamaica or some place like that, and his son, Alexander, was just a wee boy.'

'Alexander Wall, the architect?'

'That's right.'

'So it might be one of his descendants.'

'There aren't any. Not alive today.'

'Where did you see him?' Ashley demanded.

Kathleen looked up, turning the torch beam on the man in the turban again. 'He wasn't wearing a turban when I saw him, but he was sort of exotic-looking. That's why I noticed him. He was . . . outside the library.'

'He didn't come in?'

'No. You know him?'

It was Ashley's turn to look away. 'No. I saw him, too. Thought he was dead sexy. I was hoping you could give me his phone number.'

Kathleen switched off the light. 'Shall we move on?'

She led them back through the library, into the grand foyer, pointing out design features, but cutting it short when she began to suspect Ashley had already heard all this from Graeme. 'You probably already saw the Ladies' Reading Room?'

'Yeah, but I wouldn't mind looking at it again. That frieze-thing above the fireplace is gorgeous.'

'Yes, isn't it! It's by Frances Macdonald.'

'Was she local?'

'No, she was a Glasgow artist; part of Charles Rennie Mackintosh's group – his wife's sister, in fact. Both women were very fine artists. The Hunterian in Glasgow has more of her work, if you're interested.'

'I am. I'll look out for it when I go there.'

Kathleen led her visitors past the old counter that barred the way into the back, explaining that in the old days what was now the reference room would have been closed stacks. Behind the old counter she unlocked a door – a modern addition – to reveal a metal spiral staircase.

Mindful of Graeme's eagerness, and of the fact that she was wearing a skirt, Kathleen nodded at him. 'Why don't you go first, and wait for us to follow.' He sprang forward, not needing further encouragement, and she explained to Ashley, with a glance at the steps shivering beneath his moving weight, 'They are perfectly safe, these stairs, but they do kind of judder, so I worry about putting them under too much strain. It's probably better to go up one by one.'

'Do they go all the way up into the dome?'

'Oh, no. There's no way into the dome – it's purely decorative.' From the look on her face, she guessed Graeme had told her otherwise. She gave her a sympathetic look. 'I'm sorry . . . it's really not very exciting. I don't know why Graeme thinks this is such a big deal, but it won't take long.' Now that the stairs had stopped quivering, she seized hold of the railing. 'Unless you want to go first? No? Well, just give me a couple of seconds before you follow.'

The short spiral of steps ended in a long, empty room. There was a big bay window on one side which looked out into the high-ceilinged foyer. Thanks to the glass panels set in and above the doors to the Ladies' Reading Room and the main library it was possible, from here, to keep an eye on whatever was happening, with only the reference room and the museum out of sight.

'This was the old librarian's office,' Kathleen explained. 'In the old days he could come and go between his little eyrie upstairs and the counter below and never miss a trick.'

'But it's not used for anything now?'

'Health and safety regulations,' she said, waving her hand at the staircase. 'No good for storage, with staff having to haul boxes up and down those, ditto clambering up here every time you want a tea break. We couldn't provide disabled access, and I think Mr Dean – he was the previous librarian – had a problem with his hip.'

'I think it would be cool to have your office up here,' said Ashley, gazing through the window at the stained glass above the front entrance. 'It's kind of like . . . a control room in a big ship or something.'

With an odd little jolt Kathleen recalled her dream of three nights before, when the library had been a ship at sea. With an effort, she collected her thoughts and directed her guests' attention to the other interesting feature of the room, on the wall behind them. A full-sized apple tree, cast or moulded in plaster, stretched from the bottom of the wall to the top, with a few branches and leaves trailing across the ceiling.

'Weird,' said Ashley, sounding startled. 'I didn't even notice there was anything there!'

'No, the light isn't very good; it tends to blend in with the wall, especially as it's all covered in the same, cream-coloured paint,' Kathleen said.

'It's kind of like that tree above the door of that pub, you know, the Orchard? Funny they didn't paint it in different colours.'

Kathleen nodded her agreement; she'd had exactly the same thought when she'd been given her first tour of the building.

'Not much point,' said Graeme. 'The way it's placed, you can't even see it from the foyer below. I know, because I've tried from practically every angle. Yet if they'd just placed it a little farther over, more in the centre of the room, I bet you could see it from the foyer, especially if it had bright green leaves and red apples. But this way . . . well, it's for the librarian's use only.'

'Is it by some famous artist?' Ashley moved closer to peer at the bumpy texture of the bark and the smooth projecting globes that were apples.

'I doubt it. There doesn't seem to be any record of who did it, which suggests it was probably the architect himself.'

'Weird,' said Ashley again, turning away and dismissing it with a shrug.

'Well, are we ready to go?'

'There's more to the upstairs than this,' Graeme objected.

'Yes, but you can't get there from here.' She led the

way, and one at a time they returned downstairs and across the reference room, then through the door marked EMERGENCY USE ONLY and up another, more solid, set of stairs to the old meeting room.

'I'm afraid you aren't seeing this room at its best, because it's been used for storage.'

'That's the Wall collection, am I right?' Graeme gazed avidly at the glass-fronted bookcases.

'That's right. Soon to be sold off, once there's been a proper evaluation.'

'That's not right.' He scowled. 'Old Lachlan Wall donated his personal library – which included books his grandfather had collected – to the people of Appleton, for their education and enrichment.'

She suspected Graeme would not be the only local resident to object to selling off an entitlement they had never seen or previously cared about. 'Times change. Some of these books may have been cutting-edge when they were donated, but very few people are interested in reading them now. Some may be collectors' items, but others' – her eyes fell on a set of books beautifully bound in dark burgundy-coloured leather, with gilt lettering on the spines announcing *The Collected Sermons* – 'just take up space. I think most people would rather we had funds to buy more new books.'

'Most people are Philistines.'

'Well, Graeme, if you want to read any of these books,

there's still time,' she said sweetly. 'They're all in the card catalogue, in the drawer marked "Wall Collection."'

'There is one I'd like to read – I know I asked you about it – Alexander Wall's journal.'

She nodded, thinking of the handwritten book on her bedside table. 'If you'll come in during opening hours and fill out a request form, I can have it for you the next day. It can't be taken out, so you'd have to read it in the library that's the only thing.'

He still looked dissatisfied. 'I never got anywhere requesting it before.'

'That was before my time. I'm telling you how things are now.' She glanced over at Ashley, who was looking faintly stupefied with boredom. 'Come on, I'll show you the last of it . . . although unless you have a special interest in storerooms, it's not very exciting.'

'I love storage rooms,' Graeme declared. 'You never know what you might find.'

The room beyond was at least twice the size of the meeting room, uncarpeted, and furnished only with industrial-type shelving. The shelves held back issues of old magazines, box files of old paperwork, documents, issues of the local newspaper dating back to the nineteenth century, and boxes containing some of the smaller items from the museum's collection. Larger boxes and wooden packing cases were piled everywhere. The very sight made her quail at the magnitude of the task ahead.

'You don't have any idea what's here?'

She frowned, feeling her professionalism criticized. 'Of course I do. I know *exactly*. There's a list of everything in the museum collection, and the boxes are all labelled.'

He crossed to a pile of cardboard boxes and pulled open the folded-down top. Before she could say anything to stop him, he'd rummaged inside and pulled out something wrapped in a sheet of old newspaper.

'Hey, look, do you mind?'

He looked ashamed. 'Oh, sorry. But since I've got it out . . .?'

She sighed and watched as he removed a small, round, red container carved with an oriental key pattern and topped with a blossoming tree. 'It looks Chinese,' he said, surprised.

'It probably is.' She went over to read the neatly printed label affixed to the side of the box. 'Look: "Chinoiserie donated by Miss N. McLennan, ca. 1924; acquired by her late brother during his naval career."'

'But that's nothing to do with Appleton.'

'I know. People obviously had a different idea of what the museum was for in the past, so anything exotic, or unfamiliar, or beautiful . . .' As she spoke, he carefully rewrapped the trinket and settled it back inside the box.

'What's this painting?'

They both turned at Ashley's voice. She was standing by the far wall, gazing at the corner of a large, gilt frame sticking out from behind some boxes. Kathleen stared, trying to remember a painting.

'Graeme, would you help me . . .?'

Working together, the three of them quickly cleared away the obstructing pile of boxes to reveal an ornately framed oil painting. It was a big – more than three feet long – panoramic view of Appleton's harbour. In the background the hotel and the golden dome and dominating pillars of the library were immediately recognizable, as were the palm-lined Esplanade and the pier. However, the umbrella-shaded café tables in front of the hotel, and throngs of brightly dressed pedestrians strolling through brilliant sunshine seemed to have been imported from the French Riviera, and the artist's depiction of the water traffic was pure fantasy.

The view of the shore might – allowing for a bit of artistic licence – have been painted from life on a sunny summer afternoon, and the style was faintly Impressionistic. Beyond the water's edge, however, the artist's style had undergone a sea change, becoming weirdly hyperrealistic in depicting vessels and people that could never have been seen in this little Scottish town. Close in, a few ordinary old-fashioned fishing smacks lay at anchor, and there was a red-chimneyed puffer recognizable as the sort of boat that had regularly made the journey from Glasgow to Appleton from the 1880s until the 1950s. But these familiar vessels were outnumbered, and overwhelmed, by the many far more exotic craft that filled the harbour. There were dragon-prowed long ships and oriental junks, gondolas, rowboats, several basketlike coracles, a Polynesian canoe, and numerous sailing ships, from sleek little two-sailed yachts to heavy, eight-masted schooners flying flags she did not recognize. The passengers and crew of the vessels were equally varied: some were scarred, heavily armed, sinister-looking pirates, some had a royal appearance, were richly dressed, or looked like Aztec warriors, Vikings, naked and tattooed Polynesians, red-blond Celts and solemn Mandarins mingling in the scene with creatures that looked half-animal, barely human.

A small, etched brass plate screwed into the lower part of the frame identified the picture as *Fantasia: Appleton Harbour on Fair Day* by Emmeline Wall.

'Amazing,' breathed Ashley.

'Alexander Wall's daughter,' said Graeme.

'Why isn't it hanging in the museum?' Kathleen wondered aloud. She looked at him. 'Did you know about this?'

He shook his head. 'I knew she was meant to be an artist, but I've never seen any of her paintings. I never really thought about it. If I did, I probably assumed she wasn't any good, and that was why . . .'

'But this is *brilliant*,' said Ashley. 'How could they just hide it away up here? Are there any more by her?'

They spread out around the room to check the walls, peer behind piles of boxes and on top of shelves. Within a few minutes, Kathleen was satisfied there were no other hidden paintings.

'But she might have done some smaller ones; they could be in box files, especially an unframed canvas,' Ashley argued, her eyes roaming over the shelves.

'If there are others, they're listed. Mr Dean was very good about his records.'

Ashley didn't look satisfied. 'You didn't know about that painting.'

'I'd never seen it, that's all.' This was a lie; she'd no idea the painting existed. But she was sure that it was recorded in the list of museum holdings – why wouldn't it be? She rushed on, 'There's a book, a collection of Emmeline's drawings, downstairs.'

'Really? Could I see it?'

'Of course.' She felt relieved by this simple conclusion. 'Let's go.'

She ushered them back into the meeting room and locked the door to the storage room behind her. Turning back, she saw that Graeme, predictably, was reading the titles of the books displayed in the locked case, while Ashley loitered, dreamy-eyed.

'Alexander Wall's journal must be here somewhere, don't you think?'

'I think if you fill out a request form and give it to me

during my normal working hours, I'll find it for you.'

'Sorry. Sorry, sorry, sorry.' He smiled ruefully, holding up his hands in mock surrender. 'I'll go quietly now, ma'am.'

She was following him towards the door when something made her look back at Ashley. As she turned, she caught a glimpse of motion, too swift to interpret, and then the guilt that flickered across the girl's face.

'What is it?' Her voice was perfectly pleasant, but she fixed her with the look she used when some kid was trying to lift a CD, or sneak an expensive book out under his coat. 'Let me see.' She held out her hand.

Her cheeks took on a dark red stain as she raised her hand from where she'd had it hidden below the table. 'I was just about to,' she muttered. 'I just saw it . . . I was just about to say . . .' She dropped what felt like a ball into Kathleen's hand.

It was a carved and polished wooden apple, invitingly smooth and heavy, a simple thing, yet strangely beautiful. As she ran her thumb over the fine-grained wood she saw a sequence of symbols had been incised around the top.

'What is it?' asked Graeme. 'May I see?'

She gave it to him.

He held it balanced in his hand, gazing at it with a kind of awe. 'Well, well, well. This *is* a find. I wondered what had happened to it.'

'What is it?'

He pointed to the symbols. 'That's Greek. It means "to the fairest." Ashley, my dear, this was your grandmother's prize. Where did you find it?'

'It was just lying there.' She waved at the table, indicating an empty spot between two boxes of books. 'I wondered what it was so I picked it up. Just to have a look; I wasn't going to steal it!' She darted an angry look at Kathleen.

Kathleen didn't believe her. If the wooden apple had been lying on the meeting room table, she would have seen it herself before now. Ashley must have found it in the storeroom, poking into some box while her back was turned. Perhaps she hadn't intended to keep it; that quick flash of motion might have been her attempt to leave it on the table.

'But if it belonged to Phemie, what's it doing here? If it's my family's property?' Ashley had made a quick *volte-face* from the guilty to the injured party.

'The winner only got to keep it for a year.' Graeme handed it back to Kathleen. 'It would be given to a new Apple Queen at the next fair. The museum's the best place for it now.'

'I agree.' She slipped the wooden apple into one of the deep, wide pockets of her skirt. 'Thank you for finding it, Ashley. I don't know *how* I managed to overlook it.'

By the time they got downstairs, she felt apologetic. She didn't really think Ashley was a thief, and it was not surprising that she'd felt moved to pick up something so beautiful. Even now, the weight of it in her pocket drew her hand to stroke it. Maybe she really had found it on the table; Miranda or Connie or one of the cleaners might have left it there recently. She had been surprised today by a figure in a painting and a whole shop she'd never noticed before; it was surely just as likely that she'd failed to see a carved wooden object in the shadow of a cardboard box on her last few visits to the room upstairs.

In the reference room she went to the bottom shelf where the oversized books were kept, and withdrew a tall, skinny volume.

'This is Emmeline's work. Her father had it privately printed in Glasgow. I don't know how many copies were made, but the library has two.' She put it down on a table and opened it, then stepped back so the other two could look at it.

Doorways
by Emmeline Wall
Glasgow
1912

'She was just a kid!' Graeme exclaimed when he saw the date.

'You haven't seen this before?'

He shook his head. 'Never knew it existed. So, what's it all about? What sort of book would a sixteen-year-old girl write?'

Ashley had already turned the page, to a fine, detailed drawing of a heavy wooden doorway, within a carved-stone archway, immediately recognizable to any Appleton resident as the entrance to the Free Gaelic Church or 'the Tartan Kirk'. On the next page, the narrower doorway into the Lowland Church was depicted, and then those of the other three churches in town, as well as the crumbling archway into a ruined chapel on a hillside somewhere. There were other doors, to buildings both grand and humble, shops and hotels and private homes. The front entrance of the Public Library – her father's design – was faithfully reproduced, and so were the detailed carvings on the doors into the museum.

'Pictures of doors?' Graeme turned away from the table, his brow knitting.

'The book *is* called *Doorways*,' Kathleen said with a smile. 'Emmeline was an artist.' The only text in the entire book was on the title page, unless you counted the few bits of lettering above some of the doors: the date and dedication carved above the library entrance, the names of a few businesses, the shaky hand-lettered warning *Mind Yer Heid* above a low cottage door.

Hand in her pocket, she caressed the wooden apple and

felt her thumb catch on the Greek letters. 'Fancy you knowing Ancient Greek,' she said. 'Where'd you learn that?'

He ducked his head, abashed. 'Actually, I don't. I knew what was written on that apple, because I'd read about it.'

'They're not all doors.'

At Ashley's comment they looked down at a picture of the graveyard.

'Some of them you have to take metaphorically, I think.'

'So what's this?' She turned to the next page; a pile of stones in a grassy meadow, with hills rising behind it.

'Oh, you know that!' He leaned over her shoulder. 'That's where I took you yesterday – it's the reul, see there?' He ran a fingertip over the line of hills. 'And those rocks . . . well, couldn't that be the doorway – all fallen down, I admit – to one of the old stone huts?'

'Yeah, I guess.' She turned the page. 'So how do you explain that?'

The last sketch in the book was of the weird, imposing rocks that reared up beside the road into Appleton.

'Easy,' said Graeme. 'That road is the only way in or out of town – the entrance and exit – a door.'

'But you can't even see the road in the picture – just the rocks, and the sea, and the setting sun, and the empty sky.'

'Maybe she meant the sea, then,' said Kathleen. 'That

was the main doorway to the rest of the world, in the old days. Those rocks do sort of frame it.'

'Mmm.' The girl sounded skeptical. 'She should have put a boat in the picture if that was what she meant.' She shut the book. 'Well. Thanks for letting me see this. What else did she do?'

'Nothing that I know of.'

'She couldn't have just stopped – she was too good. If she was only sixteen when she did the drawings in this book . . . how about that painting upstairs? When did she do that?'

'I don't know. I didn't see a date on it. I'll try to find out.' She smiled. 'I have to thank you for making two big discoveries this morning! I'm going to get on to headquarters, see what I can find out about the painting, and get it on display as soon as possible. If we could uncover *more* work by Emmeline Wall, that would be even better. I'll let you know what I find out.'

Ashley smiled back, and she felt relieved that the brief unpleasantness about the apple had been smoothed over. It had occurred to her that she'd completely misread the whole situation. Rather than taking the apple, Ashley had been bringing it back. Maybe her grandmother had felt guilty about running off with it, and Ashley had felt moved to return it to the town – but secretly, so her grandmother wouldn't be branded a thief.

'I wouldn't get your hopes up about finding much more

work by Emmeline Wall,' said Graeme, as they walked back to the foyer. 'She died young.'

'What happened?'

'Suicide. She was an unmarried mother. Her father could forgive her anything, but I don't think the rest of the town felt that way. Could be that's why her painting wasn't on display. Bad feelings linger. Even though she was dead, the townsfolk wouldn't want to glorify someone they considered immoral – and possibly mentally unstable.'

'Are you serious? God, people can be so narrow-minded! She was fantastically talented! That's what matters.' Animated, Ashley was much more attractive, and Kathleen was startled by a sudden warm rush of affection for the girl. She wondered what it would be like to have a daughter, then backed off from the thought in alarm.

Don't go getting broody now, she warned herself. *Bad timing*!

She walked with them to the back gate and let them out, then went to lock up the library. It was only after she was back in the house that she realized she still carried the wooden apple in her skirt pocket.

She took it out and set it down on the hall table alongside her heavy ring of keys. The sight of it, first thing in the morning, would remind her to call headquarters and raise the subject of Emmeline's painting and other important questions about the museum.

From *The Silver Bough, Vol. 1: Scottish Folk-lore and Folk Belief*

by F. Marian McNeill
(William MacLellan, Glasgow, 1957)

THE Celtic Elysium was situated not, like the heaven of the hymnist, 'above the bright blue sky,' but here upon earth; but, as it was a subjective world, its location was vague ... Sometimes it was a mystic green island that drifted on the western seas. Men caught occasional glimpses of it, half hidden in a twinkling mist, but when they attempted to draw near, it vanished beneath the waves ...

The Green Island has been seen in almost every latitude from Cape Wrath in Scotland to Cape Clear in Ireland. Sometimes it was identified with a particular isle of the West.

'According to Irish tradition,' says Professor Watson, 'Arran was the home of Manannan, the sea-god, and another name for it was *Emain Ablach*, Emain of the Apples. This is, I suppose, equivalent to making Arran the same as Avalon, the Happy Otherworld.'

To enter this Otherworld before the appointed hour of death, a passport was necessary. This was a silver branch of the mystic apple-tree, laden with blossom or fruit – though sometimes a single apple sufficed – and it was given by the Queen of Elfhame or Fairy Woman to that mortal whose companionship she desired. It served not only as a passport, but also as food; and it had the property of making music so entrancing that those who heard it forgot all their cares and sorrows.

Chapter Ten

Nell was up and out of the house as soon as it was light, hurrying across the meadow and into the scented hush of the walled orchard, wondering how she could have been fooled.

She had been raised by thoroughly secular people. She'd never belonged to any church; she had no established religious beliefs to console or disturb her. But she was not an atheist, and she couldn't accept an entirely materialist view of life. She knew that her husband – and almost certainly her parents, too – had believed that death was the end, but she felt differently. People were more than their material bodies; they had souls, and those might be eternal. She'd read about karma and reincarnation and astral planes and physicists' theories of other worlds, never quite finding the answer she was looking for, but believing it was out there. As for an actual, physical Heaven, with a geographical location, that idea had seemed too naive to take seriously – until last night.

She knew the meaning of the silver bough in folklore, but what about in real life, in her own orchard? Could it possibly be a sign from Sam, an invitation to join him in the afterlife? And if so, was that more wonderful than terrifying?

And so her thoughts had run on until, at some point during the long, restless night, it had finally occurred to her that the man calling himself Ronan Wall, the man she had let into her orchard, might be responsible for the blossoming branch.

She remembered how he'd touched it – he'd wanted her to remember that. Of course it was a trick; the flowers were made of silk or paper, and he'd turn up the next day to pass himself off as special ambassador to the Otherworld. No need to ask why: he was a con man, simple as that. He'd picked her because she had money, a house, land, and, as a lonely widow without family or friends, she made an easy mark. He'd done his research and decided to use her grief, her longing, and her interest in apple trees against her. If he really was, as he claimed, a descendant of the Walls, he might be driven by more than the usual con man's desire to profit at someone else's expense; maybe he felt her property was rightfully his. Oh, but why make excuses? He was a con artist, and she'd been extraordinarily gullible. At least it wasn't too late. She wouldn't let him set any more traps for her. She wouldn't believe a word he said.

She half expected the blossom to have disappeared – otherwise, she might find it had been an illusion, convincing only in the half-light of dusk, which daylight would dispel.

But it was still there, clustered thickly along the same slender branch from which the single golden apple hung. She put her nose right up to one cluster of the creamy, pink-tinged flowers, close enough that she felt the pollen-bearing stamens tickle her nostrils, and inhaled the soft, sweet scent. It was real, all right, and the branch, too, was natural. If there was some explanation other than magic for the out-of-season flowering, she was convinced it could not be human trickery.

She aimed a mental apology at Ronan Wall, wherever he might be, and lingered to stare at the singular apple. It was ripe and ready for picking and should not be left for much longer. The sight of it made her mouth water. What a great breakfast it would be, eaten just-picked, out of doors. But superstition, or something else, stayed her hand. She didn't have to believe in magic to feel it was wrong to go against the local custom. Just because the apple had appeared on her tree, on her land, didn't make the decision of what to do with it hers alone. In the old days, the community had decided, choosing an Apple

Queen to share the fruit with her love, and their good fortune spread to the whole town – at least, that was the story. There wasn't time now to organize a competition, but there must be plenty of deserving, attractive young women about the place. She should ask Kathleen . . .

She remembered then, with a little lurch of her heart, how things were: she had totally alienated her one potential friend in this town, cutting her off and willing her to leave last night. She was on her own again. There wasn't anyone else she could ask. She thought of Jean, the woman who ran the organic shop, and remembered her broad Yorkshire accent: another incomer. So was the plumber, and that Mr Murphy who'd put up her greenhouse . . . but did it matter where they came from originally? The Murphys had been here nearly thirty years; they had grownup children, one of whom worked as a hairdresser.

She imagined going into the warm, scented air of Curl Up & Dye and presenting the golden apple to the girls who worked there. 'To the Fairest!' she might announce, and then what? Toss it like a bridal bouquet and see who managed to catch it? Suggest a beauty competition to be judged by the star of the local football team? Wouldn't they just laugh at her? And wouldn't they be right?

She left the orchard and made her way back to the house, pausing on her way to pick a handful of fat, glossy blackberries to add to her muesli. Already the day was shaping up into a fine, dry, bright one, and she guessed it would be unseasonably hot again. This late spurt of unusually warm weather wasn't enough to explain the sudden appearance of the blossom on her tree; but since she'd ruled out trickery, she had to try to think up some other, nonsupernatural, explanation for it.

As she ate breakfast, idly swirling the fragments of mint leaves in her teacup, she thought of the tree she'd found growing wild, the one she'd taken the cutting from. For all she knew it was a late bloomer, or some strange variety that customarily carried apples and blossom at the same time.

She still had the map, and a pencilled 'X' marked the spot where she'd found the solitary apple tree. It would be easy to find; she could walk there in under forty minutes. Comparing her tree with its parent might not tell her much, but it was such an obvious thing to do, she couldn't believe she hadn't thought of it before.

Two hours later, she was walking in circles, stubbornly sure of her ground, yet lost. She trudged on, wiping the sweat from her face and getting more and more thirsty and hot, and more and more cross with herself every time she stopped to consult the map. She should have been able to find the site, even if the tree itself had gone. She remembered it so clearly: on the edge of the pine plantation, near a stream, growing just beside a pile of rocks she'd decided must be the remains of a cottage, or, at least a walled enclosure. Why couldn't she find that, at least?

Of course, things did grow incredibly rapidly in this moist, mild climate, even though the soil was thin; maybe the pile of rocks she remembered was now buried beneath brambles and bracken, completely hidden from sight.

For about the sixth time she returned to the stream. Already she had traced its entire course, remembering that as she'd taken a cutting from the tree she'd heard the musical rush of water over stones like the sound of tinkling bells. Houses were generally built close to a source of water, so she felt certain she could trust her memory. But when she reached the bubbling spring that was the source of the stream, and there was still no sign of a single apple tree, she had to accept that it must have been uprooted or chopped down.

She crouched, plunged her hands into the chilly water, and splashed her face, then raised the fresh liquid in handfuls and drank. Gradually, cooler and calmer, she considered another possibility: that she'd made a mistake when she marked the map, that it was beside another stream (after all, there were plenty of them), even farther from the original orchards, that she'd found her mystery tree.

It wasn't very likely, for she was a competent map-reader, but she wasn't ready to give up and go home, so she checked the position of the next closest stream on the map, and struck out for it, striding along confidently despite the lack of a path.

Within fifteen minutes she knew that she had never

come this way before. The ground began to rise more steeply, and the terrain changed, becoming rockier and more barren. This was not land hospitable to trees. Heather and spiky broom grew in abundance, nothing much taller. She spotted one small rowan tree, its slender branches already heavy with red berries, and remembered that they grew in the most inhospitable of sites, sometimes sprouting from a covering of moss on solid rock.

She knew she would find no apple trees on such a barren moor, but she did not turn back. The weather was glorious; she enjoyed being out in the open, and found it especially pleasant to stride along quickly, stretching her legs, after creeping along, peering at the ground for familiar landmarks. It was a disappointment not to have found the tree, but it didn't really matter.

As she continued to walk, she was puzzled by the increasing emptiness of the landscape. She saw a few low, creeping plants here and there among the rocks, but no grasses – even the heathers had disappeared. The ground was hard and dry underfoot, as if it had been weeks without rain instead of only a few days. Pausing to bend and examine it she found not solid rock, as she'd half expected, but soil that had dried to a fine, powdery dust, having had all moisture leached out of it. It was like a desert. For a moment she could make no sense of it, and then she understood: there must have been a fire. Of course, wildfire, caused by lightning or a hiker's careless match, might have destroyed all local vegetation. Presumably the presence of so many streams and waterways had kept the fire from spreading very far.

She sniffed the air and realized it held an acrid, smoky tang, suggesting that the fire was very recent. She wondered if it could still be smouldering somewhere, although, looking around, she could see nothing left to burn.

Just ahead of her rose a small, bare, rounded hill. It had an odd appearance, as if some sort of path or channel had been worn into the sides, incised in a winding spiral from the base to the top. She had the vague sense that this meant something she should know, but she could not think why. The sight of the oddly shaped hill in this desolate landscape, the silence (there were no birds) and the lingering, unpleasant scent of burning on the hot and heavy air all combined to create a growing sense of unease.

Checking her map, she found the hill was named Cnoc na Beithir, and although she'd never seen it before, she remembered the name from a winter's evening of map-reading. *Cnoc* was a round hill, and her Gaelic dictionary had given four distinct definitions for *beithir*. It was 'a prodigiously large serpent' and 'lightning bolt' and 'bear' and something else she couldn't remember – some sort of fish. It had made her wonder how people could have managed with such an unnecessarily confusing language.

Which of the four definitions had given the name of beithir to this hill? she wondered. Maybe this little *cnoc* had a reputation for attracting lightning. Maybe the dead, burnt-over look of the land was not due to anything recent. But that hardly accounted for the smell. Looking up at the clear blue sky – no chance of being struck today – she ignored the urge she felt to run away, and kept walking towards the hill, bearing slightly to the left, where the spiral path – if it *was* a path – seemed to have its beginning.

At the base of the hill, just before the path began, she saw an opening, a cleft in the rock that was almost twice as wide as an ordinary doorway. She stopped short, her stomach churning. Although it was too dark to see anything inside the cave, she was *sure* there was something lurking in the darkness. The smell of burning was much stronger here, and she became aware of a sound that made the hairs stand up on the back of her neck: a low, sinister hissing.

She felt rooted to the spot by the horrible threat conveyed by the sound. Impossible, of course, but it sounded like a huge snake. Of course, there were no really big snakes in this country – adders, although poisonous, were small and shy. Maybe a nest of adders, amplified by the rock walls around them, could sound like that, but she didn't believe it. She imagined a prodigiously large serpent, more gigantic than any python she'd ever seen in a zoo, uncoiling within that dark recess, preparing to emerge and wrap itself around the hill, unwinding into the grooves it had worn in the sloping sides on other days when it lay there, torpid in the sunlight, digesting whatever it had devoured.

Only today it had not yet eaten, and would be hungry. And there was nothing in this barren region for it to eat. Nothing, except her.

Nell ran for it. There was nothing to be gained in stubbornly waiting to see what came out of that hole, and potentially everything to lose. She ran even though she didn't believe in the thing she was running from, and her steps did not slow until she reached an area – lush, green, heavily overgrown – that looked familiar to her.

She didn't know how to think about what she'd just experienced. She hadn't actually *seen* anything – she might have imagined it – was it possible that she'd been hallucinating, maybe because of heatstroke? It didn't feel that hot to her, but she had been out in the sun for hours, without a hat – maybe that was all it was. She was eager to get home, to sit in the shade and sip something cold and sweet while she read one of her library books and forgot everything else.

She was already halfway there in her mind when, approaching the garden gate, she saw someone, or something, crouched on the low stone boundary wall: an odd figure, like a gargoyle, knees raised and back hunched.

Her heart lurched and she faltered, fearful that she

might be forced to turn and run away again, this time from her own house, until she recognized Ronan. The reason for his odd posture was the large book he was poring over.

She felt a strong, half-guilty pleasure at the sight of him, which put her on her guard. Even if he wasn't a con artist, he certainly wanted something from her. She had to stay sharp, which could be difficult in the throes of physical attraction. When she was near enough to speak without shouting, she said, 'What do you want?'

He looked up and smiled as if he hadn't heard the warning in her voice. 'I've got something for you.' Unfolding lithely, he slipped down from the wall and held out a large yet slim book, taller than it was wide, and bound in a hard-wearing, dark blue material.

She frowned and crossed her arms.

'It'll interest you,' he said and, when she didn't respond, he opened it and held it up so she could see a beautiful, full-page colour print of an apple. It was not just any apple; she recognized it at once as her own mystery fruit. It was yellow-gold with a freckling of reddish blush, surrounded by soft green leaves and creamy, pink-tinged blossom all on the same branch.

Her arms came down and she took an involuntary step forward. 'What *is* that?'

'James Alexander Wall's *Pomona*. There's everything you could possibly want to know about the apples that grow here.' He pressed it into her hands, and, unable to resist such a lure, she took it.

Although she'd promised herself she would not invite him in a second time, she could not send him away with his book in her hands. The thought of standing here and quickly leafing through the book did not appeal; it was too important to skim. She was hot and tired, and still a bit shaky, after the experience on her long walk, and only wanted to rest. She took a deep breath and spoke politely 'May I offer you something to drink?'

He smiled and followed her into the garden. She stopped beside the table where she'd had dinner with Kathleen, put the book down, and gestured him to a seat. 'What would you like? Something cold? Iced tea or water or . . . some sort of fruit juice, I think. Wine? Or would you rather have coffee?'

He was watching her with a disconcertingly close gaze, as if trying to commit her to memory.

'Well?'

He gave his head a small shake. 'Whatever you're having.'

'Fine. I'll just be a few minutes.'

As soon as she was inside, she dashed to the bathroom. She fought the temptation to shower and change out of her sweaty old clothes, to brush her hair and spritz on a little Issey. *Really, Nell, could you be more obvious? You'll keep out of sniffing distance. And he is* not *coming in.*

She mixed the last of a jar of instant peach-flavoured tea with cold water and added all the ice cubes she had to the jug. Her stomach growled, and she remembered she hadn't eaten lunch. She quickly sliced some cheese and half a dozen ripe tomatoes and put them on a tray with crackers, and carried them out to the garden. Ronan was sitting with his eyes closed, head thrown back to the sun, and at this sight of him, looking so vulnerable, she again felt the treacherous stir of desire. She bit her tongue so hard it hurt.

She set the tray down, suggested briskly that he should help himself, and took up the book. 'Where did you get this?' Her suspicion that the dark blue cover was a library binding was confirmed by the old-fashioned bookplate she discovered on the inside of the front cover: PROPERTY OF APPLETON PUBLIC LIBRARY. Beneath it was a square red stamp: RESERVED STOCK: FOR REFERENCE ONLY.

'The library.'

'And she let you take it out?' This book was surely too valuable to be let out on loan; it must be irreplaceable.

'I got it for you.'

She felt a twinge of guilt as she imagined kindly Kathleen even after Sunday's disaster still thinking of something nice to do for her, asking Ronan to deliver it – yeah, sure, right. Give a valuable book to a passing stranger? The library wasn't even *open* today.

She looked at him through narrowed eyes. 'And I'm

supposed to return it to the library when I'm through with it? Or give it back to you?'

He took a drink and shrugged. 'As you like.'

'What did you bring this to me for?'

'You had questions.'

'I certainly do.' She looked down, turning the pages. The text was a shock. It was in Latin, set in a heavy gothic typeface in at least eighteen-point. She'd been made to study Latin at school, and although she'd done reasonably well at the time, she wasn't sure how much she'd retained. She looked across at him. 'Can you read this?'

'My Latin's pretty rusty, but I can probably remember enough . . .' He reached for the book as he spoke, but she pulled it away.

'Never mind. I expect I'll be able to puzzle it out myself.' She turned to another coloured plate, which showed the golden apple from different angles and also cut in half, pips appearing like sad eyes in an owlish visage. There were other coloured illustrations, but they were of different varieties, including crab apples and several varieties of domesticated red apples.

'That's the Fairest,' said Ronan, tapping one picture. 'That's what I remember eating.'

'So you never ate the golden?'

He shook his head. 'I had the chance, but . . . no.'

She closed the book and set it safely to one side before

eating a cracker and cheese. She was trembling slightly, which she hoped was simply a physiological response to low blood sugar. She drank a whole glass of tea and poured some more before she addressed him again.

'Why'd you come back?'

'To eat the apple with you.'

She shook her head impatiently. 'Why bring me this book?'

He sighed. 'You won't take my word for it, so I thought, if I could show you it's true, there's the history–'

She laughed, startling them both. 'Just because something's in a book doesn't make it true! Just because some ancestor of yours believed in magic apples – oh, honestly, trying to *reason* me into accepting the unreasonable ... Given the state of my Latin, it'll probably take me weeks to work my way through this little book. By then the apple could have rotted away. You'd have been better off relying on your native charm.'

'I don't know; you've been pretty resistant to it so far.' He spoke dryly and as their eyes met she had the sudden pleasurable sense that she'd met a good match, someone who appreciated her strengths and wasn't simply out to exploit her weakness.

Carried along on the strength of that feeling, she said, 'I'll tell you what. You don't have to try to convince me of anything. I'll give you the apple.'

He shook his head. 'That's not–'

'Don't push it, buster,' she said sharply. 'It's the best deal you're going to get.'

'It's no good to me without you.'

'Now you're being silly. Look, I don't even believe this stuff about the apple, but from what I've heard, it's not limited to certain specific people; it's any man and any woman.'

'Yes, of course it could be,' he said, a touch of impatience in his voice. 'And I've just said – I've made it clear, haven't I? – I want that man and woman to be *us*.'

'But I don't.'

'Then you don't understand,' he said. He leaned forward, looking across the table into her eyes. 'You're saying no to life and happiness – to whatever you want most in the world. You can have your heart's desire. You'll also be saving this whole community, bringing prosperity and good fortune back to Appleton, although I don't blame you if you don't care about the rest of them, since *I* don't – never mind that,' he went on quickly as she opened her mouth.

'Nobody else knows about this apple, or cares – although they should. But this town has forgotten that its fate is tied up with the apples. The old orchards are gone; the Apple Fair hasn't been held in decades, and everyone has forgotten the real reason behind it. But the magic is still here, deep in the land – and the land knows. Every so often, it offers up a magical gift. The last time, that gift was rejected, and things began to go wrong. If this one's rejected, too–' He stopped, and shook his head impatiently.

'Forget the past. I'll tell you whatever you want to know, but all that really matters is we've been given this chance. There's a golden apple growing, first one in over fifty years, and it's *ours*. Things happen when it's time for them. This is *our* time – that's our apple. There are cycles, seasons, whether we understand it or not, and that's why *you* were drawn here to plant apple trees again, so it could happen as it's meant to, and it's why I woke up one morning a few weeks ago and knew I had to get back to Appleton. I thought I'd find the apple.' His gaze became very tender. 'I had no idea I'd also find you.'

Her heart pounded unpleasantly. 'Me?' She spoke harshly. 'You don't know me. You never saw me before yesterday.'

'I knew everything I needed to know the moment I set eyes on you.'

She felt dizzy but tried to draw herself up, to sit higher in her seat, needing to look down on him, to show she wasn't taken in by him for a minute. 'Oh, really, and what was that? All the important things, obviously. Big house, land, no interfering relatives to get in the way; good cheekbones, nice legs, shame about the tits, but she's got a private income – she'll probably pay for her own implants once I convince her–'

'What are you talking about? Nell, I love you.'

'Get out. You want that apple? It's yours. Take it, and go.'

He stared at her, open-mouthed, looking as if she'd hit him in the face.

'Did you hear me? If the apple's so important, take it; find yourself somebody else to share it with.'

'I don't want anyone else. That's what I've been telling you. Nell–'

'Stop calling me Nell! I'm *Mrs* Westray. That's right – you didn't know that about me, did you? I have a husband, and – and I love him very much.' She had to stop, choking on unexpected tears. 'So I don't need you. How *dare* you! You don't know anything about me. See?'

'No,' he said flatly. His face had gone slack. 'Well, Mrs Westray, I'm sorry to have troubled you.' He stood up. 'I suggest – no, I strongly advise you to share that apple with your husband, and as soon as possible. Because there's not much time left. If it's not eaten soon, it'll be too late, and not just for me. For everyone.'

From *Recollections of Alexander (McNeill) Wall*
(unpublished; no date)

I was slow to realize that my little girl had grown to womanhood, but the reason is understandable. When you live with someone, seeing her day in, day out, your own perceptions adjust along with the tiny increments by which ageing progresses, so that the familiar, beloved person appears to your eyes the same as she ever was. In addition, Emmeline had been always a solitary child, having, by choice, few companions and no friends of the bosom, so that it was never brought to my attention, by the fact that one young lady had become engaged to be married, or another had gone to Glasgow to train as a nurse, that my little girl was just as marriageable, trainable, and generally grown-up as her friends.

My Emmeline dwelt in a world of her own, a realm of fairy tale and fantasy, made up of books and pretty pictures, old tales, songs, and the local landscape, which she was always sketching and painting and making up stories about: inside that cave slept a fire-breathing dragon; beneath that lake was a magical city where no one ever died; on that road she'd once seen the Queen of the Fairies pass on a fine white horse . . . She cared more for Fairyland than she ever could for the unhappy reality of the Twentieth Century, and, foolishly, I was happy for what I saw as her innocence. I never recognized the danger until it was too late.

I remained in blissful ignorance until May of 1916, when I slowly realized how my daughter's solitary life had changed. Every afternoon a bevy of young ladies – the very finest blossom of local society – called at the house, either to wait upon Emmeline, gossiping and giggling in the drawing room, or taking her with them on some excursion or other. She had acquired a retinue, like a young queen, and when she told me, beaming with shy delight, that at the end of the summer she was to be crowned the Apple Queen, it all began to make sense. I should have been pleased for her, that she had managed to grow from being a rather odd, solitary child into this lovely young woman, and to be awarded such an honour by her peers – but it made me uneasy.

I had no idea how the queen of the annual fair was chosen; this was a 'women's matter' and too frivolous for me to question, until my daughter was involved. By tradition, she would be crowned by a stranger, an unknown man who would step out of the Fair-day crowd at the appropriate moment. This, at any rate, was the story, but it was no more to be uncritically believed than any other bit of folklore. Young ladies of an age to be chosen for this role often had sweethearts, whether or not they were recognized by possibly disapproving parents, and even I had noticed how very often, and swiftly, past queens ended up married to the 'strangers' who had crowned them! It seemed likely, therefore, that this important role was not left to chance but was rather arranged behind the scenes, and that the 'queen' herself must surely know his identity – most likely chose him.

I felt quite certain that Emmeline had no sweetheart. She showed no interest in any of the local lads, for none of them could match in glamour the heroes of her beloved fairy tales. When I quizzed her – at first subtly and then more openly – she was amazed by my suggestion that there could be any trickery involved. There were always strangers at the Fair, visitors from far afield, and she expected it would be the same even in war-time. She told me about the girl who'd been queen two years past, who'd fallen in love at first sight with the visitor from Ireland who'd stepped out of the crowd. A month later she'd eloped with him, to the horrified consternation of both families, for her family were Free Church, and he was of the Roman persuasion.

'It often happens so,' she prattled on. 'It was fated. They say that if you share an apple with a man on the eve of the Fair, you're bound together for life.'

Although my daughter was, as I'd been forced to notice, grown to a woman's estate, she was still, in many ways, a child.

'Then you mustn't share an apple with a stranger,' I said firmly.

She gave me her mother's smile. 'Only if I love him, Daddy.'

Emmeline was oblivious to the possibility that anything could go wrong, almost feverishly excited by what was to come. As discreetly as I could, I enquired of her female friends, but they all feigned a wide-eyed innocence and pretended not to understand. I believed Emmeline incapable of sustained deception, but these young ladies I knew scarcely at all; what if they were scheming to embarrass poor naive Emmeline, or, worse, if they were out to further the fortunes of a friend, some impoverished young man who wished a wealthy wife . . .? I decided to take matters into my own hands. If there was to be a marriage it should be I, as her father, who arranged it, and no one else.

I knew a man in Glasgow, an honest, reliable merchant who'd commissioned work from my old firm and who had long been a cordial acquaintance, and he had an unmarried son who had recently qualified as a physician. I had no expectations of his forming an alliance with my daughter, but I felt I could be easy in my mind if it happened. I invited the whole family to stay with us during Appleton Fair week, explained the role the son would be expected to play; given the necessity that he should appear to be 'a stranger,' they agreed to arrive by steamer late on Saturday afternoon and make their own way to the Fair. But, as the poet says about the best-laid plans . . .

I have no heart to rehearse here the series of mishaps and misunderstandings that ensued. It's all long in the past. When Emmeline was led in her finery onto the public platform, blushing like a happy bride to the sound of cheering and applause, I was watching anxiously from a little distance. When the cry went up: 'Who will recognize this maiden?' there was a moment of silent suspense, then a murmuring and rustling in the crowd, until a man stepped forward saying, 'I see she is my Queen.'

I was too far away and the light was too dim to make out his face, but although he seemed more shabbily dressed than I'd expected, there was something so confident and educated about his voice that I did not doubt he was 'my' stranger. And when I saw how she looked at him, and clutched his hand as if she'd fall down without his support, I was relieved by my foresightedness. If she was to fall romantically head-over-heels with anyone, at least it should be a professional man from a respectable Scottish family.

When the dancing started, I lost sight of her. The glimpse I caught of her being whirled about in the arms of a dark-haired, smiling man in an old tweed jacket – looking, it hurts my heart even now to recall, more ecstatically happy than I'd ever seen her – was the last I should see of her for almost a year.

Chapter Eleven

It was only her fourth full day, but Ashley was starting to feel like she'd been in Appleton for weeks. The problem was, she'd discovered, that there was very little to *do* there. People kept going on about the great weather, but sunshine wasn't that big a deal to her. She liked beautiful scenery as much as the next person – probably more – but she didn't want to spend *every* day sketching or painting the local beauty spots. The beaches looked great, but she wasn't a surfer, it was too cold to swim, and, really, the thing that made a day at the beach fun was the company of friends and a cooler full of beer, kicking back and checking out the local talent, making new friends . . . The beaches here were way too empty. You could spend the whole day hanging out by the shore and never meet anybody but some enthusiastic dogs and their elderly owners. There weren't a lot of young people in Appleton, that was for sure. Schoolkids, their parents, and lots and lots of old people – she'd seen more *really old* people doddering along the sidewalks of Appleton in a single day than she would expect to see in Houston in a whole year, unless she worked in an old people's home – but not many people her own age.

On Tuesday morning she met Graeme walking his bike up the hill, his postman's bag hanging limp from his shoulder. He nodded to her without his usual cheery enthusiasm.

'OK?' She spoke uncertainly, wondering if he was ill.

He shook his head. 'No post. The plane should have been in just after six, but there's been no sign of it, and no word.'

She frowned. There was hardly a breath of wind, and the skies could not have been clearer. 'Maybe they had engine trouble? They'll send one later, won't they? They have to; I mean, they always get the post through, don't they?'

He shrugged. 'We haven't heard. We can't reach Paisley – that's our sorting office. No reply from any of the Glasgow area offices – even if there was a wildcat strike we hadn't heard about, *somebody* would pick up the phone. No answer from Glasgow International – none of the numbers, except the recorded messages. Those we could get, but not a single living soul. It's like, you could almost think, the rest of the world has just been wiped out by some incredible disaster that somehow missed us, and we're the only survivors–' His eyes widened at the look on her face, and he moved closer and grasped her by the arm. 'Just joking! Of course nothing like that's happened! Jings, take no notice of me, sweetheart! I never meant to scare you.'

'You didn't,' she said, coolly enough. But his words brought back the memory of an old black-and-white movie she'd seen on TCM when she was a kid, an old British disaster movie about the end of civilization. It was pretty lame, really, but it had given her nightmares about an abruptly depopulated world. 'But that is weird. I mean, can you think of some reason why the people in Glasgow wouldn't be at work today?'

'Oh, I'm sure they're all at work as per usual . . . it's far more likely there's a fault in the phone lines. We'll have to get Hamish on to it.' He shook his head, and sighed. 'Semi-retired, and never the brightest spark . . . but he's the only telephone engineer we've got living this side of the roadblock. We'll just have to make do . . . Though I suppose we could communicate with the outside world by carrier pigeon.'

'That would put you out of a job.'

'Who do you think will be training the pigeons? One of my many untapped skills.' He winked at her. 'So, what're your plans for the day? If you need a trusty local guide, I'm available . . .'

'Oh, no thanks. I'm . . . well, I've got some things I want

to do,' she said, nodding in an attempt to impart conviction.

'Well, you have a nice day, now,' he drawled in what she knew he meant for an American accent before he pushed on up the hill.

She wandered around the town aimlessly for a while, shopping as best she could. She bought a mug with a puffin painted on it, a dish towel displaying a map of Scotland, and some postcards in the newsagent's, then went into the take-away fried fish shop to buy what was called here 'a poke of chips.' The good-looking Italian boy was working behind the counter again, and his face lit up at the sight of her. She couldn't help smiling back, although the memory of how he'd practically run away from her when she suggested he join her for a drink still rankled. Maybe he felt bad about it, too, but just as he was about to speak to her, the older, grumpy-looking man snapped something brusque and incomprehensible at him that wiped the smile from his face and sent him scurrying into the back, out of sight. So she paid the older man for her chips and took the bag away.

She ate the hot fried potatoes with salt and vinegar, sitting on a bench overlooking the harbour. It was already a busier place than it had been on her arrival, the water alive with the traffic of small boats coming and going, and the pier full of people doing business. Half a dozen handwritten cardboard signs had been affixed to the railings offering water-taxi services and charter boats for hire by the day or hour. There were also a lot more small boats of different kinds, rowboats and sailboats, resting in the sheltered harbour.

She leaned out over the railing after she'd finished her snack. Most of the boats were tied up and empty, but she noticed a woman sitting, half-reclining, in a flat-bottomed wooden boat that would have been more at home on a tranquil pond. She was dressed most impractically in a long, lacy white dress, her dark hair was piled up and decorated with white flowers, and in her arms, resting across her lap, she carried a spray of white blossom. Was she about to get married? Ashley didn't see anyone else who might have belonged to a wedding party, and if there was a photographer around it wasn't obvious. The relaxed woman in white had to be waiting for someone. She tried to think who she reminded her of, and suddenly recalled Emmeline Wall's painting. She turned away, feeling a strong desire to look at that painting again. The library was about a two-minute walk.

When she got there, it was just reopening after the lunchtime closing, and she met the librarian in the spacious foyer, standing in the brilliant patches of coloured light – gold, green, and apple red – cast by the sun through the stained-glass window, a huge bunch of keys in her hand.

'Hello, Ashley! Back so soon? I thought you'd have had enough of this building!'

Ashley smiled back politely. 'Actually, I wanted to look at that painting by Emmeline Wall again.'

'Oh. Oh, dear, well.' She shook her head. 'I'm afraid that's not possible. It isn't actually on display . . . I hope it will be, very soon, but the storage areas aren't open to the public. You've had the very special privilege of seeing it once–'

'I found it, actually,' she blurted, annoyed.

The librarian's manner cooled immediately, although she still spoke pleasantly. 'It wasn't lost. You were helpful in calling it to my attention, and I'm grateful. When it's on public display, I'll let you know. Is there anything else I can help you with?'

Ashley knew she'd blown it. There was no chance she could wheedle her way upstairs now. Then she had another idea. 'Well, yes, there is,' she said. 'My grandmother Phemie came from Appleton – I think Graeme told you? I kind of wanted to do some research into her early life. I thought there might have been something about her in the local paper when she ran off – or maybe about her engagement – and when she was Apple Queen, stuff like that, you know? If I could look at the papers from back then . . .' She remembered the box files shelved upstairs.

'Of course you can!' Kathleen beamed. 'What year was it you wanted?'

'Nineteen fifty.'

'Follow me.'

She followed her back to the reference room. Instead of turning at the door that led to the stairs, though, the librarian took her to the very end of the long room and unlocked the door to her office. 'Come in. We've got bound copies of the paper from the early nineteen seventies back to the nineteen thirties in here. There hasn't been a budget for that since then, so the more recent ones are just piled in boxes.'

Oh, well, so much for that idea. She looked around the crowded, cluttered room – no coffee and pastries on offer today – and her eyes fell on the wooden apple, gleaming as if freshly polished, on the corner of the desk. The sight of it brought back the memory of the unfair suspicion and hostility directed at her by Kathleen after she'd picked it up the first time, and she clasped her hands behind her back so she couldn't possibly seem to be trying to touch it again.

'Here we are: nineteen fifty, January through December. It's a bit awkward – let's find a table for you.'

They went back out to the empty reference room, and Kathleen laid down the unwieldy, green-covered volume on a long table. 'There. That should keep you busy. Let me know if you have any questions, or if you want something photocopied, all right? There's a charge of ten pence per sheet, and I'll have to do it for you because these old pages are awfully fragile. Take care as you're looking through them, will you?'

'Sure.'

She began at the beginning, in January, turning the brittle pages carefully as she quickly scanned the headlines. Most of it made little sense to her: stories about local worthies and events, references to the politics of the wider world, market prices for fish and cattle and fruit, grainy black-and-white photographs, lists of deaths and births, old-fashioned advertisements for products that no longer existed, priced in a currency that had been obsolete before she was born. The crumbling, yellowed pages offered a murky window into a long-dead world, one that she felt so little connection with that she began to lose focus long before she reached March.

Still, she went on carefully turning the pages, her eyes glazing over as she scanned the columns of close-set type for a name she knew. Finally, in May, a photograph caught her attention.

The beautiful, dark-haired, gravely smiling young woman was her grandmother; she recognized her from other old photographs she'd seen. But she also recognized the man pictured beside her, although she'd never seen him in any photograph. He was an absolute dead ringer for the guy she'd seen from the bus, the guy she'd bought lunch for, the mysterious, sexy stranger who wouldn't tell her his name.

She read the brief announcement beneath the picture.

MacFarlane – Wall

Miss Euphemia MacFarlane, 18, daughter of Mr and Mrs Donald MacFarlane, Ballochcraig Farm, and Mr Ronan Lachlan Wall, 33, Orchard House, Fairview, have intimated their plans to be united in holy matrimony later this year. The ceremony will be performed in St Kieran's Church on 20th December. Mr Wall, grandson of the late Mr Alexander Wall, architect and philanthropist, is currently the sole owner of Wall Orchards Cider Mill, a well-known local business man who served with distinction in the Royal Navy.

Her eyes went back to the photograph. It had to be his grandfather. She didn't look much like either of her grandmothers, but this guy . . . whew, he could practically be his clone! She remembered what Graeme had said about local faces, and the way he'd identified that mysterious figure in the painting as a Wall. She could see the truth of it for herself now. No wonder her 'stranger' had known Phemie's name – but why not admit it? Why not tell her who he was? Unless his grandfather had been so embittered by his fiancée's desertion that he'd dedicated his life to revenge . . . but even if he had been, why should his runaway grandson still care?

Inspired now, she pressed on, sharp-eyed, examining

the following pages for anything else about the Walls or the MacFarlanes. Two issues later, at the end of May, she found the same picture of Euphemia and Ronan, but this time it illustrated a different story.

Apple Queen Picked

Miss Euphemia MacFarlane has been chosen by unanimous acclaim to reign over this year's Apple Fair, despite her attempt to 'de-select' herself with the claim that her recent engagement to Mr Ronan Wall should remove her from consideration.

According to Mrs R Burns, President of the local Women's Institute, only marriage itself is a bar to the chance to be 'queen for a night'. 'Phemie was the obvious choice, and I'm sure she is secretly pleased at the honour. She may have tried to turn it down because she is so modest, to give another girl a chance, but no one will have it. The crown is hers.'

When Miss MacFarlane's fiancé, Mr Ronan Wall, was asked to comment he replied, 'I can't risk losing my fiancée to a stranger, so I suppose I shall have to find myself a good disguise.'

The following week's paper had several letters on the subject of the Apple Queen:

Sir –
In light of last week's story about the young lady who feared a conflict between her affianced status and the role of Apple Queen I think your readers should be reminded that this is not the first time that this has happened. My own dear mother, Mrs Fergus Donaldson, nee Mary Ann Smith, was the Queen of the Apple Fair in 1910, and the 'stranger' who stood up out of the crowd to recognize her, was none other than 'her young man', in a borrowed coat and hat. As a disguise, it would not have fooled a child, but as no one objected to this bending of tradition forty years ago, I think it should be 'A-OK' today!

Yours, etc.
G. M. Donaldson
Clachan Farm

Sir –
My researches have demonstrated that the tradition that it should be a 'dark-haired stranger' who crowned the yearly Apple Queen was in fact seldom honoured, and only lip-service paid to it as a cover-up to allow young maidens to make matches which their families might otherwise prohibit. For a discussion of the connection between marital arrangements and superstitious beliefs, please see my article 'Women's

Rites or Women's Rights?' in The Journal of Scottish Folklore, Vol. VII, Issue 10.

It is worth pointing out, too, that, except for the case of poor Emmeline Wall in 1916, there has never been any sense of negativity or danger connected to this notional stranger at the Fair. Is she, then, the unhappy exception that proves the rule? Well, perhaps . . . however, I believe that if Miss Wall were alive today and able to tell us her tale, we might take a very different view of how her experience connects with the many happy marriages which have, over the years, been sealed with a shared apple.

Sincerely,
E. M. Whitton (Mrs)
'The Whinns'
Shore Road

Sir –
Surely I cannot be the only one to feel that to crown a 'Queen' in modern Scotland is entirely backward-looking and foolishly royalist. I am all for a bit of fun, but can't we change the offensive, outdated terminology? What is wrong with 'Apple Maid' or 'Comrade Apple' or even 'Pick of the Crop'? Let us aim to present a progressive, egalitarian, socialist

Appleton to the many visitors who come to enjoy our annual Fair.

Yours in equality,
Robert Martin
14 Fore Street

Ashley turned page after brittle page, slowly, carefully, a headache beginning to build as she swept the closely packed columns for any more mentions of her grandmother. She found Ronan Wall cited in a couple of stories, both about his business interests: *rumour of expansion unfounded; cheap foreign apples no threat to Appleton's Fairest.*

Finally there it was, the first week of October: the same picture of Euphemia MacFarlane, but this time with Ronan cropped out, above the stark headline:

Local Girl Disappears

The family of Euphemia MacFarlane, 19, have appealed to the public for help in tracing their missing daughter.

Miss MacFarlane was last seen late on Saturday night (September 30th). Her parents, Donald and Agnes MacFarlane, say they heard her arrive home at around midnight. When she did not appear for breakfast, they assumed she was sleeping in, and made no attempt to disturb her until nearly noon. At that time

Mrs MacFarlane discovered her daughter's room was empty; the bed had not been slept in, and certain of her personal possessions were missing.

Contacted at his home, Mr Wall could shed no light on the mystery. He said he had delivered her to her parents' house in his car, at about 1 A.M. Sunday morning; they had parted on amicable terms. He denied they had quarrelled, and said he believed nothing between them had changed. She had seemed happy – a statement confirmed by her friends and family members.

Police have said they entertain no suspicion of foul play. According to their inquiries, a woman answering to Miss MacFarlane's description was seen in Glasgow's Buchanan Street Bus Station on Sunday afternoon, apparently alone and in good spirits.

Mr and Mrs MacFarlane do not accept that their daughter would have left the family home without explanation, except under duress.

'It's not like her at all. There is a mystery there,' said her brother Hugh, speaking to this reporter on behalf of the family. 'She had no reason to run away. We love her and want the best for her. If she reads this, I hope she will get in touch.'

If anyone knows what has become of Euphemia MacFarlane, her parents would like to hear from them.

It was still a mystery, thought Ashley, closing the covers of the newspaper file. Although she knew what had become of Euphemia MacFarlane, she still had no idea why she'd run away like that and kept her whereabouts secret from her old friends and family to the end of her days.

Her mind flashed back to Saturday, to the stranger, and that strange link between them, and she shivered, all at once understanding why somebody might just run for it, not pausing to explain, never looking back and never taking the risk of letting anyone from her hometown, anyone who might tell *him*, know where she could be found.

She got up and went to knock on the office door.

'Yes? Oh, hi, Ashley. Find what you were looking for?'

'You said you could make some photocopies? I'd like this picture.'

'Of course.' Kathleen rose and took the heavy volume from her, opening it to the page she'd been marking with her finger. 'Wow. Your granny was gorgeous.'

'What do you think about *him*?'

'Mm, yes, tasty.'

'Recognize him?'

Kathleen frowned and peered again at the grainy old print. 'From the picture in the museum,' she prompted. 'Remember?'

'Oh, yes, that man Graeme thought had to be a Wall. I see what he meant.'

There was a brisk knock, and then a trim, auburn-haired

woman in her forties put her head around the door. She looked surprised. 'Sorry, Kathleen, I didn't realize . . .'

'That's all right, Miranda. This is Ashley, she's Shona Walker's cousin from America.'

'Nice to meet you, Ashley. I hope you don't mind if I borrow Kathleen for a few minutes?'

'I'll be right back,' Kathleen told her. 'If you want to wait here?'

'Could I have a drink of water?'

'Of course, help yourself. There are glasses in the cupboard under the sink.'

Alone in the office, she drank a glass of water, then looked around, her gaze homing in on the wooden apple. The smooth curves of it gleamed darkly. Before she really thought about it, she'd crossed the room and picked it up.

It was like the first time; the piece was irresistible, demanding to be held. *You can't put something like the apple in a museum, locked away in a case; it will be too frustrating to look and not touch; people will always be trying to break in.*

She rolled it against her cheek with the palm of her hand and enjoyed the satiny-smooth finish of the wood. Cool at first, it quickly soaked up the warmth of her skin. Her nostrils flared as she picked up a smell that was not wood or polish; something musky and sweet. She put it closer to her nose and sniffed, then drew back and stared in surprise. It smelled like apples!

She cocked her head, puzzled. Did the wood of an apple

tree really smell so much like the fruit?

She tossed it up and caught it, did it again when she felt something move, then shook it, holding her breath as she listened. She wasn't wrong. The carved fruit was hollow, and something rustled, soft as a whisper, inside. Yet she couldn't see a crack anywhere in the smooth surface unless you counted the incised Greek lettering around the top. She shut her eyes and let her fingers search, creeping over the smooth surface, pressing, prodding, and prying until at last they found the place where the two separate pieces met – a join so fine it was practically invisible. She gave it a quick, almost instinctive twist, as if the movement were one she'd learned long ago, and the apple came apart.

An odour rose: a smell musty, intense, sweet, and rotten that brought a rush of saliva to her mouth, and she shivered. Something – two things, two little shrivelled chunks – nestled within the cavity, and she dumped them into her hand. Time had desiccated them so that they were recognizable only by smell, but she had no doubt about it. She was looking at two pieces of a very, very old apple.

She resisted the idiotic urge she felt to taste one of the scraps of fruit, to lay it against her tongue the way she'd rested the smooth wood of its outer shell against her cheek. Instead, she closed the fingers of her left hand around the dried fruit, and dug into her day pack with her right.

Inside the bag was a handkerchief that had been her grandmother's. It was more than sixty years old, and the once-white cloth had turned the colour of vellum and was wonderfully smooth and soft with age. The faded pink initials in one corner – *E. M'F.* – had been embroidered by Phemie's best friend when she was eight or nine; it had been her birthday present to Phemie. The idea that your best friend might give you only a *handkerchief* for your birthday, and still remain your best friend, had been a source of great fascination for Ashley. It was the thing that made her realize her grandmother had grown up in a completely different world, a time that was now lost. It was like something out of *Little House on the Prairie*. Amused by her granddaughter's fascination, Phemie had made her a gift of it. 'I wouldn't normally, dear, but it's perfectly clean. I don't think I *ever* used it to blow my nose – it was too good for that. I kept it for best, for show.'

Ashley had kept it for remembrance. She extracted the neatly folded square of cloth from her bag, and wrapped the two shrivelled pieces of apple in it, holding her breath until the parcel had been made up and stowed safely away in an inside zipped pocket. Then she turned back to the desk and fitted the wooden apple together again. She replaced it where it had been and crossed the room to the sink, where she drew herself a second glass of water. She was just swallowing the last of it – trying to rinse away an imaginary taste – when the door opened and Kathleen came back in.

'Sorry about that—' She stopped and sniffed the air.

'That's OK,' Ashley said quickly, and tensed with the expectation of being asked about the smell.

But Kathleen didn't ask.

'Um, so, could you do me that photocopy?'

'Of course.' As she prepared to use the photocopier, which was wedged in between the door and a miniature refrigerator with a coffeemaker perched on top, she went on, 'Would you be interested in talking to someone who might remember your grandmother when she was a girl?'

'Yes! Do you know anybody?' She was curious, but skeptical that this newcomer to the town could help. She'd asked Shona, who'd canvassed the old ladies who attended her church and reported back that although a few admitted to vaguely remembering 'old Hugh's sister – that lassie who ran away,' none claimed any closer acquaintance.

'Well . . . it occurred to me you should talk to Miss McClusky. She was the librarian here for many years, and she's a local, I mean, a *real* local, one of the few you could call an aboriginal.'

'Aboriginal!' If Kathleen was joking, she just didn't get it. 'Aboriginals come from Australia, don't they?'

'The word just means original inhabitants,' Kathleen explained, grimacing slightly as she wrestled with the photocopier. 'Everyone else I've met in this town is an incomer – or their parents were.'

'Shona was born here. So were her parents. And I think my great-grandparents–'

'I'm talking about the way people talk about themselves. Most places, if people grow up in the same place their grandparents were born, they feel pretty rooted. They think this is their land. But on the Apple, two or three generations doesn't seem to be enough to stop people thinking of themselves as incomers. Ina McClusky is the only one I've met who talks about her family having lived here "for ever". Of course, she also talks as if she doesn't live in Appleton.'

'But she does?'

'Her house is just on the other side of the harbour. A hundred years ago, I'm told, people referred to this side as "the town" and that side as "the Ob" – which is the Gaelic word for bay. The Ob never was a separate town, really; it never had a church or a school, but the people who lived there felt they formed a separate community.' She handed over the photocopied page.

'Thanks. So . . . you think Ina McClusky was friends with Phemie?'

'She was the librarian here for years and years, and even though she came from the Ob, she seems to have known absolutely everyone in the town. Sharp as a whip – better memory than mine.'

'I'd like to talk to her.'

'I'll tell you what – I was planning on going to see her

today. She still comes into the library regularly, but she's getting frail. She doesn't complain, but I'm sure it's hard on her – I thought I could help her out with an occasional home delivery of new books. I could take you along; I'm sure she'd love to meet you. She enjoys company. Why don't you come back here just before five o'clock, and I'll take you with me?'

'OK. Cool. Thanks.' She shifted her bag onto her shoulder. 'See you later, then.'

It wasn't until she was out of the library and half a block away that it struck her that she'd stolen something from the library. She, who'd never been a thief, never shoplifted like some of her friends, never done anything more reprehensible than swipe a few potato chips off a friend's plate, or sneak an extra chocolate . . .

And if that wasn't really theft, was this? It couldn't be a crime to take two bits of dried-up apple! If anyone else had found them, wouldn't they have thrown them away? She didn't even want them – what on earth had come over her?

She walked on, brooding about that moment of madness. *Something* had made her take them; there must be some reason, buried deep in her brain. She knew she couldn't take them back, any more than she could throw them away, not unless she could explain what she'd done, not unless she knew what they were *for*.

She saw that she'd reached the point where the road branched, the spot where she and the stranger who looked like Ronan Lachlan Wall had parted. Where to now? Up there, he'd said, was the cemetery. She glanced at her watch, saw that she had more than an hour to kill before Kathleen would expect her back at the library, so she turned up the cemetery road.

It was a hike; farther than she'd expected. Gradually the houses fell away; and she was out in the countryside, with nowhere she could sit down and rest, and not even trees to provide shelter from the relentless sun. She was thirsty and tired. Watching a couple of cars go past, she wondered about hitching a lift. After she found her way to the cemetery – assuming she ever did – she would still face a long walk. Maybe she should turn back now? Checking her watch, she saw, to her annoyance, that it had stopped.

But then, as she rounded a bend, she saw the cemetery was just ahead; at least, she assumed those grey stone walls in the embrace of heavy dark evergreens must surround a graveyard. She picked up her pace, thinking she didn't have much time.

Gravel crunched beneath her feet as she stepped off the main road and through the open gates. The coolness inside, in the tree-shaded walkway, was as welcome as a drink of water. She breathed in deeply and smelled damp earth, vegetation, and a touch of rankness suggestive of cats. She hurried ahead, out of the dim shelter, toward ranks of graves lying like a crowded miniature suburb before her:

mostly simple headstones, but there were also a few carved Celtic crosses, some pedestals supporting urns or melancholy angels, and there were a couple of obelisks, which towered like skyscrapers by comparison with the modest scale of everything else.

She paused to read the first few stones she came to:

Erected by
Dugald Murray
in loving memory of
his beloved wife
Margaret MacDonald
who died 21st August 1941
aged 51

In loving memory of
Malcolm MacNeill
Departed
1st November 1945
aged 42
also his wife
Flora Galbraith
died 29 December 1984

She moved on past the newer-looking stones in search of something more interesting. The gravelled path wound away ahead and branched off in several directions. Some areas were well tended but plain and bare, while others, perhaps the older ones, were more picturesquely planted with trees and bushes. She left the path to scramble up a small rise, where the gravestones, instead of standing in neat rows, were more of a jumble, leaning in different directions. She spotted one almost hidden by the spiky, glossy foliage of a holly bush. Leaning closer she could make out a very weatherworn shape of a skull and cross bones, but all the writing on the pale, pitted stone – assuming there had ever been any – was completely worn away.

She straightened up and looked around, realizing that the graveyard was larger than she'd first thought. She caught sight of a walled structure not far away and, curious, headed towards it. As she drew nearer she could see that it lacked a roof; it wasn't a tomb or mausoleum after all, just an enclosure, probably a family plot, like a private, members-only graveyard within the larger cemetery. As she stepped around a small tree she could see large black metal gates across the opening in the fourth wall secured with a length of chain and a heavy padlock.

She also saw that she was not alone. Standing by the gate and peering through the bars into the enclosure was a man. Although he was turned away from her, she knew him immediately, with an almost painful surge of excitement.

She walked a bit more briskly toward him. 'Ronan Wall,' she called loudly, and saw his back stiffen. 'Ronan Lachlan Wall.'

He turned, looking defeated and sad, not so young and smug and happy as in the picture taken with his fiancée more than fifty years ago. It should have seemed crazy, but it didn't. Somehow, suddenly, she just knew he was the man from the picture, not his grandson. He was the very same man her grandmother had fled from more than half a century ago.

When they were aged about twelve or thirteen, Ashley and Freya had developed a sort of fixation on vampires. The fantasy they'd shared, part fear but more desire, stirred again in her memory as she met the stranger's gaze. She remembered confessing to Freya, who had agreed, that even though it was wrong, and scary, and deadly dangerous, she wasn't sure she'd put up much of a struggle if she ever met one.

She didn't think Ronan was a vampire. But she didn't think he was simply and entirely human, either. The lure of his difference had been tugging at her ever since their gazes first intersected, and now an impatient desire flared up in her.

She went closer to him, so close that they were nearly touching, but still he didn't move.

'It's OK,' she said softly. She put her hands on his face and kissed him on the mouth; kissed him so long and passionately that he had to respond.

Chapter Twelve

Five o'clock came and went with no sign of Ashley. Kathleen closed the library only a few minutes after the normal time, but then hung around for a good ten minutes, peering through the leaded-glass windows of the Ladies' Reading Room, expecting to see the girl come galloping along the Esplanade, breathless and horrified to discover that the big front doors were closed. It never happened.

Finally mentally cursing the breed of tardy and unreliable teenagers, she went out to her car alone. She was awfully disappointed – not so much for herself, she thought, as for Ina McClusky. The old lady would have enjoyed a new young person's company, the treat of being able to talk about the past to an interested listener.

Ina McClusky lived on the Ob, almost as far as Sandy Point, in the small fisherman's cottage where she'd grown up. Her family had lived there for generations. She was the first to get a higher education, and she'd brought it back home, getting the librarian's job in Appleton because of the wartime shortage of men. Kathleen wondered if the reason Ina had never married was that same war, which had killed so many. She thought of the engagement photograph she'd photocopied for Ashley. Ronan Lachlan Wall had come home from the war and, unlike many, he'd prospered. He'd also chosen to marry a woman fifteen years younger than himself and not someone of his own generation like, for example, the still-young librarian. There might have been class issues involved, too. Graeme had told her – before he got obsessed with folklore and geology, back when he was researching social history – that not only did the Ob and the toon keep themselves separate, but fishermen always married women from fishing families; they needed wives who understood their lives and could contribute the skills they'd learned from childhood. Ina had grown up in a fishing family, but she'd priced herself out of that marriage market. And a member of the Wall family wouldn't marry so far beneath him. He'd be more likely to choose the daughter of a well-to-do farmer, someone who would have brought her own property to the marriage.

Class barriers still existed, they'd just changed along with people's lifestyles. There were very few fishermen left; their wives, no longer needed to gut the fish or mend the lines, didn't have to be born to fishermen, only brought up expecting to work hard for little reward. And the people at the top – the celebrities – well, they married other celebrities. Rock stars married actors, or models, or others with equally famous faces; they didn't fall in love with unknown librarians.

In the nineteenth century there had been a regular ferry link to connect the Ob with the toon, carrying passengers and goods from one shore to the other; but these days, a car could make the journey on the road that curved around the head of the loch in about five minutes. As she parked on the narrow street in front of the bright blue cottage with white trim, Kathleen made a determined effort to put Dave Varney out of her head.

There was a knocker in the shape of a mermaid on the heavily varnished front door – an unusual touch of fantasy for the practical Miss McClusky, she thought, lifting the brass tail.

After a few seconds, the door was opened by a bent, white-haired old woman. Her narrow, sunken-cheeked face lit up. 'Kathleen! What a lovely surprise, my dear! Do come in.'

'Hello, Ina. I've brought you some new books.'

'Ooh!' Her eyes narrowed still more as her smile grew wider, and she rubbed her hands together. 'How nice! I can't wait. Do you know, I was just wondering what I would read tonight. Please come in. I hope you'll stay long enough for a cup of tea?'

'Thank you.' She followed her inside, noticing that the old woman seemed to bend even farther forward, her humped back even more prominent than it had been two weeks ago.

'Sit down, dear, and I'll put the kettle on. Earl Grey, or ordinary?'

'Ordinary, please. My tastes are very common.'

'My friend, when I shared digs in Glasgow, always called it "builder's tea".'

Kathleen had heard this comment before, but smiled as if it were new, and sank down onto the sturdy old two-seater sofa. The room was small and crowded with a lifetime's accumulation of things, but tidy and dust-free as always. For once there was no fire in the grate, but everything else was exactly as she remembered it, from the china ornaments on every available surface to the television in the corner which wore a lace tablecloth, as if it were a caged bird that had to be kept dark and quiet during the day.

Ina soon returned with a tea tray, and once she'd made sure her guest was comfortable, with a mug of milky tea and a pile of biscuits, both chocolate and plain, began to quiz her about the library. Even though she'd retired more than twenty years ago, she still took a keen and somewhat proprietary interest in what went on there. These conversations could be tricky when they touched on decisions made at headquarters, so Kathleen tried to restrict them to book chat and innocuous gossip about people who used the library. In a particularly enjoyed tales of visiting Americans and Canadians in search of their Appleton roots.

Evading her question about when their library would be catching up to the rest of the country by getting computers, she offered, 'We had a young American girl in today, looking for information about her grandmother. I think you might remember her – Euphemia MacFarlane?'

Ina frowned. 'You think I knew her?'

'I thought you might remember something about her. She was the Apple Queen in nineteen fifty, and–'

'Phemie! Phemie MacFarlane – I ken who you mean, now. She was the lassie who ran away. But she's much younger than I am – she was only a schoolgirl last time I saw her.'

'She's dead now,' Kathleen said gently.

Ina shrugged. 'So's the town, and long before her.' She fixed her eyes on her guest. 'She was the Apple Queen. After she left, the crop failed.'

'Oh, but that's – I mean, she couldn't be to blame for something like that. That's what's known as an act of God, isn't it? It's because of the weather, the soil, I don't know, but–'

'People blamed her.'

'That's not fair.'

She smiled mirthlessly. 'Life isn't fair – you're old enough to know that, Kathleen.'

'Do *you* think it was her fault?'

She pursed her lips and set down her mug. 'Look at it this way. She was the Apple Queen. If all had gone well, she'd have had all praise for it.'

'And if it hadn't? Look, we know the apple crop failed.'

'But it would have been all right if she'd stayed.'

Kathleen gulped her tea, wondering how soon she could leave and still be polite. Did Ina believe what she was saying, or was she playing devil's advocate? She glanced at the faded blue eyes and didn't say anything.

After a moment, Ina went on. 'She was supposed to marry Mr Wall. That was *her* choice – nobody forced it on her; if she didn't want him, there were plenty other young maids who did. He was the last of the Walls. He owned the cider mill and the orchards, and there was more – a big house, land, and stocks and savings, I've no doubt. One bad harvest didn't have to mean the end for him, not if he'd stayed. If he'd had his loving wife beside him. But she ran off and he lost the heart to stay. He was gone within a month of her. I don't know what became of him, but without him the business collapsed like a house of cards, and with it, the town.

'It wasn't just himself he took away, he took his fortune. It turned out that he'd mortgaged the mill and all his lands, bought his escape at a very high price for the town.

Except for that, it could have been very different. One bad harvest didn't have to mean the end, but there was no way to ride it out. There was nothing to secure a new loan, and there were all his debts to pay.'

'I see,' said Kathleen, taking a long, relieved breath. 'So that's why you blame Phemie MacFarlane. Wouldn't it be more reasonable to blame Mr Wall? He sounds like the villain of the piece. Maybe Phemie *had* to run away, to save herself.'

'People think too much about themselves. What about helping others? What about saving the community? Phemie was no victim. I always thought they were in it together, and they laid their careful plans, and ran away from here intending to get together somewhere else.'

'Well, they didn't,' she said firmly. 'Phemie MacFarlane married an American, a man called Kaldis. And she would never say anything about where she'd come from. Her son didn't know he had cousins in Scotland until after her death.'

'And what about Ronan Wall?'

Kathleen set down her empty mug. 'I don't know. He disappeared.' She took a chance. 'What was he like?'

Ina flinched. 'You ask me? Why do you think I would know anything about him?'

She smiled placatingly. 'I thought you knew everyone in the town – all those years in the library.'

'*He* never came in. Not that he was a philistine, mind you, but he didn't need it. He had the money to buy plenty of books. He took two newspapers, and he had a regular account with a bookseller in Edinburgh, just like his grandfather.'

'His grandfather the architect?'

'That was his only living relative.'

'Did you ever meet him? I mean Alexander Wall.'

'He died when I was a wee lass. And Mr Lachlan, that was his uncle, he died before I was born, of course; died before the library was built. Now, there was an interesting and learned old gentleman! My mother met him a few times. She used to find things for him on the shore – all the children round about knew that he was a collector who'd pay for any treasures they might find when they were beachcombing.'

Kathleen remembered hearing about Lachlan Wall's collection of oddities. 'What sort of treasures did your mother find?'

The old woman's face became even more shrivelled in thought. 'I should be able to tell you . . . but I can't rightly call them to mind.'

'It doesn't matter.'

'We could ask her.'

'Who?' Kathleen blinked in confusion.

'Who were we talking about?' Ina rebuked her. 'My mother! Would you like to speak to her?'

Kathleen swallowed hard. 'I had no idea your mother was . . . still with us.'

'Certainly my mother is still with us. She's upstairs. Will I take you to meet her?'

There being no polite way to refuse, she nodded agreement and got to her feet. Even if she'd given birth at a ridiculously early age, Ina's mother would now be well past one hundred years old, and while that was not absolutely impossible, Kathleen wondered why this was the first she'd heard of her.

She followed Ina's bent and slowly moving form out of the sitting room, into the narrow hallway, and up a short, steep flight of stairs and wondered how she managed to look after someone even older and more frail than herself. The house seemed too small to accommodate a live-in nurse, but maybe someone came in daily to help.

'Knock knock,' called Ina after pausing to catch her breath at the top of the stairs. 'Are you decent, Mother? We have a visitor.'

She heard a frail wisp of a voice reply, although she couldn't make out the words, then Ina opened a door saying, 'Now, Mother, here's a treat! Someone come to talk to you. Go in, Kathleen, dear, go in.'

The room was small, stale-smelling and murky, the orange-and-yellow curtains drawn across the window letting in only a faint light. There was a lamp beside the bed, but the combination of a heavy, tasselled shade and low-wattage bulb meant it did little to relieve the gloom. She noticed that the lamp shade also bore a thick, fur-like coating of grey dust, and in contrast to the careful housekeeping in evidence downstairs, the room was a mess. The floor and bedside table were littered with dirty plates and cutlery, empty cups, used tissues, and crumpled wads of cling film.

Lying in the long, narrow bed, propped up against a stack of lumpy pillows, with a box of tissues and a stack of magazines spilling over beside her, was a little old lady. Her eyes appeared unnaturally large and luminous in her wizened head, reminding Kathleen of a lemur. On her head she wore an old-fashioned, lace-trimmed white cap, tied under her chin, like a baby's bonnet, and her shoulders and torso were swathed in a number of pastel-coloured shawls and scarves: yellow, pink, and blue.

'Mother, this is Kathleen Mullaroy. She's the new librarian.'

The old woman shuddered, and her already big eyes became larger still. 'Ina, that's your job! Don't tell me they've sacked you? Oh, what will become of us! I suppose I shall have to go out to work again. You ungrateful girl, what–'

'Mother!' Ina spoke loudly but without heat. 'I don't work at the library any more. I retired, remember?'

'Stuff and nonsense! What did you want to retire so young for? Waste of your education.'

'Mother, I was too old for that job. They made me retire. Maybe at the time they were wrong, but now I'm not so spry. You have to admit, I'm not young any more.'

The old woman continued to direct her fierce, lamp-like gaze at her daughter, and Kathleen imagined she was gathering her resources for another attack, but finally she gave a reluctant nod, and said, 'No, I suppose you're not young. But you can hardly call yourself *old* to your mother now, can you?' She gave a dry, scraping chuckle and turned her eyes full on Kathleen. 'So, what brings you calling, Mrs Librarian?'

Ina replied for her. 'Kathleen is curious about the Wall family. I told her you knew Mr Lachlan when you were a lass. I remembered you used to sell him treasures you found on the beach, but I couldn't remember what they were.'

'Black beans,' she replied promptly. 'Those big, black hard seeds that come from foreign parts. I can't mind their proper name. Some folk call them fairy eggs, but they're not that. They're supposed to be lucky. I had a kind of knack for finding things like that, things that had a bit o' power to 'em, and Mr Lachlan liked to own them. I don't know if they brought him luck . . . it was all right through his lifetime, but the family came to a bad end.' Her head nodded up and down, and Kathleen was unable to decide if it was an intentional movement or a tremor.

The old woman made her uncomfortable; there was something almost eerie about her prolonged life. But, ashamed of her feelings, she made an effort to be sociable.

'Are you talking about . . . do you mean what happened to Ronan Wall?'

Mrs McClusky gave her a very sharp look, her head craning forward and wobbling slightly. 'You know him?'

'Oh, no.' She shook her head quickly. 'No, of course not; I don't think anyone's seen or heard from him since nineteen fifty, isn't that right?' She cast an appealing glance at Ina, who simply gazed back, impassive. 'But I'd heard that he was the last of the Walls, then he left, and it left the town in a bad way.'

'He wasn't really a Wall, although his grandfather gave him the name. I suppose it was Mr Alexander's right to do that, but it wasn't *right*, to let the inheritance fall to a bastard. The boy wasn't one of us, and he never belonged here. Nobody knew his father.'

The venom in the old woman's voice made Kathleen feel like protecting that long-lost boy. It made her realize what a hard time people could have of it in the past, for 'sins' completely out of their control. Not only for the colour of their skins, but for something their mothers had done – or had forced on them – before they were born. 'I suppose his mother did,' she said coolly.

Mrs McClusky snorted quietly and pushed herself up, quivering, against the pillows. 'Her! That Emmeline! She was a daftie – not all there – tetched in the head, away wi' the fairies – d'you ken?'

'She was a brilliant artist.'

'Artist! And what's the use of that for a woman? Oh, yes, I know her father doted on her, encouraged her, thinking that she was like him because she could draw a bit, maybe thinking she'd have a fine career. Maybe she would, if he'd sent her away, but he kept her here. Maybe, if her mother had lived, she could have kept her safe. But her father didn't understand. Mr Alexander Wall was an incomer, you know, for all that he was a Wall. He was born on the other side of the world, and then he was educated in Glasgow, so he never knew how different things are here. He didn't know the truth until it was too late. He wouldn't have listened, anyway, he doted on his daughter so. He couldn't let her go. He was bound and determined to fetch her back, no matter what the price for the rest of us.' She stopped, panting slightly, and her mouth continued to move although no words could be heard.

'Mother, we're tiring you.'

'No, no.' Her voice came out a croak and her head shook still more.

Kathleen shifted uncomfortably from one foot to the other, oppressed by the cluttered, dingy room and the old woman's prejudices. 'I can see we are,' she said. 'I really should go . . . I could come back another time,' she offered as a sop to the old woman's now vigorously shaking head.

'Mother's not used to talking so much.'

'I like it,' croaked the old woman. 'It's a treat for me

to talk about the old days and have somebody who wants to listen. What else did you want to know?' Her big eyes fastened greedily on Kathleen's face. 'Who are you interested in? Emmeline? She killed herself, you know. Drowned herself in the sea. They never found her body.' She stopped again, gasping, and Kathleen shot a look at Ina.

'Your mother needs to rest.'

'My mother could tell you more,' Mrs McClusky croaked. 'She used to do Mr Lachlan's laundry. She was in and out of his house all the time – oh, the stories she used to tell us children! Ina, fetch your granny, there's a love.'

Ina seemed unperturbed by this request, and Kathleen assumed she must be used to her mother's losing touch with the present and drifting back to a much earlier time in her head. 'Granny's asleep,' she said mildly.

'She's always sleeping! It won't do her any harm to be fetched out of her bed now. I know she'd like to see a new face.' Mrs McClusky's happy, coaxing expression darkened, and she moved impatiently against the pillows. 'Go on, then! Or do I have to get up and fetch her myself, you idle girl?' The yellow shawl slipped down her arms as she struggled to rise.

'Stop where you are, Mother.' Ina sighed. 'I'll get her. Calm yourself.'

As Kathleen watched uneasily, Ina shuffled slowly around the foot of the bed toward the massive bulk of an old wooden wardrobe. With a soft groan of effort, she tugged at one handle, and the right-hand door swung open, blocking Kathleen's view of whatever might be inside.

The old woman in the bed smiled and nodded up at her. 'Mummy's going to join us. Mummy has the best stories; she'll tell you all about those Walls.'

'Really, it's not important – I really should go,' Kathleen murmured helplessly. She tried to steal a look at her watch, but couldn't make out the time in the dim light. 'I have to get home.'

'Not until you meet Mummy. You must stay long enough to meet my mother.'

'Here we are then,' said Ina, panting as she emerged from the wardrobe with a bundle of blankets in her arms. 'I'll – just – put you down – here – on my mother's bed – eh, Granny?' Tottering under the awkward weight, she all but fell forward onto the bed with the thing she was carrying.

When she saw what Ina had taken out of the wardrobe, Kathleen was seized by a sudden attack of dizziness and blinked hard, unable to believe what she was seeing. There on the bed was what seemed at first to be a very large doll, perhaps the size of a two-year-old child. Only, as it opened filmy blue eyes and raised its head on a scraggy, shaking neck to peer around the room, it was quite clearly alive, and very far from infancy. Thin, almost bloodless lips cracked apart, and a reedy querulous voice whined, 'I was sleeping. Why've you disturbed me?'

'I'm sorry, Granny, but Mother told me to,' Ina panted.

'Who is that? Is that the doctor?' The eyes, which bulged unpleasantly from a bald, skull-like head, fixed upon Kathleen, who stood rigid with shock.

'No, Mummy.' Mrs McClusky spoke in a soft, ingratiating tone. 'This is Ina's young friend, Kathleen. She came to ask about the Wall family, and since you know so much more about them than I do . . . You'll enjoy a bit of company, and you can tell some stories about the old days.'

The little old woman made a high, gargling sound and waved a claw-like hand feebly in the air. 'Ina! Ina! Help me sit up, child!'

The retired librarian struggled to move her grandmother, and at last managed to wedge her in beside Mrs McClusky against the pile of pillows. When she was settled, the oldest woman made the noise again and clutched at her throat. 'I'm that parched after my sleep. Ina! Where's the tea? You know I always have a cup of tea first thing!'

'I'll just make some fresh,' said Ina, and Kathleen cast her an anxious look. If Ina left the room, she was going too. There was no way she was going to be left alone here with these two weird, impossibly aged creatures.

'Have a sweetie,' said Mrs McClusky, rummaging around in the bedclothes until she'd uncovered a paper bag full of some round, hard sweets that looked like sour balls. She leaned sideways and popped one into her mother's mouth. 'That'll wet your whistle.'

The tiny old woman sucked for a few moments, her eyes fluttering. Ina began to creep around the foot of the bed again, moving towards Kathleen and the door.

'Where are you going, miss?' Mrs McClusky spoke sharply.

Ina came to a halt. 'To make the tea, Mother,' she said meekly.

Pushing the hard sweet into her cheek, the grandmother stuck out her neck, rather like a tortoise, and peered around the room. 'One, two, three, four. If you're making tea for four, why not for five? Do me a favour before you go down to make the tea, Ina?'

'Yes, Granny?'

'Bring out your great-granny; she always loved a party.'

'Oh, what a good idea!' cried Mrs McClusky. 'It's been ever so long since I've seen her. Yes! Wake up my granny; wake her up, Ina, and bring her out, there's a good girl.'

Ina sighed and rolled her eyes in a put-upon way, but she was smiling as she turned and headed back to the wardrobe. 'Now then, Great-granny,' she said loudly, tugging open the other door. 'We've got a nice surprise for you.'

Kathleen bolted from the room. She couldn't bear to see a second animated mummy, a creature even more ancient and shrivelled than the two already on the bed. Between the sound of her footsteps pounding down the stairs and her own panicked breathing she couldn't hear if anyone shouted or called after her, and she was consoled by the thought that even if Ina tried to give chase, she had small chance of catching up.

She hurtled through the front door, slammed it shut behind her, and raced to her car which, having already adopted local ways, she hadn't bothered to lock. She locked the doors once she was inside, though, and, panting anxiously, started it up and drove off as quickly as she could, head down, shoulders hunched, without looking back. She didn't think about where she was going; she *couldn't* think about what she was fleeing; her heart was pounding like a drum and her single imperative was escape. It was only after she passed the filling station on the edge of town and saw the 'Haste ye Back' sign that she understood that she didn't want to go back to the library house; it didn't feel safe enough. It wasn't far enough away from the weirdness she'd just witnessed, and she was prepared to drive all the 132 miles to Glasgow, without stopping and quite possibly breaking the speed limit – until the sign warning ROAD CLOSED AHEAD forced her to step on the brake, and then, moments later, she saw for the first time the massive rock fall that made escape impossible.

'Oh *hell.*' Bringing the car to a complete and rather jolting stop, she slapped the steering wheel with an open hand. How *could* she forget?

She switched off the engine and got out, her eyes fixed

on the landslide. It was an impressive sight. At the centre of a mass of mud and rubble was one huge slab of rock, the size of a small house, which utterly blocked the road. There was no way around it. At one side of the road was the steep, forbidding cliff face, the side of a hill that had long ago been blasted and dug out when the road was built, and had finally produced this landslide. On the other side the ground dropped sharply to the rocky shore and the sea.

She looked down at the sea, perhaps eight or nine feet below. It would be possible to climb down – there seemed to be plenty of hand- and footholds in the side of the embankment – and once there, to follow the shoreline until she came to a place where she could gain access to the road again. But the exposed rocks looked awfully slippery – the ones that weren't honed to a knife-edge – licked by the waves that foamed and swirled around them. Maybe, at low tide (assuming it wasn't already low tide), with the right shoes and a helpful companion, but not now. For now she was stuck.

She stared at the massive rock in the middle of the road, chewed her thumbnail, and tried not to cry.

Chapter Thirteen

During his dinner break on Tuesday, Mario headed as usual down to the harbour. But this time he walked with his head up, looking around the crowded streets as he went, searching the faces. He was looking for the tall, curly-haired American girl who'd come into the chip shop that afternoon.

Third time lucky, he told himself hopefully.

He'd messed up the first time they met, for sure, and he'd been kicking himself ever since for his unbelievably stupid behaviour. Some sort of residual loyalty to Anna had made him resist the attraction he'd felt for the girl who'd asked him to join her for a drink on Sunday night, but minutes after walking away from her he'd realized how pointless that was. Anna didn't want his loyalty or anything else he had to offer. She'd cut him off. He was free.

It had taken him a long time to perceive this freedom as a *good* thing, but he was in a different place now. Something had been knocked loose by the earth tremor, not just the hillside that blocked the road, but inside Mario himself, shifting a whole load of mud and rock in his chest away from his heart and lungs so that he could finally breathe again and feel something other than pain.

Then, when she'd smiled at him this afternoon – and *what* a smile! – he knew she'd decided to forgive him for his clumsy retreat on Sunday. Given half a chance, he'd take it, but Uncle Tony was such a hard-ass, and he'd chosen just that moment to order him back to the kitchen to chip more potatoes.

For once he was glad this was such a small town. And thanks to the landslide, he could be sure the girl was still around. They were bound to run into one another again.

But although the streets were unusually full of people out enjoying the mild evening, he saw no one he recognized. When he reached the harbour, he found it busier than ever. Strangely, considering that the landslide was generally reckoned to have cut Appleton off from the world, the last few days had transformed the sheltered harbour from a chilly, forgotten backwater into a vibrant, bustling place that reminded him, at least a little bit, of Palermo. There were major differences, of course, but the waterfront had come to life, busier now than it had been even at the height of summer. Small craft thronged the water, dozens of battered, rather grubby working boats bobbing alongside the pleasure craft – sailing yachts and small motorboats – which were the more usual visitors to Appleton harbour. And the people – there must have been ten times as many people in and on the harbour than there'd been on the last bank holiday weekend. He wondered who they all were.

Some, clearly, were here for commercial reasons. Having scented an opportunity, they'd sailed down the coast, or motored across the water from their homes around Glasgow or Ayr to put up advertisements on the pier for 'water taxis', ferry services, and small boat charters.

But the purposes of other visitors were more mysterious. These were the oddly assorted newcomers who posted no signs, did not tout for custom or even come ashore. Whoever they might be, wherever they had come from, they were certainly not ordinary tourists. They stayed put on their vessels and gave no clue as to why they'd come, or when they might leave. They communicated with each other in a babble of different tongues, and their boats, maneuvering around each other in the increasingly restricted space of the harbour basin, occasionally drew close enough to exchange passengers. He saw women and children, too, clambering from one boat to another, and even animals. There were dogs and cats on board some of the boats; and he'd heard the cackle of hens and, he was almost certain, the bleating of a goat. The whole effect was of a floating campground or fair. Mario felt they were all just waiting for something to begin, and he wondered why he hadn't heard any gossip in the town about a forthcoming event so important it had drawn so many people from different countries.

He smelled food cooking: olive oil, onions, garlic, peppers; his mouth watered. He'd eaten fried fish and potatoes as usual, the bland stodge that filled his stomach but left him unsatisfied, yearning for the more varied herbs and spices of home. And he smelled the objects of his longing rising on the salty sea breeze, in the smoke from cooking fires and galley stoves on several of the small foreign boats.

He paused a moment and stared into the harbour, trying to pick out an identifiable flag, or maybe a boat marked with an Italian name, Palermo or Syracusa . . . But the flags were all as strange to him as the names, many of them in languages he could not even guess at. As he looked, he noticed a little rowing boat with two people in it approaching one of the yachts at anchor. As they approached, a man appeared on the deck of the larger boat. He was comically piratical in appearance in an open-throated, long-sleeved white shirt and with a red bandanna tied around his head. The man rowing the boat hailed him, and he leaned down and said something Mario could not hear. Holding up one finger, he went below.

Mario's footsteps slowed and he stopped for a second time to watch. Red-bandanna popped up again, holding a plain white carrier bag that seemed, from the way he held it, to be heavy. He leaned over the side and lowered it into the waiting arms of the man in the rowboat.

The other person in the rowboat stood up, and Mario saw it was a woman, and a very shapely one, with a shaved head. The piratical character dropped a rope ladder over the side of his boat; the woman grasped hold of it, scrambled up and aboard, and went below decks.

Drugs, thought Mario. *Drugs and prostitution*. He began to walk again, faster than before, although he was careful not to break into a run. He didn't want to do anything to draw attention to himself; he didn't want those figures to suspect there'd been a witness to their transaction. He walked with his head down, steadily, like a man with a mission, although his only aim was to get away.

His path followed the shoreline, but once past the old quay it was away from the docks, so the water was empty and quiet. He noticed there was no one fishing from the breakwater this evening, and the swings and slides in the little park on the front green were deserted except for two dogs circling each other warily. Time to turn back, he thought, but first he wanted to look at the sea without the distraction of all those people on it. He veered off the path and jumped down to the pebbles and mud on the shore. He stood for a moment, breathing in the brackish, tidal smell, his eyes drawn across the water to the other side of town. Although it was so close, he'd never been there. It had its own name – 'the Ob' they called it – but he didn't suppose it would be any different, really, from the parts of Appleton he knew.

His thoughts went back to the scene he'd witnessed, and he wondered about the shaven-headed woman. Had it been her choice to go onto that boat, or was she a victim? What was happening to her now below decks? His gaze floated unseeing on the water as possibilities suggested themselves. He imagined her mouth forming a helpless 'O,' her eyes wide, then closed, her breasts as smooth and naked as her head . . .

Something moving in the water snagged his attention, and his gaze focused. What was that, a head? A person in the water? Swimming here, so near the debris and oil that polluted the harbour, when there were plenty of clean, secluded bays not far away? Why? Unless . . .

He imagined the woman he had seen, now stripped naked, wriggling through a porthole, diving off the side of the boat, and swimming away to escape.

His hands clenched into fists at his side and he stepped forward, staring harder at the dark speck in the blue-green water. It grew larger, coming towards him, until he could see that it was a head, with a face, and it was a woman, but not the one he had seen on the boat, because this one had long glossy hair. She saw him, and lifted her hand to wave.

Uncertainly, he waved back. She beckoned more vigorously. Her shoulders were bare, no straps visible, and when she gestured again he caught a flash of bare breast. He swallowed hard. There was no doubt about it. She was not only waving, she was signing to him to join her. But why? He didn't know her; who did she think he was?

He saw her lips move: *Viene.*

He staggered back, startled. No, surely that was wishful thinking! No way did she speak Italian.

Viene. Come to me.

He didn't know if he'd heard it or only imagined it, combining her unmistakable gestures with the sexy, appealing look on her face, the speaking pout of her lips, but he couldn't be mistaken about what she wanted.

Come here, you. Don't he shy. I want you.

He felt the splash and looked down, surprised to see his feet in the water. He stepped back onto dry land, torn between his desire to swim right out to that very sexy woman and practical concerns about his clothes. He didn't want to ruin his only good pair of shoes. Besides, they were heavy and would slow him down. He bent and tugged at the laces, swearing softly at his own clumsiness.

Caro . . .

Her sweet voice caressed his ears. This time, he knew he hadn't imagined it. He looked up and saw how much closer she'd come to the shore. She smiled, her dark eyes sparkling. Her shoulders were completely out of the water, and she wasn't wearing anything on top. He saw her breasts plainly now; saw how the waves lapped at her nipples.

To hell with his shoes.

He plunged ahead just as a warning shout came from behind and a stone whizzed past his ear.

There was a splash – that was the stone – and the woman folded forward and dropped, vanishing beneath the water.

He yelled and would have gone after her except that somebody had hold of him and wouldn't let him go. He struggled, trying to pull away, shouting curses, but even though his captor was shorter than he, he was a strong, wiry, and determined man. After a few moments Mario gave up the fight, although he kept staring out to sea, searching for her at the same time as he struggled to regain his English.

'Where is she? What happened – you, did you throw that rock? You hit her! She could drown! We have to find her – save her!'

'She can't drown.'

'What?'

'Son, she was after drowning *you*. Now, come out of there, come on, and we'll talk.'

The woman had vanished. If she was dead, her body should have floated to the surface; if she'd managed to swim away, he thought there would have been some sign of her. He'd seen what might have been a large fish just disturbing the surface of the water before streaking out for the open sea, but nothing of the woman. He allowed the man who had driven her away to put an arm around his shoulders and lead him back to dry land. He'd gone hardly deeper than his ankles.

'What's your name, son?'

'Mario.'

'From the chip shop, right? You're Tony's nephew from Sicily?'

He nodded dully. The man was familiar to him by sight, a regular customer, the postman.

'Well, let me tell you, Mario, that was no woman calling to you – that was a mermaid. If she'd got her hands on you, you'd be dead. It's happened before in these parts, according to stories. Fairy stories, people say, and until this week I wouldn't have put much stock in them, either. But something's changed – *everything's* changed – we've been cut off from the world we thought we knew, and who knows what might happen next?'

He patted Mario on the back. 'Lucky I saw you. No harm done. Next time you'll know to be more careful.'

From *Recollections of Alexander (McNeill) Wall*
(unpublished; no date)

FOLK-KNOWLEDGE is acquired in infancy, from old nurse beside the fire, or in the playground. As I was born half a world away from my natural home, naturally I grew up ignorant of local custom and belief. I learned the particular folklore of the Apple when I was already in middle age, hearing it filtered through my daughter, who had a story to go along with every picture she drew or painted: these grassy mounds were entrances to underground homes where the 'old people' lived; here was a cave into which a young man had entered and never returned; this was the tree where a magic apple grew . . . I thought it all amusing nonsense, never for a moment tempted to believe it true, and Emmeline's fascination with fairy tales I thought a harmless, childish fancy she would soon outgrow.

But my daughter never did outgrow it. Instead, as she matured, so did her passion. She longed for imagined fairy realms as other girls her age longed for a husband. I don't know why it should be that she was so disappointed by our world, for I did my best to make her happy as she was growing up, and gave her everything she asked. But it was never enough. She yearned for a mysterious lover who would whisk her away from humankind, to a magical otherworld where anything could happen. And one night her dearest wish was granted. Her dearest, childish, *impossible* wish.

I believed at first that she'd been abducted, or perhaps gone away quite willingly with a handsome gypsy or a plausible chancer from the city who thought to save himself the necessity of honest labour by marrying into money, and I was quite prepared to pay him off or do whatever else was necessary to ensure Emmeline's happiness. But as the weeks and then months passed with no word from my daughter or her seducer, and no results from the private investigator, no sightings of her from anyone in Scotland, I found that fragments of the old tales I'd learned at second-hand were lodged like painful shards of glass beneath my skin: stories of fairy abductions, non-human bridegrooms, journeys made by the living into 'The undiscover'd country from whose bourn / no traveller returns.'

I don't suppose that the good folk of Appleton are any more credulous or superstitious than folk anywhere else in these isles, but certainly there are some superstitions unique to these parts. It has long been an item of faith among the locals that when their ancestors settled in these parts they made a sort of pact with the *genius loci* to grow apple trees; and that as long as these trees thrived, those who tended them would be rewarded with good fortune. This is the belief played out in the annual ritual of the Apple Queen who shares a symbolic apple with the 'stranger' who has chosen her as his bride. According to the popular superstition, these two are thenceforth rewarded with their 'hearts' desire' and their personal happiness is reflected in the continuing good fortune shared by the whole community.

For most people, throughout all of human history, I have no doubt, the heart's desire is a simple one: to prosper, staying well and free from hunger, to be loved, to live to see their children grow up and prosper . . . bearing this in mind, and the fact that Appleton has been a singularly lucky and prosperous community, it is hard to argue against the widespread belief that some sort of magic must be at work. I myself have always suspected selective memory is at work, for even in Appleton some folk go hungry, many die before their time, and not everyone's luck is good.

But there is more to this belief in a 'magic apple'. Very occasionally – once in a generation, it is said, and yet it must be rare that one would live long enough to see it happen more than once in a reasonable lifespan – a single golden apple will appear on one tree, shining strangely among the reds and greens. And as in all the old legends, this golden apple is endowed with special powers. The red apple chosen and consumed by the annual Queen is well enough for all *ordinary* wishes, it seems, granting health and fertility and so on. But the golden apple had the power to grant any wish, even those called impossible.

The apple my daughter picked in 1916 and shared with her stranger was golden.

During the long weeks and months that I waited without result to hear some word of Emmeline, I spent many hours in the library – 'my' library, as I thought of it still. I read everything Uncle Lachlan had collected on the subject of magic, superstition, fairy tales, and folklore, and I sent away to Edinburgh for other works, both published and unpublished, which treated of such subjects as the second sight, the old religions, and the fairy faith. Much of what I found was sheer rubbish, but here and there gleamed a useful nugget, which I committed to memory, and gradually I formulated a plan.

The local folk would not help me, so I recruited some builders from Glasgow to help me with my project, and took them up to the Reul, under the pretence that the land there belonged to me and that I planned to clear and build upon it. One of these builders was Irish, and as soon as he set eyes on the hummocks and cairns which Emmeline had been pleased to call 'the fairy houses', he began to cross himself and begged me not to disturb the ground. I ignored his protests and continued loudly to discuss plans for clearing away the brambles and levelling the ground, and got the other two men to agree to help, work to begin the following week, unless, I added in a clear and carrying voice, 'my daughter be returned to me, safe and unharmed, in three days' time, in which case this ground shall be left undisturbed'.

There was a terrible storm that night: thunder and lightning, torrents of rain and furious gusts of wind that kept everyone indoors, cowering in fear of the power of the elements. Rather than exhausting itself, it went on well into the next day, finally dying away at about four o'clock in the afternoon. I went out for a walk immediately the rain stopped, restless after my incarceration, and as I went past the library, I saw a huddled figure crouching on the front steps.

It was my daughter, Emmeline, but this was not the joyous reunion I had longed for. She spat in my face and cursed me for forcing her return, and wept bitterly. I thought she would forgive me soon enough, but my heart and hopes sank when I saw what she carried nestled in the crook of her arm. It was a tiny, newborn baby.

Chapter Fourteen

At last he began to kiss her in return, his mouth opening against hers, and when he put his arms around her, Ashley sagged against him, suddenly weak in the knees. He staggered a little under her weight, but she was too deliciously dizzy to want to stand alone, so she clung to him and pressed him until he took the hint, and they sank together onto the thick, soft grass.

They lay glued together, kissing passionately, and just beginning to explore each other's clothed bodies. But as her hand reached the hard, smooth bulge in his pants, he pulled his mouth away from hers with a gasp, and said, 'I don't even know your name.'

'Ashley.'

'And you know mine. So I guess … you know what you're doing?'

She widened her eyes and stiffened her shoulders in a mock display of taking offence. 'Excuse me? I'm not a virgin if that's what you mean, and I've never had any complaints about my technique before!'

'I'm not complaining. I just wondered why . . . why this sudden urgency? Have you been talking to somebody? Did someone tell you . . .? What made you decide to come and seduce me?'

She sat up quickly, feeling her cheeks blazing. For a moment she was speechless with shame; then she got mad. She stared at him, still lying stretched on the grass, looking completely calm.

'Oh, is that what this is? *Seduction*? Something I'm doing to you? Totally one-sided? You want me to believe you don't feel it, too?'

He sat up. 'Of course I'm attracted to you,' he said gently. 'Of course it's mutual, dear heart. But – correct me if I'm wrong – this isn't how you usually act when a passing stranger tickles your fancy.'

'But you're not just a passing stranger! You're—' She stopped before his steady gaze, biting her lip, reluctant to admit it, but knowing he was right. There *was* something more going on; something besides pure lust compelled her desire.

'Tell me something,' she said, changing tack. 'I want to know the truth. Are you *really* Ronan Wall? The same one, I mean, who knew my grandmother fifty-six years ago?'

'Yes.'

'But how is that possible? What are you?'

'A man.'

She looked him up and down, recalling the firmness of his body, the strength in his arms as he'd lowered her gently to the ground, and desire uncoiled in her belly. She brought her gaze back to his face. There weren't even any fine lines around his eyes. 'A ninety-year-old man who looks about twenty-five. How do you explain that?'

He shrugged. 'I can't. Can you explain how *you* look? Inheritance, I suppose; genetics. I look like my great-grandfather looked – going by his portrait. I have the look of all the Walls descended from "the stranger woman". I look like my great-uncle Lachlan, I believe, who died at the age of ninety-seven before I was born.'

'When he was ninety-seven did he look like you look now?'

He smiled faintly 'I don't suppose he did. All right. I suppose I inherit my permanent youth from my father, who wasn't human. Which I guess makes me only half-human. I wasn't born in this world, and I've come to the conclusion in recent years that I'll never die in it. I must go back to the place where I was born. It's time. I *want* to go back – back to my mother and father.' His voice was very low. All at once his face looked strange to her, altered by the swiftly gathering shadows into something alien.

She edged a little away from him. 'Did you make the landslide happen?'

'What?' He sounded startled, and once again his face was familiar, as if she'd known him for years. He laughed. 'I'm not some kind of superhero! If I could do things like *that*–' He broke off as another thought struck him, and shook his head slowly. 'Although, maybe . . . It was the land that did it, but you could be right. I might have been the trigger, coming here when I did. I might have been just what it was waiting for. And I did feel compelled to come here – I was drawn back to this place for the same reason, I think, that you've been drawn to me.'

He cupped her face in his hands and kissed her. 'Any more questions?'

It was obvious, from the way he continued to kiss her, that he did not expect her to say anything, and her body, too, was eager to get on with it. But too much remained unclear. Attractive though she found the idea of being totally swept away, she also wanted to understand why this was happening.

'Wait, wait.' Reluctantly she pushed him away. 'I still don't understand. What happens *after* we make love?'

'She didn't tell you?'

'Who?' She frowned. 'Phemie? But she never told me anything. It was only when I saw your picture with hers in an old newspaper that I guessed . . .'

She broke off, aware that Ronan had gone tense with listening to something else. She heard it, too, a noise from above them in the dark sky. She had the sense that a large flock of birds was passing overhead, but it didn't sound like birds. As she strained her ears to make sense of it, she thought she could hear screaming, and furious shouting, and thuds and crashes, heavy blows, weapons connecting with other weapons, and with flesh, in some incomprehensible battle. She opened her mouth to ask, and he pressed his hand against it, warning her to keep quiet.

They huddled together in silence for long, uncounted minutes while Ashley tried to figure out who was fighting, and where – surely it couldn't be up in the air, as it sounded. She stared up into the darkness, her eyes attempting to conjure shapes out of the emptiness, until, gradually, the sound diminished, as if the invisible battle were moving somewhere else.

'What was it?' she whispered.

'The *sluagh*,' he said in his normal voice.

'What?'

'They're some sort of spirits – some people call them the host of the unforgiven dead. They were believed to go flying about above the world in great clouds, doing evil when they could, and constantly fighting with each other. In the morning you'd see their blood splashed on the rocks. The blood of the hosts – *fail nan sluagh* – is another name for red crotal, that's the lichen used for dyeing Harris tweed.'

He spoke matter-of-factly, and she gaped at him. 'But that's a myth, right? They're not *real*.'

'How real do you want? You heard them.'

'But there must be some other explanation for that noise. I mean–'

He grasped her hands firmly and leaned in close, this time not for a kiss, but to fix her with his gaze. 'Understand: you're not in the world you used to know, not any more. We're on an island now, and it's slipping into another reality where all the things you've been brought up to think of as legends are alive and powerful. I'm very glad the *sluagh* passed over without noticing us, because one of their nastier tricks is to snatch up people, drag them all over the place, and eventually throw them down to their deaths. Telling yourself they're not real is no protection.'

She remembered the shell of the Grand Hotel, and the dance music she'd heard, the party she'd glimpsed from afar, and shivered. 'How did this happen? Why now? Is it because of you?'

'I think so. Probably. Yes.' Abruptly, he dropped her hands, and his voice hardened. 'But it's not my fault. Better blame my grandfather. He's the one who dragged my poor mother back here – and dragged me into this world where I don't belong. That's where the whole imbalance began; I'm sure of it.'

'Ronan, I'm not blaming you.' She grasped his arm and stroked it. 'I just want to understand. Is there some way of making things right, of . . . restoring the balance?'

He was silent for a moment. 'You don't know?'

She shook her head. 'I'm in the dark here.' She smiled, because it was literally true.

'When a golden apple appears, it's as if all the magic of this land is concentrated in it. The woman and the man who share it can have whatever they desire most – no matter how impossible their wish might seem. There was a golden apple the year my mother was Queen, and again the year Phemie was crowned.'

'But she didn't eat it!' She blurted it out without thinking, but he didn't question how she knew.

'That's right. She didn't want it, and neither did I – it was something the town tried to foist upon us. They were going to make me redeem my mother's mistake. My grandfather's mistake, it was, really, for dragging her back, but of course they never blamed *him* – it was she they blamed for every misfortune, and after she had died, they shifted the blame to me.

'Have you ever noticed – no, you're probably still too young; you'll have to take my word for it. People always talk about how things were different, better, *right* in the olden days, when they were young and the world operated as it was supposed to, and people all knew their places in the scheme of things. They probably talked like that when people lived in caves; how caves never used to smell or get so damp, and the animals were fatter and the fish jumped into the nets . . . they want to believe in a golden age, and blame somebody or something for the collective fall from grace.

'So, supposedly, nothing was ever quite so good in Appleton after my mother's return. When she was dead, it became my fault. I became a sort of living symbol of bad luck. Even when I was providing steady employment and bringing wealth into the town it was never enough, somehow, never as good as it *would* have been if only I'd never been born. And my one chance to make things right was to go back to where I'd come from. This was made quite clear to me. I'm sure it must have been the only time in the history of the Apple Fair when the "stranger" was chosen even before the Apple Queen! I knew what my role was meant to be. Only I wasn't ready to play it.

'And now there's another golden apple, ripe and ready to be picked. Another chance. If you'll share it with me?'

She nodded, unable to speak. He moved to kiss her, but she pulled back.

'Do we have to do it here?'

He obviously didn't understand, so she elaborated. 'We don't have to make love in the cemetery, do we? Can we go back to my place and do it there?' Her voice wavered a little.

'We can make love wherever you like. And however you like.' He stood up and helped her to her feet.

'It'll be more comfortable,' she said. She thought of the bed, and also of the pack of condoms she'd brought in her luggage all the way from Texas. It might be ridiculously petty to think about such a thing when she'd just agreed to abandon the only world she knew for him – but what if it wasn't true? What if they were both pretending? *Trust in Allah, but keep a close guard on your camel*, she thought as, hand in hand, they began to pick their way cautiously between the graves and headstones toward the gate.

'Whose grave were you looking at when I found you?' she asked, just to break the silence.

'Not a grave. The memorial tablet to my mother.'

'There's no grave?'

'They never found her body.'

'What happened?'

'They said it was suicide. I don't think so. I think she escaped.'

'Escaped?'

'She jumped into the sea. Someone saw her; it was at the roadside, by those big rocks. It's very rocky there, and the water isn't very deep. If she'd died, they would have found a body. They didn't. No one ever found her body. I think she got away at last. I think she found her way back.'

From ***Magic Islands***
by Gracia McWilliams
(Turtle Press, 2004)

Several sites in Scotland can also lay claim to being the 'real' Isle of Avalon. These include not only the mysterious phantom island of HyBrasil, but also a few places much easier to locate on the map and actually visit.

Among the most interesting to the visitor are the island of Lismore, whose name means 'Great Garden' and which was the burial place of Pictish kings; and the Appleton peninsula, which boasts 'King Arthur's footprints' on its shore, not far from a cave whose unimpressive size and appearance has not stopped it being pointed out to generations of visitors and locals alike as the one where the great king of the Britons lies in an enchanted sleep.

Although Appleton is part of mainland Scotland, its older name of *Innis Ubhall*, or 'Apple Island', suggests that this was a recent development; and, indeed, only a single, narrow road and a few hundred yards of earth and stone sustain the connection. It is not hard, looking at a map, to imagine that 'stem' severed, and if hard facts are missing to back up the perception, nevertheless local folklore is rich in reasons to believe.

During the month I stayed in Appleton I heard many stories and perhaps half a dozen explanations for why 'the apple' either decided or was forced to forfeit its status as an enchanted, drifting island. The most popular (judging from the enthusiasm of the audience at the *ceilidh* where I first heard it) was a tale of human trickery: an ordinary man, an impoverished youngest son, uses his resourcefulness and quick wits to win in a contest against a supernatural opponent. But the one I liked best (romantic that I am!) was a love story.

She was the priestess/princess on the magic isle, the youngest of three; he was a poor young fisherman who one day chanced to drift or row a bit too far from shore. They fell in love at first sight. She was a magical immortal being; he was not. However, it had always been in the gift of the priestesses to allow some worthy mortals to join them, to eat the magic apples that grew on the island, and dwell there for ever. But the two older sisters (or they may have been her mother and grandmother) refused to allow that in this case. He was only a common fisherman, not a hero, not of noble blood, and therefore not good enough for her or the island.

She did not give up. Using the birds of the air and the fish of the sea she managed to communicate with her young man, and one night in the early 1600s (unusually for this sort of story, it's set in historic times; even the year was specified, although for each storyteller it was slightly different), she ran the island aground in order to be with her lover, and the other two women were unable to shift it. This was partly because their magic powers were waning in the face of the rationalistic modern world, partly because the great love between the two young people created its own power.

Mortals came to live on the grounded island, but the old magic did not die. The youngest of the sisters had children who still carried the old magic in their blood, as did the apple trees that continued to flourish on the land. And as long as the apples grew, and lovers remembered the meaning of a shared apple, all would be well, and *Innis Ubhall* remained a demi-paradise.

Only one of the storytellers – he had to be the oldest, tiniest man I've ever seen! – sounded a darker note at the end of this tale, sorrowfully shaking his head as he warned his rapt audience of their impending fate:

'Once upon a time, the magical pact was renewed every year, when the Apple Queen shared an apple with her lover, on behalf of us all,' he said. 'But the orchards are all gone now, and although a few people still grow apples, they're hard and sour, no good for eating. It has been more than fifty years since the last Apple Queen. Ever since she ran away, refusing the gift, things have gone from bad to worse. I don't know if such a gift will ever be offered us again; but if it is, and if it is ignored again, we'll have only ourselves to blame.'

Some of the older members of the audience nodded gloomily, and everybody there seemed to know what he meant – except me. I had to ask, 'Excuse me, but what do you think will happen if this gift is ignored again?'

'I think those other two ladies will get their way and take the apple back to be an island, only this time it won't be a paradise. Not for us. Far from it.'

I asked him when he thought this was likely to happen, and he replied that it could be any day, for Appleton was living 'on borrowed time'.

Indeed, there is a general air of gloom – doubtless because of the depressed economy – throughout Appleton, which is at odds with the beautiful scenery and warmly hospitable nature of the inhabitants which should, by rights, attract loads of tourists. Forgotten it may be – and most undeservedly – but I really don't believe that scenic little spot is in any danger of drifting out to sea. It was nearly two years ago that I heard the wizened old storyteller make his dire prediction, and, as I write, Appleton is still attached to the rest of Scotland, and still most firmly on the map.

Chapter Fifteen

As she stood staring at the mass of rock and mud and rubble that blocked the road, Kathleen heard a car approaching. She didn't turn to look, but when it stopped and the engine switched off, she felt intruded upon, and edged aside, heading back for her car, hoping she could get away without the need for conversation. She was feeling decidedly fragile after her experience in Ina McClusky's house.

'Kathleen?'

Her heart gave a great leap, and she stopped and turned to face him. Dave Varney looked more tentative than she'd imagined he could, and on an impulse she said, 'Were you trying to run away, too?'

He flinched. 'Too? Does that mean you got my note?'

'What note?'

'So you weren't running away from *me*.'

'I hadn't noticed you chasing,' she said, rather tartly.

'It's not for lack of desire, believe me. Or the will. But *things* have been conspiring against me.'

'Things?'

'Mechanical things. My phone. This . . . *vee*-hicle. If I told you everything, it'd be like "the dog ate my homework, miss, and then the bus hit a dinosaur . . ."'

She laughed. He smiled, looking less strained, and as their eyes met she felt a current running between them, and knew he felt it too. 'So . . . you wrote me a note?'

'Mmm. In my old-fashioned way. Handwritten, hand-delivered – I got to the library about fifteen minutes too late, so I pushed it through the letterbox in the library house door, and hoped you were in, or would be very soon . . . and I walked around for a bit, then I thought I'd drive around for a bit; and then I saw you.'

'And thought I'd been so freaked out by your note that I was trying to escape?'

He screwed up his face, looking embarrassed. 'Well, it wasn't the response I'd hoped for.'

'Are you going to tell me what it said?'

'Not right this minute. Do you want to go somewhere? For a drink or something?'

'Sure.'

He made a gesture towards his car, but she stepped back, looking at her own. 'I'd rather not leave mine here. Why don't we meet somewhere?'

He looked uncomfortable. 'Um, if you don't mind . . . I mean, if you're driving anyway, could I come with you?'

She looked from his gleaming Porsche to her cheap-and-cheerful Micra, and she shrugged. 'I don't mind. I guess I could bring you back here to pick up your car later . . .'

'I don't want to put you to any trouble,' he said quickly. 'You don't have to do that. It's just that I'm afraid . . . I have this feeling . . . that something else might happen if we don't stick together. I don't want to lose you.'

Her heart gave a leap at his words, and she turned away, shaken. Was he for real? 'OK, let's go. Harbour Bar at the Victoria, all right?'

Neither of them spoke during the short drive back. She wondered if he felt he'd said too much already, or if she was ridiculously oversensitive, ascribing a deeply personal meaning to lightly meant remarks. At this time of day the street in front of the library was deserted, as usual, so she parked there, close to home. 'The Vic's just around the corner,' she explained.

'Your local?'

'I guess.' She didn't care for visiting bars on her own, and had been inside the Harbour Bar only once. 'The food isn't the greatest.'

'Thanks for the warning. We'll stick to liquid sustenance. The drinks are all right?'

'They don't do cocktails.'

He looked comically shocked. 'Neither do I!'

As they approached the front of the hotel they saw that two small tables for two had been set out on the pavement.

'How very Mediterranean,' he said. 'Shall we?'

'Absolutely.'

He pulled out a chair for her.

'We have to make the most of this weather,' she said. 'It can't go on like this for ever. It's *October*.'

'Are you sure of that?'

'What do you mean?'

'It may be October in the rest of the world, but is it here? Are we still following the same calendar? Are we in the same time zone? Do the same rules still apply?'

She looked at him uncertainly, but before she could say anything, a bright-eyed, fresh-faced young woman wearing a crisp white blouse and short black skirt approached their table asking what they'd like to drink.

'A glass of red wine for me.'

'My tipple as well. Shall we get a bottle?'

'If you like.'

'No, if *you* like. I won't bother unless you'll have an equal share.'

'I think I could manage a couple of glasses.'

'OK, then. Any preferences?'

'I'll leave it to you – the one you ordered with dinner on Saturday was very nice.'

As he fell into a discussion with their server about the wines on offer, Kathleen looked at her watch and saw that it had stopped. She looked at Dave's arms, bare where he'd pushed up his sleeves, showing coppery hairs and freckled, lightly tanned skin, but no watch. His hands had neatly trimmed nails and pinkish, rather prominent knuckles. He wore a plain, flat platinum band on the fourth finger of his left hand. She glanced at it and glanced away again, remembering the wife who had died so young of cancer. Kay was her name, Kay Riddle. He had spoken of her quite naturally, without awkwardness, during that first evening they'd spent together, not dwelling on it, but letting her know about his loss, and thereafter able to say 'we' or refer to Kay without further explanation. That he'd loved his wife very much – that he loved her still – she didn't doubt. The sight of his wedding ring gave her a small pang, but it was only a small one. After all, they weren't kids, they both had their private histories, and there was no sense in being jealous of a dead woman.

'I did try to call you,' he said quietly, and she flashed him a startled look, feeling uncomfortably as if he'd just homed in on her innermost feelings. 'I couldn't get through. Is your phone working all right?'

She thought of the trouble she'd had in the library. 'I'm not sure.'

'I can't use mine at all. No network coverage for the

mobile, and I had to unplug the landline because otherwise it would keep ringing, and–'

'And?' she prompted after a few seconds.

'And nobody there.'

She didn't think that was what he had been going to say, but their server was approaching with a bottle and two glasses on a tray, and by the time he'd tasted the wine and approved it, and two full glasses had been poured, the moment when she might have quizzed him had passed.

They toasted each other silently and drank. The wine was soft and delicious and she relaxed and sighed with pleasure. 'It's like being on holiday.'

'Could be a permanent state.'

'What do you mean?'

'Well.' He looked into his glass and took a gulp before he went on. 'Have you heard of HyBrasil?'

'I don't think so.'

'A travelling island that appears and disappears. It could never be reliably charted because it kept moving, and was often surrounded by mists. It's seen mostly by sailors, a few of whom managed to land on its shores; it's also been seen on occasion by people from the coasts of Ireland and Scotland. The same sort of story used to be told about *this* place, the island of apple trees, *Innis Ubhall*, Avalon, the island of the blessed, where no one ever died or had to wear themselves out labouring, because there was magic in the very soil, or at least in the apples that the inhabitants dined upon, until, whether because of a navigational error, or interference from some sly culture hero, Avalon ran smack into the coast of Britain during a mighty storm and was ever afterward stuck fast. Stop me; you look like you've heard this one before.'

'Sort of. There's a man who comes into the library most days, doing research for a local history he's writing – Graeme Walker.'

'Graeme-the-Post. An absolute mine of local information. I was amazed to find out he's a transplant from Glasgow. I'd thought his roots must be centuries deep. So, he told you the legend?'

'Not as a legend. He says he's got geological evidence that this area used to be an island. He says there's no historical evidence for its being here before the sixteen hundreds. It's certainly not shown on the oldest maps of Scotland.'

He leaned across with the bottle and poured her some more wine. She was surprised to realize she'd already finished her first glass and resolved to slow down.

'Does Graeme have a theory about the original inhabitants?'

'The people who were here before the incomers came?'

'That's it.'

She shrugged.

'They were supposed to be immortal,' he said. 'Once the island was grounded, though, they lost that magical protection and became more like ordinary folks. They began to age, and suffer from ordinary infirmities. They intermarried with the incomers. According to the stories, some of them became Christians and were happy to exchange their pagan immortality for life everlasting. As for the others – well, they didn't die, but they kept getting older, and after a hundred or a hundred and fifty years they began to shrink and shrivel, getting smaller and smaller until they were no bigger than newborn babies. Their children and grandchildren and great-grandchildren had to look after them as they aged, but since they ate less and slept more, like the babies they began to resemble, they weren't much trouble to keep. Even so, as the years went by their descendants tended to forget about them, and instead of recognizing them as their ancestors, they thought these tiny little people living in cupboards and odd corners of the house and garden were some sort of supernatural beings, elves and fairies, to be treated with great caution – Kathy, what's wrong? You look like you've seen a ghost.'

The memory of her experience in Ina McClusky's house came back in a rush, sending a panic flood of fear all through her.

He put a hand on hers, warm and solid and comforting. 'Hey. Kathleen?'

'Something weird happened to me today.' She grimaced. 'What you said reminded me of it, but – it's crazy.'

'Tell me.'

'I don't think I've had quite enough to drink yet.' She laughed a little.

'Drink up, then. Listen, I've never been a particularly credulous or superstitious kind of guy, but today, some of the things that've been happening . . .' He shook his head.

'Like what?'

'You'll think I'm crazy.' He smiled at her, teasing, and she smiled back, her fear eased by the pleasure of his company.

'Try me. You tell me yours, and I'll tell you mine – unless this is just a trick.'

His eyebrows shot up. 'How can you be so distrustful when you hardly know me?'

'I had a big brother.'

'Oh, man, please tell me that's not how you think of me! As your *brother*?'

'I was using that as an example of – I promise you I don't.'

'Good. Because I really don't need another little sister.'

'Are you going to tell me about the weird things that happened to you today, or have we moved on to the subject of sibling rivalry?'

'OK.' He took a fortifying gulp of wine. 'Well, apart from the general cut-off-ness that's descended on the Apple – no grocery deliveries, no post, no phone service, *et cetera* and the fog–'

'What fog?'

He gestured out at the lights of the harbour, and she was surprised to see night had fallen already. 'You can't see it from here, but if you go up in the hills, to any height at all, there it is, out at sea, a line of fog, like heavy, low cloud, on all sides. We're surrounded by it, much as we are by the sea.'

She frowned, feeling the same uncanny prickling at the back of her neck as she'd felt on entering the library that morning. The feeling – she'd nearly forgotten after everything else – similar to what she'd experienced in Nell's orchard, as of some other, nonhuman presence nearby. She pushed the thought away, determined to be reasonable. 'That's probably just a weather system, isn't it? You often get fogs at sea, and if the air is warmer than the land . . .'

'There could be a natural explanation. I'm just telling you, I've never seen anything like it – the way it's stayed out there, in the same place, all day. It struck me as weird. Another thing – I don't know how well you know Appleton yet, and I could be wrong about this, but I've seen things – buildings, mostly – looking like they've been in place for ever, that I would swear I've never seen before.'

She thought of the strange little shop she'd seen yesterday morning.

'It doesn't sound like much, I know.' He frowned down at his wineglass, moving it between his fingers. 'But I have the feeling it's all connected, and that it means something. A change.'

'Like, the Apple is becoming an island again?'

He looked at her and nodded.

'Do you believe in magic?' As soon as the words were out of her mouth she felt embarrassed by them. She didn't think she'd asked that question seriously in her adult life – although as a child she had believed in magic, passionately, and would often quiz others to find out if they felt the same. She held her breath, waiting for his reply.

He took it seriously. 'Before . . .' He shook his head. 'I'm not really sure what I thought before. But here – now – yes.'

She felt certain that the few things he'd mentioned wouldn't have been enough to change his mind. 'Something else happened.'

He hesitated a moment, then, reluctantly, nodded. 'Phone calls. The phone would ring, and . . .' He frowned, looked away, swallowed hard. 'The voices . . . they couldn't hear me, I don't think; it was more like I was overhearing a conversation, half a conversation.' He stopped and drank some wine.

'Did you recognize the voices?'

It took him a moment to find the words. 'They were . . . yes. People I'd known, been close to. They were all dead. But I could hear them talking.'

She told him then about what had happened at Ina McClusky's.

'I never thought the end of the world would be like this,' he said when she'd finished.

Her heart gave an uncomfortable jolt. 'It's not the end of the world!'

'The end of the world *we've* known. I guess it's also the start of something new, one world dying, and another busy being born.' He shook his head thoughtfully. 'There's something going on that we don't understand. I have a feeling we're just glimpsing the tip of an iceberg, and it's huge, and it goes down deep, into regions we can only guess at, or glimpse in dreams.

'I keep being reminded of stories I read as a kid . . . the old legends that people used to believe were true. What if they *are* true? After all, even if magic doesn't work in *our* reality there might be other worlds where it does. And what if Appleton used to be part of another world that somehow slipped or strayed into this one, and now it's being pulled back again–'

'But why should it be? Why now?'

He shrugged. 'Why do apples ripen in September and not in May? It could be a cycle that makes perfect sense, if we could see it from the right perspective. Maybe it's happened before, but only once in so many hundreds or even thousands of years.'

'Atlantis?'

He nodded. 'Maybe.'

'But didn't Atlantis sink into the ocean, or blow up, or

something awful? Avalon was paradise. If we're going to find ourselves living in paradise, it should be wonderful, not sinister.' She thought of the old women in the wardrobe, and Dave's phone calls from the dead, and a shiver ran through her.

'I'm not sure it will be paradise, not for all of us. Probably not even for most of us. I think it has to be too much to hope for, that we'd all be allowed to share in the bliss, all three thousand plus of us rewarded with paradise just because we happened to be living here on this little spit of land at this moment. That doesn't make sense to me. In the old stories it was never a matter of chance; people were *chosen*, and they had something to show as their mark of favour – usually a blossoming apple branch.'

His words brought back a vivid memory of Nell's orchard. 'Would the branch have fruit on it as well as blossom?'

'It might.'

'Because I *saw* a tree like that, on Sunday. Just one branch of the tree was in blossom, but it also had a big yellow apple on it.'

'Where?'

'In Nell's walled orchard. Nell Westray; she's an American who settled here – she bought Orchard House a few years ago. It didn't have any orchards left when she came, but she started growing apples.'

'So there are apples again in Appleton. I wonder . . .

What did your friend say about the blossom? Was she surprised?'

'I don't know. She was pretty calm at first, so I couldn't tell if it was new to her or not. She said something about the unseasonable weather to explain it. But after that, she changed. That could have been the reason. She'd been so friendly before, and after that . . . it was like she couldn't wait for me to leave.'

'I'd like to see that branch. Orchard House – where is that? Could you take me there?'

She looked from his intent, questioning face to her almost empty wineglass and winced. 'You know, I'm probably not in a great state to drive . . .'

'Hey, neither am I.' His hand came down again on top of hers and gently pressed. 'There's no big urgency. I don't *have* to see this apple tree. I wouldn't know what to do with it. I can't help being curious, that's all. I think it must be connected to everything else that's been happening. But, listen. First things first. We should get something to eat. I don't know about you, but with one thing and another, I missed lunch. Do you want to chance the kitchen here, or go somewhere else?'

'My house is right around the corner.' Her heart gave a hopeful, fearful thump as she said it. 'If you don't mind something simple – pasta or an omelette – I'll cook.'

'That would be great.'

He poured the rest of the wine into the two glasses just

as she pushed her chair back from the table. 'Hey, no hurry. We've got to finish this.'

'I'm just going to visit the ladies' room.'

'Oh. Well, don't be long, huh?' She thought he looked oddly nervous, but then he winked, and said, 'Or I might drink the rest of the bottle myself. If you see our waitress, send her out and I'll settle up.'

She saw herself in the restroom mirror: rosy cheeks, sparkling eyes, tousled hair, lips wet and reddened slightly from the wine. For once, she had no fault to find with her looks. She looked as happy, as desirous and desired, as she felt. *He* liked the way she looked; he liked *her*. All they had been talking about, the roadblock, the telephones, the fog, Ina McClusky's ancient relatives, passed through her mind without making the impact of a single, lingering look from him. Something had happened; something was going on, but at the moment, befuddled by lust and wine, she couldn't seem to get to grips with it. Maybe it was too big to take in all at once. If Dave was right and Appleton had entered another realm, a place of myth and magic, it seemed to her that taking a fatalistic attitude might be best. You had to go with the flow and try to stay sane while accommodating such a huge shift in reality. What would be, would be, and she would just have to fit her life into the changed circumstances as best she could. She couldn't imagine herself as either the hero or the villain of Appleton's tale, which would surely have unfolded in the same way without her. But whatever was to happen, she was grateful to the fate that had brought her together with Dave Varney.

On the way back through the dim corridor from the toilets she passed their server.

'Excuse me – could we have the bill? Out front?'

'He's paid already,' said the girl with a flick of her wrist. 'He was in a hurry. I left your glass.'

When she got outside Kathleen saw their table had been cleared except, as the girl had said, for her own, half-empty glass of wine. There was no sign of Dave.

She told herself he'd probably just gone to the men's room – he'd be back in a minute – but, with a painfully hollow feeling in her chest, she stood beside the abandoned table and looked around. Over by the quay, across the wide Esplanade, she saw a group of people, perhaps half a dozen, walking away toward the town centre. Because of the darkness and the distance, she couldn't make out any details about them. But there was one man, walking a little behind the group and hurrying as if to catch them up, whom she knew, even at this distance, by the set of his shoulders, the way he moved, and the ponytail that hung down his back.

She swallowed down a bitter taste and stared, her hands clenching at her sides as she willed him to look around and wave to her, to come back, to *explain*. He'd just seen someone he had to talk to, someone he wanted her to meet . . .

But as she waited and watched, the whole group crossed over another street and they all, Dave included, passed out of sight.

She turned on her heel and hurried away in the other direction, towards home, blinking hard against tears of shock. She felt eviscerated; in pain, then numb, then, gradually, she started to get mad at his pointless cruelty. It wasn't like he owed her any explanations. If he didn't want to have dinner with her, if he couldn't bear another five minutes in her company, the briefest, most banal excuse would have done the trick, leaving her disappointed, yes, but not devastated. Was he under some compulsion to toy with women and leave them humiliated? She was not giving him another chance. She didn't care *what* he said; there would be no next time. She remembered how he'd walked away from her so abruptly that first time in the library and felt she should have known from that what he was like.

His letter lay in wait for her: a square blue envelope all by itself on the hall floor.

She picked it up and held it between thumb and forefinger like something contaminated. It would be full of lies and seductive promises meant to affect her like a cunning, slow-acting poison. She remembered he'd been afraid reading it had made her determined to run away from him. No. That's what he'd *pretended* – to find out if she'd read it. Probably so he wouldn't slip up and contradict himself. The thought of so many layers of deceit made her tired. She didn't have to read his lies. Curiosity was weakness, another chink in her very, very rusty old armour.

She took it into the kitchen and walked straight over to the bin without switching on the light.

But there was already a little light in the dark room, a shaft of it spilled through the window, coming from the library which should, at this time of night, have been completely dark. She froze, then slowly turned her head to look. Across the garden, a single lighted window blazed like a sheet of gold set in the dark stone of the long building. Strangest of all, the light came from a window that did not exist; an opening high on the side of a wall that, earlier this evening, had been solid, unbroken stone.

Chapter Sixteen

Nell regretted her words as soon as Ronan walked away, but she resisted the temptation to call him back and explain. She was mad at herself for invoking Sam like that, for waving the flag of her supposed marital status – 'I'm Mrs Westray' – as if she belonged to one of those primitive cultures in which a woman's only protection was what her husband could provide. And yet there was a sense in which she was still, and would always be, Sam's wife. She would never marry again and was incapable, she believed, of ever loving anyone else with the whole-hearted, passionate commitment she had felt for him. There was absolutely no point in admitting to Ronan that her husband was dead; what she'd said was emotionally true. Being widowed had not made her available. She might be sexually attracted to him, but she wouldn't act on those feelings, especially not after what he'd said about marriage. There was no *way* she would ever marry him.

He'd really effected her. She tried, when she was alone again, to forget about their meeting, but the memory of him haunted her. The sound of his voice, the faintly honeyed smell of his skin, seemed to hang in the air of her garden and made it impossible for her to concentrate on any of the tasks that normally absorbed all her attention. The weather bothered her, too; it was far too warm for the time of year, and even the level of daylight seemed wrong.

Despite the disturbing memories that lurked within its walls, she forced herself to go into the orchard again. There were apples that needed to be picked. She looked at the mystery tree first, wondering if anything would have changed, and noticed at once that the blossom, while it still thickly decorated the branch, no longer looked as vigorous. The petals had spread open more widely and were beginning to look slightly tattered. The apple itself had never looked more beautiful, and she sensed that it was at its very peak, almost ready to fall from the tree. If she so much as touched it, it would drop into her hand. She was very tempted to do so; to eat this singular apple all by herself. Ronan Wall certainly wouldn't bother her again, and if it brought her bad luck, well, when had she ever had any other kind?

But once again she turned away from temptation and set about picking another tree's heavy, ripe crop, settling each glossy red apple carefully in its nest of shredded paper as she fought off memories of how he'd looked at her; his eyes and his smile. But she had sent him away. It was pointless. She would never see him again.

Another question began to bother her. Why had she planted these apple trees? Why had she gone to so much trouble in her quest to reproduce Appleton's Fairest? With what purpose? Who was it *for*? Not just the golden apple, but all of them, more apples than she could eat by herself in a year. If it was just a way to pass the time, more interesting than playing endless games of solitaire, but at base no different, then her life *should* have ended when Sam's did, and she was still alive, a prisoner serving out her term only because she was a coward, frightened to kill herself, yet too scared to live.

It was not the first time she'd had such thoughts, but it was the first time she'd seen, opposed to death and time-serving, a real alternative, an opportunity she could reach out and take, if only she was brave enough.

She carried the heavy trug full of apples out of the walled orchard, across the meadow, and into her garden, where the sight of the large, blue-covered book lying on the table claimed her attention. She decided to take it back to the library, where it belonged. It was a relief to have a simple, straightforward task to perform, a release from thoughts that had begun to circle upon themselves and become obsessive, and the prospect of seeing Kathleen again was unexpectedly cheering. Maybe it wasn't too late to apologize and make up for her antisocial behaviour; maybe a friend was just exactly what she needed.

As she was turning the car on the paved area in front of her house, preparatory to driving down the steep hill, Nell noticed a line of fog hiding the horizon. More surprisingly, the fog had rolled in to land just beyond the place where the road was blocked, cutting off her view of the road beyond Appleton, yet the road on the near side of the landslide, going into town, was clear. How peculiar.

She couldn't see any fog at all after she'd descended her hill. As she pulled up and parked on the empty street in front of the library she realized it was shut. It was obviously later than she'd thought. The clock in her car – a venerable secondhand Volvo – didn't work, and she didn't wear a watch because she didn't have to; she'd always had a pretty good sense of time. She could look at the sky and judge the hour within five or ten minutes; just now, she thought it could not be later than half past five.

She got out of the car, the book in her hand, thinking that she could try the library house, which was the building abutting the museum at the end of the road. Turning in that direction, she noticed a small child standing on the corner: a little girl dressed in a stained pink T-shirt and shorts, with dirty bare feet, scabby knees, and scratched legs, her hair a long, uncombed brown tangled cloud who stared at her with a fierce, accusing glare. She felt a startled, queasy jolt of recognition, a start of anxiety, almost as if the child was her own long-forgotten responsibility.

It was ridiculous. She'd never had or wanted a child; she didn't even *know* any children. Yet as she continued to look at this one – who stared angrily, implacably back – the feeling of recognition didn't decrease, and her anxiety grew. The kid couldn't have been much more than five. What was she doing out on her own? And those bare feet – she could gash her foot on a broken bottle or, worse, step on a rusty nail. Somebody should be looking after her. Where were her parents? What were they thinking to let such a young child out on her own?

There was no one else anywhere in sight; there was no one but Nell to take responsibility, so she did, stepping forward, making an effort to fix a friendly, unthreatening expression on her face. 'Hello, what's your name? I'm Nell.'

The little girl's eyes widened. Without answering, she whirled around and ran across the street. Halfway up the next block she stopped and looked over her shoulder: a look that dared, or invited, Nell to follow.

Nell didn't have to run. For all the energy the little girl poured into her movements – arms and legs both pumping away – she was not moving very fast. By walking briskly Nell was able to close most of the distance between them, at which point she slowed down again rather than catch her up. She didn't want to frighten the child.

They passed a church and a tennis court, then a block

of flats built half a century earlier in ugly, utilitarian concrete. She wondered if the child's home might be there – it was the sort of place anyone might run away from – but the little girl dashed by without giving it a second look. She only paused at the top of the hill, where there was a choice of directions. To the right, the road ran down toward the town centre; straight ahead it offered access to a crescent of handsome old houses and a hotel, while on the left it doglegged down the hill again, past more houses, before joining the wide Esplanade that followed the coastline.

It was the downhill route the girl chose, but she did not stick to the road for long. Abruptly she swerved into a driveway or alley running between two houses. It was paved, but only wide enough for a single vehicle and heavily overgrown with bushes and trees of various kinds. A crookedly leaning sign near the entrance announced in faded letters: ACCESS TO HOUSES ONLY, KEEP CLEAR. NO PARKING.

To enter the narrow, shadowy lane was to plunge into twilight. Up ahead she saw the pale pink of the little girl's T shirt, and she had an unnerving flash of *déjà vu*. Although she did not remember it herself, she'd been told by relatives that for almost a year after her parents' death she'd refused to settle down, taking off every few days without a word of warning and with nothing but the clothes she was wearing – once it had been her pyjamas and bunny slippers – to walk and walk in an endless, hopeless search for 'home'. She either did not understand, or could not accept, that the house where she'd lived with her parents – the only place that meant 'home' to her – was not only occupied by strangers now, but was also hundreds of miles away, in another city.

The alley ended in a cul-de-sac; straight ahead she saw a row of four identical, run-down, dingy white cottages, the spaces in front of them taken up by as many parked cars. The little girl had stopped running, but Nell could not guess if that was because she had come home, or because she'd only just realized she was trapped. Fencing ran along behind the terrace of cottages and on either side, marking off property boundaries. Her only escape was back along the narrow road by which she'd come. Nell stopped still in the mouth of the alley, conscious that she was blocking the girl's retreat, and waited.

The girl walked towards the end house, then paused and deliberately turned and looked back at her. She might have been trying to communicate something by her intent gaze, but Nell didn't know what. Still without a word, the child turned away, took a few steps forward, and vanished into the house.

Nell followed, and, then, as she went closer, she stopped and stared in surprise. The house on the end of the row was a mere shell. No one could live there. Although the outer walls remained standing, the roof was gone, and there was not much left of the interior.

Hide-and-seek, she thought, and stepped forward, up to

the gaping doorway through which she'd seen the child go, eager now to bring the game to an end. But the girl had vanished. Inside the ruined building were some piles of rubble overgrown with weeds, and nothing else. Nothing larger than a cat could have hidden there. She gazed all around, dismayed and a little frightened as she understood who the child reminded her of, why she'd felt such a strong jolt of recognition. It was herself, of course. There was a picture of her taken shortly before her parents' death that showed a cleaner, happier child, but one with the same fierce gaze, scabbed knees, and long brown hair.

Just to be sure, she searched every inch of the ruin, and even went behind it in case a real child had tricked her by slipping through the back window and was crouching out of sight. She was still pursuing this pointless search when a large, slatternly-looking woman came out of the house next door to ask, in a pointedly hostile voice, if she needed any help at all.

'I'm sorry – I thought I saw a little girl go in there. I was worried in case she was lost. But I guess . . . I must have been mistaken.'

The woman's hostility cleared away at the sound of an American accent. 'You'll be a visitor, then? I thought you'd all left on Saturday night. Dunno why *you* stayed. There won't be any more planes now, you ken. You'll have to take whatever happens along with us.' The woman's eyes alighted on the large book she was still clutching.

'Is that your book of maps? It looks an old one. That's probably how you came to get lost. Shall I show you where you are?'

She responded without thinking to the outstretched hand and gave her the book. 'It's not maps,' she said, uneasily. 'And it's not mine. It belongs to the library. I was just going to return it. It's about apples.'

'Apples! Now there's something my family used to know something about – or so they say. It's from our library here, you say? Do you mind if I look?'

'Sure, go ahead.'

The woman opened it to the first illustration and sucked in a long breath of appreciation. 'My! That *is* fine! No one's seen one of *them* in fifty years.'

The woman herself could not have been much more than forty, and Nell narrowed her eyes skeptically. 'But you know what it is?'

'Oh, yes. Me mum had a picture – not as nice as this, mind, but we always thought it was something special. And of course we knew the stories. Me granddad came from one of the families that planted the first orchards here.'

'I've seen an apple just like that hanging on a tree,' said Nell, suddenly glimpsing a way out, the chance to hand over responsibility to someone who knew what to do with it.

The woman eyed her calmly. 'But you haven't picked it.'

'I wouldn't know what to do with it.'

'Sure you would.' She closed the book without looking any further into it, gave it a soft tap, and handed it back to Nell. 'You'll have read all about it. You know that you must share it with your man.'

'My man's dead.'

'And you think the world came to an end, aw, poor you,' she jeered gently. 'But the world didn't end, did it? You went on living. And now it's time for you to find a new man. Just get on with it,' she finished impatiently. 'There's not much time left, you know.'

'You're not real,' said Nell suddenly. 'I'm imagining this, just like I imagined that little girl.'

The woman laughed, showing crooked, overcrowded teeth. 'You think I'm your conscience? Well, listen to your conscience, dearie!' Her hand darted forward and she seized a bit of flesh on Nell's arm and gave it a vicious pinch.

Nell fell back, shocked.

'There, you felt that, didn't you?' The woman laughed again and nodded with satisfaction. 'This is no dream. Its all really happening – yes, lots stranger things than meeting me, I'm sure! You've been chosen.'

'Why me? I don't want it. You have it. Share it with your man and have your heart's desire.'

'*My* man. Oh no, oh no.' She chuckled.

'Well, why not, if it's supposed to be so wonderful? You ought to leap at the chance.'

'And I would've, ten or fifteen years ago. But I kicked

out my last worthless boyfriend two years ago and – funny thing! – nobody's shown any interest in me, 'less I'm buying a round. I've got four kids, and nobody but me's interested in them, neither. I couldn't leave 'em to fend for 'emselves, now, could I? Reckon it was one of mine you saw just now, playing some trick,' she added, nodding in the direction of the ruined house.

Nell didn't bother to argue with her. 'Thanks for your help,' she said flatly turning away.

'Thanks for yours, and all,' the woman called after her. 'You'll do what's right, in the end. You're pretty enough to be the Apple Queen.'

It was still light enough to be considered daylight in front of the houses, but a few seconds later, as she emerged from the gloomy, tunnel-like driveway onto the road, night had fallen. She sucked in a shocked breath and looked around, wondering if she was starting to suffer blackouts. How long had it taken her to walk those few short yards? She couldn't even guess what time it was now, but it was certainly well after sundown. The streetlights were on, and away down the hill she could see the glimmer of lights strung along the pier. Here and there in the harbour the lights on the boats gleamed like fireflies in the darkness of sea and sky. She shivered, chilled in spite of the warm, still air, and set off at a brisk walk for the library house, praying that Kathleen would be in.

Just as she reached the street that ran along behind the

library she saw a bright light come on in the garden – probably a motion-sensitive security light. Going closer, she saw a figure standing in the library garden, and, as she reached the iron gates, recognized the librarian standing very still and staring up at a lighted window in the side of the building.

'Kathleen?'

The woman started violently.

'Kathleen, it's me, Nell – can I come in?'

'Nell! Oh, thank goodness! Just wait, I'll unlock the gate.' She hurried over and grappled noisily with the cumbersome lock before finally managing to swing it open. 'Oh, my, it's good to see a friendly face!' She peered up at her earnestly. 'Can I ask you to do something for me? Just look over at the library and tell me if you can see a light from *inside* the building.'

Nell glanced across at the lighted window and shrugged. 'Yes.'

'You do see it?' At her confirming nod, Kathleen sighed. 'So at least I'm not hallucinating.'

'You must have left it on.'

'No, absolutely not.'

'Do you think somebody broke in?'

'I don't know what to think.' She sighed and squared her shoulders. 'I'll have to go in and find out. I know it's a lot to ask, but would you come with me?'

Although Nell wasn't bothered by the prospect, she felt

she had to say, 'Shouldn't you call the police?'

'I don't think so. You see – it's kind of weird – that window shouldn't be there. It wasn't there this morning. I never saw it before.' She sighed. 'I don't know why you should believe me.'

'Because there's no reason for you to lie, and I'm sure you're not hallucinating.' And she no longer thought she had been suffering from heatstroke on her walk through that mysterious wasteland, or that the golden apple in her orchard was descended from anything that had ever been sold in a supermarket. The world had changed around them, as if they were living in a fairy tale. She wondered who they'd find inside the library, waiting for them in a room that did not exist: Rapunzel? Or the wicked witch? Or someone closer to home?

She thought of Ronan Wall with a stab of longing and held out the book she'd been clutching to her chest all this time. 'Here, Kathleen, this came from your library. A man gave it to me yesterday. It looks valuable; I think he might have stolen it. Maybe he broke into the library – I wouldn't put it past him. And maybe he's inside there now.'

Kathleen gasped. 'This is someone you know?'

'Not really. He just turned up at my house on Sunday, wanting to see my orchard. He said his name was Ronan Wall.' She hesitated. 'You know that branch? There wasn't any blossom on it before he touched it.'

'Ronan Wall,' Kathleen said slowly. 'That name keeps

coming up. Well, I'd like to meet him. Shall we go and find out if you're right?'

'I'm ready if you are.' They grinned uneasily at each other, and she was surprised by the excitement that surged through her. There was nothing in it of fear. Kathleen's company lifted her spirits and made her feel like a schoolgirl embarking on some slightly mad adventure.

Kathleen lifted her large key ring and led the way to the back doors. As soon as they were inside – wincing at the noise the old locks and heavy doors made – she switched on some lights.

'Anyone would have heard us come in, so there's no reason for us to creep around in the dark. By the way, if we *do* need to call the police, here's my mobile.'

Nell took it a little awkwardly, then looked around for somewhere to deposit the book she still held, and decided it should be safe enough on top of the old counter that separated the entrance foyer from the reference room. She followed the librarian around the back of the counter and watched as she unlocked another door. If someone really had broken in, they'd gone to a lot of trouble, locking doors behind them. Behind the door was a narrow spiral staircase, rising into darkness until Kathleen touched the switch on the wall at her side. Anyone upstairs had to know they were coming by now. As she watched the librarian mount the stairs, Nell was reminded of her own worried foray on the night of the earthquake and guessed Kathleen felt a protective love for the library similar to what she felt for her orchard. She clutched the phone more firmly as she followed behind, ready to press 999 at the first sign of trouble.

The room at the top of the stairs was empty of furniture, but it was decorated with a life-sized 3-D mural of an apple tree on one wall, so vividly painted that the apples appeared positively to glow: two red, and one golden. Kathleen was standing stock-still and staring at the tree as if she'd never seen it before.

'Did that just appear?' Nell asked in a whisper.

Kathleen shook her head. 'But I never knew it was a door,' she murmured. She reached out her hand to the golden apple, the lowest of the three, and as she pressed it there was a click, and the door that had been hidden in the wall swung open.

It revealed a second spiral staircase, this one well lit by the light that flooded down from above. Kathleen started up the stairs, moving in a slow, oddly dreamy way, and Nell, close behind, had to take care not to bump into her.

The stairs took them up into a wide and spacious room filled with a faintly golden light. It was a round room and, as she looked up at the high, curved ceiling, Nell realized they must be inside the golden dome that made the library such a famous landmark in the town. The other thing she noticed immediately, as distinctive as the room's shape, was the smell: oil paints and turpentine. Even before she took in the number of painted canvases, resting on easels or stacked against the gently curving walls, she knew this was an artist's studio.

She looked at Kathleen, who looked back at her, pupils dilated in shock, clearly even more astonished than she was by the discovery of this secret atelier. Then they both turned and stared at the artist who was very much in residence, and deeply engrossed in her work, painting away at a canvas resting on an easel. The unfinished painting, largely composed of shades of green and brown, seemed to depict a grove of trees. The artist wore a multicoloured, striped, long-sleeved, knee-length smock over a long dress or skirt. She was turned away from them, so they couldn't see her face but only a mass of light brown hair loosely fastened behind her head.

Kathleen cleared her throat. 'Hello?' Her voice sounded soft and weak. 'Excuse me,' she went on, more determinedly. 'Would you mind telling me who you are, and what you're doing here?'

The artist gave no sign that she'd heard. The librarian walked right up to her and reached out to touch her. Nell, who stayed put, admired her nerve, and was not at all surprised to see her hand pass right through the artist's colourfully striped shoulder.

Kathleen reeled back in shock, then suddenly giggled. She walked all the way around the working artist, looking at her from every angle, but keeping well clear of her, taking no risk of trying to touch what looked so solid yet had no mass. When she'd completed a circuit she looked back at Nell. 'You see her, too?'

She nodded.

'She doesn't look like a hologram projection. Not like anything I've ever seen. She looks absolutely real. I wonder, can she see us? Hear us? Or . . . are we ghosts to her, too, only she's used to ignoring us so she can get on with her work?'

'She's very industrious.' It felt wrong to talk about the artist as if she wasn't there – but, probably, she wasn't. 'Any idea who she is?'

'Emmeline Wall.' She took a step back, her eyes fixed on the ghost as she spoke the name, but it seemed to have no more power than any other words.

'I never heard of her.'

'Daughter of the man who built this library.' As she spoke, Kathleen moved away from the painter and began to prowl about, inspecting the paintings on display. 'She was never famous but I found a really interesting painting by her tucked away in the storage room. Oh, and she was the mother of Ronan Wall.'

Ronan's mother.

Although the information made her focus once more on the back of the oblivious artist, Nell still did not move. She had a strong feeling that they were trespassers in this room. They hadn't been invited, and even if she was unaware of them, even a ghost deserved courtesy.

'Hey, look at this!'

'Kathleen, I think–'

'Come here – it's a portrait of her son. See if you can recognize him.'

Despite her unease, she couldn't resist, and crossed the room to Kathleen's side.

'That's Ronan, isn't it?'

She looked at the canvas Kathleen had found and could only nod, speechless, as she recognized the man who had offered her the chance to have her heart's desire, the man she had sent away yesterday. The painting was fairly small, no more than eight-by-ten, a head-and-shoulders portrait of an unsmiling, darkly handsome young man.

'How weird is that,' said Kathleen, sounding awed. 'I thought it was, you know, because I just saw a newspaper photograph of him from nineteen fifty, when he would have been in his early thirties, and he looked just like that. But Emmeline didn't live to see her son grow up. He was only about three years old when she killed herself. So how could she have known?'

Obviously, thought Nell, the picture had been painted by Emmeline after her own death, when she was a ghost, drifting about the town unseen, still watching over her orphaned son. As the image formed in her mind she felt sorry for the sad little boy who'd lost his mother at an even earlier age than she had. 'What happened to him? Was he adopted?'

'He was looked after by his grandfather, but not with much affection. I've been reading his diary, and it seems that he just couldn't warm to the boy. I guess he couldn't forgive him for what happened to Emmeline.'

Nell thought of Ronan, and her heart ached for him – and for herself. She remembered her child-self – dirty and desperate and doing her best – and felt ashamed of the foolish coward she'd grown to be. Once she had not been afraid to take chances, to try to achieve the impossible. Maybe it wasn't too late.

'I think we should go now. Kathleen?'

The librarian had drifted away. Nell called her name more loudly, but she seemed nearly as oblivious as the ghost, and Nell could see no other way of getting her attention but to go after her and take hold of her arm. It was a relief to feel warm, solid flesh beneath her fingers.

'We have to leave.'

Kathleen looked puzzled; Nell had the idea she wasn't sure who she was.

'Kathleen,' she said, more urgently. 'Let's go.'

Her face cleared. 'Oh, that's all right! You go; I don't need you here.'

'Come with me. We don't belong here.'

She laughed. '*I* do! I'm the librarian. I've got a job to do. Just look at all these paintings! Absolutely none of this stuff has been catalogued; can you believe it?'

For a moment Nell was tempted to leave her to it. But

she knew it would be wrong. Even though Kathleen looked happy enough, she clearly had no idea where she was or what had happened. She was in a dream-state; she hadn't made a conscious choice.

'Well, before you get started, we should finish downstairs. We have to make sure everything is all right downstairs, all the books and everything; make sure nobody broke into the library.'

She frowned. 'Broke in?'

'Remember? It's late, Kath. You're not supposed to be working now. You'd gone home, and then you saw a light on–'

'Oh, I remember! But we came up here–' She broke off and looked around uneasily. Her gaze fell on Emmeline, still working away at a mass of green in the centre of her canvas, and she shivered. Without another word she headed for the door.

Nell hesitated, drawn by her own curiosity about what the ghostly artist was actually painting. But she recognized the danger in that and would not let herself be distracted. She hurried down the slightly swaying staircase after Kathleen and, after a moment's uncertainty, left the hidden door ajar before descending the second staircase. She did not believe that Emmeline Wall could pose a threat to anyone save herself, and did not like the idea of her poor ghost being trapped up there if she couldn't manage to open the door from the inside.

Once they were back on the ground floor, Kathleen shut the door behind them and locked it, her trembling hands making it a difficult enterprise. There was no talk of searching the library for other intruders; they were both eager to get away.

It had been dark when they entered the library, but now it was light – light enough, at least, that they could see their way around outside. But it hardly seemed like morning. There was a dim grey half-light that might have come just before dawn, but with an odd greenish tinge.

'How long were we in there?' Kathleen said, sounding bewildered. 'What time is it? Darn this cheap watch! Do you have the time?'

Nell shook her head.

'We must have been in there for hours! The whole night! And it felt like minutes – I'd still be in there, if not for you. Look, the window's disappeared!'

Together they stared up at the side of the building. Where the glowing rectangle of an upstairs window had been there was now nothing but solid reddish stone. Then Nell staggered slightly as Kathleen threw her arms around her and gave her a strong hug. 'Thanks for being there. Thanks for getting me out,' she murmured. Then, letting her go, she said, 'Want to come in for a drink?'

'Thanks, but I have to go. There's someone I have to find, if it's not too late.'

From *Popular Superstitions and Festive Amusements of the Highlanders of Scotland*
by W. Grant Stewart
(Archibald Constable, 1823)

In the former and darker ages of the world, when people had not half the wit and sagacity they now possess, and when, consequently, they were much more easily duped by such designing agents, the 'Ech Uisque', or water-horse, as the kelpie is commonly called, was a well-known character in those countries. The kelpie was an infernal agent, retained in the service and pay of Satan, who granted him a commission to execute such services as appeared profitable to his interest. He was an amphibious character, and generally took up his residence in lochs and pools, bordering on public roads and other situations most convenient for his professional calling.

His commission consisted in the destruction of human beings, without affording them time to prepare for their immortal interests, and thus endeavour to send their souls to his master, while he, the kelpie, enjoyed the body. However, he had no authority to touch a human being of his own free accord, unless the latter was the aggressor. In order, therefore, to delude public travellers and others to their destruction, it was the common practice of the kelpie to assume the most fascinating form, and assimilate himself to that likeness, which he supposed most congenial to the inclinations of his intended victim.

The likeness of a fine riding steed was his favourite disguise. Decked out in the most splendid riding accoutrements, the perfidious kelpie would place himself in the weary traveller's way, and graze by the road-side with all the seeming innocence and simplicity in the world . . . he was as calm and peaceable as a lamb, until his victim was once fairly mounted on his back; with a fiend-like yell he would then announce his triumph, and plunging headlong with his woe-struck rider into an adjacent pool, enjoy him for his repast.

Chapter Seventeen

Dave's letter lay on the kitchen floor where she'd dropped it when she saw the light from the library. As Kathleen bent to pick it up she remembered the last she'd seen of him, running off with some strangers only minutes after agreeing to come back with her for dinner. But before she could get too indignant over the way she'd been abandoned, she recalled the compulsion she'd felt to stay in that room on top of the library, the room that did not exist. If not for Nell, she'd be there still. Strange things were happening, undoubtedly. She couldn't presume to judge his behaviour without more information.

So, instead of throwing it away as she'd meant to do earlier, she slit open the square blue envelope with a table knife, took out the folded sheet of paper it contained, and held it up to read by the murky light that filtered through the kitchen window.

Dearest Kathleen,

Although I haven't seen or spoken to you since Saturday night, you've hardly left my mind. I tried to call several times, but 'No network coverage' said my mobile, and my landline has become even more mysteriously unreliable than usual. My noble (and formerly trusted) steed took me only as far as the sign which always makes me think of Virginia Woolf before collapsing.

I'll spare you the mechanical details. Suffice to say it has been repaired, I have wheels again, and I really should have managed, as intended, to turn up at the library before it closed today.

The reason I didn't is because of you, actually, and I hope you'll forgive me when you know why.

I've written a song.

(I feel those words should leap off the page in neon lights, at the very least!)

It's the first song I've written in over three years, and it's for you.

I must see you. I won't leave Appleton until I do. I'll be back shortly.

Your

Dave

She gulped. Her heart was fluttering; she felt like someone in an old-fashioned romantic novel – no, like the teenaged fan she'd once been. He'd written a song for her!

Again she recalled her last sight of him, the greying reddish ponytail bouncing against the back of his smart leather jacket as he walked quickly, almost running . . .

He'd been running *after* that crowd; he wasn't with them; he'd been struggling to catch up, while they'd strolled on, completely unaware . . . Who were they that had drawn him away, that he'd been so desperate to reach?

She thought of the ghost and the secret room inside the library dome. She'd had Nell to draw her back to reality, but Dave was on his own. She grabbed her purse and her car keys and went out to find him.

Even in a small town it was hard to know where to begin.

Since her car was still parked in front of the library, she had only to drive half a mile and turn left on the Esplanade to find herself back in front of the Victoria Hotel, at almost the same spot where she'd had her last sight of Dave. The hopeful attempt at a pavement cafe had been dismantled, the outside lights were off, and the hotel looked dark and deserted in the cool grey light.

She took the second turning at the pierhead circle, but was then stymied in her attempt to retrace his steps. Half a dozen smaller streets branched off it, and he might have taken any one of them. Yet it hardly mattered, for they all joined up with Main Street, and from there . . . Flipping a mental coin, she turned right, taking the road out of town as far as it allowed. Dave's car was still parked where he'd left it, the glossy red paint softly beaded with moisture: dew or sea spray. She noticed a soft grey fog hanging over the sea, gradually creeping closer to the land. At last she made sense of the strange light and odd, muffled atmosphere hanging over the town: fog.

Wrapped in the dim, foggy silence, the town slept. She met no one on the road, and the shops were all shut up tight. The clock in her car had chosen this inconvenient moment to die, and when she went past the town hall she saw the hands on its clock face both pointed straight up at twelve.

She shivered uneasily. It could not be mere coincidence. What sort of power would stop every clock in town? Or had time itself been suspended?

She felt a sudden, childish urge to hurry home, lock the doors, crawl into bed, and put her head under the covers. She wouldn't be surprised to learn that was what practically everyone else in the town was doing at that moment, waiting and praying for the return of normality. Unless, of course, they were all innocently asleep as they would be in the middle of the night, and it *was* still the middle of the night, despite this strange, sourceless grey light.

On her first drive along the Esplanade, past the harbour,

she'd noticed people hanging around on the pier. So, having found everywhere else so deserted, she was drawn back there. Slowing her car to a crawl along the Esplanade, she peered out at the dockside activity, and her unease grew. *Who are all these people? And what are they doing, so alert and busy, while the town sleeps*? Then, at last, among all the strangers she glimpsed a single familiar figure: an old codger in a filthy old sweater and knitted cap, with a pipe sticking out of the side of his mouth as if growing there. He was often to be seen on a bench gazing out to sea, or loitering on the pier, offering advice to visiting sailors, and on very wet days he'd sometimes pass a whole afternoon in the library, poring over the latest issues of *The Fishing News*. As she parked her car nearby and walked back to the pier, she searched her memory for the old man's name.

'Mr McNaughton!' she called out brightly, the name popping into her mind just in time. 'Good morning!'

'Is it?' He levered himself slowly off a bench, peering at her suspiciously from beneath bushy white eyebrows.

'I'm Kathleen Mullaroy, from the library,' she said, thinking he hadn't recognized her.

'Aye, I know fine who you are.'

'I'm looking for someone. I wondered if you might have seen him go past. Dave Varney is his name, and he's–'

'Mr Varney as stays out at White Gates?'

'You know him?'

He gave a grunt and shifted his cold pipe in his mouth. 'Not to speak to. I knows him by sight.'

'Did you see him? It might have been a few hours ago . . . possibly with a group of people.'

The old man removed his pipe and went and knocked it sharply against the back of the bench. 'I saw them, all right. Took it he was going home. Time I was off myself.' Replacing the pipe in its accustomed place, he steadied himself and began to walk away with slow, careful steps. After four or five steps he stopped and turned back. 'You want to get yourself home, too. Don't hang about here – it's not safe.'

'Why?' She couldn't stop herself glancing around at the other people. There were now only a few left on the pier; the others had returned to the boats lying at anchor, or otherwise melted away out of sight.

He shook his head slowly. 'You've seen the fog, haven't you?'

'It's not so bad.'

'It'll get worse. And if you get yourself lost in it – well. You don't want to be out alone when the fog comes in. You don't want to get yourself lost. Go home.'

'I'll be careful. Did you speak to Dave, Mr McNaughton? Did he say anything?'

'Go home,' he said again, and turned away.

But going home was not an option – not until she knew Dave was safe. She went back to her car and headed for the hills. She had only a rough idea where White Gates Farm might be, but as there were so few roads on the Apple, even a rough idea should be good enough. If Dave had struck out for home on foot, there was a chance she'd meet him on the way.

She allowed herself this hopeful fantasy: finding him a mile or two outside of town, standing sheepishly with his thumb out, tired and confused but suffering from no more than inconvenience and embarrassment. And then she'd take him home.

'Next time, *tell* me before you go off,' she said, like a bossy mother, addressing the imaginary hitchhiker. Next time, next time . . . Unexpected tears sprang to her eyes. 'Oh, Dave,' she cried out as if he could hear her. 'Dave, Dave, where *are* you?'

As the empty miles clicked past, her hope withered. There were no other cars on the road at all, and this new day – if it was day – was weirdly birdless. The only living creatures she saw as she drove past fields and farmland were a lot of bedraggled sheep, two pale horses, and a herd of black-and-white cows.

Thick clouds hung overhead, making the sky seem unnaturally low, as if a huge, opaque bell jar had descended upon the land, isolating it from all the known world.

The road gradually rose, and farmland gave way to rough, rocky moors. She drove past a pond – what they called a 'lochan' here. The water looked very still and deep and gleamed like a black mirror beneath the paler sky, and for no obvious reason she felt oppressed by the lonely sight. Then, on the other side of the road, she saw the sign: TO THE LIGHTHOUSE and the line from Dave's letter came back to her; she could practically hear him saying it, 'the sign which always makes me think of Virginia Woolf . . .'

Her heart leaped, and, in a surge of giddy excitement, she pressed down too hard on the accelerator.

It should have been all right. There was absolutely no traffic; she hadn't encountered a single car or person since she'd left Appleton, and the road stretched reasonably straight and empty ahead. But suddenly out of nowhere, a huge white horse stepped out onto the road in front of her.

She slammed on the brake; the car wobbled, fishtailed, and slewed around. Wrestling for control, she managed to bring it to a halt, but not before it had gone off the road, canting to one side, one wheel hanging in open air above the steep ditch.

'Oh, shit!'

She switched off the engine, yanked on the emergency brake, and then, terrified, scrambled out the passenger-side door, expecting all the time to feel the car shudder and roll over. It seemed a sort of miracle that she managed to escape unharmed, and that the car remained precariously balanced.

The horse was standing in the middle of the road, looking at her.

'Well, thank you *very* much,' she said, in a voice at least an octave higher than normal. She looked back at her car. Amazingly, it appeared undamaged, but clearly she would not be able to get it back onto the road by herself.

Looking back at the horse – undeniably a handsome animal – she realized it was saddled and bridled, all ready for riding, and a small note of alarm sounded in her mind. She scanned the other side of the road for a fallen rider, but there was no sign of anyone, either lying injured or stumbling after a runaway mount.

'Where's your owner?'

The horse whickered and moved toward her. Wary, she backed away. It appeared friendly, but then so had the Shetland pony who'd nipped her painfully on the arm when she was ten, establishing her lifelong attitude of extreme caution around all members of the equine race.

Perhaps sensing her unease, the animal stopped. It dropped its head, then angled around to present its side to her as if inviting her to mount.

'Oh, yeah, and what'd you do with your last rider? No thanks.' She turned away to peer anxiously along the road again, longing for the sight of someone, anyone, who could help her. An ancient noisy tractor, a taciturn shepherd with dog riding pillion on his quad-bike, even a limping teenager screaming abuse at her runaway steed.

'Hello!'

A man's voice boomed right behind her, and she whirled

around, shocked, to find a very fit young man beaming at her. Looking back, she could see no other vehicle but her own drunkenly leaning car; even the horse had disappeared.

'Where did you come from?'

He pointed in the direction of the lochan.

'You live over there? Very near?'

He nodded, still smiling in his open, friendly way, and she sighed with relief.

'Thank goodness! That's my car,' she explained. 'I need help. Is your phone working? No? Ah, well, do you have a car? Truck? Tractor? Anything, really . . .' As he went on cheerfully shaking his head, she bit her lip. 'Well, you must know somebody who does! All I need is something to pull the car back up onto the road – if we had some rope—'

'I could get rope,' he volunteered.

'But not a car? Don't you drive?'

'Never have,' he admitted cheerfully.

She sighed. 'Actually, even a horse might – hey, did you see it? That beautiful white horse? Was it yours?' It was suddenly obvious, explaining the mystery.

'Want to come back to my place?'

She was taken aback. It was clear what he meant from the way he eyed her, and in another situation she might have been flattered that such a handsome young hunk found her attractive, but under the circumstances it just made her nervous.

'No, thank you,' she said cautiously, with an appeasing

smile. 'Actually, I'm expected somewhere – White Gates. They'll be wondering where I am – probably come out to look for me soon! Do you know White Gates?'

He nodded slowly. 'I know. I could show you, later, after we go to my place. I've got rope there – you said you wanted rope?'

'Rope's not any use to me without a truck or a tractor to pull my car up,' she explained. 'Or a horse – if you think your horse could do it.'

He scowled in confusion. 'I thought you didn't want the horse.'

Oh, dear. 'I just want my car back on the road.'

That seemed to cheer him up. He looked past her, down the road at her precariously tilting car. 'I could do that for you.'

'I wish you would!'

Keeping a slight distance, she followed him back to her car and watched without saying anything as he made a half circuit of it, bending and peering as he made his own sense of its position. Then he clambered down into the ditch, set his shoulder against the front end, and, with one mighty heave, levered the car up and onto the road.

She stared, openmouthed. True, the Micra was a small car, but the strength that must have taken . . .

'That was amazing,' she said as he came bounding back.

He grinned broadly. A light sheen of perspiration stood out on his brow, but he wasn't even breathing hard. 'That was easy. I'm strong. Anything else I can do for you?'

She shook her head quickly. 'No, I don't think so. You've already done so much!' She edged toward the driver's-side door, trying to keep cool although her heart was hammering. There were so many ways he could stop her leaving if he wanted to . . .'I'd better check that everything's all right, that it'll start after that . . .' She slipped in behind the wheel, and turned on the ignition as he watched blankly. The engine caught immediately.

'Great!' she cried. 'Thank you so much!'

He seemed to take in for the first time that she was leaving, and sprang forward, hand out to seize the door handle, but she'd already stomped down on the accelerator, and the small car shot away out of his reach. She felt a tiny twinge of guilt for treating him so callously when all he'd done was help her – she didn't *know* that he'd meant her any harm; despite his lustful gaze and stupendous strength, maybe all he wanted was to take her home for a nice cup of tea and introduce her to his hardworking mother. Her eyes flashed to the rearview mirror. She expected to see him standing desolate in the road, staring after her, but there was no sign of him, nothing there except the large white horse she'd encountered earlier.

Startled, she stepped on the brake, and twisted around to make sure of what she'd seen. Where had he gone? And where had the horse come from? She couldn't see anywhere to hide on this stretch of empty road and moor.

The horse suddenly veered about and galloped off the road, heading straight for the lochan. It didn't stop at the water's edge, but plunged straight in and, while she gaped, disappeared in a churning spray, beneath the silvery water. She went on watching, expecting the great head to erupt, snorting, above the surface as the horse swam across, but all that happened was that the choppy waves gradually died away, and the ripples of disturbance grew smaller and slower until finally the water in the little lochan was again as still and calm as a dark mirror.

Shivering, she turned around in her seat again and discovered that the engine had died. This time, when she tried to start it, there was no response. For the first time in their happy, four-year relationship, her dear little car had let her down.

Although it seemed to be totally dead, she went through her repertoire of psychological voodoo tricks: letting it rest, turning the key in different ways, jiggling the gear stick, promising various rewards if it would start and punishments if it remained stubborn.

Finally, she had to get out and start walking. She felt very exposed without the protective shell of her car, and walked as fast as she could without actually running.

She had read somewhere, or been told that, despite its small size, the Apple contained such a variety of landscape features that it reflected Scotland in miniature. It offered mountains, moors, bogs, lochs, rivers, forests, and farmland, as well as both rugged coastline and sheltered bays, sandy beaches, and rocky cliffs, all compressed into such a small space that the scenery changed dramatically almost minute by minute as she travelled through it by car. She felt grateful for that scenic diversity now, as the bleak empty moorland gave way to mixed woodland.

Only, as she glanced into the shadowy depths of the forest, she saw flickers of movement deep within, and realized maybe the change wasn't such an improvement. She froze at the sound of snapping twigs, the crunch and clatter of disturbed undergrowth. There was something large moving in there among the trees, and it was coming her way.

She still hadn't decided what to do when he came crashing out onto the road: a man wearing muddy blue jeans and a once-smart, now sadly battered, leather jacket; a man with long, greying red hair, which fell in tangled strands around a flushed and weary face; a man who looked worn-out, middle-aged, totally uncool, and unutterably dear to her. Her heart turned over. 'Dave!'

His head came up and he looked around, his eyes wide but unseeing. 'Kathleen? Where are you?'

'I'm right here.'

He put his arms out like a blind man. 'Keep talking, so I can find you.'

A lump rose in her throat; she thought of Jane Eyre finding Rochester at the end, and could not speak.

'Kathy?'

'To – to your right, and straight ahead. Just a few steps – here—' She stepped forward to meet him, and then they were in each other's arms, clinging together.

She closed her eyes and rejoiced in his solid, real presence, breathing in the smells of leather and damp cloth and his warm, perspiring flesh.

'Oh, God, you're real. It's really you. Kathleen. How did you find me?'

'I don't know.' She pulled away slightly to look at him. 'What happened to your eyes?'

'My eyes? Nothing.' They were more green than she'd remembered.

'You can see me?' Even as she asked the question she knew there was nothing wrong with the eyes that looked back into hers. 'Why couldn't you see me before?'

'Well, because it was so dark!'

'It's not dark.'

'No, not now,' he agreed, looking around, then back at her, with a warmth in his eyes that made her go weak in the knees.

He let go of her and stepped back, looking around, getting his bearings. 'I think I know this wood, but I'm not sure. Do you know where we are?'

'The sign for the lighthouse is back that way.' She pointed back the way she'd come. 'Maybe a mile.'

He whistled. 'I did get turned around. Still, that's not too bad. Where's your car?'

'Not going anywhere.' She explained about it breaking down, describing its position in relation to the lochan, but not mentioning the man who'd turned into a horse.

'OK, so we walk – it's a couple of miles to my house, but there's nothing else any closer.'

He took her hand and they began to walk along the road. For a while they went in silence, matching their steps, developing an easy rhythm that made them comfortable with each other.

'I owe you an apology, and an explanation,' he said at last. 'You know about Kay.'

'Your wife.'

'My late wife. She died a year and a half ago. I loved her very much, and I still miss her, but – she's dead.' He sighed. 'Start again. Do you remember when we first met?'

'In the library, with the heavy reference book?'

He grinned. 'Nearly knocked *me* out, anyway. So I started flirting with you—'

'Never!'

'Don't tell me you didn't notice?' He gave her a sidelong glance, fluttering his eyelashes.

'That's not what I meant. I thought it was *me* flirting with you.'

'Snap. So, there we were, both of us enjoying ourselves, when that grumpy old man came and banged his book down on the counter to get your attention.'

'The ever-patient, soon-to-be-sainted, Mr Rand.'

'The book had a picture of a swan on the cover.'

Unable to remember, sure it could not be important, she shrugged.

He went on: 'Swans mate for life.'

'Oh?'

'So I've heard. And when one of them dies, the other one just pines away. No second marriages for Mr or Mrs Swan. That's the thought – well, the association – that came into my mind at that moment, and it hit me like a ton of bricks. I was really, really attracted to you.' He cleared his throat. 'I mean, more than just appreciating your looks and charm and wit – it was . . . I hadn't felt like that about anyone for a long, long time. Not since I first met Kay. And – when I made that connection, well, it really did my head in. I had to turn around and walk away just to get some kind of control – that's why I wasn't there when you'd finished dealing with Mr Rand.'

She tried to pull her hand away, but he held it more tightly. 'Do you mind letting go my hand?'

'Why?'

'It just seems very inappropriate for you to be holding my hand while you tell me why there can never be anyone in your life but your late wife.'

'That's not what I'm telling you.'

'No?'

'No.'

He stopped walking to face her and gazed intently into

her eyes. 'I thought I was supposed to be good with words; I don't know why I'm doing such a rotten job of explaining.'

She thought she saw fog creeping in from the seaward side, but when she turned her head to look, it wasn't there. But the air seemed thicker, somehow, and the light more dim. 'I think we should keep walking. And go faster.'

'OK. Can we still hold hands?'

She didn't object, and they went on as before. She liked the comfort of his warm clasp, even when her heart was aching.

'What I'm trying to say, in my clumsy way is that I'm not, and never could be, a swan. I'm a faithful type, but, well, death is the end . . . at least as far as *this* life is concerned, and I'm not planning to go celibate to my grave.

'Kay and I had even talked about it. She'd expected I'd get married again – she thought I was good husband material, despite my many flaws – too good to stay on the shelf. And I started dating about six or seven months ago, but more because it seemed like I *should* and friends kept wanting to fix me up with all these amazingly gorgeous, kind, single women. But nothing clicked. I was just kind of going through the motions, and, frankly, it was kind of depressing.

'That's actually why I came back here. I wanted to get away by myself and think about what I was going to do with the rest of my life – whether I should sell White Gates . . .'

'Because it had been Kay's place?'

'No.' He sounded surprised. 'I'd been coming to Appleton before I met her. The thing was, I'd had the old barn converted to a recording studio, with the idea of making it a commercial venture. I didn't go ahead with that because – well, because then we'd got Kay's diagnosis. I decided to spend a few weeks here, to get the feel of whether or not it could work for me, living by myself and working at White Gates.'

'And then the landslide happened.'

'And then I met you.' He squeezed her hand.

They walked on a little way more in silence. 'So why did you run away from me last night?'

'Not away from you. It was such bad timing.' He took a deep breath. 'I saw Kay. I knew it couldn't be, but – there she was, across the Esplanade, walking past the harbour with a group of people. One of them I recognized – my old mate, Mickey Stark.'

She recognized the name of a pop star who'd taken a fatal overdose twenty years ago.

'So you ran after them.'

'Kathleen, what would *you* have done? If two people you had loved, and thought were dead, went past on the street? Wouldn't you go after them?'

She tried to imagine it, but everyone she'd ever loved was still alive, apart from her grandparents, and she barely remembered them now. She picked him up on his phrasing. '*Thought* were dead?'

He sighed. 'OK, *knew*. I was with Kay when she died, and I had no illusions that Mickey could have been spirited away to Tibet, but – I damn sure knew I wasn't dreaming. I couldn't just let them go without trying to talk to them, find out what it meant, what was happening.

'I yelled out Kay's name. She heard me, I'm sure, because she stopped and looked around. I was waving my arms and jumping up and down like a crazy, but, I don't know, she never would wear her glasses except for driving, and her long-distance vision wasn't great, especially at night. When she turned her face toward me, I knew beyond any doubt that it was Kay, not just somebody who slightly resembled her.

'If you'd been there – but you weren't. I thought it wouldn't take more than a couple of minutes. I'd catch up to them, I'd speak to *her* – and then I'd come back.'

'So what happened?'

'I can't explain it. Even though they seemed to be strolling along, and I was walking as fast as I could, I never could catch up to them. Kay never paused or looked back, no matter how I shouted. I didn't realize how long I'd been chasing them until I was right out of town, in the middle of the dark countryside. And then . . . not only did I realize that I was totally lost, but I had a moment of clarity when I understood that not only was I trailing along after phantoms, but that there was something sinister going on. I'd been lured away from *you* – the very person I should have been looking after – I wondered what might have happened to you. So I turned around and tried to make my way back to you, tried to find you – and it just got darker, and darker – until, in the end, I heard your voice. It was *you* who found *me*. You saved me,' he finished, simply, squeezing her hand.

She could think of nothing to say.

'So what happened to you?' he asked, and she told him about her adventure in the library.

'Mm, I can't help wishing I'd been there. So now I'm forever in Nell's debt, for saving you. Here we are, this is my road,' he said.

She saw a small sign announcing PRIVATE ROAD emerging from the mist, and realized at the same moment just how thick the fog had become. Looking back, she could see only swirling white clouds, masking everything else.

'We won't get lost as long as we hang on to each other and stick to the road,' he said, reading her thoughts. 'It'll take us right to my door. It's less than half a mile now.'

'What happens if you hear your wife calling to you from over there somewhere?'

'I'll cling all the more tightly to you. And if you see anyone, or any mystery lights, don't go following them, all right? We'll keep each other safe.'

She realized as he spoke that she didn't feel frightened. Whatever was to come, they would face it together.

They made it to the house without incident. Inside the large and welcoming farmhouse kitchen – it reminded her of Nell's, only without the decorative stencil work – she gazed at the windows and saw nothing but the pale mass of fog on the other side of the glass. Behind her, Dave cursed softly.

She turned around. 'What's wrong?'

'Electricity's out. Damn. I really wanted some coffee. Shall I open a bottle of wine?' She shook her head.

The silence stretched between them. He looked pensive. 'I could probably rustle up something to eat . . . otherwise, there's water. Normally, I'd put some music on . . .'

'Why don't you play me my song?'

'What?'

'Your new song, I mean. You did say it was for me.'

He glanced away. 'So you did get my letter.'

'Well?'

'Oh, well, it needs a lot of work yet. I'm not really sure about the bridge . . . and a couple of the words . . . besides, I'm a lousy singer, and it should have a string section and a piano. It has to be orchestrated–'

'So it was just bullshit, your letter.'

'No!' He looked hurt. 'God, Kathleen! I poured my heart out to you–'

'You really wrote me a song?'

'Yes.'

'And you won't even sing it to me?'

He sighed, capitulating. 'OK, but be gentle with me. I can't sing for toffee.'

'Hey, I'm your biggest fan! Besides, nobody's ever written me a song before – how could I not like it?'

The sitting room was smaller and darker than the kitchen, but the walls lined with shelves full of books, records, and CDs, the comfortable-looking chairs, sofa, floor cushions, and oriental rugs on top of a pale, thick-pile carpet, gave it a cozy, appealing atmosphere. Dave picked up the guitar resting across the arms of one chair and sat down with it. She settled down nearby to listen.

The song was about someone walking home at night and losing his way; stopping to ask a stranger for directions, he finds that she seems to know who he is and where he lives, and she takes him by the hand to guide him home. The road they travel is at once familiar and strange, and the house she takes him to is *her* home – a place he's never seen before, but which he knows at once is where he wants to spend the rest of his life.

He had a pleasant, unemphatic voice, not especially melodic, but he could carry a tune. She was completely unable to judge the song by any objective standards. How could she compare it to others when this was *her* song? When it was so simply and openly about his feelings for her?

When he finished he looked at her, and she didn't make him wait. She opened her arms and looked at him with all the love in her heart. 'Let's go to bed.'

From *The Woman's Dictionary of Symbols and Sacred Objects*
by Barbara G. Walker
(HarperCollins, 1988)

MUCH of the reverence paid to the apple arose not only from its value as food, but also from the secret, sacred sign in its core: the pentacle, which is revealed when the apple is transversely cut. Gypsies claimed this was the only proper way to cut an apple, especially when it was shared between lovers before and after sexual intercourse. At Gypsy weddings it was customary for the bride and groom to cut the apple, revealing its pentacle, and eat half apiece. Such marriage customs may suggest the real story behind Eve's sharing of an apple with her spouse: an idea that developed quite apart from the biblical version, in which there is no mention of an apple, but only of a 'fruit'.

Chapter Eighteen

After making love, Ronan fell asleep, but although she was tired and physically sated, Ashley was too preoccupied with thoughts of what was to happen next to do the same. It wasn't that she wanted to back out, but what had she gotten herself into? All his talk about 'your heart's desire' – what did that mean? What *was* her heart's desire? Was it, could it be, this strange man lying warm and close beside her? Did she need to have a particular wish in mind when she ate the apple, or would blind faith be enough?

She listened to his breathing as it slowed and deepened, and when it became a mild snore, she edged away from him, slipped out of bed, and padded quietly out of the room, pausing to shut the door softly behind her.

She felt starved. There was a box of Cheerios in the kitchen; she carried it back to the sofa, turning on the

TV as she passed from force of habit before remembering what her cousins had said about there being no reception in the area. Nevertheless, she clicked through channel after channel of hissing grey visual static, just in case, until she was rewarded at last by a picture, an outdoor scene on a beach with glittering white sand and brilliant sea beneath a wide blue sky She opened the box and seized a handful of Cheerios while gazing with mild, detached interest at the scene.

Scottish Cheerios were different from the ones she was used to; they had a sweet frosting. She was surprised, but too hungry to mind, and she munched away as she tried to figure out what she was watching. A movie or a commercial? She couldn't identify the soft music in the background, although there was something hauntingly familiar about it, and she thought she almost recognized the scenery, too. She had an idea it was a beach where lots of stuff had been filmed, maybe an island in the Caribbean, or maybe Hawaii.

People – all fit and healthy and young – strolled past occasionally in couples, or ran down to the water in small groups. By her third handful of Cheerios she was growing impatient. What was the point of this undramatic scenery? Cut to the chase, she thought; show us the star, or make the pitch. Even if she'd tuned in to a local community access channel, and this was somebody's holiday video, there ought to be somebody who'd pause and mug for the camera. Only the fact that there was nothing else on, and that it seemed too much trouble to pick up the remote and switch off, kept her watching.

Finally, the camera began to close in on one of the young people on the beach. A girl in a bikini, a young woman with long blonde hair, almost a standard-issue beach babe, except that her breasts were smaller than the Hollywood norm, and she could have been Freya's clone.

The half-chewed Cheerios turned to sugared sawdust in her mouth. She tensed and leaned forward, blinking in disbelief. As if in response to her wish, the camera zoomed in closer and closer, and with every magnification the likeness to Freya was more staggeringly complete. That was her best friend's slightly heavy-footed walk, her smile, even the tiny mole beside her left eyebrow . . .

What *was* this? Could it be, somehow, film from a family holiday? But Freya's family didn't go to exotic beach resorts, and no way was that pale sand and azure water on the Texas coast – if Freya had ever been anywhere like that in her life, Ashley would have known all about it. So how – where – when . . .? Ashley gave a soft whimper of disbelief and struggled upright on the lumpy old sofa. Was it possible that her friend was still alive? That the reports of her death, the funeral, all the grief, had been some gigantic con? A guy came running up, grabbed Freya's hand, and off they ran together, laughing, to splash through the surf. Their backs, receding from her, were golden-brown and dusted lightly with sand, so real and close she could practically smell the suntan lotion, and it hit her: this was *now*, not something filmed in the past, but the present moment, a glimpse of Freya's present, ongoing life. To ancient Celts, heaven was to be found on an island in the west.

With a sharp whine, the television screen went blank; at the same moment, the table lamp and the light in the kitchen both went out, and she cried out as the room was plunged into darkness.

She made herself stay where she was, getting her bearings. It wasn't as dark as all that; the living room curtains were heavy, but the kitchen window was uncovered, and she could make out a faint, murky glow. Gradually, as her eyes adjusted, she realized it was no longer night-time. Hours had passed; she must have slept, even though she thought she hadn't.

'What's wrong?' A pale, naked figure appeared in the doorway.

Her face felt stiff as she tried to smile. 'Nothing. I was startled. We've lost electricity.'

He came farther into the room and held out his hand to her. She let him pull her up off the sofa. As soon as they touched, her nervousness went. She kissed him where a crease line from the pillow marked his cheek, and felt beard stubble against her lips.

'Come on,' he said gently, drawing her back to the

bedroom. She went with him eagerly, but as she began to caress him, he caught her hands to stop her. 'Get dressed.'

She pouted. 'Why?'

'It's late. There's no time to lose. We have to go.'

Unease roiled and clenched in her stomach, matching the tension in his voice. She watched him gathering up the clothes he'd abandoned so hastily a few hours earlier, and she thought of Freya running on that beach, wherever it was, wherever *she* was.

'Just before the electricity went off, I saw my best friend on television – she was on a beach – I think it was real, and I think it was now – but she's dead.'

'This upset you?'

'Ronan, she's dead! She's not romping around on some island paradise—'

He straightened up, holding his shirt. 'Don't you believe in Heaven?'

She scowled at him uncertainly and shrugged. 'I guess.' Her belief was halfhearted, at best. At worst, when someone said Heaven she thought of cartoon angels standing around on fluffy white clouds; she was more than half-afraid 'gone to Heaven' was no more than a euphemism, a weak attempt to comfort children for the loss of pets and grandparents, not a rational explanation.

He pressed her. 'Do you believe there's a life after death?'

'Well . . . I think there has to be *something*,' she admitted, for how could there be nothing? How could this earth be all that there was? A soul's existence could surely not be bound and limited entirely by one single fragile body.

'And your friend was a good person?'

'Of course!'

'She looked happy?'

'Yes.'

'Then I don't understand.' He tilted his head to one side. 'What's bothering you?'

'If that was Heaven – or wherever Freya is now – how could I see it?'

'I'd guess . . . well, the normal barriers are down now. Maybe . . . maybe you're nervous about coming with me, and your friend wanted to show you there's nothing to fear.'

She felt dizzy. 'So that's where we're going? To Heaven?'

He gave her his full attention. 'We're not going to die. Stop worrying.'

'So, I'm not going to die, but I'm going to see Freya again?'

'If that's your dearest wish, then yes.'

Of course she wanted her best friend back, but that was impossible. As for joining Freya where she was now – that had to mean dying; there could be no other way.

'How?'

He shook his head. 'Don't ask me – it's magic. This is the year of the golden apple, and anything can happen. It will give you whatever you want the most.'

You don't know what that is, she thought. I *don't even know*. Her mind went blank. Why did she trust this stranger? What was going to happen to her?

'Put your clothes on, love,' he said gently.

Stalling for time, she said, 'I'll take a shower first.'

'You can't.' He met her glare with a mocking smile. 'It's electric.'

She gave in to the inevitable and went to the dresser to hunt out fresh underwear and a clean T-shirt. The jeans she'd worn earlier, damp and grass-stained as they were, would do.

He sat on the edge of the bed, putting on his socks. She sat down beside him and took a deep breath. 'Be honest with me.'

He turned to face her squarely, unsmiling. 'Of course.'

'Why did my grandmother run away? Why didn't she go with you when she had the chance?'

'Her ambitions were worldly. I wasn't her heart's desire. Nothing on offer here was. She was more interested in Hollywood than Paradise. She was only nineteen.'

'I'm nineteen.'

'I know.' He patted her knee. 'Put your shoes on.'

She pulled her leg away, resenting his patronizing attitude.

'Tell me what happened. What was she afraid of?'

'She wasn't afraid,' he said, sounding weary.

'Why did she run away from you?'

'She didn't run away from *me*. Just from this place. The expectations and limited horizons . . .'

'Not from you?'

'I'm the one who *helped* her. Who do you think gave her money enough to go to America?'

She gaped at him, abruptly unbalanced, feeling all her preconceptions overturned. 'You did? I don't understand . . . why?'

'We formed an alliance. We were friends – partners – united in the wish to get away – not lovers. She set out to seduce me. I was tempted, sure, and flattered, but I was no despoiler of innocent young virgins, and I had no intention of getting married. When it didn't work out as she'd planned, she was straight with me, told me what she wanted, and I agreed to help her out. We announced our engagement.

'I don't know how the Apple Queen was chosen – men didn't know; it was the women's business. They chose their representative each year, and of course *she* chose her partner, the man she wished to share the apple with, even though it might appear, to an outsider, to be the other way around. Until nineteen fifty when the rare golden apple appeared, the first since my mother was the queen, and the powers that be in this town decided that their best interests would be served by using me. I don't know why it never occurred to them that I cared for most of the local people as little as they cared for me, and that the winning of *my* heart's desire might not be in their best–'

She interrupted. 'But you didn't eat the apple! So you didn't get your heart's desire, so–'

'Oh, but I did. My heart's desire was to get clear of this place *and* take my revenge on it. Phemie didn't need any magic for hers, either. All she asked was to escape, with the chance to try her luck in Hollywood, and I gave her the money to do just that. We didn't need a magic apple to give us anything, because going out in the world and getting it for ourselves was what it was all about. Just in case the old stories were true, and our good luck would be shared in by the town, I practised a bit of sleight of hand and substituted another apple – not even locally grown! – and that was what we ate in front of the crowds.'

His expression hardened. 'For once in my life, that night they didn't hate me. They thought I was finally doing something right. They needed some powerful magic to revive the local economy. If they'd only realized how much I'd done for this town over the years, how much Appleton's fortunes were tied up with my business, they wouldn't have been so eager to see the last of me. But I had no intention of leaving my inheritance behind. I planned my escape. I spent months shifting my money around, out of the business, and by the time I left Wall's Cider was mortgaged to the hilt and the notes were due. There was no money to pay employees, and the orchards had to be sold to pay off the mortgages – sold at a loss because the trees weren't bearing and nobody wanted them. It was over; all the while they'd been complaining, they'd never realized how good life really had been. Things could only get worse. But not for me – I'd bought myself a new life, to live wherever and however I wanted.'

Watching him, hearing the pain from the past still ringing in his words, she felt her emotions toward him shift and change. He wasn't the powerful being she'd imagined, and she wasn't in his thrall. She almost pitied him.

'So why did you come back?'

'I nearly ruined this town – maybe now I can save it.' He stopped and looked searchingly into her face. 'I mean, of course, *we* can. This is what I came here for, I know it now, and you were called, too, for the same reason. You felt it.'

She shook her head. It hadn't been like that for her at all; there'd never been any compulsion. It was all a matter of impulse, drifting, whims, and chance. You went to Scotland because your father gave you the ticket, and you didn't have anything better to do. Her ties to Appleton were recent and tenuous; she couldn't get all emotional about it. And as for Ronan, well, he was definitely hot, but that didn't make him the great love of her life.

But he didn't want to hear her protests, her second thoughts, her stumbling explanation; none of that mattered. She realized that he didn't really care how she felt, or what she wanted; he was just using her because he needed a woman, because the magic would not work for him alone. For all she knew, his dearest desire might be death – after all, despite his vigour and youthful appearance, he'd been living in this world for ninety years. And if he was wishing for death and all she could think of was her dead best friend–

He got up and pulled her to her feet.

'Wait!'

He waited.

'Look, I'm just not sure . . .' She heard how weak she sounded and was annoyed with herself for being so pathetic. After all, she reminded herself, she'd started this. And maybe it was too late to back out. But she needed more encouragement from him.

'Ashley, we're running out of time.' He gripped her hand more firmly and looked deep into her eyes. 'You're thinking we're not the great loves of each other's lives, but we do all right.' He pulled her to him, then, and did what she'd been hoping he'd do. He kissed her long and hard, so she didn't have to think.

After that, he let her pause just long enough to tie her shoelaces and grab her rucksack before they left the house.

Outside, she was startled by the fog hanging like heavy curtains on all sides. Walking through the weirdly muffled streets they met no one; not another living thing was stirring, only the slow, ominous, wavelike movements of the occluded air. It was like being in the clouds, and as they headed out of town on the main road, it got worse.

The numbing, comforting quality of his kiss had worn off. She was very aware of the chilly touch of the fog, and felt uneasy at the way they were rushing ahead so blindly. She pulled at his arm, trying to get him to slow his pace. 'Where are we going?'

'To get the apple, I told you.'

'Where is it?'

'Orchard House.'

'I don't know where that is.'

He sighed. 'On a hill at the edge of town. Can't you walk a bit faster?'

'Does it have to be that apple?'

'Of course it does. It's not just symbolic, you know. Eating an ordinary apple wouldn't–'

'Not an ordinary apple – Phemie's apple. Would that work?'

He stopped short and pulled her around to face him. 'Are you telling me she kept it all these years? And you've got it?'

'I've got it. It's all shrivelled up – more than fifty years, no wonder! – but it smells heavenly.' She moistened her lips.

He didn't look delighted, or kiss her as she'd hoped. Instead, his eyes narrowed suspiciously. 'Show me.'

She shrugged off her backpack and reached inside,

found it at once, and handed it to him in the folded handkerchief. 'I should have told you before. We could have eaten it in bed.' She gazed up at him hopefully, still waiting for her reward, but he only stared at the little parcel in the palm of his hand, his nostrils flaring at the scent.

'Well? Will it do?'

'Yes,' he said flatly. 'Of course, this will do. Why not? We'll eat Phemie's apple, and we don't go back to *her* orchard – let her eat her own apple; let her share it with whomever she will.'

She felt her hackles rise with possessive jealousy. 'Her? Who are you talking about?'

'Never mind.'

'But I mind—'

'Forget it; come on.' He pulled her along, not even pausing when she stumbled.

'But where are we going?'

'We need a doorway.'

'What do you mean? What kind of doorway?' She felt breathless, trying to keep up with him.

'Like the one my mother used – in fact, it might as well be the same one. Its not far now.'

Chapter Nineteen

When Nell left the library in the strange, murky half-light that seemed to belong properly neither to day or to night, she felt more powerfully alive and sure of herself than she had in years.

Her impulse was to hurry, but she forced herself to take it easy, driving at a sedate and careful speed through the sleeping streets of the town, determined not to risk an accident. The odd light made everything so uncertain; she kept glimpsing strange shapes and movement from the corners of her eyes, accompanied by the feeling that *something* – animal? human? – was about to dart out into the road, but when she hit the brakes and took a second, sharper look, she saw that the movement came from a plastic bag caught and flapping on a bush, the lurking shape was only a child's toy lying abandoned in the gutter.

As she turned off the main road onto her driveway her sense of urgency increased. From the top of the hill, in front of her house, she usually had a good view of the sea, but today there was nothing to be seen but thick, white fog. Appleton was thoroughly isolated. This little spit of land, this almost-island, was being claimed – perhaps reclaimed – by a different reality. Was it her fault, had she brought this fate on them all by growing the apple in the first place, then refusing to share it with Ronan?

But how *could* it be her fault, when she'd known nothing about any of it? No, more likely, she'd been used. She'd been the unwitting instrument by which the golden apple could return; then Ronan, who could have had his pick of women in the town, had wanted to use her – and now, although she'd refused him at first out of pride and fear or sheer stubborn will, she'd made up her mind to use *him*.

If only it wasn't too late.

She jumped out of the car and, her heart pounding and breath catching as if she'd already run a mile, she raced around the house, through the garden, across the meadow, and into the familiar close, scented warmth of her walled orchard.

The apple was still there, the smooth golden skin glowing softly out of the shadows. Her deep, heartfelt sigh of relief stirred the thick blossom and sent a few fluttering gently to the ground.

It was still here. That meant that *he* would have to come to her again to get it. She only had to wait.

It should have been easy but, for the first time since she'd planted her apple trees, she drew no comfort from standing among them. Instead of feeling safely enclosed within the walls of her orchard, she felt dangerously isolated.

She looked at the apple again. There could be no magic without it, no rescue, no miraculous escape, no winning of her heart's desire – or his. He *had* to come here, towing along whichever young lovely he'd managed to seduce; she only had to wait, and step forward when he came through the door in the wall, and offer herself – she had no doubt that he'd forget the other woman immediately and share the apple with her instead.

Still her anxiety grew. She thought of the fog creeping in outside the sheltering walls, and, as she gazed at the golden apple, more blossom fell like snowflakes to the ground. What if it was too late? Or what if Ronan, as stubborn as she, refused to make another choice, or to return here uninvited?

Abruptly she turned on her heel and headed for the door in the wall. She was no good at being passive and simply waiting for others to decide her fate. As soon as she'd left the walled orchard she felt better, more hopeful, certain she'd made the right move. If there *was* some great power at work that had directed her steps so that she'd found the wild-growing apple tree to take a graft from when it was needed, maybe it would help her find Ronan.

She had no plan beyond going down the hill and driving around, but even that turned out to be impossible: her car was dead. She wasted no time in trying to fix it, seeing in its failure the hand of fate once again. In a car, in such a fog, she might so easily drive past him. If they were both on foot, they might be drawn together . . .

The fog had grown thicker. At the bottom of the hill, she couldn't see more than a foot in front of her. And the world was eerily silent. There were no crying seagulls, no sound of wind, not even the crashing of wave against rock, which she'd normally expect to hear along this stretch of the road. There was nothing but a briny tang in the air to indicate the nearness of the sea. Maybe everything else had vanished, leaving her alone in the fog, she thought. Maybe this was death.

And then she heard voices. She stopped and held her breath, straining to hear. She could barely make out the words, but one of them was his.

Her heart leaped, and her footsteps quickened, and all of a sudden, there he was, a familiar shape in the thick, foggy air.

'Ronan!'

The joy that lit his face when he saw her told her everything she wanted to know, but she asked anyway. 'It's not too late?'

He made his face a blank. 'Too late for what, *Mrs* Westray?'

'To save myself.'

He said nothing.

She went on, 'I've changed my mind. I will share the apple with you.'

The woman beside him clutched his arm and pressed against him possessively. 'It *is* too late,' she said. 'Too late for you, anyway. He's with me.'

Nell took her in with a single glance. Tall, slender, with a mass of curly black hair and full, pouting lips – she was just a pretty child. No competition. She met Ronan's gaze again.

'I shouldn't have sent you away. If what you told me is true . . .'

'I couldn't lie to you.'

'I won't lie to *you*,' she responded, making a swift decision, hoping she wouldn't regret the easy lies she *could* have told him. 'My husband is dead, but I still love him. If I could have my heart's desire, that stupid accident would never have happened, and I'd still have my life with him – I'd never have come to Appleton, never planted my orchard – there wouldn't even be this apple that you want, understand?'

He shrugged. 'I'm not sure . . .'

'I want back my life with Sam – *that's* my heart's desire; not you.'

All of a sudden he smiled, and the incredible tenderness in his expression took her breath away. 'All right. If I can give you that, I will.'

'No!' The girl yelped. 'Are you crazy? She doesn't even want you! She loves somebody else – so why would you want her?'

He gently disengaged his arm from hers, and looked down into her eyes. 'Well, then, I have to ask: why would you want *me*?'

The girl gave a sharp gasp, as if she'd just been punched, and tears filled her wide, shocked eyes. In spite of her own concerns, Nell felt sorry for her.

'Because I love you,' she whispered.

'No.' Ronan looked at her without any obvious emotion. 'You don't love me, Ashley. You'd like to be in love and lose yourself in it. You gave yourself to me because you're a lovely, warmhearted, generous girl, and I thought I needed you. But I don't; and you don't love me.'

He left her then and slipped his arm around Nell's waist, and almost immediately they were striding through the pale, obscuring clouds. It was like travelling in a dream, she thought, for although she could see no more than a foot in front of her, she had no fear, certain she was protected by the strong, warm arm around her waist, and that no misstep was possible.

Her thoughts flew ahead to the orchard where, once before, she'd imagined making love with Ronan beneath the fragrant trees. She felt a pleasurable tingle. This time she would not resist. This time, she would let it happen. But even as she glimpsed the sign for Orchard House looming out of the mist, he was pulling her past it.

'Hey, where are we going? That's the bottom of my driveway.'

'I know. It's not much farther now. Hard to tell in this fog, but I think we're nearly there.'

'Where? The apple's still in my orchard; I didn't bring it.'

'That doesn't matter now.'

He sounded confident, and she'd already made up her mind to do whatever he said, but she felt the faint, chilly touch of uncertainty, something colder than the fog wrapping around her, insinuating itself damply into her skin. 'So where are we going? We can't go much farther; we're nearly at the landslide now.'

'I think those are the rocks,' he said. 'Can you see them? Like warped church spires, pushing through the clouds.'

She knew the rocks he meant, those strange shapes looming over the road on the seaward side. At the sight of them, she stopped short, her heart pounding harder with a sudden unease.

'Don't stop now, come on, just a little farther,' he said, pulling her with him off the road, onto the grassy verge. She dug her heels in, resisting.

'What's wrong?' He spoke gently.

'This is where his mother jumped off the cliff.'

Nell started at the sound of Ashley's voice, so close to her ear.

She'd had no idea the girl was still following them; the fog muffled everything.

'Ashley, go away,' said Ronan.

'I won't. You have to tell her the truth. It's not fair. It's not right to try to trick her into it. Like you were going to trick me.' She turned her face to Nell. Her eyes looked huge, and two dark red spots burned in a face that was otherwise very pale. 'He told me we had to go through a doorway. Did he tell you that? I bet you didn't know that his mother did a whole book of sketches called *Doorways*. The very last one in the book was a picture of the rocks and the sky and the sea, seen from the side of the road. Right here.' She stamped her foot on the ground and waved at the wall of mist obscuring the sea. 'It was a picture of the sea and sky framed by those big pinnacles of rocks. And guess what? That's where she killed herself. She jumped off the cliff between those rocks. That was her doorway out of this world.'

Feeling a little sick, Nell looked at Ronan.

He kept his eyes calmly fixed on hers. 'She did jump. She did leave this world. She didn't die.'

'Just because they never found her body – *if* that's even true – it doesn't mean she was OK,' Ashley cried desperately. 'Please don't jump. Ronan, I don't care if you like her more than me, you can share the apple with her, I don't mind. But don't jump. At least wait until the fog clears.'

'You don't understand. It'll never clear if we don't go,' he said flatly. 'Now back off, Ashley. This is nothing to do with you.'

The tone of his voice made her back up a pace or two, but the girl didn't give up. Nell saw that she was trembling but determined as she stared at her. 'You're a sacrifice – did you know that? He thinks the two of you have to die to save this place.'

Ronan touched Nell's chin to make her look at him. 'We're not going to die,' he said quietly. 'There's no death. It's a new life for us both. *Will* you share this apple with me?'

Confused, she saw that he was holding two little dark brown crescents of dried fruit. Where had they come from? She thought of the fresh, ripe apple still hanging on the tree, and was sorry that she would never taste it. Although she could not see anything but fog on either side of them, she could feel the nearness of the sea, and she knew that the land dropped away very suddenly. A few steps in that direction would end in a nasty fall. Was that the plan?

She said, uncertainly, 'Couldn't we go back to the orchard? I thought . . . don't we have to make love first?'

He grinned. 'Is that disappointment I hear in your voice, my sweet? My, my, what would your husband say?'

Her face felt hot. She opened her mouth to make some snappish retort, and as soon as her lips were parted, he pushed the dried apple through, and, with his other hand, popped the other half into his own mouth.

The taste was astonishingly intense; her mouth flooded with saliva, and at once she smelled apples everywhere, as if she were standing in a small, unventilated room where the walls were lined with shelves and racks full of ripe fruits, some of them so overripe they were beginning to ferment. She chewed, quickly, and the taste became even richer, headier, alcoholic.

A ray of sunshine cut through the fog. Turning her head, she saw not the sea that she knew had to be there, but a narrow pathway stretching ahead, winding and vanishing in the mist and clouds. She smelled apple blossom and knew that somewhere very near was a springtime orchard.

Ronan gripped her hand. She didn't hesitate. They walked forward together.

Then she was falling.

She gasped and flailed her arms, but the emptiness had gone; she was contained, held, safe in his arms. Although she was still feeling giddy, she knew it would pass. There was no danger. It was only a brief dream of falling. She was grounded, alive, at home, where she belonged, naked in her lover's arms, and the smell of his warm skin was sweeter than apples, more intoxicating than wine. The great upwelling of love that overtook her was so powerful, her pleasure in his touch so complete, that she couldn't think of anything else. And yet there was no urgency, no hunger in her love for him; although it was intensely sensual and physical, it was not sexual in the usual way. His warm, close presence was all that she desired.

Gradually that feeling began to ebb. It was another dream, like the previous nightmare of emptiness and falling, but it was more meaningful, more true to her life, and she did not have to let it go entirely. It became a happy memory, part of the background, as the reality of her present surroundings intruded and gradually overwhelmed everything else.

It was her real life. She was waking. She was lying inside an enclosed space, on a thin foam mattress and pillow, cocooned inside a sleeping bag. She knew she wasn't on solid ground as she became aware that the strong, irregular motion in the background was not a dream. Finally, smell, that most potent sense, kicked in and she inhaled salt water, varnish, and a whiff of mildew. Then she knew for certain that she had been sleeping alone: his close, warm weight, that naked body, had been only a dream.

Groggy and confused, she opened her eyes and sat up carefully, aware now that she was exactly where she should be, in her bunk on board *Circe*, Sam's boat. Well, *their* boat, technically, since he'd with all his worldly goods her endowed in the marriage ceremony more than two years ago, but she still thought of it as his.

'Sam?' Her voice bounced back to her, muffled and weak in the close confines of the cabin. Where was he? Why was she alone below decks?

She fought her way free of the sleeping bag and rolled to her feet just as an especially strong wave hit the boat and jarred her sideways. She banged her arm painfully on a bulkhead as she struggled to keep her balance, and the pain was enough to assure her that this was no dream. Why had she thought it might be? Her mental disequilibrium increased. Of course she knew where she was, *when* it was – that other life, that other person was just a dream.

But what kind of a dream? How was it possible for a mere dream to make her feel that five years or more had passed in a single night?

She'd been a different person in the dream: older, harder, sadder, living a very different, solitary life. She'd never had a dream remotely like that before. In the dream – she felt sick to remember it – she was a widow, Sam had died in an accident on this very boat, on solitary watch during a storm like the one that it seemed, from the boat's pitching and heaving, they were going through now.

Her stomach lurched. Panic gripped her. She prayed it was not already too late, the dream a premonition of what was to come. With trembling fingers she managed to zip herself into her heavy weather gear, then she scrambled up the steps, out through the hatch, and immediately found herself in a different world of wind and noise and water.

Sam was above her, on the forward deck, struggling to batten down the mainsail, and as she saw him she was seized by a powerful, sickening sensation, a sort of mental double vision, as she *remembered* what was just about to happen.

But forewarned was forearmed. She knew, and so she screamed out a warning: 'Sam! Get down! Look out! Get down *now*!'

Even if her precise words didn't reach him, he heard and responded to the terror in her voice, immediately letting go of the rolled and partly fastened sail and coming towards her. He moved a full second before the mast snapped, sending one of the metal stays whipping down and around. In another lifetime, another reality, the chunky metal clip on the end of the wire had struck Sam with deadly force in the back of his head; he'd staggered and fallen, unconscious, into the sea, where he drowned.

But it didn't happen like that – not this time, not in this world.

He'd moved in response to her scream that vital second *before* the accident, and now he was bending down to her, puzzled and concerned, holding her hands and gazing into her eyes as he asked her what was wrong.

She burst into tears. 'You're all right!'

'What's wrong? What made you scream?'

'I thought the mast was going to come down – it could have hit you—'

He grunted, surprised. 'Silly old sausage! I'm fine! But your hands are freezing – you're shaking – let's get you below and warmed up, shall we?'

She could never explain to him why she was crying, or what had made her scream like that. He didn't believe his life had ever been in danger – at worst he might have got a bit of a knock from a stay. It wouldn't have *killed* him. It wasn't like her to get so upset about a dream – and, really, how could she have dreamed that for the past five years she'd been living in Scotland and growing apples?

'Now, what's so scary about that?' he demanded.

'I thought I'd lost you – I thought you were gone—'

'Well, I'm here now. Need me to prove it to you?'

'Yes, please.'

They snuggled together into the narrow bunk, lying as close as two spoons, loving each other while the storm raged unnoticed outside. And that was the night their child was conceived.

Chapter Twenty

The Syracusa Fish Bar had vanished. Mario stood at the intersection of two narrow, winding, cobbled streets and stared disbelievingly across at the wretched, thatched-roof hovel that filled the space that should have been occupied by the chip shop, with its blue-and-white sign displaying an improbably joyful fish.

When he'd finally managed to get free of the helpful postman, he'd kept walking, in no hurry to get back to the heat and stress of his job, hoping to clear his head before he had to face all that again. With his mind on mermaids and other such mysteries, he paid little attention to where he went. It wasn't necessary. Appleton was a small town, and as long as he stuck to her boundaries and did not stray into the hills and trackless countryside, he could not possibly get lost. Even if he was drunk or half-asleep he knew he could count on his feet to carry him home, like a faithful horse. Over the past three months they had mapped out every street, path, and alleyway in the small town, tracing and retracing every possible route.

And so, when darkness fell with what seemed quite shocking and unnatural suddenness, he was sure he did not have far to go. His uncle would be furious, no doubt, because even being a few minutes late was a big crime in his reckoning. Mario had no idea what time it was. His watch had stopped working; he supposed the salt water must have damaged it.

Somehow, incredibly, he was lost.

Nothing was where it should be; everything was strange. It was as if he'd turned a corner on a familiar street in this little Scottish town and found himself abruptly somewhere else, in the heart of the ancient quarter of some very large, old city – Rome, maybe, or Prague – although not as they were now, when you saw them on TV, but more as they might have been hundreds of years ago.

But that was crazy.

Trying not to think about it, blurring over the fearful possibilities in his mind with the bland assurance that he'd taken a wrong turning, and things looked different in the dark, he hurried back the way he'd come. If he could just get back to the last place he'd recognized, it didn't matter if it was a shop or a hotel or a street sign or a distinctive doorway, he'd get his bearings and find his way. He hadn't been paying attention to where he was going and he'd become confused; it could happen to anyone. And in this darkness . . .

He came to a crossroads and peered along the road to the left, then to the right. In both directions, high, featureless buildings lined a narrow, cobbled street that curved away out of sight. His skin prickled with unease. He had never seen a street like it anywhere in Appleton. There were no streetlights, and no cars parked in front of any of the buildings, which were all at least four stories high, and, in the darkness at least, presented a blankly identical appearance. He'd never seen a street like it anywhere, he thought, and yet there was something naggingly familiar about the setting, as if he had encountered it before, seen it in a movie, or a painting, or perhaps a dream.

He decided not to turn to either direction, and kept going straight ahead. But the street frustrated him, curving around in a loop that offered him more chances to turn off onto more streets, but never one that he could recognize. They were all narrow, all weirdly empty of cars or people. Some were lined with tall, blank-faced buildings, others with smaller cottages and houses. None had streetlights, and apart from an odd, sourceless illumination from above – which could have been a full moon through light cloud cover, except he recalled no such moon from last night, which had been clear – the only lights were those which spilled out through windows or open doors.

Maybe someone could direct him, he thought, and so he paused by the next open doorway and, instead of striding past, he looked inside. A cozy, old-fashioned scene met his eyes: a group of people gathered around a glowing hearth in a long, low-ceilinged room. The smell of chicken broth made him feel hungry; then, although he'd said nothing, done nothing to attract attention, a young woman rose from her seat and approached the door. She held a fragrantly steaming bowl in one hand; with the other she beckoned to him. Her lips and eyes shone in the firelight, and although her face was mostly in shadow, he suspected she was beautiful. She wore a long, full-skirted dress and although he could see she had a slim waist and what seemed a shapely bosom, he could not see her legs, and there was no sign, beneath the skirt which rippled slightly where it brushed the floor, of feet. As she beckoned to him again, holding forward the bowl as if to attract him, as she might tempt a dog or cat, he thought of the mermaid and backed away.

She wanted to pull him in, to pull him under and keep him there – he began to walk more quickly, not quite running, but hurrying on to the next street, then the next.

Despite his growing bewilderment and fear he managed to keep his head. Common sense told him that if he went straight for long enough he must emerge, if not beside the sea, then onto the main road. In one direction it wound up into the hills of the interior; in the other, it would take him to the roadblock. Although he could no longer distinguish such directional points as north or west, at least he knew when he was continuing in the same direction and when he was being forced by these maddeningly twisting streets into doubling back on himself.

For what he judged to be an hour or more he wandered through the dark, unfamiliar streets, growing footsore and feeling a gathering sense of dread that he would never be able to escape this strange urban maze. Where was the sea? In Appleton, the scent of the sea was always in the air, however it might be masked by the tarry smells of smoking chimneys, car exhaust, petrol, or fried food; and if he could pick up which way the wind was blowing, he thought he should be able to trace the salt smell on the breeze to its source.

Now, though, the night was still and windless, and he was often distracted by other smells, which drifted out of open doorways – roasting meat, baking bread, beer, pipe tobacco, a woman's perfume. He made himself hurry past without so much as a glance inside. Sounds attracted him, too – music, laughter, and once, singing so beautiful it brought tears to his eyes, and as his footsteps slowed, he had to force himself, weeping, to run away.

He couldn't resist forever; there was no point to this

endless wandering. He grew weary. If it was a choice between curling up on the hard, cold ground by himself, or walking into one of these inviting homes . . .

And then the darkness lifted. Just as suddenly as the night had descended, it was ended, replaced by an eerie grey half-light. It was not a normal morning any more than what preceded it had been a normal night, but Mario was grateful. His footsteps slowed and he peered around, newly hopeful of seeing something he recognized. He glimpsed a flash of green, sudden bright life in contrast to the pale dull stone of the buildings, and as he walked toward it, he saw there was a gap between two houses, and beyond it was grass.

Relieved by the sight of something different, an end to the monotony of the never-ending, mazelike streets, he went toward it. When he walked between the houses, he came out on the edge of the school's playing field. At last he could orient himself. He recognized a nearby housing development as the one still referred to locally as 'new,' and beyond that was the main road.

He did not look back. He'd dropped the idea of finding the fish bar, or going back to his uncle's house – he wanted out. He crossed the playing field, heading for the main road out of town. He was determined that the landslide would not stop him escaping. If he couldn't manage to scale the cliff and get over it that way, he'd climb down to the rocky seashore and follow it until he could rejoin the road. After that he might hitch a ride, or walk all the way to Glasgow if he had to.

The fog that came rolling in did not deter him. As long as he kept to the road he should be all right. After another ten minutes or so he thought he must be getting near to the roadblock. The fog pressed in on all sides so that he seemed to be walking through a tunnel of cloud. He could smell the sea nearby and hear the faint muffled pulse of the waves. He thought he heard voices; but, afraid it might be another trap, he ignored them and pressed on.

Someone had left a car parked in the middle of the road, and it was absolutely the car of his dreams. He stared at it suspiciously, torn between desire and caution. Who would abandon a beautiful Porsche like that? Of course, the road was blocked; anyone determined to get away, as he was himself, would have to leave the car and go on foot.

A woman's scream, very close by, made him whirl around, heart hammering. The fog was thinning, dissipating with remarkable speed. It revealed a girl standing on the grassy verge, near a tall, jutting spire of rock, her back to him as she stared over the edge at the sea below.

'Ronan?' Her voice, shaky and uncertain, wafted to him on the sea breeze. She had a mass of long, curly black hair. He looked at her blue-jean-clad legs, and her feet in blue-and-white Nikes, and knew she belonged to the same world he did. He took a few steps towards her. 'Hello?'

He saw her tense before she whirled around. As soon as he saw her face he recognized her – she was the American girl he'd been looking for earlier – and he broke into a smile.

Her expression remained strained and suspicious. He tried to think of something to say to make her relax, but he'd never had a gift for light, flirtatious banter, and probably this wasn't the time or the place for it anyway. He didn't know what she'd been through during the brief, unnatural night that had just passed, but it could be that it would make his adventure seem a playground game by comparison.

'Are you OK?' he asked. 'I heard you scream.'

She was silent a moment longer, assessing him with her eyes. Then she said, 'I just saw two people drop off the cliff here. But if they fell, I should be able to see them down there – and I can't.'

'Want me to look?'

He felt grateful when she nodded. He hurried up beside her, and stared searchingly at the rocky coastline below, taking his time about it before shaking his head. 'I can't see anything. We could climb down there, but . . . are you sure . . .?'

'I'm sure. I was standing right behind them, close enough to touch, when it happened. But I guess I shouldn't be surprised. He as much as said it was magic – they were going to another world. And I guess they did.'

'They weren't real.'

She turned on him indignantly. 'They were so! I knew them – well, I knew *him* – at least, I thought I did.' From her expression he guessed that the unknown man had been her lover. He looked away, embarrassed, and noticed the Porsche again.

'Was that his car?'

She followed his gaze. 'That? Ronan's? God, no, he didn't have *anything*. Not enough for a cup of coffee. I had to buy him lunch.'

'Who was he?'

'Ronan Lachlan Wall. My grandmother's fiancé.'

He must have looked astonished, because she laughed. 'True. It's a long story.'

'I'd like to hear it.'

She nodded at the road, looking back towards town. 'I could tell you while we walk. I'm guessing you're going that way.'

His urgent desire to leave had vanished. 'Sure.'

'Do you think any of the shops will be open?' she asked. 'I'm dying for something to eat.'

He smiled. 'I can help you there. I have the keys to the chip shop. Come with me. I'll cook you whatever you like. On the house.'

'You mean it?' Her face lit up. 'OK, then, you're on!' She gave him her wonderful smile again, like a gift.

Chapter Twenty-One

Something softer than a whisper woke her; the sound was deeply familiar, yet felt rare, entirely unexpected. She opened her eyes, and there was Dave, head pillowed beside hers, gazing at her with fond, sleepy eyes.

A rush of happiness made her forget everything else.

'Do you hear something?' he asked.

'Mmm-hmm. I was just wondering . . .' As she spoke, she knew. 'It's raining!'

'Not that. Something inside – closer – a humming . . .' He rolled onto his other side and reached up to the bedside table. A moment later, music entered the room, a cascade of high, bright piano notes.

'Well, well, we have electricity,' he said. 'And broadcasts from the BBC.' He gave her a wistful look. 'Something tells me we're not in Oz any more, Dorothy.'

'I guess that means I have to go to work today.'

'No hurry, surely?'

She smiled and snuggled into his arms, then winced as she remembered, 'My car! I left it on the road – I don't even know if it'll go. You don't have a car here, either, do you?' She sat up. 'I'd better move – it's a long walk into town.'

'Easy.' He sat up, too, and put an arm around her. 'Assuming the phone's working again, it won't take long to get this sorted. Why don't you go and have a shower, and I'll find out whether it's too early to make a few calls?'

When she emerged from her shower, the radio announcer was giving the time as half past eight, and the rich aroma of fresh coffee filled the kitchen.

Dave put two slices of bread in the toaster and turned to smile at her. 'Jamie McKinnon – he and his wife look after this place for me – is going to find your car. If it's running, he'll drive it here; if not, he'll come here and pick us up and take us to where I left *my* car. Either way, you won't be late for work.'

'Thank you.'

He sketched a bow. 'Ever at your service, ma'am. Now: would you like eggs with your toast?'

'Just toast is fine. And some of that coffee – it smells wonderful.'

'It's made from magic beans,' he said, handing her a plain white mug.

'Dave . . .'

'Hmmm?' He plucked two pieces of toast, hot from the toaster, put them on a matching white plate, and gave her that as well. 'Butter, jams, marmalade on the table. Tuck in. I'll be with you in a second.'

When he had joined her at the table, she began again. 'What happened? I mean, what do you think has been happening over the past few days?'

He looked searchingly into her eyes. 'You have to ask?'

'I don't mean to *us*.'

'But I don't know what's happened to anyone else.' He grinned. 'They should all be so lucky!'

'Telephone lines, TV reception, electricity.' She ticked them off on her fingers. 'We were cut off – Appleton was cut off from the world, starting with the landslide and spreading. I don't know, *maybe* there will turn out to have been logical explanations for why nothing was getting through, but it seems to me that this whole place genuinely disappeared. People outside either forgot we existed, or simply couldn't get through the – whatever it was, invisible barrier, fog, or magic that surrounded the Apple. I think this whole little spit of land moved into another dimension, another layer of reality, something – it sounds like science fiction, but—'

'More like a fairy tale, and I agree with you, by the way. The kind of fairy tale people long ago used to believe about this place. We were taken out of the modern world and set adrift in another sort of reality, where the normal rules don't apply. And then the fog . . . when that came in, I thought things were going to get a *lot* more unpleasant. I thought it might be the end.'

'Maybe it was. The fog was a curtain coming down on this little play – like *A Midsummer Night's Dream*—'

'And returning us to our regularly scheduled reality?' He shook his head. 'Why? I think we were headed for a much more permanent end. Until somebody did something to stop it. Maybe whoever started it off?'

'Something happened while we were asleep . . .'

He held up his hand. 'I didn't sleep. I just lay there and watched you.'

She felt heat rise in her face. 'All night?'

'Not that long. An hour, hour and a half. I didn't want to risk going to sleep not knowing what I was going to wake up to find. I thought that as long as I didn't lose sight of you, at least we'd still be together, whatever happened.'

She felt as if something inside her that had been broken – all jagged fragments that had jostled painfully in her chest, making it difficult to breathe comfortably for so long – had been joined together, each piece slotted smoothly back where it belonged. For some reason, she thought of the wooden apple, imagining that it was not solid, but had been constructed in two parts that fit so well it seemed only one.

'Maybe what happened was *you*,' she said softly.

'Us?' His eyebrows rose and he looked at her tenderly. 'You changed *my* world, for sure.'

'What happened overnight?'

His left shoulder rose and fell. 'There wasn't a night.

While you were asleep, say it was an hour, the light hardly changed at all – it was the same murky foggy glow from the window. Then, maybe it got just a little bit darker, and it started to rain. It was about then that I heard the humming of the radio alarm clock, too; normally I wouldn't notice it, but after no electricity, the sound caught my attention. You opened your eyes a few minutes later.'

'Thanks for watching over me.'

He smiled. 'It was no hardship, believe me. There's nothing else I'd rather do.' He stroked her arm and cleared his throat. 'Now, eat your toast. I don't want you going to work on an empty stomach.'

A few minutes later, Kathleen heard the familiar friendly growl of her car's engine in the yard outside.

'There's my man,' said Dave, springing up. 'Are you ready?'

Jamie McKinnon was a wiry, freckled little guy accompanied by a black-and-white sheepdog.

'Hope you don't mind Meg being in your car, missus,' he said immediately, before Dave had even introduced them. 'I put a blanket down for her, and she behaved herself.'

'That's fine, I don't mind, I'm very grateful to you for getting the car started,' she said, scratching Meg behind her ears.

'There was nothing wrong with your car at all. Started sweet as a whistle.'

He went on to explain that he'd left his vehicle parked beside the road where hers had been, and they dropped him and the dog back there on their way to Appleton, with grateful thanks. Kathleen stole a quick look at the lochan as she drove past. It was as silvery-grey and still as ever beneath the cloudy morning sky, but it no longer appeared as sinister. Was that because the world had changed, she wondered, or only her personal situation? The last time she'd come by here, searching for Dave, could have happened in another lifetime. Already in her memory those strange events – the old women at Ina McClusky's house, the ghost of Emmeline Wall, the water-horse – had taken on the quality of remembered dreams, and she didn't know how long she'd be able to believe they'd really happened.

They drove into the changed, familiar town. The holiday atmosphere had vanished with the sunshine. The people on the streets this morning wore their sober, everyday clothes: hats and waterproofs against the expected return of rain, or scarves and sweaters against the first, faint touch of winter on the wind from the sea. She turned on to the main road, heading out.

As she caught sight of the faded, leaning sign for Orchard House, she made a split-second decision and swung right, turning into the long, uphill drive to Nell's house.

'I hope you don't mind if we make a little detour – I'm just thinking about a friend of mine. I told you about Nell. I'd like to know she got home safely.'

'Hey, would you look at that!' Dave was turning in his seat, winding down the window, craning out for a better view.

'What is it?' Nearing the top of the drive, she slowed. Something about the house ahead didn't seem quite right, but his excitement distracted her from thinking about it.

'You can see the roadblock from here.'

She pulled up on the level, paved area in front and stopped the car. He got out immediately, his attention caught by the view of the road at the bottom of the hill, and she followed him.

'Your car's still there,' she said, catching sight of the bright red Porsche and thinking he must be concerned about it.

'Yes, yes, but look at the *other* side.'

She raised her eyes beyond the mass of rock and earth, looking farther, and could just see part of the road on the other side of the blockage, her first glimpse of the greater world beyond Appleton since she'd looked down from this very spot on Sunday evening. At that time, the road on both sides had been deserted. Now, the other side presented a very different picture. There were trucks, cars, and a huge, orange digger, as well as at least a dozen men scattered about on foot, oddly insect-like in their bright yellow reflective jackets and shiny domed hard hats.

Dave seemed fascinated by the distant scene. 'Wonder if they're using dynamite? I think they'll *have* to blow it, no other way to shift it. You don't happen to have a pair of binoculars with you?'

'Sorry, no.' She smiled, amused by his boyish enthusiasm, and left him to it. She turned back to the house and, as she really took in the sight of it for the first time, felt a cold hand clutch her heart.

Nell's house had been painted a subtle, elegant shade of moss green with cool grey on the trim; it had looked fresh and immaculate. This house, although it was the same solid, two-storey wooden building, had been neglected for years. It was a worn and faded white, with a darker, greyish undercoat showing through, and on the shabby front door and crumbling window frames, ancient black gloss paint had cracked and peeled. The windowpanes were filthy, and one had been replaced with a piece of thin board. Several of the paving stones at the front of the house were broken, and all sorts of weeds grew in the gaps between them.

She stared at the evidence of desolation and mentally retraced her route, trying to convince herself that she'd taken a wrong turning, driven up the wrong hill, but knowing she had not.

Dave put a hand on her shoulder. 'Your friend lives here?'

'She did on Sunday. But it wasn't like this.'

'Shall we try the door?'

'Let's go around the back.'

She could almost have convinced herself that she'd

misremembered the front of the house, fooled by the lovely interior redecoration into thinking the exterior was in better condition than it actually was, but about the gardens there could be no mistake. They were Nell's pride and joy, and she remembered eating dinner on a little patio, close enough to the herb garden to inhale the varied, heady scents . . .

There was no patio, no table, no herb garden, no vegetable garden, no greenhouse, nothing but waste ground turning rapidly to wilderness. Where the paved area had been were clumps of stinging nettles and giant hogweed; instead of carefully tended roses, a tangle of brambles; cow parsley and dandelions flourished where the vegetables for their dinner had been grown, and a pile of old bricks, rotten timbers, and odd bits of scrap metal took up the rest of the space.

'It's impossible. I was *here* on Sunday night! We sat out eating dinner – eating vegetables she'd grown, right there.' She waved her hand at the impossible wilderness the well-tended garden had become. 'She had a greenhouse, over in that corner, and – I mean, you can knock things down, but thistles and giant hogweed don't spring up overnight!'

'Did you know this woman before the landslide?'

She frowned, understanding the implication. 'I didn't *imagine* her – and she wasn't a ghost!'

'Kathy, you don't have to justify yourself to me. Was she an old friend?'

She sighed, shook her head. 'Sunday was my first visit. But loads of people knew her – she'd been in Appleton for years, fixing this place up. I knew her from her visits to the library – she requested some things we had to get through Inter-Library Loan, specialist articles, mostly, about apple-growing.'

'Apples! Was she the one you told me about, with the tree bearing fruit and blossom at the same time?' He began to look around. 'Where was that tree? Can you show me?'

'She had an orchard inside an old, walled garden. Down there somewhere.' She pointed, wincing at the prospect of fighting their way through the trackless wilderness. 'I wish I had my high boots on.'

'Never fear, fair lady, I shall break a path for you,' he said with a bow, and they made their way slowly and carefully across the inhospitable wasteland, to the walled garden. She was relieved to find it still there, but as soon as he forced open the warped and battered old wooden door in the wall, her hope died.

The apple orchard was gone, as if, like everything else Nell had repaired, changed, built, planted, and tended, it had never been more than a fantasy. Instead of rows of carefully nurtured trees, the enclosed space was a mad confusion of growing things, some of them survivors of the garden that had once been here, others incomers from seeds dropped by birds or rodents, or blown in on the wind. The garden was protected on three sides only; the fourth wall was crumbling, half-caved-in, the bricks furred with brilliant green moss and sprouting a crop of hardy weeds, even a slender sapling rowan tree.

As she gazed around, comparing this reality to the picture in her mind of Nell's orchard, she could feel the remembered image crumbling like the old brick wall, overwhelmed by the pressure of all this real and growing vegetable life.

'Here's the apple tree,' said Dave.

'What?' She turned and stared, but couldn't see what had caught his eye. As she began to move towards him, a thorny tendril caught at her leg. She unhooked herself, wincing. 'How can you tell? Are you sure?'

He gave her a sardonic look. 'It has an apple growing on it.'

She forgot all concern for her clothes and bashed through the undergrowth to reach his side. The tree he'd discovered was very small and looked ancient: gnarled and bent low to the ground, with flaky white scales erupting here and there along the crooked branches, and brown-spotted leaves. It didn't look very healthy, but the single apple that it carried was beautiful, without a blemish, smooth and yellow and inviting.

She reached for it at the same moment that he did, but his hand closed about it first, and he was the one who plucked it from the tree.

'Halvsies?' he said, and she nodded, feeling suddenly oddly breathless, on the brink of something momentous.

He pulled a folding knife out of his pocket and cut the apple in two.

'That's the wrong way to cut it.'

He shrugged. 'I always liked to do it that way, to see the star in the middle.' He handed her a piece, and she saw what he meant. The fruit felt warm, as if it had been resting in the sun rather than in this shady place, and a subtle yet heady aroma rose from the cut flesh.

Her mouth watered but, afraid of disappointment, she hesitated. 'It's probably some old cooking apple, incredibly bitter–'

'Oh, I don't think so. I think this is the apple that made Appleton famous – the last of its kind – incredibly delicious – but we'll never know unless we try.'

'Together?'

At his nod, they each bit into the apple. It was sweet, yet sharp, with a surprising complexity of flavour that defied simple analysis. She swiftly took another bite, then another, until she'd eaten it all except for the seeds.

She looked at Dave, who took the hand with the seeds in it and, clasping it tightly, whispered, 'Make a wish.'

She could think of nothing to wish for. She had what she wanted: this man, this feeling between them, this moment and hope for more like it. She was happy, and she knew it. She smiled at him, and he smiled back.

'Now kiss me,' he said.

Eight Months Later …

Chapter Twenty-Two

Kathleen settled the last of her newspaper-wrapped dishes into the cardboard box, closed the flaps, and reached for the tape dispenser. A ribbon of shiny brown squeaked out, then snagged. It was the end of the roll.

She sat back on her heels and looked around the living room, nearly filled with carefully packed cardboard boxes, and had a flash of *déjà vu*. A year ago, she'd been confronted by this same sight, only then the chore ahead of her had been to unpack and find a place for everything in the bijoux Library House which was to be her new home. Now, sooner than she'd expected, she was moving on. A tingle of nervous excitement ran through her at the thought of what the next year might bring. To live in a library had been her childhood wish come true, but to be moving in with the love of her life – well, that truly was her heart's desire.

In any case, she would have had to vacate the Library House, because it was going to be needed for office space. There were big changes coming to Appleton Public Library; not only a new computerized system, and computers with free Internet access for the public, but more staff, longer opening hours, and substantial redevelopment plans for the museum.

Glancing at her watch, Kathleen rose to her feet, stretching the kinks out of her arms and legs. It was too early for lunch, but since she was going to have to go out to buy more tape, she thought she might as well take a break. With her own cups and kettle packed away, she had the perfect excuse for visiting the new café that had just opened on the high street. Called The Magic Bean, it advertised an interesting list of specialty coffees and teas, and looked surprisingly cosmopolitan for Appleton.

But Appleton was changing. The Magic Bean was only one of several new businesses to have opened in the past few months, and throughout the town centre other commercial properties, long vacant, were being refurbished and redecorated as shops, restaurants, or offices as people scented new possibilities in the air. Kathleen recalled how last September, while most people were complaining about the inconvenience of being cut off, a few had suggested that the landslide might be the best thing to happen to Appleton in a long time. Now it seemed that they had been proved right. Newspaper articles and television features about the isolated little town had attracted a lot of interest. After one celebrity couple chose to get married on Southport Beach, near King Arthur's footprints – musical accompaniment to their 'traditional Celtic handfasting ceremony' provided by a local band, who were immediately signed by a major label – the area became even more famous as a destination for a romantic short break. The local hotels had their busiest 'off-season' ever, and it was widely expected that this year's tourist season, just beginning, would be a stunning success.

The front door of the Library House opened onto a quiet back street, and it was still quiet on this cool morning, but as soon as she turned the corner toward the town centre, Kathleen could feel the buzz, the positive life force which had recharged the whole area. The physical changes might be small – a new sign here, a new coat of paint there – but Appleton was very different from the faded, forgotten backwater it had been a year ago. The atmosphere was utterly changed, filled with a new hope and optimism, and this time Kathleen knew she wasn't simply projecting her own emotions onto her surroundings.

She went into the newsagent's where she bought the tape she needed and a newspaper. During this brief transaction three people came into the shop, and every one of them greeted her. It gave her a good feeling, to be recognized and liked, and she knew she was now really part of the community. She would have gone with him anywhere, but she was glad that Dave wanted to stay at White Gates.

She saw more people she knew outside. It was easier for her now to recognize the visitors in the busy streets. She enjoyed her status as a local all the more among the crowds of tourists admiring the scenery and wistfully fantasizing about giving up their stressful existence in the city for a new life here. Such visitors were often to be seen standing outside the estate agent's window, viewing the details of properties for sale as longingly as kids in front of a sweet-shop.

As she approached it now, Kathleen cast a quick, amused glance at the people standing outside the window only to stop, startled, to look again before calling out, uncertainly, 'Nell?'

The tall, willowy brunette turned in response, and at the sight of her face, Kathleen had no doubts. 'Nell Westray! It *is* you! Where have you been?'

There was no answering recognition on Nell's face, although she smiled back, a bit quizzically. 'I'm awfully sorry, but I don't remember . . . how do we know each other?'

Well, of course she doesn't remember, because it hasn't happened, thought Kathleen, dazed all over again as she confronted an impossibility. There was no proof that anyone named Eleanor Westray had ever lived in Appleton – she wasn't in the phone book, or in the card catalogue of library members, and everyone she asked assured her that Orchard House had stood empty for years, an unsaleable white elephant that had just been put back on the market this month. The only evidence – if you could call it that – was Kathleen's memory, and that had grown steadily more tenuous, less clear, until the sight of this woman brought the past rushing back.

'I'm Kathleen, Kathleen Mullaroy,' she stammered. 'I'm the librarian.'

'The library – isn't that the wonderful building with the golden dome on top?' At her nod, a line appeared on Nell's brow. 'But . . . we haven't been in yet. We thought we'd go in after lunch, didn't we, Sam?'

At this she finally noticed the man who stood beside Nell, his hand on her shoulder: dark brown eyes in an open, rather boyishly good-looking face. 'Hi, Kathleen. I'm Sam. I don't think we've met?'

'No, we haven't. I'm glad to meet you.' He had a firm handshake; strong, somewhat callused hands: nothing ghostlike about him, she was relieved to note.

Nell had continued to stare, and now something kindled in her gaze. 'I think I *do* know you . . . I sort of remember . . . didn't I invite you over to dinner once? Where was that? I was living alone . . . it must have been in America; you're American, aren't you?'

'That's right.'

'It must have been a long time ago! Well, of course, since you don't know Sam. Was it in Boston? When was it?'

She shook her head and shrugged, unwilling to lie yet unable to tell the truth.

'Well, obviously it was B.C. – before children. Do you have kids?'

'No.'

'Well, I don't want to put you off, but I honestly think childbirth causes brain damage. I don't know if it's the hormones or what, but I lost so many brain cells that it's like I can't remember anything from entire *years* of my life. But all the same, it's worth it.' She smiled suddenly, dazzlingly. 'You haven't met my other sweetheart. Ronan, say how do you do to my friend Kathleen.'

Kathleen froze at the sound of his name, but it was not a man who stepped out from behind Sam, but a slight, dark-haired, four-year-old boy who clutched his mother's hand for security before looking up at her, and murmuring, 'Pleased to meet you.'

'Good boy,' said Sam, touching him gently on top of his head.

'I'm very pleased to meet you, too, Ronan.' She looked at Nell. 'His name . . . do you mind me asking? Where did you get it?'

'From a book,' said Nell, shrugging as if it was unimportant; but Kathleen thought she looked uneasy.

'We wanted a name that wasn't ordinary, but wasn't too weird or too hard to spell,' Sam explained. 'We had a shortlist of about half a dozen each, boy and girl, and couldn't make up our minds. Ronan's an Irish name; it means "little seal", and that's just what he looked like the minute that he came into this world – just like a little pink seal. So we knew that was the right name for him.'

Ronan was gazing up at his father, obviously enjoying a story he had heard before. 'And I can swim just as good as a seal, too,' he volunteered. 'And we're going swimming today, you promised.'

'Yes, we are – if you'll be good for just a bit longer.'

'I'm good – I'm very good!' the little boy said, sounding both proud and indignant.

Nell crouched down to give him a hug and a kiss. 'Yes you are indeed,' she said.

Feeling she was intruding on this happy family scene, Kathleen stepped back. 'Nice to see you,' she said. 'I hope you'll come into the library while you're here.'

'Of course,' said Nell. 'We'll see you again.'

'You can count on that,' said Sam. 'Nice meeting you.'

When she had gone half a block Kathleen stopped and looked back, just in time to see the Westrays disappearing through the doorway of the estate agent's.

So they weren't just wistfully fantasizing about a new life in Scotland like a lot of other visitors, but might actually be planning one. Orchard House was still empty. She wondered if they would buy it, and if they'd plant apple trees there again.

Wait and see, she told herself, and walked on.

From the Appleton Advertiser

Full Steam Ahead

The Bride of Lammermoor, the historic sea-going paddle steamer which carried passengers between Appleton and Glasgow three days a week while the road was closed, is set to return next month, 'due to popular demand.'

According to a spokesman for the company which owns the vessel, 'We had so many enquiries from individuals and tour groups that we have decided to offer a regular service again, beginning at the end of May and running through September. Although the road is now open again, many people have said they prefer this more peaceful and luxurious way of travelling to going by bus.'

Sailings will be every Tuesday, Thursday, and Saturday, leaving Appleton Pier at 9:15 A.M. The return from Glasgow will arrive at 5:30 P.M.

Tickets may be purchased on the pier or in advance from the Tourist Information Office.

'Grand' Hopes Revive

A successful Glasgow business man and hotelier seems to have set his sights on Southport, with the recent purchase of the cliff-top property including the ruined Grand Hotel.

James MacAlister Bruce would not confirm or deny any definite plans to re-open the hotel, saying only that 'I own quite a bit of property. It's a matter of sensible investment, and being ahead of the game. I am always on the look-out for places with potential.'

Asked to comment on the 'potential' of Southport, he remarked that the beautiful beaches and the fine old golf-course were 'hidden treasures'. He went on to say, 'I understand there's a strong chance of a ferry link between Appleton and Northern Ireland, and that would expand the tourist base tremendously. The hotels now in Appleton could not cope with the boom.'

Museum Developments

Ever since the discovery by head librarian Kathleen Mullaroy of a secret entrance into the public library's 'golden' dome – long believed to be purely decorative – speculation has been rife about when it will be open to the public.

As previously reported in these pages, Mrs Mullaroy found that the hidden room had been used to store a cache of paintings by local artist, Emmeline Wall, and a writer for this paper suggested recently that the best use of the domed enclosure would be as a gallery to display those works.

Fraser Mann, head of library services for the county, replies, 'Unfortunately, the restricted access to the dome makes it impractical as a public gallery. We are, however, planning changes to the interior lay-out of the library which will allow for expansion of the museum, and the permanent display of many of the paintings.

'We have recently learned that our application for matching grants from the Scottish Arts Council and the European Union have been successful, and this, along with a substantial donation from an anonymous benefactor, will allow for some exciting new improvements. We have been interviewing candidates for the position of Curator to the Appleton Museum, and hope to announce an appointment very soon.'

Watch this space!

Acknowledgements

Most of the books I've referenced in these pages are likely to be found only on the restricted-access shelves in Appleton Public Library, but I've used brief quotations from two books still in print and protected by copyright; wonderful, scholarly works I heartily recommend to anyone interested in myth, magic, and folklore. These are:

The Silver Bough (Volume 1: Scottish Folk-Lore and Folk Belief) by F. Marian McNeill (William MacLellan, Glasgow, 1957, pages 102–3).

The Woman's Dictionary of Symbols and Sacred Objects by Barbara G. Walker, copyright (c) Barbara G. Walker 1988 (HarperCollins, London, 1995, page 480).

And the description of the kelpie I've quoted on page 273 is from *Popular Superstitions and Festive Amusements of the Highlanders of Scotland* by William Grant Stewart, originally published in Edinburgh and London in 1823.